Beast

Other Books by Lexi Blake

ROMANTIC SUSPENSE

Masters and Mercenaries
The Dom Who Loved Me
The Men With The Golden Cuffs
A Dom is Forever
On Her Master's Secret Service
Sanctum: A Masters and Mercenaries Novella
Love and Let Die
Unconditional: A Masters and Mercenaries Novella
Dungeon Royale
Dungeon Games: A Masters and Mercenaries Novella
A View to a Thrill
Cherished: A Masters and Mercenaries Novella
You Only Love Twice
Luscious: Masters and Mercenaries~Topped
Adored: A Masters and Mercenaries Novella
Master No
Just One Taste: Masters and Mercenaries~Topped 2
From Sanctum with Love
Devoted: A Masters and Mercenaries Novella
Dominance Never Dies
Submission is Not Enough
Master Bits and Mercenary Bites~The Secret Recipes of Topped
Perfectly Paired: Masters and Mercenaries~Topped 3
For His Eyes Only
Arranged: A Masters and Mercenaries Novella
Love Another Day
At Your Service: Masters and Mercenaries~Topped 4
Master Bits and Mercenary Bites~Girls Night
Nobody Does It Better
Close Cover
Protected: A Masters and Mercenaries Novella
Enchanted: A Masters and Mercenaries Novella
Charmed: A Masters and Mercenaries Novella
Treasured: A Masters and Mercenaries Novella, Coming June 29, 2021

Masters and Mercenaries: The Forgotten
Lost Hearts (Memento Mori)
Lost and Found
Lost in You
Long Lost
No Love Lost

Masters and Mercenaries: Reloaded
Submission Impossible, Coming February 16, 2021

Butterfly Bayou
Butterfly Bayou
Bayou Baby
Bayou Dreaming
Bayou Beauty, Coming July 27, 2021

Lawless
Ruthless
Satisfaction
Revenge

Courting Justice
Order of Protection
Evidence of Desire

Masters Of Ménage (by Shayla Black and Lexi Blake)
Their Virgin Captive
Their Virgin's Secret
Their Virgin Concubine
Their Virgin Princess
Their Virgin Hostage
Their Virgin Secretary
Their Virgin Mistress

The Perfect Gentlemen (by Shayla Black and Lexi Blake)
Scandal Never Sleeps
Seduction in Session

Big Easy Temptation
Smoke and Sin
At the Pleasure of the President

URBAN FANTASY

Thieves
Steal the Light
Steal the Day
Steal the Moon
Steal the Sun
Steal the Night
Ripper
Addict
Sleeper
Outcast
Stealing Summer

LEXI BLAKE WRITING AS SOPHIE OAK

Texas Sirens
Small Town Siren
Siren in the City
Siren Enslaved
Siren Beloved
Siren in Waiting
Siren in Bloom
Siren Unleashed
Siren Reborn

Nights in Bliss, Colorado
Three to Ride
Two to Love
One to Keep
Lost in Bliss
Found in Bliss
Pure Bliss
Chasing Bliss
Once Upon a Time in Bliss
Back in Bliss
Sirens in Bliss

Happily Ever After in Bliss
Far From Bliss, Coming 2021

A Faery Story
Bound
Beast
Beauty

Standalone
Away From Me
Snowed In

Beast

A Faery Story, Book 2

Lexi Blake
writing as
Sophie Oak

Beast
A Faery Story, Book 2

Published by DLZ Entertainment LLC at Smashwords

Copyright 2019 DLZ Entertainment LLC
Edited by Chloe Vale
ISBN: 978-1-942297-28-4

Sign up for Lexi Blake's newsletter
and be entered to win a $25 gift certificate
to the bookseller of your choice.

Join us for news, fun, and exclusive content
including free short stories.

There's a new contest every month!

Go to www.LexiBlake.net to subscribe.

Dedication

This book is for Liz Berry, tireless champion of authors both big and small—and for her Wine Wednesday girls. Ladies, I believe you'll find this one goes with a nice red.

Dedication 2019

I originally dedicated this book to a woman who had become a good friend at the time. I liked Liz Berry. She was funny and sweet and loved books. It's been nine years since that first email between us and my sweet, funny friend has become a force in the industry she loves. I've watched you take a dream from an idea that maybe, might, if you hoped enough, work, to one of the best run companies in the publishing industry. You are still sweet and funny. You still love books. And you are fierce, an example for all women of how to value ourselves and each other. You are both beauty and beast. I love you, sister of my heart.

Prologue

The Werewolf Plane

Kaja looked up into the eyes of the woman who had raised her. Helga had not been a kind mother. The older wolf wasn't her mother at all. She'd been designated by the First as her keeper when Kaja had been orphaned. But Helga had been the one to ensure Kaja survived. Helga had given her food and grudging shelter when the weather was too cold for any wolf to stand. Helga had only beaten her when there was no other option. Kaja was aware that she was far too thin for a woman of four and twenty, but that was only to be expected. She had no mate, and Helga must think of her own children first.

"What does it mean?" Kaja asked.

She didn't understand what had happened. It made no sense. Her hands shook as she pulled the thin shawl around her shoulders. She thought about changing. She always changed when she felt this anxious. Fur and fangs and four strong paws seemed more solid than her two-legged body. She held fast to her human form since she needed to understand how her life had changed following the wise woman's pronouncement.

The wise woman, a large, sturdy wolf, had stood up in the middle of the evening meal and spoken. Kaja had been at the edge of the dining hall, as was customary. She wasn't allowed to eat until the rest of the pack was done. Though she hadn't been able to hear everything that was said, she'd felt the eyes of the pack turn, seeking her out. They had stared, some with open sympathy, most with sneers.

She did not understand what was happening.

Helga's eyes were anything but kind as she looked at Kaja. "It means you are outcast. Do you understand the word, girl? You are no longer welcome in the pack. I risk the First's anger by even speaking with you, but you are too stupid to be expected to understand on your own."

"Why?" Her voice was as small as she felt.

She ignored the insults. They were as ordinary to her life as breathing. She'd never been particularly welcome in the pack, but it was the only home she knew. The world was a cold place. How would she survive on her own? It was winter, and there was barely enough food to feed the pack. She couldn't compete with the warriors on her own. If she was outcast and they caught her poaching in their territory, they would kill her.

Sven would kill her.

Tears pooled in her eyes at the thought of the handsome Second. He was every inch his father's son. He would be First someday. She'd fought him, but he hadn't taken no for an answer. She'd hated the mating, but somewhere in the back of her mind she'd wondered if Sven wouldn't help her. He desired her. That had to mean he cared about her. She had always known that Sven would not ask her to be his permanent mate. He would select a much more suitable she-wolf for that honor. But he had promised her the role of concubine. It was not without its benefits. She would be respected as the Second's mistress. She would be the she-wolf who held his heart. She would be fed and have a place of honor.

"Sven will not allow it." Kaja felt her face firm as she said the words.

He'd said she was beautiful. He wouldn't allow her to be thrown out of the pack. He couldn't. He'd been the one to pursue her. Surely that meant he cared.

Helga sighed. "He's done with you, idiot child. He's going to permanently mate with the wise woman's daughter. Did you think she would allow her daughter's future husband to keep you as a

14

concubine? That is an embarrassment she could not endure. You should never have given yourself to the chief's son."

"I did not realize I had a choice," Kaja said bitterly.

She remembered that first night. She had not been given a choice. Sven had come for her with his friends at his side. His friends had held her down as Sven took her. She had fought, and she had lost.

Helga frowned, and for the first time there was sympathy in her dark eyes. "You didn't, child. You haven't had a choice in anything. It would have been kinder if the chieftain had left you on the mountainside to die as I suggested. Now, go. I will not risk my place for you. I am fourth among the women now. I am the keeper of this long house. I eat well and have good shelter. I will not lose my standing for the daughter of a traitor. You must go."

Kaja turned. There would be no moving her foster mother. When Helga had mentioned her father's perfidy, she knew there was no argument that could sway the older woman. Her father had challenged Sven's father and lost. That was what made him a traitor. Kaja knew if she'd been born male, she would have been slaughtered along with her father. Perhaps that would have been easier.

As her father's female pup, she'd been allowed to live, but never given a place in the pack. Now that she thought about it, she'd been outcast all of her life.

She looked around the long house. It was the only home she'd ever known. She was allowed to sleep in the back where they kept the cattle. Kaja never told them that she didn't mind. It was warmer near the cattle.

Where would she sleep this evening?

She was pulled from her misery by a rough hand. Kaja looked up and saw it was Sven's closest friend, Stellan. He looked sad with his unkempt beard and dark eyes. Though his hand was tight around her thin arm, it was not painful. "Come. You must go now."

He began to drag her along. She saw the door to the long house. It was dark outside, and she could feel the cold from here. Once she left, she knew she would never be allowed back in. "Please, take me to Sven. He won't let this happen."

Stellan sighed. He stopped and looked down at her. "Oh, little one, who do you think ordered me to escort you out?"

She felt sick to her stomach. All around her the pack was watching with judgmental eyes. She was weak, and they hated weakness.

"Out!" one of the women shouted. She tossed a rancid tomato at Kaja's face. It struck her firmly and her eyes burned from the juice it spat out.

Stellan hurried them along.

Others joined in on the fun, and she was covered in food and bruised by the time Stellan maneuvered her out. The cold struck her as hard as any of the objects they'd thrown at her. The snow was deep, and she had no shoes. Shoes were a luxury. She was barely allowed food. When she turned, she saw the light glowing from inside the long house. Her heart ached. She had not known an ounce of real kindness there, but it was safe. It was warm.

"Sven is an ass," Stellan said, not unkindly. He shrugged out of his fur-lined coat. "He never keeps a mistress for long. You were an easy one to get rid of. I would offer to keep you myself, but he's made it impossible." He held out the coat, easing it around Kaja's shoulders. "You have to run. If they find you, they will tear you apart."

"I've never been on my own," Kaja muttered, feeling the cold seep into her bones. Though she had not been particularly welcome in the pack, she had never been without them. She had always been surrounded by wolves.

"That's funny because I would say you've always been on your own. Perhaps Freya will be kind. Perhaps she will show you the way to a better place as she showed the People when we left the first plane. There are other planes with other people."

Kaja felt her eyes go wide. "That is sacrilege. There is only this world."

"No, they want to keep you ignorant. This is a barbaric world, but it is home. My father traveled to other planes. He went to many worlds, some of which he should not have gone." Stellan smiled a bit at the thought. He pointed to a place far in the west. "Beyond that mountain, that is where he said the door is. If you can find it, a whole new world waits for you. Do not waste yourself trying to get back into favor with the pack. They will never accept you. Find a new pack."

Kaja stared at the mountains to the west. They loomed in the distance, mighty giants rising from the ground to touch the sky. Could she make it? Were the stories real? She shook her shoulders and let Stellan's coat slide off into her hands. She gave it back to him. She wouldn't need it.

In a blink, she changed. Her limbs neatly adjusted themselves, and she was wolf. Her senses were a thousand times sharper, and she no longer felt the cold as keenly.

Stellan shook his head as he looked down on her. "Sven thinks the wise woman ousted you for her daughter's sake. I believe differently. You are strong. If they ever fed you properly or gave you a moment's training, you would be First among the women. Perhaps even the men, and that is what they all fear. Go, little wolf. Your destiny is not here."

Kaja ran, her wolf legs eating the distance despite the thick snow. She ran, and she did not look back. Stellan was right. There was nothing for her here.

Chapter One

The Vampire Plane

Dante Dellacourt watched his family and friends as they stared at the floor-to-ceiling projection from the comfortable seats of Dellacorp's media room. The room that was normally used for conferences had been done up for a party, but he was worried no one would want to celebrate at the end of the show. His whole family, a large group of their friends, and several key members of the corporation were rapt with attention, watching everything that happened on this final episode of the most popular DL in the States.

Dante tried not to laugh at the image of himself pondering the decision he was about to make. The producers made sure he thought about the intensely important life decision he was making via reality television in various states of undress. During filming, he'd spent an awful lot of time with his shirt off, but he had to admit, he looked good in a tux, too. He stood at the edge of a lovely, romantic pond, surrounded by greenery and flowers, waiting for the helicopters that would bring the two final women to him.

Dante took a long drink of Scotch as he watched the drama play out. He hoped the alcohol would relax him fairly quickly. He hadn't had much of an appetite. He desired neither a meal pill nor an actual warm-blooded dinner. His gut was not in a good place. On an empty stomach, the Scotch should work fast. He had the feeling that he was going to need it once his parents saw the way the final stock ceremony ended.

On the high-definition screen, the luxury helicopter landed, and a gorgeous vampire stepped out showing off her long legs and perfect figure. She wore a designer gown and looked like a woman on a mission. *Veronica*. Even her name made him shiver.

"I knew it." Susan practically shouted at the screen. Dante had to grin slightly. His big sister was a high-octane, type-A version of himself, right down to her red-and-gold hair and green eyes.

His sister hadn't liked Veronica at all. It had been a mistake to put two alpha females in the same room together. They'd practically had a knock-down, drag-out when he'd brought Veronica home to meet the family. The producers had been thrilled. It made for excellent television.

"They always dump the first one," Susan said with a vicious fist pump. "Take that, bitch! I knew my brother would pick the consort."

Susan's husband, Colin, gave his wife an affectionate pat. He nodded Dante's way. "Thank you. She would be impossible to live with if you brought that one home again."

Dante noticed his mother was crying slightly. It made him nauseous at the thought of disappointing her. Her manicured hands came out to pat his shoulders. "I knew you would make the right choice. The consort is lovely. I can't wait to begin planning the wedding. I know you're contractually obligated to stay apart from Sheila until after the final airing, but I wish she could have been here. I can't wait to welcome her into our family."

On the screen, Veronica was rolling her eyes and vowing corporate vengeance. Her long red nails reminded Dante of talons. She'd actually scared the crap out of him. He'd been afraid to dump her before the final ceremony. More than one corporate war had been started because of this particular series.

His father walked up behind him and gave him a hearty pat on the back. He could feel the satisfaction coming off his father in waves. "I didn't think this was a good idea. Your mother had to convince me this wouldn't ruin our corporate image. Playing around in hot tubs is no way to find a wife, I say. You should have done what your cousins did. You should have bought a consort at the marketplace. Still, I liked Sheila. You did good, son."

There was a loud snort from the back of the room. Dante looked up and saw his aforementioned twin cousins sitting in the small crowd with their market-bought wife between them. Six months of marriage had only brought the three of them closer together. Cian, the more sarcastic of the two, was watching the screen raptly. It didn't stop him from making his opinion plain.

"I think you're all crazy," Cian said, his musical Fae accent filled with humor. "Do any of you know Dante? Seriously? I bet you all a thousand gold that he dumps them both."

"Shut up, you bastard," Beckett Finn said, slapping at his brother playfully. "You don't have a thousand gold."

"He won't need it. Let him make the bet," Meg Finn pronounced, her eyes narrowing on Dante. "He dumps them both."

On the screen, a second helicopter was setting down on the top floor of one of the most luxurious high-rises in Manhattan. Dante had been happy the producers of the DL had chosen to film the end in New York rather than his own hometown of Dallas. Romantic music was playing. Sheila, a consort from the Faery plane with an amazing backstory to go along with her sweet good looks, got out of the helicopter. Her face beamed as she looked up at him.

"I'll take that bet, Cian," Dante's father replied, his Texas accent thick with pride. "There's no way my son lets a consort that beautiful get away. She saved twenty children from the civil war. She's a healer and a philanthropist. She's everything a vampire could want in a consort. Sheila reminds me of my wife. She's quiet and elegant. She's a true lady."

"Now, you see editing can really change a person's perception. They leave out all the bitchy parts," Dante said, feeling a bit hot under the collar.

He thought Sheila had been reading far too much of her own press material. She was stuck-up. When the cameras weren't rolling, she'd barely talked to him except to ask about his cousins. She was interested in the true kings of the Seelie Fae. Not so much in him.

It didn't matter. He knew what was coming. At the time, it seemed like a funny adventure. He hadn't expected everyone to get caught up in it. He certainly hadn't expected his parents to get invested in a made-for-DL relationship.

His sister was standing now. Her mouth thinned as she studied him. "You asshole! Ci's right. You dumped both women. How could you?"

Dante pointed to the screen where the quiet, demure consort was slapping him silly, completely forgetting that oath she had taken to do no harm. She pushed him back until he fell ass-first into the romantic koi pond that would have made an awesome place to propose had he actually fallen in love with someone. "Does that look quiet and elegant? They don't show you the fact that she tried to throw one of the cameras in that pond with me. She tried to electrocute me. And they totally made her look like she wouldn't put out in the fantasy suite, but she did."

Susan gasped. "You slept with her?"

He shrugged. It should have been obvious. He'd spent six weeks shooting a reality DL. What the hell else had there been to do? "I slept with all of them, sis. Haven't you read the tabloids? My point is she's nothing like mother. Mother would never try to electrocute a man."

Alana Dellacourt stood. Her gray eyes were stormy as she stared his way. "Maybe you don't know me as well as you think. You wouldn't like what's going through my head right now. I have to make sure my clothes are ready for tomorrow's luncheon. I will have many questions to answer. The Malones are coming over. Their JT recently married a consort, a lovely woman from the Earth plane named Dana. I thought I would be able to announce your engagement, too."

The Malones ran a rival corporation. His mother and Ava Malone were friendly but deeply competitive. It would bother his mom to have to listen to Ava rave over her son's new consort. She brought herself up to her full regal height and sauntered out of the room with dignity.

The room was buzzing all around him as many of the corporate attendees followed his mother out. Some stopped to shake his father's hand, their sympathy utterly apparent. Damn, he was truly fucked. He was going to have to charm the hell out of his parents.

Susan followed their mother, giving Dante a look that made him take a step back.

"Man-whore," she accused as she stalked past him.

Colin hurried to catch up, but not before throwing his brother-in-law a slightly sympathetic look.

"We're breaking up?" Cian asked, sounding disappointed. "But I wanted to watch the episode where all the women yell at each other. It's my favorite part. I still can't believe they found twenty females who would actually fight each other to date Dante."

His lovely wife took his hand. She seemed to understand that the evening had taken a distinctly bad turn. "Come on, baby. We'll watch it in our room."

Beckett stood with them. Dante didn't miss the way he slid his hand playfully across his wife's curves. Beckett Finn was a happy man. Beckett Finn was a man who wasn't about to get his ass chewed out.

Dante sighed as the Finns left, and he was alone with his father. The room, which had been alive and full moments before, was now as quiet as a tomb. Someone had been smart enough to turn off the sound, but the video was still running. It played pictures of himself and the women he'd turned down one after another.

His stomach sank as he looked at his dad. He loved the man, he truly did. But he didn't understand him most of the time. Donald Dellacourt had taken Dellacorp from a small-time cattle farm to one of the largest conglomerates on the plane. A few years back, he'd handed over the daily operations to Susan. Dante didn't blame him. Susan was a better CEO. He wished his father could see that he had something to provide, too.

Like tabloid scandals and a constant stream of mistresses.

"This is the end, son." His father didn't yell. It was a bad sign. Donald Dellacourt was a larger-than-life man. He yelled. He screamed. It almost never meant anything. When he was quiet, that was when Dante knew he was in trouble.

"The end of what?" He heard the irritation in his voice. It was a typical reaction. He'd never been one to take punishment well. "I'm thirty years old, Dad. You can't send me to my room."

"I can kick you out of your room."

He swallowed once, and then twice. He was joking. He wasn't actually going to kick him out of his home. This was beyond bad. "You can't be serious."

His father poured a couple of fingers of Scotch and took a long swallow. "I am deadly serious. By your age, I had already founded a company, married your mother, and we had Susan. I've given you all the time you need to mature, and you keep acting like an idiot. Tomorrow morning, you're going to be utterly reviled in the press."

He was worried about that? He'd weathered many a scandal. "They'll find a new story the day after. It's not a problem, Dad. I'll go down to the surface and pose with poor children. I'll donate some meal pills to the homeless shelters. It'll blow over."

His father brought his fist down on the bar, making the crystal shake. "It will not blow over! It won't blow over for me or your mother or your sister. All of your life you've had everything given to you. You went to the best schools. You've always had the best money could buy. You never have to go to the surface for anything but a photo op. I lived on the surface, son. It's harsh, but it makes a man out of you. If I don't do something about it, you'll stay a boy the rest of your life. I don't want that for you."

He didn't like where this conversation was going. He had plans, big plans, that did not involve getting cut off from his inheritance.

Six months before, something amazing had fallen into his lap, and he was close to a major breakthrough. "Dad, give me three more months. The sunscreen Meg brought back is going to sell like gangbusters. The bio-med guys almost have it reverse engineered. There are some compounds in it that don't naturally occur on this plane, but we'll make it work."

His father sighed. He suddenly looked wearier than Dante could ever remember seeing him. "I have no doubt that the chemists can make it work. Don't try to sell this as some big job. Meggie gave you the sunscreen, and you passed it off to the bio-med team. It doesn't make you a businessman. You spend far more time partying than you do in the office."

Humiliation flashed through his system. Everyone discounted him. Even his own family. "How about all the marketing research I've done? I can sell this. I can make this our biggest seller within a year. I've done the financials. Sunscreen tech can be the most profitable arm of Dellacorp within five years. Bio-med has been our weak point. I can make us a leader in the market."

His father looked far past his sixty-five years as he shook his head. His anger seemed spent, replaced with something he could only term as disappointment. "No. You're off the sunscreen project. You'll bring too much bad publicity. It's best if you take a break. I'll make you a deal. Get married, and I'll let you back in. A wedding would mollify the stockholders. They'll think you're finally settling down. Look what happened to Malone Corp when JT married his consort. Might I add, she was pregnant at the time and it wasn't his kid. Poor thing got hauled off the Earth plane in a delicate condition and JT stepped up to the plate and made his family proud. Got some great PR, too. You know the more I think about it, the more I like this plan."

"I don't want to get married," Dante said. Even when he'd accepted the DL gig, he'd known he wasn't ready to be anyone's husband. He was barely thirty. He was still a kid. Maybe JT was ready to be someone's dad, but the thought horrified Dante.

His father shrugged and scrubbed a hand across his face. "Then I would start looking for a job, son. You have a business degree. I made sure of it."

His father walked out, leaving Dante stunned in his wake. On the screen behind him, the women were beginning to shout at each other.

Dante slumped into the first chair he found, utterly shocked at the events of the evening.

It had been a stupid idea. He should never have gone on that dumb show. He'd reacted to his cousins' happiness. He knew his father would never believe it, but he was jealous of what Beck and Ci had found with their bondmate. Meg was a hell of a woman. She was tough and funny, and he genuinely liked her as a person. He hadn't found anyone as interesting as Megan Finn. He doubted he ever would. How was he supposed to get married when he was half in love with his cousins' wife?

He'd been looking for a connection. He could lie to everyone, but he knew the truth deep down. He hadn't found it. He probably never would. And his father sure as hell couldn't force it on him.

Something wicked and angry took up residence in his gut.

If he couldn't have love, he decided, he could have the next best thing. Dante pulled out his tablet and dialed up his latest mistress. He was sure his father would disapprove, but he needed to let off some steam.

* * * *

Two hours later, he let his head rest against the back of the chair as Amanda King teased the head of his dick with her talented tongue.

"He seriously expects you to get married?" She emphasized the "you" part. The question vibrated against the sensitive skin of his cock.

Dante took a long swallow of Scotch. He knew he probably looked every bit the decadent, care-for-nothing no-good his father had portrayed him as. He was sitting in his mistress's suite, which he paid for, drinking and letting her pleasure him. The worst part was the fact that while his cock was engaged, his fangs hadn't popped out yet. He was distracted. Or getting old.

Maybe he really should think about taking a consort. JT Malone seemed happy with his consort. "I got a lecture about how marriage can settle a man down. He threw the Malones in my face. Again."

The Malones ran a rival corporation and their twin sons were roughly the same age as Dante. They'd been in some of the same schools together, but he'd never gotten close to them.

"You know I heard that he married a chick from the Earth plane, but the twist was it was the same girl he grew up with on this plane," Amanda murmured against his cock. "It was one of those mirror things. Except the girl he grew up with died when they were teens and then this one shows up and he lost his mind. I wonder if I'm out there somewhere."

He didn't even want to think about it. He was probably living it up on the Earth plane, and no one would tell him what to do. It was probably paradise.

Then Amanda ran her tongue from the base of his balls to the crown of his cock, and he wasn't thinking much anymore. She was extremely good at giving head. What right did his father have to tell him he was useless simply because he liked to party and kept a mistress? He worked hard. Sometimes. Didn't he deserve to play? Besides, he considered himself a mentor to his mistress. Amanda was a young woman trying to put herself through school without the aid of family or corporate funds. It was a given in their society that she would find a wealthy patron to help her. If she'd been born in a royal line, he would never have touched her, but Amanda was a lovely peasant girl. She knew the score. He could never marry a peasant. It would be a royal or a consort for him.

Even if she'd been a royal, he wouldn't have considered her. Amanda was all right, but he didn't love her. And she sure as hell didn't love him. He suspected she didn't like royals at all.

His father had been born a royal, but one without money. His father had pulled his entire family off the surface with willpower and intelligence. He was never going to live up to his father.

"Have I lost you?" Amanda stared up at him, her brown eyes questioning. Her hands were on his thighs. He hadn't even noticed that she'd stopped. What was wrong with him?

He shook his head and stroked her hair. She was a sweet girl, and she'd been good to him in her own way. He didn't want her to feel insecure. "I'm sorry, sweetheart. My mind is on the problem. Don't stop. I need this tonight."

She winked up at him and lowered her head, talking as she pressed kisses along his cock. "You know all the eligible American royals. I doubt any of them will be willing to date you after your *Bachelor* debacle. Way to break the consort's heart, by the way," Amanda pointed out as she cupped his balls.

He stared down at her, reclining in a comfortable chair, watching as the blonde beauty worked. She looked thoughtful. He knew she was contemplating his trouble when she should have been paying attention to his need, but he was practical. She was in this for the cash. If he got married, she had to look for a new "mentor."

"Are you going to go international? There might be some royal on an island somewhere who didn't see the show."

"I'm not going at all," Dante replied, thrusting his hips up. He relaxed back as her head bobbed up and down. She settled into her task. "I'm not going to let him force me into something I'm not ready for. Just because he wanted to get married and start a family at such a young age doesn't mean I have to. Oh, yeah. That's it, sweetheart."

This was what he needed. He tangled his hands in her hair as his fangs popped out. It had taken them long enough.

He felt her tongue whirl over and around his dick, and he started to thrust into her mouth with purpose. Her mouth was small and warm, but he wanted more. He wanted to give her an orgasm, to remind himself that he could still do something right.

"Come on," he ordered, pulling her up and into his lap. "Ride me."

She straddled him obediently. Her brown eyes were warm as she lined his cock up and sank onto him.

Dante forgot about the fight with his father. He forgot about the potential for disaster lurking in the background. He forgot about everything but the need to come. He let his hands trace the lithe lines of her body, guiding her up and down.

He worked his hand in between their bodies. He rubbed his mistress's clitoris forcefully and was pleased when she came with a mewling cry. He let himself go and groaned as the orgasm took him. He bucked up and held her hips. Amanda fell forward into his arms.

He rubbed her back gently, but his brain was working overtime again. He should be content. He should be basking in the afterglow, but all he could think about was how he was going to face his family in the morning knowing he now had an expiration date. How was he going to find a job in a company his father didn't own? He seriously doubted Susan would give him a decent reference as anything but a man-whore.

"You need to find someone completely unsuitable." Amanda's words were sighed against his neck.

"What?"

She sat up and put her hands on his shoulders. "Look, consorts are hard to come by ever since King Torin closed off Tír na nÓg."

"You mean Torin the Pretender." The words were harsh to Dante's ears. Torin had killed his aunt, uncle, and cousin, Bronwyn. Torin was the reason Beck and Cian were in exile. He would not hear him honored with a title. "The kings of the Seelie Fae are King

Beckett and King Cian."

Amanda's mouth formed a perfectly shocked *O*. It didn't surprise him. He rarely sounded serious. His cousins' throne was one of the only things he was damn serious about. One day he would convince them to take it back. He wouldn't be satisfied until Beck, Cian, and Meg wore their rightful crowns and led the Seelie plane.

"Of course," she said politely, scrambling off his lap. She quickly recovered. She pulled her robe around her and poured Dante another drink. Her smile was gracious as she passed it to him. "I apologize, baby. As I was saying, once the Pretender closed off the homelands, consorts became rare. I hear there are many who come from planes we would never have considered before."

Dante zipped up his pants. He would take a shower before he headed home. The last thing he needed was his parents to catch him reeking of sex and Scotch. And it was probably time to begin to ease his way out of the relationship with Amanda. He would pay for her last year of school. Maybe it was time to be alone for a while. "Yes, the Planeswalker clans are making a fortune off Torin's miserliness. I don't see how this helps me."

It limited his options. Now that he really thought about it, he supposed he'd always planned on finding a consort eventually. Almost all vampires of royal lines married a consort. There were several reasons for the practice, the chief being all the physical benefits a vampire received from taking regular blood from a consort. It elongated the life of the royal vampire. A typical vampire's life span was roughly a hundred years. It doubled when a royal dined regularly on a consort.

A consort was a special type of male or female, usually of Fae lineage, though he'd recently discovered humans could be consorts, as well. Something about their blood strengthened the vampire. In return, the consort remained young and vital from sexual relations with the vampire. Torin was attempting to sway the Vampire plane to his side by cutting off their access to suitable consorts.

It was starting to work. There was a large part of the plane that called for turning over the royal twins to Torin. If Torin was satisfied, he would open Tír na nÓg and trade would flow once more.

It wasn't going to happen. They would take his cousins over

Dante's dead body.

"A Fae consort is trained." Amanda's musing brought him out of his dark thoughts. "Even Colin, who wasn't aware of his status until he came to our plane, was taught manners and proper etiquette. He was educated. Your father might have come from meager beginnings, but he has high standards. If you brought home a completely unsuitable wife, he would be horrified."

His mind raced with the possibilities. Amanda was right. His father would die before allowing an uneducated rube into his precious family. Perhaps he could use the current state of trade to his advantage. "He might even let me get her a house somewhere far away."

Amanda rolled her eyes. "He might let you cast her aside. You can then go back to your former playboy lifestyle, having done your best to satisfy your father."

It could be the perfect solution, though he doubted he would ever cast a woman aside. It was a terrible thing to do in his culture and brought great shame to the woman being cast aside, but if he could convince the consort to work with him, then that was another story. It wouldn't be a marriage as much as a partnership. He would marry the woman, and then she would prove to be completely unsuitable. Perhaps he could find a human like Megan. He knew he wouldn't find anyone as beautiful and sexy as Meggie, but humans seemed a reasonable race. He could certainly work with one. Together, they would ensure that she was an embarrassment to everyone. His father would understand that they should live apart, and Dante would be free to live his life as he always had.

"You're a genius," he said with a smile. He got up and kissed her briefly.

"That's what the IQ tests tell me," Amanda quipped.

He winked at her as he made for the door. He had a lot to do. He could shower later.

* * * *

The minute the door slammed, Amanda made the call. She didn't bother to change into more professional clothes. It wasn't like the man on the other end of the line hadn't seen her naked. It also wouldn't hurt to remind him of what he was missing while she was on this particular job.

"What is it?" Chalen Palgrave asked, his voice rough. There was an edge of impatience to his tone that never left no matter what the situation was.

He had picked up immediately and that told her he'd been waiting for the call. He'd been waiting for any kind of information she could dig up on the Dellacourts' son. She was slightly satisfied that his eyes went immediately to her breasts. There was a bank of windows behind him that let her know he was still in his office. He rarely left it these days. Since his brother had disappeared six months before, Chalen spent all his time at work. He had to if he wanted to keep Palgrave Industries from going under.

"He's been ordered to get married or face disinheritance." Amanda sat forward, waiting for his approval.

It was not forthcoming. "And this is news? What could you expect after the disgraceful way he behaved this evening? His father should have disowned him right then and there. It proves Donald Dellacourt's poor morality that he did not. The Dellacourts have no honor. What should we expect? They're one generation off the surface. Dirtwalkers, every one of them."

It took everything she had not to roll her eyes. She'd rapidly discovered that royals thought along different lines than commoners. They only saw the big picture and rarely thought about how important small cracks could be. A peasant understood all about small cracks. Amanda's whole life had been a delicate balance.

"If he's invested in finding a wife, I think his newfound work ethic is going to get shelved. He's been much more serious about work in the past six months. He thinks he has something going in bio-med," she explained. "He can't work too hard if he's looking for a wife. He'll let his guard down. Better yet, if his father does kick him out, he'll be vulnerable."

"Why wouldn't he marry the first consort he sees? I would," Chalen pointed out.

"You don't know Dante the way I do. He's furious at the thought of being put in a corner. He's going to choose someone guaranteed to enrage his father." She held up a small recording device. "And I've got the proof. How is Donald Dellacourt going to react when he hears his son plotting to embarrass the family he worked so hard to elevate? The press will eat it up. He'll get kicked to the surface, and the Dellacourts will have more to worry about than the political situation on Tír na nÓg. Dante Dellacourt will be vulnerable, and the Finn twins will lose their biggest backers. You can push the government to declare for Torin. It won't be long before all three are dead."

"I want the girl dead, too," Chalen said between clenched fangs.

She was a bit startled by that pronouncement. The girl in question was a consort. Meg Finn was valuable. If her husbands were dead, she would be fair game to any royal vampire without a consort. Consorts were precious. A royal even considering harming a consort was a shocking thought. She carefully schooled her features. "I'm sure that can be arranged. Are you still in contact with the king?"

Chalen nodded. "I speak with King Torin daily. I am attempting to convince him to make his plea directly to our government. The twins are accusing him of all manner of crimes. He needs to show that he is the one who turned over the tyranny of their father's reign."

"Do you actually believe that?"

"Of course not. He killed his own brother and would have murdered his nephews if he hadn't proven incompetent. This is about perception, not truth. If I can move the members of the senate to Torin's side, I can isolate the bastards responsible for my brother's death."

She didn't bother to point out that Kinsey Palgrave's body had never been recovered. He'd simply vanished after telling his brother he was going after a consort on the Refugee plane. Chalen Palgrave had figured out the consort his brother had been interested in was Megan Finn. As Meg Finn's husbands were alive and well and his brother was missing, Chalen had drawn certain conclusions. He was going to have his revenge on the Finns and the Dellacourts. He was willing to do whatever it took to get it, even placing his own "beloved" mistress into his enemy's bed. He would not be swayed by anything as simple as logic.

"I need a copy of that tape," Chalen ordered. His face softened for a moment. "You've done well, Amanda."

31

She kept her eyes demurely down. "Thank you, sir. I only hope to serve you."

She would never, ever let him know that Dante Dellacourt was ten times the lover he was. She would never let him know that she actually kind of liked the bastard. This was war, and her personal feelings would only get her in trouble.

"Keep me updated," he said before cutting the connection.

Amanda sighed and stood. One day she would have a nice, normal job with Palgrave Industries. She would get married to someone of her own caste and live in the happy normalcy of the mid-levels. She would never go to the surface again, but she'd learned that living in the upper heights with the royals was too dangerous for her.

She stared down at the tape that would likely cost Dante Dellacourt his lofty position. It wasn't fair, but she downloaded it and shipped it to Chalen Palgrave's address. She hoped it was all over soon so she could get on with her life.

Chapter Two

Dante rubbed his head as he walked into the small kitchen the next morning. He didn't actually eat solid food. He dined on prime-grade meal pills, but there was an ultramodern food preparation appliance in deference to the home's inhabitants with fully functional digestive tracts. He glanced around, slightly relieved to see that his mother was not present. Only Cian sat at the table, munching on a piece of toast and drinking fragrant tea. Dante poured himself a cup and thought briefly about adding some Scotch. Just a nip.

"I wouldn't if I were you," Cian said, never looking up from the book he was reading. Dante caught sight of a bunch of equations that would make his head hurt even more. "It will get back to your father that you're drinking before noon, and you'll never hear the end of it."

Dante groaned, but his tea was alcohol free as he sat across from his cousin. "Fine. I'm in enough trouble as it is. What are you doing up so early? Shouldn't you be screwing your wife or something?"

Cian grinned as he looked up. He didn't even come close to taking the bait. "Meggie's tired. She had a long night. I thought I'd let her sleep in. You look worse for the wear, cousin."

"Thanks." He hadn't slept well, but he didn't need to be reminded by Cian. His cousin looked fresh as a daisy. Cian looked every bit the young royal. He was dressed in casual clothes, but there was no doubt the man was a king. He simply lacked his throne.

Cian formed the intellectual half of the king. He was one half of symbiotic twins, a rare condition in Fae royals. He shared a soul with his twin, Beck, who formed the warrior half of the duo. Of the two, he'd always felt closer to Ci. Cian had been his playmate when they were young. Many summers had been spent at the White Palace playing with Cian and Bronwyn. Dante's heart clenched at the thought of sweet, mischievous Bronwyn. She was gone forever, killed by her own uncle's thugs.

"If it's any consolation, I think you did the right thing," Ci said in his musical accent. "None of those women were right for you."

"My father would disagree," Dante replied, thinking about the fight last night. It didn't seem real, but his father had been serious. He had to get married or get out.

Cian shrugged negligently. "I've found parents don't always know their children the way their peers do. I wouldn't have picked any of those women for you, cos."

He was curious. "Who would you pick? What's my type?"

"Someone like Meggie," Ci said. There was nothing about his attitude that made Dante think he was anything but serious.

Dante felt himself flush. He thought he'd kept his crush to himself.

"Meg isn't anything like the women I date," he muttered. Meg was far smarter and kinder than the women he dated.

Cian laughed. "No, she isn't. That's the trouble. Everyone you meet here is going to be influenced by your name. They might hate you or want you, but somewhere in there, they're reacting to the fact that you're Dante Dellacourt, heir to Dellacorp."

Dante snorted. He didn't mention to his cousin that he might not be heir to anything at all soon. "So, that's the way it is. I can't fix that problem."

He wasn't going to meet anyone who didn't know who he was. Even among the Fae, he was known as the kings' cousin. There were few places worth visiting where he wasn't known for something.

"Meggie didn't know who you were, and she couldn't have cared less," Cian pointed out. "She likes you for who you are and what the two of you went through together."

"She told you about that?" Dante was surprised.

He and Meg hadn't talked about the day in the forest when they'd saved Beck and Cian's lives. He knew Meg still had nightmares about how close they came to losing them. He tried not to think of it. That day had pointed out all the things wrong with his own life. Meg had been perfectly prepared to die if it meant saving her husbands. He didn't have anything he was ready to die for.

"Of course," Cian replied with a sarcastic lilt. "I know that Meggie nearly died killing the hag, and you took care of the hag's wee kitty cat."

Dante sat up and pointed a long finger. "Hey, that was a damn vicious cat. I had scars for…well, a couple of minutes. I can't help it if I heal quickly. I still don't like cats."

He shuddered slightly. He did have some nightmares about that cat.

Cian was smiling. "Nonetheless, your relationship with my Meg is based on mutual affection. It has nothing to do with your wealth or the company. It's why you've spent the last six months mooning over her."

"Am I that obvious?" Dante asked, conceding the point.

"Not to Beck or Meg," Cian offered. "But I know you better than they do. I also know that you're not truly in love with her. She's just the first woman who you could be sure liked you for you. You need to find someone who has no idea who you are."

"And that female exists where?" It was a stretch to think he could find such a woman. He wouldn't be going to any of the far-out planes soon, and it was a real hassle to get to the Earth plane. It would require a Planeswalker, and they tended to charge. Those demons didn't accept money, only souls.

"You'll find her," Cian said with a smooth smile. Dante was glad his cousin was so very sure. Cian set his ridiculously advanced math text aside and looked slightly thoughtful. "We're leaving for home tomorrow. Do you want to come with us? We have a meeting with the king of the Unseelie in a few weeks. I'd love for you to be there. You won't even have to sleep in the barn. We added an extra bedroom. One of these days, we're going to need it."

Did he want to meet with the Unseelie? Fuck yeah, he wanted to be there. If Beck and Ci were willing to meet with King Fergus, it meant one thing. They were willing to talk about taking back their throne. *Politics.* That really interested Dante. It also wouldn't hurt to be gone for a while. Maybe his father would cool down...

Beck strode into the kitchen along with his wife. He held Meg's hand, and the look on his face was that of a satisfied man. Meg was still yawning, but she was adorable to Dante. "I'm afraid we have to cut our visit short, brother."

"What's wrong?" He sat up straighter, focused despite the slight hangover he had. Torin was always a threat. He would feel better if his cousins would simply move into the Dellacorp building, but they had obligations to their people.

Beck snatched the toast out of his brother's hand, earning him a dirty stare. He merely smiled and chewed gamely. Meg rolled her eyes and set herself on Cian's lap. She happily nuzzled his neck while Beck explained the situation.

"I got a call from Reeve at the auction house. He's got a serious problem. The Planeswalker brought him a bondmate from a plane he is unfamiliar with. She's causing trouble. She won't talk or eat, and she's attempted to kill the few men brave enough to come near her," Beck explained.

"What does he expect?" Meg asked, sounding irritated. "Who knows what the poor woman was doing when a demon kidnapped her. Maybe she was about to buy a really nice pair of shoes. Now she'll never get those shoes."

"I'm sorry, lover," Cian replied, running his tongue over the shell of her ear. "I can't make up for your footwear. It's a tragedy."

She slapped playfully at him. "You know what I'm saying. It's not easy to be in that position. I should know. It can be scary."

Beck smiled down at his bride, his eyes lit with love. "Yes, you seemed entirely frightened by me. I remember you spitting bile at me the first time we met."

Meg reached up and touched her warrior husband's cheek. "I remember that encounter differently, husband. But I was frightened. I didn't understand what was happening. I didn't even know there were other planes of existence. I want to help this woman."

Beck nodded, his face tight with emotion. "I understand, love. We'll do what we can."

"We're going to the marketplace to talk to her. It might help to talk to another female," Meg said. "They say she looks human, so she might talk to me. The gnomes aren't threatening, but they seem weird if you haven't seen them before. Reeve says she's violent and should be put down."

"He wants to kill her?" Dante was shocked at the thought.

The woman hadn't asked to be brought to another plane and sold in the marketplace. Most of the women who were sold at the market actually requested the sale. It was considered a reasonable way to find a mate. If a man had enough money to buy a wife, it probably meant he could afford to support one. In the Fae world, outside of nobility, it was a common practice. Only bondmates and consorts from other planes were brought in and forcibly sold. "Why doesn't he let her go?"

Beck sighed. "For several reasons. He's been contracted to sell her. Those demons are damned serious about their contracts. If Reeve simply lets her go, he'll be in violation. There's also the fact that he has no idea what he'll be setting loose. He doesn't know how to get her back to her home."

"We're going to find a way," Meg vowed. Her face was solemn. "I won't let anyone put her down like an animal."

"Of course not, darlin'," Beck agreed, but there was worry in his eyes. Sometimes it wasn't easy to be the king. "We'll figure out some way to help the poor girl."

"You say she's violent?" His brain was working overtime. A violent woman who could serve as a consort. A woman who frightened the gnomes. A woman who tried to kill the men who touched her. She sounded awful—and a little perfect.

"That's what Reeve said," Beck corrected. "He says she's out of control. The women can't get close to her cage."

The words were music to his ears. "And you're sure she's a consort?"

"Again, according to Reeve, she is. The demon said she glows. I could tell you if she was a bondmate. Bondmates can usually pass for consorts, too." Beck's voice became suspicious. "Why? Do you want to come and help us, then? You could tell just by looking at her."

Cian was staring at Dante with narrowed eyes, but he said nothing.

Dante shrugged. He would be able to tell if the woman was a consort by her glow. It appeared as a slight halo around the consort's form. It was a lovely, infinitely appealing sight to the royal vampire. "Sure, why not?"

It wasn't like he had anything better to do. It wouldn't hurt to go take a look at her. He got up to follow his cousins out. At the very least, he would meet someone who didn't know who he was.

* * * *

It was late in the afternoon when Dante found himself walking through the marketplace following Beck as he strode toward his goal. The door between the Vampire plane and this plane—a refugee plane—was easily accessible. There were hundreds of ways to get to different planes. Vampire scientists had theorized that there were still thousands of planes yet to be discovered. Many scientists would love to work with the Planeswalker clans to map out all the different doors. Unfortunately, the Planeswalkers came from a plane called Hell, and they didn't have a problem with eating scientists.

Reeve of the Gentle Hills had the largest and most impressive tent in the marketplace. There was no question the gnome had done well for himself in the years since the civil war in Tír na nÓg.

Reeve's tent was at the center of the small village, and everything had built up around it. Dante liked the marketplace. It was filled with the weird and wonderful things that could be found across the planes of existence. He even liked the feel of dirt beneath his feet. The surface on this plane was radically different from his home. It was closer to Tír na nÓg. This particular plane had been deserted when Beck and Cian had fled their home. It had been used by vampires as a place to hunt in the old ways and to raise cattle.

There was no smog here. The sun was bright and everything was open and airy. At home, the surface was tight and confined.

Sometimes, the sun didn't get past the clouds of pollution that clung close to the surface. It was why most vampires who could afford it never left their high-rise homes.

Dante adjusted the hood of his jacket to better cover his pale skin. The sun was stronger on the Faery planes. His sunglasses had already adjusted to the light. The nanites in his clothing adapted quickly to keep his temperature in an optimal range and ensure the ultraviolet light didn't burn him.

But what would it be like to walk unclothed in the sunlight? What would it be like to laze about unencumbered by clothing while the warmth of the sun kissed his skin? He would never tell anyone, but that was what had attracted him to the sunscreen project. It hadn't been the money they could make. It had been the possibility of experiencing something he never had before.

"What do you think you're doing, cos?" Cian asked. He'd allowed Beck and Meg to get ahead of them.

Dante hoped he projected an air of curious innocence. Ci was right. Ci knew him far too well for comfort. "I wanted to come along. It might get dangerous. You never know. You and Beck might need backup."

Cian's gray eyes rolled. "Yes, the warrior king requires backup. He's not only the greatest warrior to rise from the Seelie in a thousand years, but he's a Storm Lord, too. I think he can handle one small female. Now, spit it out, cos. What happened with your dad last night? Don't lie. I know that look on my uncle's face. I saw it when he caught me and Beck with his personal assistant ten years ago."

That was news to him. How had he missed that bit of gossip? "You two did Helena? Seriously? How did I not know that? She's twenty years older than you."

Cian's smile was slightly lecherous. "She was very experienced. We were just young lads looking to learn. It was a beautiful afternoon that we got our asses kicked for. Uncle Don had that look in his eyes last night. What's going on?"

He shrugged as they passed a goblin vendor selling all manner of odd items. "He was a bit upset. He thinks there's going to be some bad press about the DL."

"Yes, I caught some of that this morning. Meggie likes to watch the DLs when she's here. I believe the talk shows labeled you 'Asswipe of the Year,'" Cian confirmed. "I didn't think that was a term serious journalists would use, but they seemed happy with it."

"Stupid tabloids." They were always on his back. The paparazzi waited to capture his fuckups for the world to see. "What do they want me to do? I didn't even like many of those women. Most of them weren't looking for a mate. They wanted to be DL stars. Should I have asked one to marry me so I didn't look like a jerk and then break it off later?"

"Maybe you shouldn't have gone on the show in the first place," Cian said with a sensibility that set Dante's fangs on edge. "I find it hard to believe you were serious about finding a wife from twenty females desperate enough to share one man."

He hadn't been serious. He could admit that to himself. It had seemed like a fun way to waste some time while the bio-med unit worked on the sunscreen project. Dante had been surprised at how joyless dating twenty hot chicks was when there was always a camera around.

"Besides," Cian was continuing, "it works better the other way. You only have one dick, man. How are you going to keep that many women happy? It takes two of us to keep Meg satisfied. If you really want to go down that road, you should find a friend and get a woman between you."

"I don't want a ménage," Dante growled. The last thing he needed was some dude in bed with him. It worked for Beck and Cian because they shared a soul. Dante had never shared anything and wasn't about to start now. "I don't want anything at all, if I'm honest. But I don't have that choice anymore."

Cian stopped in the middle of the street, the dust churning under his feet. "What does that mean?"

"It means my father ordered me to get married or else," Dante admitted harshly.

"Are you serious?"

"Do I look like I'm joking?" Dante sighed and began walking again. "He kicked me off the sunscreen project. He told me I can't get back in until I have a consort at my side. He apparently thinks getting married will make me seem less like an asswipe."

"You can't get married just because your dad tells you to," Cian insisted.

Dante snorted inelegantly. That was the pot calling the kettle black. "I don't know why not. You were certainly going to, or have you forgotten a frigid filly named Maris? Are you trying to tell me it was your idea to bond with her?"

Before the civil war, Beck and Cian's father had arranged their bonding with no thought to love. Dante remembered Maris. She'd been a highborn bondmate. She'd also been one of the coldest women he'd ever met. Cian couldn't stand her. Many nights, Dante had listened to his cousin bemoan his fate.

"That was different," Cian insisted.

A wave of rising irritation nipped at his patience. "Sure, cos. It was different because it was your father threatening you and your inheritance at stake. I remember how much you hated that woman, and you would have married her if fate hadn't stepped in. I'm sure you would have stood up for yourself in the end. You would have told your father and Beck to go to hell because you wanted to marry for love." Dante's sarcasm flowed through the room.

"That's not fair." Cian frowned.

"None of it is," he shot back.

"And it *was* different. There was a kingdom at stake. I'm not trying to say I'm better than you. I don't think that at all. I'm trying to point out that you have choices. You have more freedom than Beck and I had."

Naturally he had it better off. "Stay out of it. I'm going to do what I need to do, and that's that. My father has always complained that I wasn't willing to do what it takes. Well, I'll show him."

Dante hurried along, leaving his cousin with the perfect wife and happy life behind. He didn't need a lecture from Cian. Cian was happily married. He had his brother to depend on. Dante's sister treated him like he was still five years old. Come to think of it, everyone treated him like he was a child. He was thirty. He ran a business. Well, he ran an arm of the family business. Of course, he had a manager who did most of the daily work, but everyone had help. Not everyone was as efficient and organized as his sister. Not everyone wanted each minute of the day planned out to model efficient time management.

What did Cian expect him to do? Should he tell his father to go straight to the Hell plane and righteously pack his bags? Where would he live? How would he survive? He'd never gone without a day in his life. He liked being rich, and he was good at it.

A long wail split the air around him, and Dante stopped. It was the howl of an animal in pain.

"What the hell was that?" Cian asked with a hitch in his breath.

"I think that's our guest," Beck replied.

Beck broke into a run, his long legs eating the distance to the tent. Meg struggled to keep up with him. While Beck ran ahead, Cian took their wife's hand and hurried her along. Dante jogged, easily catching up and matching Beck's stride.

There was a crowd outside the large tent, though he noticed they gave the place a wide berth, as though what was inside was too terrible for them to get too close to. It was easy for Dante to push his way to the front.

All around him, the people and creatures whispered in hushed tones. They talked about the animal in her cage and wondered if the bars were enough to keep her from their children. Savage, one called her. Brutal. Some spoke of her attempting to eat the gnomes assigned to care for her.

Maybe he would rethink the whole getting-married plan. Maybe Reeve had another, less hostile consort he could buy. He didn't need to die to prove this point to his father. A nice, homely, uneducated rube would do nicely. He wanted her to shock his father, not cannibalize him.

"Reeve, what's going on now?" Beck asked.

A small man with a pointy red hat moved toward Beck and Cian, who had taken his place beside his brother. Dante felt Meg at his side, but he was watching the gnome. Reeve of the Gentle Hills, who had served the Finn family for decades, bowed deeply.

"Your Highness," the gnome said, nodding to each of the Fae royals. "I am sorry to have bothered you, sir. I simply do not know what to do with the lass. She's completely feral. The demon gave us a potion to keep her weak. We've given it to her every day, hiding it in the water she drinks, but I fear it doesn't work. She wouldn't eat for the first three days she was here until Cara had the idea to give her raw flesh. She is an animal, sire. Though I am loath to do it, I must ask you to put her out of her misery."

"No," Meg argued instantly. She rushed to her husbands.

Dante held his tongue. The sounds coming out of the tent made him think that maybe Reeve was right. There was a long, loud howl. He wasn't sure how a sound like that came from a thinking being. It was primal. The sound was pure rage.

"Meggie, calm down," Beck commanded, his voice dropping to a low, dark bark. Meg's head dropped immediately.

"Yes, sir," she said quietly.

Beck's hand came out to lift her face up. The harsh lines left his brow, and he kissed her forehead. "I'll do what I can, Meggie mine. Trust me."

She smiled up at him, though Dante could see tears unshed in her eyes. "Always, baby."

Beck looked back at the gnome. He pulled his sword off the scabbard on his back and held it at his side. "Let's see her, then."

The flap of the tent was pulled back, and Dante found himself following his cousin.

To his heightened senses, the room was quite pungent. *Whoa.* He checked his gag reflex.

"I am sorry, sire," Reeve apologized, his face reddening. "We have not been able to clean her. She is filthy. When we attempt to get close, she tries to bite and scratch. She growls like an animal. It is the only language she seems to know."

"I thought I gave you translator implants," Dante heard himself saying. His eyes adjusted as the sunglasses flowed back into his jacket. It was dark in the tent. All of the flaps that would allow light in had been closed. There was a single candle burning, and only a bit of light filtered through the canvas at this time of the day. The place felt a bit like a pit. Or a tomb.

Reeve snorted. "As if we could get close enough to get one in her. We've barely managed to keep her fed and to give her the medication the demon claims she needs. I don't know what the bugger was thinking bringing me an animal to sell. She's not fit for any society."

Whatever else was said, Dante missed because he caught his first glimpse of the female in question. Through the gloom, he caught sight of a slender figure. He could see nothing of her face, but her form moved, flowed, toward the front of the cage.

The cage was the largest of the ones kept in the tent. A "mate cage," as the Fae called them, was supposed to be for show. It was a tradition that was passed down through the centuries. They were richly decorated. There were carpets covering the dirt floor and soft mattresses with fine blankets for the women to rest on. The blankets and pillows had been torn apart in the girl's cage. It was a chaotic mess, but still neater than the female herself.

She glowed. Like all consorts, there was an aura about her that a vampire couldn't mistake. His cousins might need to physically touch her to know that she was an adequate bondmate, but Dante could plainly see it. She glowed like Meg glowed. He wondered, seriously wondered, exactly how sweet she would taste. After she'd been properly cleaned, he thought with a shudder.

Dante's eyes adjusted to the low light. He studied the woman.

Her brown hair was matted. He couldn't tell how long it was, but there was an awful lot of it. She was covered in dirt and other things Dante didn't want to recognize. He was surprised to find her naked. Reeve would have given her robes to wear when she wasn't on display. Her small breasts were round, and he couldn't help but think they would make a sweet handful. She was slender, but her hips flared in a pleasing way. She would be lovely when she was clean. She sniffed the air around her and growled low in her throat at the newcomers.

"You see, Your Highness, she is completely feral. There is no intelligence," Reeve said.

"Bullshit," Dante muttered, not taking his eyes off the woman for a second. The woman in the cage was baring her teeth, but he was looking at her eyes. They were a startling blue. They looked like seas of the tropics on his home plane, blue and clear, and he felt like he could see deep down to her soul. He stared, quite caught in her eyes.

The woman rattled the cage viciously. Her small hands wrapped around the bars as though she could pull them apart with nothing but her own will. She howled, but Dante could hear something beneath the seemingly chaotic sounds.

"*Befria mig.*" She said it over and over again. He didn't recognize the language, but it was there all the same.

"*Befria mig?*" Dante tasted the words, trying to make sense of them. Vampires were known for being talented with languages, and his innate skills told him that this seemingly feral woman was trying to communicate.

The female stopped suddenly, her hands falling away from the bars. She stood up, where before she seemed inclined to prowl, as though more used to four legs than two. She stood properly now, and all of her attention was on Dante.

"*Hjälp mig, var vänlig min herre,*" she said plainly. Her stark blue eyes were filled now with tears.

"Not intelligent?" Beck asked. Dante could feel the iciness in the query.

Reeve sputtered, staring up at his king. "Sire, I…"

Dante ignored the small argument between the Fae. He stepped toward the woman, trying to ignore the smell. "I don't speak your language, sweetheart." He pulled a translator implant out of his pocket. He always had a couple. He held it up. "I need to place this behind your ear." He pointed to a small spot behind his own ear where the translator would be deployed. "Then we can understand each other."

"*Befria mig?*" the woman asked, her voice almost timid now, as though she didn't quite believe him. This close, Dante could see her high cheekbones and the delicate planes of her face. Her cheeks were soft and her chin a stubborn line.

He gave her his most reassuring smile. He could handle this. He could handle this better than Beck, who had just planned on brute force. Dante could show them all that diplomacy and charm worked even better. "Sure, sweetheart. Let me get the translator in and we'll '*befria mig*' all you like."

"Mr. Dellacourt, I would not do that if I were you," Reeve warned him.

"It's fine." He had this. He moved toward her. "Give me the keys."

Reeve pursed his lips together as though he would argue further.

His small hands didn't move toward the keys on his belt. Dante gave his cousin an impatient glance.

"It's one small female, Beck," Dante said, irritated that yet again someone thought he couldn't do something. She was petite, and her eyes were soft and pleading. "I think I can handle her."

"Well, if you can't, I'm sure I can," Beck allowed, his hand still on the sword, but his arm had relaxed. He stood in the center of the room, blocking the way out. He was a broad, reassuring figure. "Reeve, open the cage. Let Dante have a try with her. I would hate to kill her if this is all a misunderstanding."

The gnome didn't hesitate when his king ordered him. Reeve moved immediately, pulling the correct key off his belt and turning it in the heavy lock that separated the female from her freedom.

Dante watched her, strangely fascinated by the creature in the cage. Every muscle in her slender body was taut as the small gnome slowly pulled back the door. Her eyes flicked suspiciously about the room as though she were waiting for something terrible to happen. Was she frightened? She'd been thrown into a world she obviously didn't understand. At least Meg had spoken the language. This poor thing didn't even have that comfort. Dante felt a wealth of sympathy rise for her.

Moving cautiously toward her, he kept his hands out, attempting to show her he had no weapons, only the tiny translator that would painlessly burrow into her and attach itself to her brain thereby allowing her to understand the known languages of the planes. He hoped it worked as quickly as it was supposed to. Even if the language was unknown, the computer would decode it. It shouldn't take long before he could talk to the little creature in front of him. Then they would discuss hygiene.

She took a step back when she realized he was coming in. She went down on her feet. She crouched low, her knuckles grazing the floor. She looked tense, as though prepared to pounce.

"It's all right," he cajoled. He suspected she was quite lovely under all that grime. The bones of her face were delicate, but well defined. Her eyes were wide and her lips…he knew a lot of women on his plane who paid money to get lips like that. And she was young. She was too young to have eyes so wary.

He saw the minute her eyes changed from wary to aggressive.

Beck had moved closer, and the female had caught a glimpse of the sword in his hand. She growled and went after the only target she could get to—Dante.

"Wait," he tried desperately. The translator fell from his hand as she leapt from her crouch and pounced.

Chapter Three

Dante felt his head smash against the iron bars of the cage as the female slammed into his body. She was slight, but he was shocked by the strength in her delicate frame. She didn't feel insubstantial as she pressed down on him. She wrapped a hand around his throat.

"Get away from him!" Beck's command roared through the tent.

The woman snarled as she looked to the king of the Seelie Fae. *"Låt mig gå, eller ska jag döda honom."*

Dante's head throbbed, and there was something about the hand at his throat that was bringing out the beast in him. He looked up at the slender feminine body that crouched in a dominating fashion, and he felt something break inside of him. *Too much.* It was too much for a man to take. First his father, then Beck, and now this slip of a woman thought he was less than a man. His heart began to pound. His fangs lengthened in anger rather than arousal, though he admitted that was present as well. He could smell her now. He smelled past the filth to the woman under the dirt. The smell was strangely familiar, as though something primal in him recognized her on a base level.

Beneath the filth, there was a sweetness. It was there, hidden under the dirt and bravado. She thought she could hide it from him? A dark need began to twist in his gut. It was totally foreign and a bit frightening.

And it was far too powerful to ignore.

"Dante, stay calm, and I'll get you out of this." Beck's words were meant to be reassuring, but all Dante heard was that Beck intended to get between him and the female.

The female had attacked him. She'd put him on his back and laid her hands on his throat as though he were some submissive, soft thing to bargain with. He didn't know exactly what her words meant, but he understood. She was using him. She was threatening to kill him if Beck didn't back down and allow her to flee. He was her pawn, her weak pawn.

She was afraid of Beck, but Dante wanted her afraid of him.

His claws popped out, an ancient gift from his royal ancestors. Almost no vampire used them now except in the arena when they fought for a mate. It was considered impolite to show one's claws, but there was nothing polite about this situation. His fingertips hurt where the claws had burst, but he made no sound. He felt his vision expand and knew that his eyes had bled out, filling the orbs with a deep green as his irises expanded. All of his senses opened up. He could see the heat pouring off the female, and he knew she was different. She wasn't vampire or human or Fae.

But she was his.

Her hands tightened around his throat. She didn't bother to look down at her prey. *"Jag vill döda honom."*

The female sounded in control now. The frightened girl who had pleaded with him was gone. Her brilliant blue eyes were still on Beck. Beck seemed to be the only thing in the room she found worthy. Dante needed to make a few things clear.

The growl that came from his throat was both foreign and deeply satisfying. His people had left their primal selves long ago, but now he allowed instinct to take over, and it felt good.

Shocked blue eyes glanced down at him, as though she was surprised he was still there. He opened his mouth and bared his long fangs. In a single move, he flipped her over on her back and straddled her hips. He didn't try to hide the erection he was sporting. He ground it against her, further intimidation he could use. He genuinely enjoyed the fear in her eyes. It meant she was finally aware of him.

"Don't try that again, sweetheart," he said harshly through his fangs. She squirmed under him, getting him harder. Her hips bucked up, and Dante ground her down. "I'm a little on edge. Let's try to start over."

She kicked up neatly, catching the edge of his cock as she shoved him to the side. Pure agony bloomed across him and Dante gasped, falling over.

She was on her feet in the blink of an eye. Dante heard Beck shouting and the clang of metal against the iron of the cage. Ignoring the pain in favor of the righteous anger that now burned through him, he followed. He hissed at the ache in his groin, but he was on his feet immediately. The female ran through the cage, seeking her freedom. Dante followed, knowing he would never permit it. She would not get away from him.

Beck's face was savage as he drew the sword over his head.

"No!" Dante screamed the command in a voice that didn't sound like his own. Beck froze. The sword in his hand hung in midair. The entire tent seemed to still as though time itself was taking a short break. Dante stared at his prey. "I will handle her."

The woman looked between Dante and Beck. Her eyes darted between them as if she couldn't figure out who was the bigger threat.

"I can't let her go," Beck said quietly. Every bit of Beck's focus was on the woman. "Meggie and Ci are out there. I won't take any chance that she hurts them."

He understood. If there was the smallest chance that Meg or Ci could suffer a moment's discomfort from this creature, Beck would kill her without a second thought. His cousin loved few people, but those Beck did love had his whole heart. His cousin would kill for him, too. But Dante needed something besides his cousin's sword this afternoon.

"I will take care of her." He had to speak carefully. Forming the words around his fangs felt alien to him, but he forced them from his throat anyway. She was his responsibility. She had been from the moment he'd heard her plea. He was the only one who had understood she was intelligent, and he was the only one who could save her now. Though she might not like how he did it.

50

Beck snarled, frustration pouring off him as he lowered his sword. "See that you do, and quickly."

Dante knew how hard it was for his cousin to stand down. The warrior king was used to taking charge. Beck's eyes were narrow and focused solely on the female. He was waiting and watching for her to make a single wrong move. Dante would have to be careful. Beck nodded to him and moved to block the entrance to the tent.

The woman turned and squared off against Dante. She moved, her limbs fluid and close to the ground. She circled him, her every step a testament to grace and potential violence. Dante watched, taking in the way she stalked around until he had the rules of engagement down. He could take a sword from Beck, but that would only prove that he had better weapons than she did. He needed to take her down in a way that left no question who was in charge. The instinct to dominate the lithe creature in front of him was overwhelming.

Dante mimicked her, allowing his body to flow in a predatory fashion. He felt an almost drugged sense of peace as he gave in to his primal urges. This was a simpler place. The world narrowed to include only two people.

The female seemed to realize his intent. Her eyes formed slits, and her mouth firmed stubbornly. She reached her hand out as though to swipe at him. He reacted instantly. He batted her hand down. Dante didn't hold back. He heard the smack as his hand slapped viciously against hers. She pulled it back quickly, clearly surprised at his violence.

"*Är du Första?*" She bit her bottom lip as she asked the question.

"You will kneel and take the fucking translator," Dante declared.

He moved his hand down in a gesture she couldn't possibly mistake. He wanted her on her knees in front of him. She might not know why he wanted her to do it, but she would know where he wanted her. "Reeve, get the chip. Get it now."

She backed up, but she didn't back down. Her eyes slid between Dante and the door that was guarded by Beck. It was obvious she was trying to decide between fight and flight.

"Kneel!" He would allow her neither option. She would kneel and submit. There was no other acceptable outcome.

She turned and ran. He jumped into action. Before Beck could draw his sword, Dante was on the woman. He wrestled her to the ground. He pulled ruthlessly at her arms, gathering her wrists behind her back and shoving her breasts into the hard dirt of the floor. He used his weight to cover and control her. She fought, but his hold dominated her petite body. She spat out curses until Dante had finally had enough of her rebellion.

He gathered her wrists in one large hand. He used his other hand to shove her face into the ground and, running on primal instinct, placed his fangs directly over the delicate bones of her neck. He bit down with a gentle but unmistakable force, careful not to break the skin. She stilled beneath him. The only movement from his prey was the breath rattling in and out of her chest. She was obviously aware that he could break her neck with the slightest force. She was at his mercy.

"Jag lämna," she said breathlessly. She relaxed beneath him.

Dante had the insane urge to press his victory. The pretty predator lay still and silent beneath him. Even her words sounded submissive. The impulse was there to pull off his slacks and pound into her softness, claiming that which he had conquered. He could spread her thighs and take her. She was his by right of battle. She would accept him now.

Instead, he took a deep breath and sat up, releasing his hold on her neck. He hadn't broken the skin, but there were twin indentions where he'd pressed his fangs. He stared at those marks, allowing his finger to trace them. If he'd used a bit more force, her blood would have flowed into his mouth. *Consort blood.* He'd heard the stories. Consort blood was sweet, sweeter and richer than any meal pill. If the stories were true, her blood could make him stronger and faster than he was. Every instinct in his body screamed at him to plunge his fangs in and drink his fill. He wanted so badly to feed in that moment, though it had nothing to do with hunger.

But he wasn't an animal. He was a modern man, and he had a job to do.

"The chip," Dante commanded, holding his hand out.

Reeve responded immediately. The chip was in Dante's palm, and he placed it against the delicate skin right behind her left ear. The chip disappeared, burrowing painlessly through skin and bone and into the brain.

"My consort needs a bath. See that it is drawn." He didn't move from his position. Now his hand moved forward, rubbing across her neck. She was still beneath him, her eyes closed, her posture utterly submissive.

It filled something inside him he hadn't known was missing.

"Your consort?" Reeve asked. There was no mistaking the shock in the gnome's voice.

"Dante, what are you saying?" Beck asked.

"You heard me." Dante grinned, looking at the gnome. "I'll take her. Do you need cash or will credit do?"

* * * *

Kaja sat quietly as the First checked the water. She wasn't sure why he needed such a large bowl, but many things in this odd world confused her. She kept her eyes on the First. She thought about running again, but he'd caught her so quickly. She still remembered the moment when he'd placed his fangs against her neck and proven himself to be alpha. She'd been wrong. She had thought him weak, but he was obviously the First in this pack.

"Bath," he said.

There were many more words in that strange language he spoke, but the word "bath" seemed to stand out. He spoke rapidly to the creature in the pointy hat. Kaja's stomach growled. The little ones were fast. She hadn't been able to catch one yet. Perhaps now that she was out of their cage, she could make a meal of the fat one. She would only feast on the male, though. He was the one who spoke to the thin man with the sharp claws. The male had been the one who had locked her in the cage. The female had brought her fresh meat and sang while she worked in the tent. Kaja had found the sounds soothing. The small female had talked to her. Kaja hadn't understood her words, but there seemed to be kindness behind them. Kaja knew she shouldn't have, but she had grown fond of the female and wouldn't eat her.

Of course, she wouldn't do anything yet. The First kept his eyes on her. Anytime she attempted to stand, he moved over, placed his hand on her neck, and forced her back down. He said something called "wait." Kaja thought that meant to sit. He was First here, so she did.

When they had walked in, she'd believed the large man with dark hair and the sword was the leader. Now she utterly discounted the fact. He didn't even have fangs or claws so far as she could tell. He had the sword because he could not fight with his hands. The one with the reddish-gold hair, he was the leader. He'd been the one to force her to submit. He hadn't used magic to do it, either. If he had, she would still fight him as she had fought her captor and the little ones. She would respect this First's dominance because it was natural.

It wasn't anything like the Nightmare Man.

Kaja let herself think about it for once.

It hadn't taken long to get to the mountains Stellan had spoken of. She had stayed in her wolf form, preferring it greatly in the cold forests. So far from the small valley she'd grown up in, Kaja had seen many wonders. There had been frost giants in the mountains, their massive forms almost too much for her eyes to take in. She had hidden her body deep in the snow, and they had passed her by. She took it as a sign from Freya that her quest would be fruitful.

She had hunted freely. Without the restrictions of rank, she had eaten far better than she had with the pack. Rabbits at first, and then small deer had been her prey. When her strength was up, she'd taken down a buck on her own. Oh, she had feasted. Her belly had been full for the first time in her life. The week she had spent traveling to the mountains had been strangely fulfilling. On her own, she felt strong and capable. Her foster mother had been wrong. She had not died. She had not faded. She had been lonely. But then even among the pack, she had been lonely.

She'd searched for the magical doorway Stellan had spoken of, but the Nightmare Man found her first. He had been tall, not as tall as the frost giants, but much taller than Kaja. His stick-thin body belied his strength. Kaja had underestimated him, as she had underestimated this First. She should have run, but she'd attacked the thin man instead. Still, if it had only been a battle of strength, Kaja knew she would have won. The Nightmare Man had a weapon. There had been a terrible sting when he had shoved it into her arm. She had felt her strength fade, and she changed without willing it. One moment she had been a strong wolf, the next she had been small and frail and freezing in the snow. Kaja could still remember the way the air and snow had bitten into her skin. It had been so cold it burned. She had tried to change. She had needed her fur.

"It's no use, shining one," the thing above her had said. He spoke her language perfectly when he wanted to. "You can't change. Don't fight it. I'll get a good price for you. One of these days my clan will have to thank that jackass Torin. We've made more money off the slave trade in the last ten years than we could have imagined. Behave now, little dog, and soon you'll have a new master to take care of you."

The Nightmare Man had picked her up and carried her. Her weight hadn't slowed him at all. He'd found a cave, but the entrance shimmered and when he'd walked through it, Kaja had found herself in another world. The new world was warm, without a hint of snow. It had taken a day to get to the village and her cage.

She shook her head and pulled herself back into the present. She had worried at first that she was in Hel, the place where wolves went to die, but this male made her doubt it. He must be the master the Nightmare Man had spoken of. She watched him, trying not to let her appreciation show. She had seen several males over the days she'd spent in the cage. None of them had shown her his glorious fangs and claws. All the men had seemed appalled with her. They looked at her with disdain, as the pack had. This First wasn't afraid of her. He'd fought her. He'd fought *for* her.

"Come," he said, his voice taking on that deep cadence that pulled at her.

Kaja's eyes went wide. That word made sense to her. "You want me to come?"

"That's just cool," the second man with midnight hair said. There seemed to be two of him.

After she had calmed and accepted the First's dominance, the second man with black hair had been allowed inside the tent along with a pretty red-haired woman. The two men wouldn't let their woman get as close to Kaja as she obviously wanted. The woman had complained but backed down when the one with the sword growled.

"I am not cold at all," Kaja said. Their words suddenly made sense. They seemed to be learning her language. Or perhaps there was some magic at play, after all.

The second dark-haired man smiled broadly. He seemed to do all the smiling for the two. "I wasn't talking about the temperature, dear. I've spent too much time with my wife. It's a human saying. It means I think the technology is very advanced. I'd like to take one apart and figure out how it runs."

"Small words in the beginning, Ci," the First said. He frowned. Kaja liked the fine line it put in between his eyebrows. "And she won't understand slang at all."

"What is slang?" Kaja asked.

The First turned to her. His eyes seemed kind as he walked over and knelt down. He took her hand in his. His skin was cool to the touch, but she liked the feel of it against her own. "It means this is going to be hard, sweetheart. Trust me. There are going to be words you don't get."

She didn't "get" half of what he'd said. She did understand the request. He'd asked her to trust him. She breathed in. He was so close to her. She opened her senses and let him fill her. Oh, she liked his smell. She leaned over and let her nose run against his neck. He smelled of many interesting things. Beneath all of it was a scent that was uniquely his own. She sighed as she caught the scent of his arousal. He was interested in her. She felt her own body respond, softening and preparing. The First wanted her.

"Hey!" the black-haired man—the irritable one—called out.

"Back off, Beck." The First held still and let her smell him. He honored her by allowing her this close. And in front of his kin. No one allowed her so close in her own pack. "She isn't doing anything to hurt me."

She reveled in him for a moment. It was the closest she'd been allowed to another being. Even when Sven had taken her, he had simply shoved her on her knees and thrust in from behind while some of his kin held her down. He hadn't allowed her the intimacy of rubbing skin to skin and covering herself in his scent. She liked this First's warmth and the faint sound of his heartbeat. She breathed him in, memorizing his smell. Like a memory, a smell was something to think upon long after the action was done.

After a moment, she leaned back. The First stared down at her, a curious look on his handsome face. He was so beautiful, with vibrant green eyes and sensual lips. His face was not covered in hair. His skin was perfect, and she longed to trace the utterly masculine line of his jaw.

"I hope that wasn't some formal greeting, sweetheart," the First said with a chuckle that did strange things to her insides. "I'm afraid I won't be able to return it right now. You stink something horrible, love."

She frowned, her heart sinking. He did not like her scent. It was a bad sign. She swallowed down her emotions. She should have known. The pack had always told her she was cursed. No one would want her. She should have stayed alone rather than trying to seek out a new pack. Now she was alone in a world that she couldn't understand. She couldn't even change anymore.

"Hey," the First said quietly. He placed a hand under her chin and forced her to look up. His voice had shifted to a musical, cajoling tone. "It's all right. We can get you clean, and then I'll sniff you all you like. You can teach me all your kinky ways. You'll find that I'm a tolerant man. It's just customary where I come from to not reek of…all the things you reek of. Come on."

He stood up, his muscular frame unfolding gracefully. Kaja took a moment to study him. He did not seem to require immediate compliance. He seemed a patient First. Perhaps it was why the others followed him. He was tall, perhaps a full head taller than Kaja. When she stood, her head fit neatly under his chin. She appreciated his lean build. He had taken off the strange clothing that covered his chest, and now she could admire the strong muscles found there. He was different from the males of the pack. He had no hair on his chest. She found she liked it. His skin was pale, almost luminous. There was no fat on his body. Only long, muscular lines. His stomach was covered in muscle that led to lean hips. His pants covered the part of him she wished to see. She was curious if he would allow her to look at his male parts. Were they as beautiful as the rest of him?

He grinned down at her. "I'm glad you like the package,

sweetheart. It'll make things a lot easier between us. Now let's get you cleaned up."

She gasped in happy surprise. She understood. He wanted her to groom herself. It was easier when she was in her wolf form, but she could do it if it pleased him. She nodded and decided to start with her hands. She licked one hand and frowned. She did not taste very good.

"Whoa!" the First said. Kaja looked up. He seemed positively horrified.

"Do you think she was raised by wolves?" The red-haired female's eyes were wide as they studied her. Shame washed over Kaja. She was as stupid as the pack said. She did not understand even the simplest command. It must have shown in her eyes, because the female softened. "I'm sorry. I wasn't trying to offend. We don't lick ourselves clean."

"Sometimes you do, lover. Beck often orders you to lick him clean," the softer of the two dark-haired men said. It earned him an elbow in the ribs from the woman.

The First frowned at his lessers. "Nice, guys. Make her think we're all pervs."

"She'll find out soon enough," the man said and stepped back to avoid another elbow. His twin laughed aloud.

The First sent them a dirty look. His eyes softened when he turned back to Kaja. "What's your name, sweetheart?"

"Name?" She did not recognize the word. The magic they employed only worked part of the time. She still was confused by much of their talk.

He patted his chest. "Dante. That's what people call me. What do people call you?"

The People called her many names. She flushed thinking of all the things she had been called. She had chosen her own "name" at the age of eight, though the members of the pack still refused to use it, preferring to call her "that creature." She did not have to tell him that. She could hide her shame here. "Kaja. I am Kaja. I like it. It means pure."

She'd always liked the way it sounded.

"Kaja, that is ironic." The First laughed. Kaja felt a sweetness center in her chest. It was the first time she'd heard the word she called herself from another's lips. The First stopped and smiled down at her. He touched his chest. "You are Kaja, and I am called Dante."

"Dante," she said, trying the word out on her tongue. Dante, the First.

"Come," the First said. He held out his hand. Kaja let him pull her up. "Meg, do you have anything with you that will take the stink off her? I think there's a pretty woman under here somewhere."

The female handed the First a square. It was pink, and Kaja could smell a pleasant floral scent. She hoped they didn't want her to eat it. It didn't look like something good to eat. The First held his square and began pulling her toward the water. Perhaps she was supposed to take a drink. She leaned over and smelled the water. It seemed fine, though it was a bit warm.

"No, sweetheart," the First said. "Get in. I want you to bathe yourself."

Her eyes went wide, and she pulled her fingers out of his hand. He wanted her to immerse herself in water? She'd seen two members of the pack fall through the ice into water once. They'd struggled and fought and finally went under never to be seen again.

"No," Kaja said, shaking her head.

She would not allow him to drown her. She would not be put down. She'd done nothing wrong. She planted her feet to stop from coming one step closer to that small pool.

"Yes," the First sighed. "Look, this isn't going to work if I can't convince you to stay clean. Vampires are fastidious creatures. Heightened senses and all. Let's get you cleaned up, and then we can talk. I have plans, you see, and you, darling, figure into them."

She wouldn't be able to talk. She would drown. She pulled back and tried to change. A growl of frustration started low in her throat. Her limbs would not change. She was weak in this form. Why, oh why, could she not change? She tried to pull away from the First's hold on her. She wanted so badly to run. She would run and never come back. She would find a place with a forest. She would live alone forever.

"Stop fighting me," the First said, sounding tired. He wrapped his hand around her arm and tried to haul her to the pool.

"Tell her, Dante." That came from the dark-haired man with the

59

sword.

The First refused to give up his hold on her. They were at an impasse. She struggled against him. "I just did that, Beck."

"No, you didn't. You were polite. That's not what she needs. She didn't respond to you until you forced her to submit, and then she followed you like a sweet girl. Dogs are like that. They fight and bite until you show them you're their master."

"She is not an animal." The First sounded irritated.

"Neither is Meggie, but trust me, our lives got easier once I took control," Beck offered.

The red-haired girl snorted. "As if."

The one called Beck stood too close now. He stared at the First. "Tell her what to do. If she doesn't do it, make her do it. She needs it. She's scared. We have no idea where she came from or what she's been through. She calmed down once she realized you were stronger than she was. It makes her feel safe. She needs dominance first and then kindness. Take control or I will."

Kaja fought harder. She didn't like the look of that one. He was larger than the First and probably cruel. What was this kindness he spoke of? The word did not translate. Why would the First let her close and then kill her? Tears formed in her eyes. She hated them. Helga used to slap her every time she cried. It was weakness. She growled low in the back of her throat to cover them up.

"No." The First growled right back. "You will do as I say. Don't make me hurt you. I don't want to do that, but I will if it means keeping you alive. If you get away, Beck will hunt you. Do you understand?"

His words were too fast, and she wasn't truly listening. The man—Beck—had his hand on his sword again. Meg was pulled behind the soft one. Kaja kicked out, trying to hit the First in the groin again. She was surrounded and she couldn't change, but she wouldn't go down without a fight.

The First roared at her, and she was on the ground once more. She felt the hard dirt against her skin and his hand on her neck.

"You belong to me," the First snarled at her, his breath hot against the back of her neck. "You will do as I say. If you don't, we're going to have a problem. I might not have played at BDSM, darling, but I assure you I can spank that sweet ass of yours if I have to."

Kaja went limp. The tears began, and they wouldn't stop this time. Perhaps it would have been better if they'd left her to die after her father's betrayal. She'd been a newborn babe. She wouldn't have cared. She would have given in to the snow sleep and never woken up.

"Damn it." The First pulled her up. His arms wrapped around her. She was filled with his scent once more. She didn't struggle. He was warm and smelled so good to her. She cried and let him settle her on his lap. "Why are you fighting me, sweetheart?"

"I do not wish to die," she said quietly. She didn't know why. Valhalla had to be better, but she worried she would be given to Hel.

The First's face was wide open. "What? I'm not trying to kill you. I'm trying to get you clean."

She stared up at him, sensing no lies. "Other pack members have drowned when they have fallen into the water."

His hand caressed her cheek. "I promise, I won't let you drown. Here's what's going to happen. You'll get in the tub and wash the filth away. Reeve is already preparing water for a fresh tub. We'll haul away the grimy water, and I'll soak with you for a while. Would you like that?"

She didn't see that she had much of a choice in the matter. He was the only thing she'd found to cling to in this odd world. If he betrayed her, at least it would all be over. But if he was not lying, perhaps she had found something good.

When he got up, she followed.

Chapter Four

"What the hell do you think you're doing, Dante?"

Dante forced himself to turn around. He didn't want to. He was enjoying the picture that Kaja made as Meg soaped her hair. It had taken Kaja a while, but she was finally settling in to the business of getting clean. He'd had to stroke her and hold her for the longest time. It was the only way to calm her. Her bright, blue eyes had pleaded with him to keep her safe, and he couldn't deny her. He'd felt his heart tugged by the sweet whimpers she'd made as she'd tried to adjust to the water. He'd let her know how pleased he'd been with her for being so brave. He hadn't been joking or sarcastic. It really had taken a lot for her to get into the tub.

Now her eyes were closed as she allowed Meg to rub her scalp. There was a dreamy look on her face. She seemed to enjoy the contact. *What a sensual little thing.* If she liked having her hair washed, how much would she like a massage? He would like to rub his hands across her soft flesh and feel her respond.

"Dante." Beck's voice pulled him out of that fantasy. "I asked you a question. What are you thinking buying that woman? Have you lost your mind?"

He took a deep breath. Yelling at his cousin would only scare Kaja. "I bought a consort, cos. Vampires do it every day. Do I need to remind you that you bought Meg in this very tent?"

"I fought for Meg," Beck corrected. "As you should be forced to fight in a tourney for Kaja. The reason you aren't fighting is that no one else is willing to take her. That should tell you something."

It was traditional for the gnomes to collect an entry fee for the tournaments they held. The prize was a consort. A large tournament could attract twenty to thirty combatants. He kind of thought it was a plus that he didn't have to get his clothes dirty. He didn't mention this to his warrior cousin.

"I agreed to pay a measure of gold equal to ten tourney fees," Dante assured him. "Reeve will be able to give the demon a proper cut. This solves the problem for everyone. Stop worrying."

Beck's mouth tightened. "I wasn't worried about Reeve. I'm worried about you. You can't seriously believe she will make you a fit consort. She didn't even know what a bath was."

"Meg wasn't from this plane, either," Dante pointed out. He was rapidly getting irritated with his cousin. It was irrational. He should be thrilled. It was exactly the reaction he was hoping for. She was spectacularly unsuitable. He couldn't have dreamed up a less suitable candidate if he'd tried. Yet Beck's assessment of her rankled.

"Meg is highly intelligent," Beck said in a wholly lofty voice, the arrogance of it setting Dante on edge. "She might have come from a different plane, but she had a working knowledge of the creatures around her."

"Yes, that's why she nearly let a kelpie eat her," Dante shot back. It had taken Meg a while to get used to her new home.

Beck shrugged, his eyes straying to his wife. "I didn't say she always used it intelligently. She adapted quite nicely. She's making an excellent queen. This Kaja is never going to adapt. She's practically feral. How is she going to live on the Vampire plane? Do you honestly think she'll be happy in your penthouse, going to teas with other consorts, and attending charity balls?"

Again, that had been a part of the plan he'd formulated to get around his father's edicts. He struggled to see her sitting in the penthouse's large, elegant parlor having drinks with his parents, sister, and her consort before the consorts were called in to dinner. He would sit with his father and sister and discuss business while she was led to the sumptuous dining room and did whatever consorts did while they ate. More than likely they talked about fashion and the latest DLs. She wouldn't know what a DL was. He wasn't sure she knew what clothes were.

"You see my point?" Beck asked, not unkindly. "Look, Cian talked to me about what Uncle Don is doing to you. You might not like to hear this, but I think he's right. You do need to find a consort. It's far past time, but Kaja isn't the right one. I've discussed the situation with Reeve, and if your family will pay her fee and put a hefty down payment on the next suitable consort to come through, Reeve will give you the first look. He'll make it a private sale contingent on your father's acceptance of the female. I'm sure your father will agree to it. It isn't a deal Reeve would make with another vampire family. I'll take Kaja and find a place where she'll be happy. You'll get your consort, and Kaja will be free."

His claws popped out as the words from his cousin's mouth sank in. His hands twitched with the need to wrap them around his cousin's throat. A righteous sense of possessiveness swept across him. It was primal and like nothing he'd ever felt before. "I bought Kaja. I paid her full price. I used my own fucking money to do it. I signed the paperwork not ten minutes ago. Is Reeve threatening to revoke her sale?"

Beck took a step back, his eyes wide as he glanced down at Dante's hands. "Not at all. Look, cos, no one is telling you that you can't have a consort. One comes through every couple of weeks. Be patient."

His cousin patted him sympathetically on the shoulder, and without a thought, Dante batted his hand away. Beck held his fisted hand by his side, but Dante could see the impulse to fight in his cousin. Part of him hoped the big Fae gave in to it. He was sick of being treated like an idiot. "Stay out of my marriage. If you won't accept Kaja, then get your ass back to your kingdom. I'll take care of my consort."

He turned and noted Meg's white face. She watched the confrontation with a worried air. Kaja's eyes had come open, but she didn't look worried. She was watching Beck with narrow eyes, as though prepared to attack should he take a step toward Dante.

"It's all right, sweetheart." He took a deep breath and calmed a bit. She didn't need more drama tonight. She needed to see that he was calm and in charge. The gnomes were coming in with the second tub. The water she'd cleaned herself in was grimy. She needed a bath from her bath. "Beck isn't going to hurt me. He's leaving."

"We're leaving?" Cian asked, walking in with a bucket of hot water.

"No," Beck replied with a frown. "Dante is being unreasonable."

Meg got up and fetched a towel as the wee ones made the clean tub ready. Kaja stood up.

"Hey," Dante said, quickly covering her in the towel. He hadn't thought much about her nudity before. She'd been covered in filth. Now that her pale skin was clean and glowing like a pearl, he had problems with it. "We have guests."

She nodded. "Yes, I can see them. Meg, Cian, and Beck."

She smiled as she pointed to each and seemed pleased to have remembered their names.

"Yes, and the men have no need to see what belongs to me," Dante muttered. "They should leave."

"You see what I mean?" Beck asked, looking at his brother. "Unreasonable. He won't listen to me, Ci. Talk to him. She's wild. She needs to roam. She needs a home with lots of land and places to run. I was thinking of the woods outside the village. As long as she promises not to attack our villagers, it would be perfect. There is plenty of game in the forest. Would you like that, Kaja? Would you like to be alone in the woods?"

Dante felt her small hand slip into his. She clutched the towel around her. Her smile had disappeared. "The First does not want me?"

"First?" Beck asked.

She inclined her head toward Dante. "Yes. I thought the First wished to mate with me. He allowed me intimacies. Do I not understand? Does he already have a mate? Our First is allowed to mate with any of the women. I am clean now. I will stay clean if that is what you require."

Her big eyes were killing him. What was it about this petite woman that kicked him in the gut? And the cock. Damn, she was beautiful. She was utterly different from any woman he'd met before.

He put his hands under her arms and lifted her out of the water. The gnomes immediately took the filthy tub away. The new tub was ready. Dante could see everything he had asked for, including his Scotch. There was a glass of water for Kaja. "I do have a mate, though we use the word consort where I come from. You are my consort, Kaja. I signed the papers a few moments ago. You legally belong to me. Do you understand?"

Her smile was back, and this time there was a bright happiness to her face. Her chestnut brown hair was starting to curl up, and he couldn't help but stare at the graceful line of her neck. "You claim me?"

He gave into the temptation, touching her porcelain skin lightly. "I claim you. I'll take care of you."

"You don't know what you're saying," Beck interjected.

"Leave it, brother," Cian said in a firm, authoritative voice. "Dante knows what he's doing. If he doesn't, he'll figure it out. He'll take care of her."

There was a long moment between the twins. Dante was surprised to see Beck back down. He nodded briefly. "All right, then. We'll leave you to your wedding night. We've been given a tent next to this one. You only have to call out and I will come."

"I don't need you to save me from a woman," Dante winced. It sounded whiny even to his own ears.

Beck studied Kaja carefully. "I hope that's all she is, cos. Come on. Let's go settle our wife in for the evening."

Cian grinned brightly. "Aye, she definitely needs some settling."

Meg shook her head but threw her husband an affectionate look. She crossed to Dante. "Are you sure about this?"

"You, too? Don't think I can handle her, do you?"

"No, I was thinking of her, actually. She seems oddly innocent."

Kaja frowned. She seemed to be trying to figure something out. "The First told you to leave. Do you not fear the First?"

Meg had the audacity to grin. "Fear Dante? Only if I were a cat. Or a bottle of Scotch. He can tear through that, if you know what I mean."

Kaja shook her head. "I do not."

Meg sighed and stepped back. "I know. I'll see you in the morning, Kaja. If you need anything, we'll be in the tent next door. Good night."

Kaja let the towel drop the minute the others were gone. There was no exhibitionism in it. She simply seemed comfortable with her nudity. Dante wasn't comfortable with his own state of dress. His cock was trying to tunnel out of his pants.

"You should beat them more often. I do not think they properly fear you." She leaned over and sniffed at the Scotch. She wrinkled her nose and moved to the water, drinking it down.

He couldn't help but laugh at the suggestion. He also couldn't help but notice that he was alone with a naked female whom he was practically obligated to fuck. He'd signed papers promising to fuck her and fuck her often.

"Beck, Ci, and Meggie are family, sweetheart. I scarcely think I'll be beating on them anytime soon." He turned and pushed the pants off his hips. He tossed them to the side, but the clever nanites readjusted themselves, folding the pants neatly in a square.

Kaja stepped back. "The coverings are magic."

It was going to be fun to show Kaja his plane. "I'm sure they seem that way to you. Would you believe me if I told you they're tiny machines that a rival corporation makes? We tried to make a competing line at Dellacorp. They developed their own intelligence and attacked the people wearing them. That was a lawsuit, let me tell you."

Kaja stared at the pants. "What is a machine?"

He decided to leave that part of her education for another time. He sank down into the tub, hoping the heat would wilt his raging erection a bit. He found it necessary to talk through his fangs. The damn things wouldn't go away. "Don't worry about it. Come here, Kaja."

She didn't hesitate. She gingerly stepped into the tub and placed herself between his legs with her back to his front. She leaned against him and sighed. "I like the warmth. It is very cold where I come from. I've never known I could feel so warm."

Her shoulders rubbed against his chest, and her little ass nestled against his cock. Nope, the heat wasn't helping at all. His cock was long and thick against her skin.

"This home you were taken from, do you want to go back?" He needed to ease his conscience. If she had a home and a husband, maybe he should think about asking Beck to help her find her way back. His cock protested mightily.

"No," she said quietly. "I do not wish to go home. I do not truly have a home."

"Why do you call me First?" He was curious. "Is that what you call the leader of your people?"

He didn't mention that he wasn't the leader of anything. Or had that changed? When he thought about it, he was kind of the leader of her.

"The First is the most important," Kaja explained. She spoke slowly, as though measuring each word. "He is First among the pack, though his mate is usually First among the women. He selects a strong mate. Because they are First, they get the best of the meat and the warmest place to sleep. The Second gets the next best, you understand?"

"Yes." He let his hands cup her shoulders, reveling in the smooth skin. He breathed in her scent. Her head rested close to his face. Now she smelled of citrus and soap. It was the same cleanser Meg used, but it smelled different on Kaja. "So does everyone have a number? What number were you, sweetheart?"

He felt her deflate. "I had no number. I was not allowed to ever move up, so I did not need a number."

"What do you mean?"

"My father, he attempted to become First. He lost. The pack executed my brothers and my father. My mother died while birthing me. I was alone. I was female. They allowed me to live, but I had no place in the pack."

Her words were even, as though she was working hard to cover her emotions, but Dante could feel her hurt behind them. He thought about the strange connection he'd felt to the female from the moment he'd seen her. A restlessness stole over him. He preferred to think about screwing her. That didn't bring forth any odd, protective instincts in him. He understood sex, but he felt the need to set the ground rules first.

Kaja was smart. She would understand the bargain he wished to make with her. They could be partners.

"I'm sorry about that. I don't pretend to understand your people, though I suppose my people are just as brutal in a way." When a rival corporation went under, no one came out to help the family. He recalled a man he'd gone to school with. He'd had a bad run and ended up moving down from the penthouse level almost to the street. Dante was sure no one he knew had spoken to the man again. They weren't so different.

She sighed and wriggled against him. "Now I am here. Stellan was right. It is good that I left my home. I will be your mate. I will make sure you have the finest meat and the nicest bed to nest in. I think the fat one will make a good feast. I will catch him for you tomorrow."

Dante stilled, caught between laughing and being really fucking shocked. "Are you talking about Reeve?"

"I do not know his name. He is small and vicious but has much meat on him. Now that I am out of that odd cage, I'll surely be able to catch him for our meal."

"Whoa, sweetheart. You can't eat the gnomes," Dante explained quickly. She turned her head to face him and seemed confused. "The gnomes are our friends. We can't eat them." She still looked unsure. He decided to follow some of Beck's advice. He allowed his voice to deepen. "You will not eat anything that talks back, Kaja."

Her lower lip pouted sweetly, but she nodded. "Yes, I understand. I do not see why, though. They do not even have fangs or claws. It would be easy to…"

"I said no," Dante replied firmly. He pulled her back into his arms. He rather liked being forceful with her. It was nice to have someone take him seriously for a change. He let his arms drift around her torso. She was a lovely armful. She relaxed against him as his palms found her round breasts. She gasped as his thumbs drifted over her nipples. "Kaja, did you have a lover?"

She seemed distracted by his fingers plucking at her nipples but managed to answer. "Only one. Only the Second ever managed to catch me and hold me down for the mating, though he required help. I eluded the rest."

He was rapidly discovering a distaste for whatever plane she had come from. "Do you intend to run from me, sweetheart?"

He wouldn't allow it.

Her sigh was happy. "Oh, no. You have claimed me. You use my name. I eluded the others because they did not intend to claim me. They wanted to use me and then move on."

A nasty feeling hit him square in the gut. He was using her, but she was going to use him, too. She would get something out of their arrangement. "Maybe we should talk about things for a moment. We might have very different ideas about how this whole mating thing works. We're married, in a sense, but we should keep it light, you know? Married people on my world don't necessarily stay together forever."

She sat up suddenly and turned. Her eyes were wary now and steady on his face. "Say what you need to say, Dante."

He swallowed a hefty amount of Scotch. Kaja might be uneducated, but she was far from stupid. He thought briefly about lying, but he owed her the truth. "Look, I was ordered by my father to find a consort. You're the first one I saw, so I bought you. The truth of the matter is I don't want to be married. I don't see the advantage."

Her face went strangely blank. "You do not wish to mate with me."

That wasn't exactly correct, as his dick would attest. "I would love to fuck you, sweetheart. But we don't know each other well enough for me to think I'll never, ever want to fuck anyone else. In fact, I can pretty much guarantee that I will. I've never been good at keeping it in my pants, so to speak." He gave her a smile, trying to coax one out of her. "It doesn't mean we can't have fun. We'll be married, but we can do as we like. I need for you to live at home with me for a while, but after that I'll buy you someplace nice."

It was a good plan. There were still places on his plane that were wild. Once his father decided to scoot his unsuitable daughter-in-law out of the family, Dante would be allowed to buy some land and settle her there. He could still visit. They were married, after all. Besides, if she was on the surface, there would be little chance of her encountering another royal who might decide to take his chances with adultery. It was strange, but he didn't like the idea of his wife fucking around. "There are some nice places. Most of Canada is still a brutal hellhole, excuse me, lovely wilderness. We can get you a nice cabin up there."

She stood suddenly and grasped the towel.

"Hey," Dante protested, pulling at her hand. "I thought we were talking."

"I'm tired. It has been a long day," Kaja said without a hint of emotion. "Which corner is mine?"

"What do you mean which corner? There's a perfectly fine bed here."

She shook her head. "I am not First. You will have the bed, and I will find a corner. I prefer a corner."

He had a sudden flash of intuition. She preferred a corner because she would only have to protect her front. He got the feeling Kaja slept with one eye open. He sighed inwardly. He'd made a mess of this. He should have been less honest. It would have been kinder. He could have eased Kaja into the life he wanted, but no, he'd bungled it. "You sleep with me. I'm your husband."

She shook her head, a wealth of sorrow in the gesture. "No, you are like the rest. You would use me and cast me aside when you are finished. I cannot risk it. If a pup were to be born, she would be outcast, too."

Dante stilled. He hadn't even thought about children. The women on his plane used birth control until such time as they desired children. He had never had to think about it. Kaja wasn't on anything. If he slept with her, he could make her pregnant. If he wasn't ready to be a husband, he was really unready to be a father.

She wrapped the towel around her middle. Her eyes studied him, and he had a bad feeling she could almost read his mind. "See, you do not wish for my pups." She stepped out of the tub. "I will speak with your Second. I'll go to these woods of his and be alone. I will cause no trouble."

Dante was on his feet in an instant. He didn't care about his nudity. He wasn't about to let her run off to some faery forest. "You are not going anywhere with my cousin. I bought you, and you're coming home with me. I'm sorry I'm not Prince Charming, but we'll find our way. If, and it's a mighty big if, you become pregnant, I would never deny our child. Our child would be a royal. He would have the best of everything. He would not be outcast."

He would attempt to avoid it, of course. He doubted he could live apart from her if they made a baby. He wouldn't have his child grow up in the wild, and he couldn't imagine having to separate a child from his mother. Kaja would have to adapt. He reached out and grasped her hand. He was surprised to find it was shaking. "Kaja? Are you all right? Sweetheart, you're burning up."

"No," she said, shaking her head. Her knees buckled, and Dante had to catch her. Her eyes went to the glass of water.

Reeve had said he put the medication the demon gave for her in the water. *Damn it.* He should have made it clear he didn't want her drugged.

Kaja began to shake all over.

Dante carried her to the bed and thought maybe he would let her eat Reeve after all.

Chapter Five

"**S**on of a bitch," Dante cursed as the computer reported on the "medicine" the demon had given to the gnomes. "It's colloidal silver and a freaking aphrodisiac."

The gnome paled, his ruddy cheeks turning stark white in a second. "I did not know silver was in the solution. I was only told that it would keep her weak. She was frightening, even in a weakened state. If I had allowed her to achieve her full strength, I feared she would kill us all. I was only following instructions. I certainly didn't know it contained silver."

Beck stood over the gnome. His massive frame seemed to be a weapon of intimidation. The gnome practically cowered as Beck spoke. "If Dante had fed from her, he could have died. Vampires are allergic to silver."

Dante looked down at the readout from his tablet again. He forced himself to take a deep breath. If he'd followed his instincts, he would have taken Kaja that way. The instinct to feed from her immediately had been almost overwhelming. In the past, he'd always considered feeding an intimate act he wasn't interested in. He'd never taken a female that way, never sunk his fangs into a living creature and drank. He realized his father fed from his mother, and that Susan fed from Colin, but he didn't find it intriguing. It was brutal and primal, and made him squeamish. It had, until he'd placed his fangs on the back of Kaja's neck. She glowed, and he knew she would taste sweet. She belonged to him. Her blood belonged to him.

He shook off that dark thought. He wasn't some primal seeking out the blood of those around him, keeping virtual harems of females to feed him. He was modern. He got his nutrition from meal pills.

"I am sorry, Your Highness," the gnome was saying. His head was down in supplication. "The demon told me it would keep her quiet. Given the fact that she was terrifying on the drug, I did not want to see her without it. I thought it best to keep giving it to her as I was instructed. The Planeswalker warned she could escape if I did not make sure to keep it in her system."

Dante glanced at Kaja. She was curled up on the bed the gnomes had brought in for them. It was the equivalent of a nice pallet. If he'd been thinking, he would have brought his own equipment. Then Kaja could have a proper bed to cry on.

"I need to change," she whimpered over and over again.

He sat beside her and ran a hand through her clean hair. Someone had done a number on her. "No, you don't, sweetheart. You're fine the way you are."

"Please let me change." Her clear blue eyes were narrowed in pain.

"Don't you feed my consort that shit again," he said, turning back to the gnome because he couldn't stand to see her in pain. He felt utterly useless. If he'd been at home, he would have doctors to care for her. Here, there was nothing. She shook and seemed to be running a fever.

The gnome looked to Beck. "Sire, this is not a good plan."

Dante stood and showed his full fangs to the Fae. He enjoyed the gnome's wide eyes. "Kaja is not married to Beckett. He has no authority over her. I own her, and you will follow my instructions. If I discover you have drugged my consort in any fashion, I'll drain you. Do you understand me?"

He might not feed from living creatures, but he would make an exception in the gnome's case if he didn't follow instructions.

The gnome quaked and averted his eyes. Dante noticed the gnome's wife, Cara, enter. She went to the bed and covered Kaja's forehead with a cool rag. "Yes, sir. We will leave the care of your consort to you, Mr. Dellacourt."

Dante was satisfied with the gentle way Cara was treating Kaja. But he wasn't about to treat her husband in the same fashion. There was more than just the silver in Kaja's system. "Now, explain to me why you fed my consort an aphrodisiac."

The gnome swallowed several times.

"Answer him," Beck ordered.

"I wanted the sale to go through," Reeve replied.

"Bastard," Cara spat even as she rubbed her small hands across Kaja's back. Dante was grateful to the female gnome. It was obvious to him that Cara had been kind to his consort. Kaja wouldn't allow Reeve near her, but she clung to Cara's hand.

"How could you?" Cara seemed to wait for Reeve to explain. When he didn't, she took over, turning her head to lock eyes with Dante. "If you bedded down with the consort tonight, you wouldn't be able to revoke the sale in the morning. You have a night to decide, but if penetration occurs, the sale and marriage are final by Fae laws."

"Get out," Dante snarled. He longed to wrap a hand around that male gnome's throat and squeeze.

The Fae still looked to his king. Beck stared down at him. "I would go if I were you. We will discuss your methods in the morning. You have contracts with the demon clan, but you are still my subject. You are still bound by my laws. Cara, can you take care of the woman?"

The blonde gnome nodded as her husband retreated. "I will aid the vampire. The silver should be out of her system by morning. She was to be given the elixir every morning and every evening. The demon said it would keep the change from happening."

Dante exchanged a glance with his cousin. He was certain they were both thinking the same thing. They had dealt with a creature that had two faces not six months before. "Is she a hag?"

Cara shot him a dirty look. "Of course not. Have you ever heard of a hag who could serve as a consort?"

"No," he replied. "But then consorts don't tend to change forms. How do I know this isn't a trick of Torin's?"

Torin was dead set on killing Beck and Cian. He'd sent a hag to do the job last time. He might think to try it again. The thought of

Kaja being one of Torin's goons unsettled him.

"I gave her a purgative when she came here," Cara explained. "I give it to all the females to make sure they are free of any spells or hexes. There was not a hint of magic on her." She looked thoughtfully at the woman in her charge. "I would say she is a shapeshifter of some sort, but she isn't Fae. The demon said she came from a far-off plane. The females there must be consorts as well."

Dante accepted that explanation but worried all the same. He really didn't know what Kaja was. "So the silver will be gone by morning. What about the aphrodisiac?"

Cara's mouth turned down. "It will only be in effect for a few hours, but it will be painful for her. It is a strong mix, if I am correct. She needs to have physical relations or she will feel like she is burning inside. My husband was trying to make sure she didn't resist you." Cara walked over to Dante. "If you are intending to revoke the sale, it would be best if you would allow me to find her a male."

"I will take care of my consort." Did he need to tattoo it on his forehead or something? He was getting damn tired of having to remind everyone of his rights.

Cara craned her neck to look up at him. "I understand, Mr. Dellacourt. Do you require anything?"

"I think I have the proper equipment."

"Come along, Cara," Beck said with a slight smile. "You can stand guard outside. If my cousin needs anything, he will let you know. Dante, I happen to know the drawers in the back are filled with…helpful items. Many a wedding night has occurred here. I will make sure she isn't given the drugs again. She's my cousin now, too."

Dante nodded, happy with Beck's acceptance. He wondered what Cian had said to turn the warrior king around. The flap to the tent slapped shut, and he was left alone with his wife.

He knelt down, placing a hand on her naked back. The towel had fallen away, and she writhed on the bed. He saw her pain. He also saw her body. His fangs lengthened, and he cursed himself for being a selfish bastard. This was not the way he wanted his first time with his wife to go.

"Kaja," he said carefully through his fangs. "I need to take care of you."

She shook her head. "It hurts."

She covered her pussy with her hand, showing him where her pain was greatest.

It struck him suddenly that there was an easy solution. Why wasn't she masturbating? Dante shoved his hand under hers and cupped her pussy. Her eyes flew open.

"No," she said helplessly. She seemed to know she couldn't fight him so she played to his sympathy. In this case, he didn't have any. "No mating."

He kept his eyes and voice soft as his hand rubbed against the flesh of her pussy. She was soaking wet. He let his hand dip into the crevice and felt his dick get hard as a rock. It was going to be a long night. He couldn't take her. She hadn't given him permission. The drug didn't change that. He would take care of her, but he would be going without. He refused to be one more person who took from Kaja and gave nothing back.

She tried to push his hand away, her legs rubbing restlessly. "No. Leave me alone."

Dante had to wonder. She was obviously in extreme pain. She wasn't a virgin by her own admission. Why was she fighting him? Why wasn't she trying to take care of herself? He tried to remember her words from before. "Kaja, you will mind me. Be still. Tell me something, sweetheart, when the Second held you down for the mating, did he pleasure you?"

Her eyes were feverish, the pupils large. "Women receive children from the mating. Men receive pleasure. Everyone knows this."

He felt a slow smile spread across his face. That door he'd slammed closed with his idiotic admission had swung open again. He let his thumb drift up. He felt her plump clitoris and sighed. She had all the parts for an orgasm. She simply needed someone who knew what he was doing. He wasn't the greatest businessman in the world. He wasn't CEO material like his sister. He couldn't recall amazing amounts of data like Cian or wield a sword like Beck. There was one thing he was confident in, though.

"Sweetheart," he cajoled softly as he circled that nubbin of flesh he intended to get acquainted with. "Those men were idiots. They were boys with tiny dicks who didn't know how to please a woman. I assure you, I'll take care of you."

He grinned and forced her legs apart. The night was looking up.

* * * *

Kaja felt like she was on fire. Her insides were burning. *Poison.* Someone—that mean gnome—had poisoned her. She groaned, and her legs drew up. She tried to slap away Dante's hands, but he did something and it felt so good, she moaned. He was slipping his fingers into that secret part of her.

"No," she whispered. "Don't."

He didn't want her, not really. He might wish to slip his male parts into her, but he would walk away. She wasn't sure why he was playing with her. Why would he wish to put his fingers inside her woman's place?

"Stop it, Kaja," he said in a deep voice.

She looked up and saw his magnificent fangs on heart-stopping display. They were long and so white it made her sigh. He was beautiful. She loved his lean body. It was so different from the bulky bodies of the pack males, but no less strong. The First's body was elegant. He wouldn't overwhelm her with his weight. His eyes were the green of the forest. She enjoyed looking at him. At Dante. She knew she would not enjoy the physical process of mating, but he did not seem like a man who would walk away when he was done. He had allowed her to be close to him. Perhaps the mating would not be so bad if he wrapped his arms around her afterward.

She'd been overjoyed at the thought of mating with such a creature. Then he'd told her of his plan, and she'd known. She was in the same situation she'd been in with the pack. He didn't want a family with her. He only wanted his pleasure. He wasn't any different. She didn't belong here, either. This place was filled with pain.

She tried to move away from him. He was caressing her in a way that made her uncomfortable. It was too intimate. He shouldn't do such things.

"Why not, sweetheart?" Dante asked, and she realized she'd said what she was thinking. He was merciless. One hand was on her stomach holding her down while the other did strange things to her. She squirmed, trying to unseat his probing fingers. "Don't you like it?"

She didn't. It was disturbing. His hand covered that part of her that was aching. She needed to cool it down, but he blanketed her instead. She didn't like the way he rubbed her. And then she did. He rubbed the pad of his thumb firmly across her core, and she cried out. A heat poured from her center. She moaned as he continued.

He was smiling down at her, looking pleased with himself. "See, you liked that, didn't you? You are ridiculously wet. You would feel so good. Your little pussy is tight as a fucking vise. This Second of yours, he was an asshole, you know that, right? If he'd done that to you here, he would be arrested and tossed into jail."

She didn't understand half of what he was saying. Her body twitched from his magic.

"What is this feeling?" She panted as she asked the question. Her body felt pleasantly soft. His motions slowed and became languid.

"It's called an orgasm," he replied in that silky way of his. She loved his voice when it got thick like honey. Most of the time he spoke so quickly she lost track. She liked it when his tone got deep and husky. "You should have one every time a man touches you. If you don't, punch him in the face. And that includes me."

"I don't want to punch you," she replied honestly.

Dante's green eyes were wide before he filled the room with his laughter. "Well, I'll count myself lucky then. Kaja, I know you told me no just then and I kept touching you. I need you to understand I only did that because you're in pain and you don't understand how I can help you. You understand now, right?"

She nodded. He could give her...orgasms. She liked that word. She definitely liked that feeling.

He stared into her eyes. "Good, then you should understand that you can tell me no at any time. I signed papers to take care of you, but you get to pick this. Your body is your own. No one here can take that from you. It might have been normal on your plane, but we're not criminals here."

"He was the Second," she tried to explain.

His hand came up to cup her face. "And you are Kaja Dellacourt. You are better than him. No one gets to take that from you. Not even me. Do you understand?"

She didn't but she liked how she felt when he looked at her like she was worthy. Maybe this place wasn't so bad if she truly got to choose. "Yes, Dante."

"I doubt that but I'll make sure you do before all of this is over. Are you feeling better?"

He released her. Kaja missed the feel of his hands on her body. What was wrong with her? She forced herself to sit up.

"Yes," she said quietly. The weakness was there, but the terrible burning between her legs was gone. She felt a fresh rush of arousal as Dante drew his fingers into his mouth. His tongue came out, and he licked his fingers clean. That was her essence on his fingers. It was dirty. She couldn't take her eyes off the sight.

He leaned forward. She could see her moisture on his lips. "What do you expect, darling? You taste good."

She bit her lip, chewing nervously. "Do you taste good?"

The question was out before she could recall it. She had seen the fluid men left behind when they reached their pleasure.

"I have no idea. I've never tasted myself or any other dude. I don't swing that way, though I've heard it's pleasant. I like women, despite what the tabloids will tell you. Lay back. Do you remember what I said? About you not having to obey me? You can tell me no at any time and I will honor your wishes. I want you in this with me. But if you do as I ask, I promise there's more orgasms for you."

She did as he told her, aware that she was submitting. She knew she shouldn't. It was an act of respect that he hadn't earned beyond being able to hold her down, but she did it anyway. She found she didn't want to break the contact they had. His hands felt so good on her skin. Sometimes it felt like she'd gone her whole lifetime without the sweetness of another soul brushing against her body. She sighed, all the while knowing in the morning she would leave. She wouldn't wait to speak with Dante's Second. Her senses told her there were forests nearby. She could lose herself there, but this night she would revel in the feel of his hands on her. She would pretend their mating was real.

"I want to make you feel good," Dante was murmuring. She liked the way his eyes roamed her body. There was approval in them. "I think I need to teach you how we do it where I come from. What you call mating, my people call sex or fucking or making love."

"Making love." She tried the words out on her tongue. Dante's hand cupped her breast. She felt herself swell in his palm. He stroked his hand around her flesh, his fingers lingering on her nipples.

"See, you're a sensual thing," he commended her. "Sex isn't merely about penetration. It should involve all of the senses." He straddled her. His knees surrounded her hips, and she liked the way he filled the space. He leaned over and ran his nose along her neck, breathing in her scent. She shivered deliciously everywhere he touched her. "You smell awfully good now, Kaja."

She let his scent waft over her. He smelled so good, clean and masculine. She allowed her hands to drift up and touch his red-gold hair. It felt odd. Parts were slightly stiff, but she did not sense he was dirty.

"It's called mousse. This hair doesn't look this good on its own," Dante explained with a smile. "You're going to have to deal with my hygiene ritual, darling. We'll make an appointment with a stylist when we get home. You'll like spas."

She wasn't sure what a spa was, but she liked the way his face felt buried in her neck. She felt his fangs graze her skin. Was he going to bite her? She shivered at the prospect and wasn't sure if she wanted it or not. She decided to distract him. "Is your pack nice?"

She wondered why his father did not wish for him to mate with one of the females of his pack.

Dante pulled his face from her neck. "Darling, I don't have a pack. I have a family." He looked at a loss for a moment. "You have no idea what I am, do you? Have you ever heard of a vampire?"

She shook her head.

He rolled off her and propped his head on his fist, lying on his side. His shirt was off, but he'd covered his lower body before calling in the wee ones. He kept his free hand on her stomach as though he didn't want to break the contact, either. "Well, I'm different from you. I don't eat meat."

"How do you survive?" Only prey animals ate no meat. Animals that lived off fruits and grasses were prey. She couldn't imagine Dante was prey.

"I live off blood." Dante grinned and showed off his fangs. They were so much longer than hers or any of the pack males. She reached her hand out. He allowed her to touch them. When she pulled back, he continued. "My home plane is very advanced. It's probably going to be a shock and seem like magic to you, but you'll adapt. You'll like it. My people used to drink the blood of animals to survive. I'm a little different than most vampires. I'm what's called a royal. My fangs are specialized. I can feed from other vampires or species without ripping them apart. Most vampires can't do that. They kill anything they feed from. I can take my nutrition from either animals, other vampires, or consorts, like you. I haven't actually tried another sentient being, but I'm certainly thinking about it now." He moved his hand up to her throat. He looked at it with great longing, his thumb moving across it like he was tracing a line. "You see, you're what my people call a consort. Your blood is rich, and for someone like me, it can do some awesome things."

"You wish to eat me?" Kaja began to scramble off the bed. She wasn't sure of what he meant.

Dante was on her in an instant. He flipped her over and held her down with his weight. He put his fangs against her neck until she calmed. "I wish to feed from you, Kaja. It is an intimacy between husband and wife. In return, I'll open a vein and let you taste me. You'll heal faster and stay young longer with my blood in you. I won't hurt you."

"I am afraid," Kaja answered honestly. "Your fangs are long. It will hurt."

"No, it won't, and I won't do it until you're comfortable with the idea. I would never harm you. Vampires take their consorts seriously. Trust me, from the way Colin moans, you'll love it. Once we're home, I'm going to force my parents to move my rooms. I hate listening to my sister have sex. It's gross." He stroked his hands along her back. She could feel that hard male part of him against her rear. He still wore his pants and made no move to divest himself of them, so she calmed. "Besides, I want you to be able to scream without any worry. I think we're going to fit together nicely. I would try to convince you to let me taste you tonight, if it wouldn't almost certainly cause my horrible death. I hope when I go I don't explode the way some do. It's nasty. Unless someone murders me, of course, and then I hope I cover the fucker."

That horrible burning was back. It started as an itch and quickly grew, tormenting her center. What had Dante called it? He'd called it her pussy. Her pussy ached. She felt the hated tears start.

"Kaja?" Dante flipped her over. "It's starting again? Don't worry." He slid down her body, spreading her legs as he went. "I'll take care of it. I can do this all night, you know."

"What are you doing?" She was a little panicked when she felt his breath above the dark curls of her pussy. "You should not."

She looked down, and Dante's gaze was savage in the dim light of the tent. Full night had fallen. The only illumination was candles and a strange device that held fire. Dante's eyes seemed to glow in the darkness. He growled low in his throat and sounded nothing like the slick man he was before.

"You would rather ache and burn than let me help you? Give over to me. I can top you, Kaja. Don't doubt it. Say yes and let me show you how good this can be." He stared at her for a moment.

Kaja believed him. She stilled but not before she'd nodded her assent. He slid his fingers through her pussy, causing her to let her head fall back. How did he do that? She had never felt such sweet pleasure. The men of the pack had lied about what a female should expect. She wondered what else they had lied about.

"Feel better?"

She moaned her answer. He parted her and slid his fingers in. She couldn't help the tremor that raced through her. She wanted more. She wanted more than his fingers.

"We're going to wax you here, love," he chuckled. "I like a bare pussy. It makes this easier, but I'll suffer through tonight."

"Oh," Kaja exclaimed as she felt something lovely slide across her supersensitive skin. She looked down and saw Dante licking her, his tongue coming out of that sensual mouth of his. Her body began to shake. The burn was turning into something sweet.

"See, you like this," he whispered. His words sizzled across her flesh. She could see her cream on his face. He lapped it up like it was the sweetest nectar. She watched as his tongue came out and swiped across her in a way that made her eyes blur. "This jewel is called your clitoris. Your clit is a sweet piece of flesh, love. You can touch it yourself, but it's better if I do it for you. That way you can lay back and enjoy."

This time when he placed his tongue on her clitoris, he also worked a finger into her pussy. Her hips moved of their own accord, seeking a harder rhythm. She was closing in on something. She wasn't sure what, but she needed to find out where he was trying to take her. She felt so close. Close to pleasure. Close to him.

"Yes, baby," he encouraged her. She noticed he was trying to watch her face. "Fuck my fingers. Show me what you need."

She pushed against him as he adjusted his pace. He added another finger, stretching her. She felt him thrusting harder into her while his tongue was planted firmly against her clitoris. She was close, oh so close, to that lovely place. She let her feet find Dante's shoulders, using his body to anchor hers. She gave over to the instincts riding her body. She fucked his fingers and his tongue. She liked that word. She liked fuck. Fucking felt like heaven, and she wondered what it would feel like to have him thrust his man part into her. She thought she would like this better because she could see him. When the mating happened, he would be behind her. She wanted to see his face.

Kaja pumped against his fingers. When her body felt like it would split in two, she let herself fall over the edge. What had he called it? Orgasm. Orgasm felt like a sweet wave across her body. It was better than anything.

Her body went soft, and she couldn't help the giggle she felt. She never laughed, but now she understood the impulse. Laughter bubbled over, and she couldn't stop it. She was happy. *Happy*.

Dante laughed against her skin, his every touch a little aftershock. When he finally moved up her body, he looked lighter and happier than she could remember seeing him.

"Do I please you, Kaja?"

It would be simple to hurt him as he'd hurt her. She had what she needed. He didn't want her, but he asked for her acceptance. It would be simple to deny it.

"Yes," she said dreamily. Her arms drifted up and around his neck. He didn't want her for more than a night or two, but she would take them. She would take the night and hold it close to her heart. When the lonely days came again, she would dream of his green eyes and strong arms. She would pretend she was still his. "Yes, you please me, Dante."

"I am glad, consort," he said with a grin. He had the sweetest dimples in his cheeks when he really smiled. Kaja traced them with her hand. Dante leaned down and pressed his mouth over hers. Kaja gasped in surprise. "I suppose the Second wasn't great at kissing, either."

"What is kissing?"

His smile was pure decadence now. "Let me show you, wife."

He leaned over again. Kaja could taste herself on him. He thrust his tongue inside her mouth, and it rubbed against hers. Kaja sighed. Whatever this kissing thing was, she liked it very much. Dante's arms went around her. She was covered by him. His skin touched hers. His scent filled her senses. His tongue mated with hers. So close to him. It was almost as though they were one person, and she was no longer alone.

After a long moment, he came up for air. He pressed his lips against her once more and then got up.

"Wait here, just a minute," he commanded.

He jumped up. His man part was fully extended. It tented his pants admirably. Would he thrust it into her now? She would allow it because he had brought her such pleasure, but she dreaded it. Dante crossed to the chest Cara had pointed out before. He came back with a smile on his face and what appeared to be an egg in his hand. Were they going to have a meal?

"Vampire tech," he said. He seemed excited. She wondered what he intended to do with the egg since he did not eat in the normal way. Then he turned it, and it began to vibrate. "We're going to have so much fun, Kaj."

Kaja lay back and closed her eyes. She trusted him and was ready for this fun he spoke of. When he placed the egg on her, she was sure she'd found Valhalla.

Chapter Six

Dante swatted at whatever weird bug was trying to wake him up. He groaned and tried to turn over in bed. He kept his eyes closed to hold on to sleep. If he woke up, he would have to deal with the fact that his dick was still hard eight hours after his wife's marathon orgasm session.

The bug tickled his ear. He tried turning over.

He hadn't come once. Well, he had, but it had been an "oops" kind of orgasm, so it didn't count. He'd come in his pants like a horny teenager.

He sank down against the pillow. Light was starting to stream in from the openings above. He clenched his eyes closed and thought about the fact that he had a wife now.

Kaja had been so fucking hot, it was inevitable that he would come in his pants. Her pretty pussy had taken everything he'd given her. He'd fucked her with his fingers, his tongue, several vibrators, and a glass dildo. And he hadn't even gotten to her sweet ass yet. He needed to spend the morning working a plug into it.

Gods, he wanted to fuck her. He wanted to shove his cock into all her hot holes and leave a piece of himself behind. He hadn't expected to want her so badly, and not just because she was lovely and female.

He liked Kaja.

This wasn't going the way he had planned. Luckily his pants cleaned themselves, or he would be asking the gnomes for some shorts.

He snuggled down on the pallet and reached for his wife. He would pull her close, and maybe he could convince her to have some morning fun. She would be out of the influence of the aphrodisiac now. He could cuddle with her and kiss her neck. He would kiss her and lick up to her ears where he would nip at her lobes before taking her mouth. She loved kissing. Every time he kissed her, she softened and flowered open. If she asked him to fuck her this time, he could do so in good conscience. He was a married man. The thought ran through his head with no small bit of satisfaction. He'd taken a consort. His future was secure. The sunscreen project would be back under his management in a week or so. In the meantime, he would enjoy his bonding time with a little bump and grind. He would have to make sure she got off first, though. He was pretty sure he wouldn't last long once he got inside her.

"Kaj?" He lifted his head when he couldn't feel her next to him and frowned.

The night before, she'd fallen asleep in his arms, completely exhausted from the pleasure he'd given her. The aphrodisiac had been strong, taking hours to leave her system. She would settle down from one orgasm, and the fever would start again. He'd been relieved when she finally closed her eyes and let her head rest on his chest. He'd been proud of the smile that curled her lips up as her breathing had become soft and even. He'd put that smile there.

And now she was gone. Dante forced himself up.

"Kaja? Holy crap!" What the fuck was that? He started to back up, but realized he was already against the edge of the tent. He wondered briefly if he could tunnel under. It seemed like a bad idea to turn his back on the brown wolf sitting on his bed. A wolf. On his bed. He held his hands up. "Nice doggy."

He said doggy, but he knew what was sitting on his bed. It was a wolf. It was an elegant, lovely wolf that was probably going to kill him and eat him for breakfast. He wondered how the hell something so predatory had managed to get into the marketplace. There was supposed to be some form of security.

Kaja. Dante felt his heart clench. Where was his consort?

He didn't see his wife's bloody body anywhere. He had to assume she'd gotten away. She might have given him a heads-up on the carnivore using their bedroom as a hunting ground, but he was just relieved she wasn't dead.

The wolf sat back on its haunches. Dante went still. Maybe Kaja had gone to get Beck. Yes, Kaja had managed to sneak out, and she would bring his warrior king cousin. He hoped it was Beck and not Cian who rushed in to save him. If Ci came running, Dante would likely get a lecture on the habits of wolves while Cian cowered behind him hoping to get eaten last. Beck was the only way to go in a situation like this.

He stared at the creature because he couldn't help it. The wolf was beautiful. Her brown coat was glossy and looked incredibly soft. Something about her, and he knew the wolf was a female, called to him. She had to weigh at least a hundred pounds. Her face was delicate, and there was an intelligence about her that drew him in.

"Hello, girl," he said quietly.

The wolf sat patiently. She made no aggressive moves toward him. He knew he should try to get away from the vicious predator that had made her way into his bed, but he felt compelled to put his hand out.

The wolf immediately placed her head under his outstretched hand. She pushed against him, begging him for a pet.

"Oh, you're a sweet thing, aren't you," he said, stroking the wolf. He grinned, fairly certain she wasn't going to tear out his throat. She wanted some affection. Her fur was like silk under his fingers. "I always have had a way with the ladies. Apparently my charm crosses over to all species."

The wolf snorted.

Holy shit. There was no mistaking those arctic blue eyes.

"Kaja?" Dante felt his heart beating. This was what she had meant the night before when she'd begged to change. Cara had been right. His consort was two-natured.

Kaja laughed, the sound pealing like a happy bell as she fell forward into his arms in human form. The change was so effortless he almost didn't notice it. One moment there was a furry wolf begging for his attention, and the next, his wife's naked body fell laughing into his lap. His hands came up to catch her.

"You should have seen your face," she said, covering her mouth. Her eyes were full of mischief. "You looked like you might pee yourself in your fear. You did not expect that."

"No, Kaja," Dante said, still trying to get over his shock. His wife could change into a wolf. "I did not expect that my bride would greet me with fur and fangs."

She sat up, all joking gone. Her face fell. "You do not like my fangs?"

His heart warmed, and he pulled her close. She was such a sweet thing. He pushed her hair back behind her ears. Her hair was soft, a deep, rich brown. "I love your fangs. You're beautiful, and you know it."

"Am I?" She cuddled close, breathing him in. She didn't seem at all self-conscious. He let his fingers tangle in her hair. He loved the dark-brown softness. "I would not know. One cannot see oneself."

He chuckled. Her plane really was backward. "Wow. So no mirrors on your plane, then. I have no idea how I would survive without a mirror. Wait here."

He forced himself out of bed. He knew there was a handheld mirror in the dresser, and he brought it back to Kaja, who lay on the bed watching him. He appreciated the look in her eyes. She was watching her lover move. He knew the feeling. Now, he needed to show her how gorgeous she was. He sat down and held the mirror out. "This is you, Kaja."

She gasped and sat up. Staring into the mirror, she leaned forward. Dante couldn't help but watch her breasts. They were soft and round, with pretty pink and brown nipples that hardened at the merest whisper. She touched her face as though unsure of the image before her.

"Do you see how beautiful you are, consort?"

A slow smile parted her lips. He felt the air around him, and she was a wolf once more. She nosed the mirror playfully.

"Yes, you're fucking amazing in this form, too," he conceded, wondering if he was making a monster. Would he have to fight her for the mirror in the morning? He stopped himself. It wasn't like he was going to live with her long-term or anything. They were only having fun.

The flap to the tent opened, and Meg walked in.

"Good morning," she said with her usual exuberance. "I came to take Kaja to breakfast. Holy shit!" She backed up, never moving her eyes off the wolf on the bed. "Dante, stay calm. I have the gun in my backpack. I'm going to back out, and I'll go get it. Don't make any sudden moves, okay?"

Dante laughed and petted his wolf-wife. Kaja's head cocked as she looked at Meg, curiosity in her eyes. He wondered if Kaja saw her differently in her wolf form. There were a lot of questions he had for his wife. He put a hand on her fur and leaned toward Kaja. "She thinks you want to eat me, love. Actually…" His mind went to all sorts of dirty places. "No, that borders on bestiality. You're going to have to do that as a human. There are levels even I won't sink to, love. Though, not many."

Meg's eyes went wide. She stopped in her tracks. "Are you trying to tell me that's Kaja?"

"I'm not trying to tell you anything," Dante said with a frown. "I'm trying to enjoy being in bed with my consort, even if she is shedding. I think she's trying to get rid of her winter coat." He brushed some stray fur off the bed. He was going to have to tell the housekeeper to upgrade the vacuuming robots if Kaja ran around the penthouse in this form very often.

Meg ignored him. She approached Kaja, who sat up regally. Kaja cocked her head as though asking a question.

"Wow," Meg said softly. "That's a werewolf. That is so cool. I can't begin to describe it."

"Werewolf?" He'd never heard the term. "I don't know if I like that. I was going to suggest *shanimal*. You know, *she* because Kaja's a girl, and *animal* because, well, there she is."

Both females turned to him. He knew what they were thinking. He knew when someone thought he was a dumbass. He shrugged. "Fine, werewolf it is then. But it's not catchy like shanimal. Don't expect it to seep into our cultural lingo or anything."

Kaja greeted Meg with a heavy thump of her tail. The wolf's

mouth opened, and her tongue panted out. She appeared to be smiling. It was a sweet expression. Meg's eyes were filled with wonder. Kaja didn't need to worry about Meg accepting her. Meg loved the strange creatures of the planes. Vampires, on the other hand, might see her as a lesser being. His people weren't known for their easy acceptance of the odd and different. Especially in high society.

And that was why his plan would work. So why did his stomach turn at the thought of judgmental eyes on his Kaja?

"You're an idiot, Dante. Werewolf is what she is. You don't have werewolves on your plane?" Meg asked, though she never took her eyes off Kaja. Kaja nudged her hand, an invitation to pet. Meg ran her hands down the wolf's strong back.

Dante wondered if he could get her to do that when Kaja was in human form. It would be way hotter that way. His brain was on sex. "No, we don't have hot chicks who run around in fur. Well, not if they don't want to get coated with blood. PETA. They should be arrested for wasting the blood." He thought for a moment about Meg's statement. "Is she from the Earth plane?"

Meg's hazel eyes were staring into Kaja's blue ones. "No, they're a legend where I come from. Though I thought about her a lot last night. When she was talking, before the translator took over, it sounded like she was speaking Swedish or maybe Finnish."

Dante shook his head. "No idea. Everyone speaks English on my world. You know, language of the conquerors and all."

Meg's hands worked over Kaja's fur. His wife seemed to love it. "How does the whole door thing work? When I left from this plane, I ended up in Fort Worth. The Vampire plane is very similar to the Earth plane. If we found a door from your plane to mine in Dallas, would I end up in another Dallas?"

Dante laughed at the thought. "No, it's far stranger than that. While the planes might look similar, they aren't. Didn't you notice that the time of day shifted as we went from the Vampire plane to this one? It's several hours off. And there's a door in upstate New York that leads right off a cliff into an ocean. Some corporation managed to put in a slide. They sold tickets for a while. Then some plesiosaur ate a couple of kids. You know how it goes."

"So Kaja is from someplace like Sweden, but not Sweden."

Dante didn't care. All that mattered was that she was here now.

Meg seemed content to continue her intellectual exercise. "Of course, it makes you wonder. Maybe they started out on the Earth plane and fled because humans can be real assholes, you know. And maybe there are still werewolves on the Earth plane. After all, there are vampires. Maybe they hide like the vamps. Because again, humans can be assholes."

"Yes," Dante agreed readily. He arched a single eyebrow. "They can also really interrupt an interesting morning. Tell me something, Meg. Did I interrupt your opportunities for hot sex with your new spouse the morning after your wedding?"

Meg flushed. "Oh, I'm sorry. I thought that since... Cian told us what was going on. I thought you probably wouldn't be doing that."

He stared at her like she was a crazy person, which was exactly what she sounded like. "You thought I wouldn't have sex with my consort. I have sex with everything that allows me to, but you thought I wouldn't fuck my own wife?"

He firmly intended to fuck her at every given opportunity. He knew he should play it cool, but he also knew himself. He wouldn't be able to hold back, and he didn't really want to try. This crazy possessiveness was only a phase. Fucking Kaja would put it all back on an even keel.

"Fine, you're a man-whore," Meg said, flustered. "I thought you would want to get to know her, that's all."

Dante sent her a questioning look.

"Not in a sexual way," Meg complained. "Men. Have you even talked to her? Have you asked her about her home plane and what she misses about it?"

"Of course," Dante retorted. "It sucked, and the men there sucked in bed. Then she just moaned a lot. Don't look at me like that. I learned an enormous amount of information about her from those moans. I learned that she likes the middle setting on a vibrator. A nice twist and midlevel hum and she goes off like a rocket."

Meg rolled her eyes. "You are useless, Dante. Fine. I'll go, but when you're done, please send Kaja to my tent for some breakfast." Meg looked down at the wolf with a friendly smile. "We can have some food and get to know each other. We're family now. It's so awesome. I have a werewolf in my family."

Dante felt another surge of irritation. "You have a vampire as well. I don't see you gushing over me."

Meg shrugged. "Vampires aren't as cool as I expected them to be. In romance novels, vampires are all dark and broody and sexy. In real life, you talk an awful lot about stocks. It was a definite disappointment. But Kaja there seems like a real werewolf. I can't wait to get to know her." She turned and started to head out. "Oh, and we have to stay close to the market today. Beck and Ci got called away. There's some trouble in a Fae encampment on the other side of the plane. Something about fields and starvation and stuff. Cian needs to do his Green Man thing. Beck is worried about him being alone too far from civilization. Can you believe he used that word to describe this place?"

Dante rolled his eyes. "You can stay here all you like. I'm taking Kaja home. I'm not spending our bonding time on a pallet in a marketplace."

He wanted to get her in a real bed. He wanted to see her laid out on sumptuous sheets with her hair haloing around her pretty face.

"You walking then?" Meg asked with a shit-eating grin.

What the actual hell? He was going to have a talk with his cousins. "Damn it. Why did they take both bikes? They fit on one." They'd traveled to the marketplace on two of his customized Harley hover bikes. Each one seated two, but no, his cousins had to take both, leaving him stranded.

"They fought about who would drive. Cian says he's the obvious choice, and Beck won't give up control, so they took both. Besides, I think they think you'll babysit me. As if."

Meg walked out, and Kaja changed immediately. She ignored the argument. She seemed to have other things on her mind. Her eyes stared at the door Meg had disappeared behind. "She likes me, Dante. She wishes to dine with me and speak with me. I should hunt and get her a good meal for our breakfast."

Her pretty face was flush with excitement. He couldn't help but smile back. "Meg is a nice lady. She'll be a good friend to you, but you don't have to worry about hunting, love. Food is taken care of."

"What is friend?" Kaja sat back. She looked eager to learn.

Lustful thoughts fled. "Damn, love, what was that place like for you? A friend is someone you can depend on, someone you share your life with and talk to and stuff. It's different for a girl. Guys hang out and watch sports and bail each other out of jail. It's more intimate with women. You talk about feelings and stuff. And you apparently buy a lot of shoes."

She opened her mouth to ask another question.

"Meg would be better to explain the whole shoe thing, sweetheart." His lustful thoughts were back, and he didn't want to talk fashion with her. She was lovely and naked and sitting on his bed. She was completely out from under the influence of the aphrodisiac. All he had to do was convince her that making love was a good idea. He leaned over and ran his hand across the soft skin of her arm. She shivered slightly. "Why don't you come back to bed, Kaj?"

Her eyes narrowed, wariness clear.

He patted the place next to him. She wouldn't be beside him for long. She'd be under him as fast as he could get her there. He felt his fangs lengthen. The silver was obviously out of her system, too. It was what had kept her from changing forms. There was no good reason not to sink his teeth into her smooth white skin. He could see the faint blue vein that ran up the side of her neck. There was another vein in her thigh that would work as well. He could drink his fill, all the while breathing in the scent of her arousal. His mouth would fill with her blood, and they would be married in the traditional way of a royal vampire.

Gods, he was suddenly so fucking hungry. For the first time in his life, he knew a meal pill wouldn't do. He wanted her. He wanted to take her blood and then fill her with his cock.

"Your eyes are strange," Kaja whispered.

There was the faintest hint of fear in her voice. She backed away slightly. His irises were bleeding out, and his entire eye would be a vivid green before too long. He'd only seen himself that way a few times. He knew he would look alien and dangerous to Kaja.

Dante didn't like her backing away from him. She was drawing something primal out of him. He was a good-time lover. It had always been that way. He enjoyed the sex and had kept many mistresses, but he could easily walk away and find another if they showed they didn't want him. It wouldn't be that way with Kaja.

"It means I want you. My eyes change when I want something very badly. Look at me." It was an old trick royals used on peasants to draw them in for a nice meal. He'd never felt a compulsion to try his hand at persuasion, but the impulse was there now.

Kaja did as he asked. She stared into his eyes, and he knew the moment he caught her. A savage sense of satisfaction filled him.

"Come to me," he commanded in a voice that sounded foreign to his ears.

Kaja moved forward and placed herself in his arms. She cuddled close to him, tucking her face into the crook of his neck. "You are working magic on me."

He forced her head up. "Do you want me to stop?"

She considered the question for a moment. "Yes and no. Yes, because my heart will ache when you set me aside. No, because my heart already aches when I think of never touching you again."

He pressed his lips to hers. "Don't think about the future. Can't we enjoy today? And I would never cast you aside. I just think we should let all of that sort itself out. Whatever happens, whatever we decide, I promise, I'll take good care of you."

"For as long as you want me," Kaja said with a little bitterness.

Dante felt the ache she talked about. He didn't know what she wanted. "Isn't that all you can ask of a man? I promise to be good to you even if things go wrong. You won't ever want for anything again."

"But you will not give me your heart." It wasn't a question.

He sighed. He could give orgasms all day long, but he had no idea how to deal with this. "I don't think I have one, sweetheart. Can't it be enough that I'll give you what I have?"

She seemed to come to some inner decision. She pressed her lips to his. "Mate with me."

Her lips were closed against him, but he took advantage anyway. He pressed her down and covered her small body with his. Dante knew he should feel triumphant and thrilled because the night before had been difficult for him. Yet all he could manage was a strange sense of awe. Her clear blue eyes were open as she looked up at him. He didn't need to remind her what he wanted from her. She spread her legs willingly. There was so much honest, open desire in her face that he almost turned away. It was too much, but he wanted her more than he'd ever wanted a woman before. Looking down at her, he realized he'd only wanted sex before. Now he wanted Kaja. It was a disturbing feeling.

"What's wrong?" Kaja asked. There was worry all over her face.

He pushed down his unwanted emotions. This was sex. It was just sex between a vampire and his consort. It was the most natural thing in the world. He gave her his surest smile. "There's nothing wrong, love. Everything is perfect now. The only problem is these pants of mine. They seem to be in the way."

He ground himself gently against her, letting her feel his hard cock.

She sighed. "How do you do this to me? Already I feel some pleasure."

"I told you, love. I know what I'm doing," Dante replied. He felt surer now. The need to fuck was riding him hard. He wasn't thinking about the future. He was thinking about how damn good it would feel to pound away at his wife.

His hands reached down to unbutton his trousers. He didn't want to take the time to get out of them. He'd shove them down enough to free his cock and then work his way inside. The second time could be slow. They had all day.

Kaja stopped suddenly, throwing her hands to his chest and pushing him away.

"Don't, baby," Dante said, not giving an inch. "I promise I won't hurt you."

"Dante, something is coming," she said, trying to get up.

"Yes," he coaxed. "You can come first. Then I'll come, and then I'll rest, and we can both come again."

The tent flap opened, and Meg ran in. She turned slightly when she saw the erotic scene before her, but she didn't leave.

"Dante, there's an ogre coming," she said breathlessly. She had her gun in her hand. "He's attacking the marketplace."

In the distance, Dante heard the screams begin. He rolled off his bride and fastened his pants.

That ogre was going to suffer.

Chapter Seven

The world seemed filled with chaos. Every sense Kaja had was on overload as Dante tossed back the door to the tent and walked through. His magic went to work. The shirt he wore grew a hood that he pulled up to cover his head. A strange black object flowed over his face, covering his beautiful eyes.

Screams filled the air along with a terrible roar that seemed to come from every angle. There was a predator nearby. She sensed it deep in her bones. And he had a strong odor. Whatever attacked the small village reeked of decay.

Reeve ran up to them, his hair in disarray. His eyes were flared, and he'd lost his cap. "You must run, Mr. Dellacourt. And my queen. You must run for your lives."

"Which way? He sounds like he's coming from all sides." Dante was frowning, his face set in fierce lines. He held his hand out to her. "Stay close to me, Kaja."

She moved to the First's side. *No. Dante.* He was Dante. And she was practical. "We need only be faster than the little ones. This beast will dine on them first. We should keep Cara close when we find her.

I can run very fast. I will carry her."

"No, miss," Reeve said. "I have a place to hide, but it is small. You must save yourselves—all of you. I cannot hide until I find my wife."

Reeve disappeared, his small body fleeing through the labyrinth of tents.

There was a loud roar that sent Kaja's hands flying to cover her ears. That sound made her ache.

"Where the hell did that ogre come from?" Dante got to his feet. He stood behind one of the high tents and poked his head around the side as though trying to look but not be seen. "Holy fuck, that thing is huge."

Kaja stood beside him and stared out as well. She swallowed as she took in the sight before her.

She couldn't see its whole body, but it was massive. It wasn't as big as a frost giant, but a frost giant had some intelligence. This beast looked like a creature that only lived to kill. "What is it called again?"

Dante stared up at it, his mouth slightly open. "It's called an ogre."

Kaja felt Meg's hands on her shoulders, steadying herself there as she, too, took a look at the mountain of flesh currently destroying everything around it. The ogre was much taller than the tents, his torso barrel shaped and naked. Thick cords of muscles crossed his body. His arms were bigger around than Kaja's waist and covered in flesh that had a greenish cast to it.

She did not see how they could battle the creature. Not without a pack. The pack could take out much larger creatures, but there were only three of them. Meg didn't even possess claws and fangs.

"I think we could safely call it Godzilla," Meg said. Kaja wondered what the strange silvery item in her hand was. Meg clutched it, holding it close to her body. "Cian didn't say anything about ogres when he lectured me on all the things to stay away from."

Dante turned back around. His hand was tight on hers. "That's because it shouldn't be here. It's an Unseelie creature."

"What is Unseelie?" Kaja's heart was pounding, but she couldn't let the unknown words pass. She needed to understand.

Dante began walking close to the walls of the tent in the opposite direction from the screaming. "Meg, stay close. Beck and Ci are Seelie Fae. It's basically a tribe. The Unseelie are the other tribe of Fae."

Kaja's bare feet sank lightly into the dirt beneath her. "This is a war between tribes?"

"No, it can't be," Meg said. "I don't understand it. We have a meeting with the Unseelie king in a few weeks. Why would they attack us? And why send an ogre?"

Dante stopped. Up ahead was a wide road. They would be without cover until they reached the forest. As they stood there, the ogre was tossing about the things it found. Large items like tent poles and cages and wagons were being thrown toward anyone who tried to flee. "There's no reason to send an ogre. An ogre is chaos. No one can control it. It would just as easily turn on the Unseelies. It makes no sense."

"And it only helps Torin," Meg said. "King Fergus hates Torin. He would never aid him. Fergus's daughter was trapped on the Seelie plane when the civil war broke out. He's had men looking for her, but he can't get an army on the plane. He's sent assassins, but they haven't returned."

Ah, now she understood. It was a bit like a pack war. Packs had territories. The Firsts often fought over those territories. These Seelie and Unseelies must be like packs, and Torin and Fergus were the Firsts.

This was not her fight or Dante's. They were free to leave.

"We should go to the woods." Kaja pointed to a spot of green trees beyond the tents. "We can hide there."

They would have to be fast. Even as she thought the words, she watched a creature fall beneath a large wagon that had been thrown into the fleeing crowd, but there was no other choice. They had to get to the forest. Once there, she could hunt for them. She knew forests. She would be valuable to Dante and Meg there. She wouldn't be a hindrance in the wild. She wouldn't feel like a fool there.

"I hate camping. I am going to kick my cousins' asses when they get back," Dante muttered. "All right. We need to get out of here."

Kaja turned back and looked at the tent where she'd learned about pleasure. Dante had made himself plain. He wished to use her for a while, but perhaps a bit of affection was better than none at all. She wasn't ready to be done with him. She knew she should run on her own, but she couldn't leave him yet.

"Cara!" Reeve could be heard calling for his wife. His voice had taken on a desperate wail.

All manner of creatures were running for the forest now. They bumped against her in their frantic flight from the ogre.

"Cara!"

The ground beneath Kaja's feet shook.

"He's coming this way." Dante started to lead her out. "We're going to have to make a run for it. Meg, can you keep up? I don't want to explain to your husbands why I lost you to an ogre who seems to be practicing his left-handed slider."

Meg seemed to steel herself. "I'll keep up. You won't lose me that easily."

Dante's hand squeezed Kaja's, tightening as though he was afraid to let go. "Stay together. Kaja's right. We only really have to be faster than the gnomes. They're short. The ogre should catch a bunch of them, and while he's eating his appetizers, the main course will be fleeing as fast as our feet can take us."

Kaja got ready to run, but a thin wail broke through the chaos around her.

"Cara, no! No!"

Kaja turned and saw the small blonde gnome who had been so kind to her. She was trying to get away from the ogre. Cara ran down the road, moving toward them, but it was clear that she would not make it. Her legs were too short. She wasn't quick. The ogre roared and stamped his foot. It looked to be roughly the size of Cara's whole body. He would crush her beneath that foot.

Dante's hand tugged insistently at hers. "Kaja, let's go."

In her pack, the weak were allowed to fall. They were considered an insult to the pack. If a wolf fell, it was because they were not strong enough, not worthy.

The strong wolves of her pack were the same ones who spit on her. They were the same ones who tossed her out. Cara was not strong. She had no fangs or claws. She could not change. The gnome would be a liability during the hunt. But Cara was the one who'd held

100

Kaja's hand when the world had seemed filled with pain. She'd brought her raw meat when it was so obvious to Kaja that Cara had been disgusted by it. Even as she'd tossed the raw meat in, Cara had begged her to eat. Cara had cared that she was hungry. She'd shown Kaja true kindness. In the pack, kindness was considered weakness.

Kaja no longer believed in the pack.

With a single thought, she changed. There was a moment of pain, but she'd come to almost enjoy it. That brief flaring of heat through her system brought with it a certain freedom. Her limbs shifted, joints popping into place in a quick change. Her hand became a slender paw that slipped easily from Dante's hold. She fell from two legs to four.

"What are you doing?" Dante seemed so tall when she was in her two-legged form. Now, he truly towered over her. He looked down, indignation plain on his face.

Kaja barked. She didn't have time to explain. He should run. This debt was hers and hers alone. Perhaps she could also provide the distraction required for Dante and Meg to get away.

She turned and began to run toward Cara.

* * * *

Dante felt his heart threaten to explode as Kaja sped away from him toward the really pissed-off, man-eating ogre.

What was wrong with her? Did she think that the ogre wouldn't eat her when she was in wolf form? If she'd asked, he would have explained that the ogre would eat anything he could catch. And the ogre was definitely going to catch Kaja because she was running toward it.

"What happened?" Meg asked. She had turned toward the ogre. She had to scream the words now because there was so much chaos around them.

"Kaja went insane." Dante reached out to hold Meg's hand. There was a crowd rushing toward them. If he didn't hold on to her, he would lose her in the chaos. He watched as Kaja slipped nimbly in and out of the crowd.

He felt a growl start deep in his throat, and that ridiculous beast that had taken up residence in his body the minute he'd laid eyes on

Kaja seemed to be clawing to get out. She wanted to run from him? He would show that wolf her place. She would be at his feet and begging for forgiveness before she could even scent the freedom she seemed to want. She belonged to him.

Only one thing kept him from immediately tearing after his wayward wife. He needed a place to stash Meg.

Meg held on to his hand for dear life. She used her free hand to point to a spot close to the tent where he and Kaja had spent the night. "It's Cara. She's going to try to save Cara."

Dante pushed against the crowd. It was like swimming upstream. A troll with atrocious body odor nearly flattened him against a tent pole. He used a good portion of his strength to keep Meg close. He had mere seconds before Kaja made her way to the ogre.

The ogre. It was huge. It was strong. Perhaps Beck could handle the ogre, but it would be a battle. Kaja was tiny compared to that monster. What was she thinking? The ogre's only weakness was its utter stupidity and a Fae creature's aversion to cold iron.

Cold iron.

"Meg, what does that gun of yours shoot?" Dante asked.

He'd played around with the gun. Meg had taken him out behind the barn and shown him how to use the weapon. He'd been quite good with it, or so she'd told him. He had a good eye and a steady hand. But did he have the right ammunition?

Meg's mouth dropped open as she seemed to reach the same conclusion as Dante. "After I taught Cian how to use the gun, he figured out how to make new bullets. The blacksmith forged them from cold iron. He thought it was the best way for me to protect myself if Torin attacked. It should work on the ogre. Get me close enough and I'll take the shot."

Dante barely averted rolling his eyes at her. "You're not going to do anything, sweetheart. It's not like he'll go down from one bullet. You'll only piss him off. He might be dumb, but he has spectacular survival instincts. The minute you start shooting, he'll turn on you. I can't risk that."

He opened the flap to the tent they were close to and shoved her inside. "You have to stay here. I can't take care of you and save Kaja. Please, Meg. I need you to give me the gun and promise me you'll stay safe. I'm begging you."

He was in an impossible situation. He owed Kaja his protection, whether or not she wanted it. But he was responsible for Meg, too. It wasn't a position he was comfortable with. He'd spent his life without any kind of responsibility at all. Now two women who he cared about could die without him.

"I'll stay here," Meg said. She placed the gun in his hand. "But you can't expect me to hide if you go down. I'll stay out of sight until you need me."

It was the best he was going to get. Dante steeled himself and began to push through the crowd. He could hear Kaja's bark. She was on the edge of the throng, making her way toward Cara. He began to shove people aside. The ogre roared, making the tents shake and the air smell fetid and rank. The big creature reached down and picked up a tent by the large pole that held the center up. He tossed it toward the field. Another scream reached his ears, this one smaller and weaker. He watched in horror as the ogre picked up a small brownie who had been hiding in the now defunct tent. He lifted the brownie's delicate body and tossed it into his mouth. In a second, the brownie was gone, lost to the ogre's never-ending hunger.

Kaja broke free from the crowd and raced toward Cara. The gnome seemed frozen in terror, looking up at the monstrous form above her. Kaja's sleek body was utterly graceful as she raced toward the gnome. The ogre looked down, and his hand reached out to grab Cara, but before he caught her between his thumb and forefinger, Kaja struck. Her body forced Cara's out of the way, and the two of them went tumbling to the left of the ogre.

He needed a plan and quick. A single bullet wouldn't get through all that muscle. It would, however, piss the creature off, and then he would go straight down the ogre's gullet. Dante pressed past the last of the fleeing Fae.

The ogre now stood above his wife. Kaja had placed herself in front of the gnome. Even from his position, he could see Kaja's sharp white teeth were bared, her body utterly rigid. She was prepared for attack, but he couldn't see how his small wife was going to take down the mountainous ogre.

Her head turned slightly, and those arctic eyes found his. Though her stance didn't change, there was a softening in her face. Her eyes ate at him, the plea in those blue orbs so apparent he suddenly wished he could hide.

What did she want from him? He wasn't a hero. He wasn't a warrior. He was only a man, and his greatest talent was being able to give a woman multiple orgasms. And he liked it that way, damn it. He didn't want to be Beck Finn. He wanted to have fun.

But now he wasn't just a man. He was a husband. And he couldn't fail her.

Running on pure instinct, he took off. He felt the claws in his hands pop through his fingertips, the pain barely registering. He shoved the gun in his pants pocket. He couldn't use it from a distance. He needed to be close. There was really only one place where the cold iron bullet would work fast enough to save them all.

But it was going to be a bitch to get that close.

The ogre threw his head back and let loose a mighty shout as his foot came up. Kaja moved back, Cara staying behind her. The ogre's foot came down, and Dante feared the ground would open up, but it gave him his shot. He leapt onto the ogre's calf, digging in with his claws, using those primal gifts the way a mountain climber used an axe.

He heard Kaja barking. When he looked down, he saw her darting up to bite the hell out of the ogre's toe. She came back with a bit of flesh in her mouth.

"Kaja, you do not eat that!" he yelled as he climbed. "You have no idea where he's been!"

She would need a full round of antibiotics, but she'd done her job. She'd distracted the giant. The ogre didn't try to brush Dante away. The big guy was far too busy attempting to kill his consort.

Dante held on for dear life as the ogre brought his foot down again. Kaja darted in between and around that massive foot, her quickness keeping her alive. Dante found a foothold on the back of the ogre's knee and moved up to his thigh.

The smell was really what got to him. He couldn't breathe this close to the damn thing. He pulled himself using sheer upper-body strength. At least he'd always been vain enough to work out, though now he would definitely spend more time on chin-ups.

"You stay alive, Kaja! Do you hear me?" He was climbing up an ogre's ass for her. He really wanted the chance to kill her himself. Gods, he hoped the damn thing didn't have gas, but it was far better than having to crawl too close to the monster's junk.

Dante cursed the entire way up the ogre's backside. The ogre, massive as he was, moved somewhat slowly. It aided him in his climb. The ogre twisted and turned, trying to find Kaja. He roared when Kaja's teeth bit into his flesh. It was a perfect distraction. The monster didn't seem to care that there was a vampire climbing up his back.

But he was about to. Dante made his way to the back of the ogre's neck. He wouldn't be able to hide now. He had to get to the ogre's vulnerable spot and take his shot. One shot straight through the eye and into the dumb asshole's dim brain.

That was all he had to do. No problem.

He was going to spank his consort. If he lived.

Dante climbed onto the ogre's skull and found a nice piece of thick, scraggly hair. Luckily, the ogre hadn't bothered with a comb-over. What hair the beast had was long and went every way possible. His stomach clench when he realized how high he'd climbed. If he fell, it would be painful, though not for long since he would be flatter than one of the pancakes Meg liked to eat. The minute he hit the ground, the ogre would crush him.

He wound his hand around the chosen piece of the ogre's hair just in time to tumble off the creature's head. A huge hand came out to swat at Dante, barely brushing past him. With his free hand, Dante pulled the gun and swung out, trying to get to the ogre's face.

Fetid breath, as rough as any strong wind, blew from the ogre's mouth, making him gag, but he held it together.

One shot. One shot to live. One shot to save his wife.

At least it was a big damn target.

Dante pulled the trigger as he passed by the ogre's eyes, the black pupil huge. He swung by the second eye, but already the ogre was faltering.

Those eyes flared, a trickle of blood flowing from the injured one. The ogre made a terrible sound that blew back Dante's hair. Then the light fled in the ogre's eyes, and the monster was falling to the ground below.

And Dante was falling with him.

Fuck.

The ogre hit the ground with a resounding thud. Dante hit it with barely a whisper compared to the ogre's, but it felt like he'd broken every damn bone in his body. The air rushed from his lungs, and he struggled to take in a breath. He noticed Cara running to Reeve. At least the gnomes were safe.

A warm tongue licked at him.

"Oh, you are not getting off that easily, love. We are going to have a serious discussion about this whole First thing. If I'm the First, then I get to decide if you're going to run off and try to kill really disgusting things. I think my spine is crushed," Dante complained.

It wasn't, but that didn't mean he didn't ache. And it was more than his muscles. Something was definitely wrong with him. Seeing Kaja in danger had done something to him. He couldn't make his heart stop racing. He couldn't seem to come down. He needed something.

He needed her.

Dante began to force himself off the ground. He needed a long bath. Since Cara owed him her life, he wasn't going to feel guilty about asking her to set it up for him. He would get the stink of ogre off of him and then settle down to have a long discussion with Kaja about what it meant to be his wife. Beck had the right idea. Dante would make sure Kaja's backside was red, and then he would fuck her until she forgot a time he wasn't shoving his cock inside her pussy.

Then maybe he would calm down.

Kaja whimpered, her nose nuzzling him.

"It won't work, Kaj," Dante said. "You can't turn those puppy eyes on me and expect that all will be forgiven. You disobeyed. You put me and Meg and yourself at risk. You're going to have to take your punishment."

He'd never wanted to punish anyone before. He was a good-time guy. If a chick didn't do what he thought she should, he left.

He couldn't leave Kaja. He couldn't walk away this time. She looked at him with those same eyes he'd claimed wouldn't move him. She was alone in the world. She didn't have anyone except him.

He brought his hand up to give her a pet, to let her know that he could be mad at her but not leave her, when she growled. The sound came from deep in her throat. Her spine straightened, and she seemed to focus on something.

"I would have your dog heel, Mr. Dellacourt." A proper British voice filled the courtyard now. Dante looked up to see a group of vampires in gray-and-green fatigues.

"What the hell is this?" Dante asked, pushing to his knees. He stared at the group of ten mercenaries. They appeared well armed, with swords and Taser units at the ready. Where the hell had they been when he needed them? "You're late to the party, boys."

He moved to reach for the gun, which had fallen behind him, but Kaja was quicker. She covered it with her body and laid down, head on her paws.

"Kaj?" Dante asked.

Kaja barked as though trying to tell him something.

"I think we're right on time, Mr. Dellacourt," the leader said. "Bring her."

Dante got to his feet as he saw two soldiers leading Meg toward him. She was safe and whole, and tied up with a gag in her mouth. She fought against her captors, but they were bigger and meaner. "What the hell is going on?"

"A successful operation, Mr. Dellacourt," the leader said. "We have the queen and you, and soon we shall have the rebel kings, and trade will flow between the Seelie and Vampire planes once more. I admit, I rather thought the ogre would kill you. Would you like to explain how you managed to take it down?"

This was bad. This was way worse than the ogre.

Beck was going to kill him.

"Fuck you, mercenary," Dante shot back. Kaja was covering the only weapon they had. Smart girl, his wife. And they had no idea she was anything but his pet.

"Yes, I heard you would be trouble."

The leader gave a signal with his hand, and a large, righteously ugly dude stepped up. Dante saw what was coming and tried to hold up his hands in the universally acknowledged sign for "don't send ten thousand kilowatts of pure electricity through my body."

"I'm not going to be trouble," Dante started.

But the Taser flared and sank into his flesh. Dante held on as his body spasmed, and he fell back to the ground.

His last thought was of Kaja and those blue eyes.

Chapter Eight

Chalen Palgrave stared at the monitor with something close to happiness. He would never allow himself actual happiness because emotion would prove that he was undisciplined, and he was nothing if not disciplined. But still, the sight of Dante Dellacourt lying on the dirt floor, his perfect hair a mess, brought a bit of joy to his heart. Dante's hands were tied behind his back, and he lay at an angle that would surely be painful if he were awake.

Of course, the Taser would have been intensely painful, too.

"And you have the female?" Chalen asked.

The feed from his mercenary's tablet turned. Former Sergeant Major William Roan nodded shortly, his manner as crisp as his clothing. Chalen doubted the man would get dirty even in the middle of a war. "Her Highness is secured, though I will say, sir, she has quite the mouth on her for a royal."

"Yeah, well, she's a cut-rate royal at best," Chalen shot back. "The twins had to make do with a woman from the Earth plane. I believe they call themselves humans. Ever since Torin shut the borders, finding a consort has been difficult at best. I heard even the Malone heir recently took one as his consort. It's ridiculous that we have to lower ourselves this way. Once the twins are dead and Torin reopens our trade routes, I'll be a hero."

And his stock would be up.

And his brother would be avenged.

He wasn't absolutely certain if Beck and Cian Finn had a direct hand in Kinsey's death, but they were undoubtedly the reason his brother was dead. He didn't need to see a body to know that his only brother was gone. Kinsey had understood the obligations of family and business. He would never have walked away.

Chalen still remembered the last time he'd seen his brother. Kinsey had been filled with hope. He'd promised to bring back a beautiful consort named Meg.

He'd never returned.

The fact that the Finns had not accepted their place—that was what had truly caused Kinsey's death. If they had accepted the stronger man as their king, there would have been no need for his brother to seek out a consort. Kinsey would have done what should have been his right. He would have purchased the finest consort money could buy. He wouldn't have died trying to marry himself off to a disgusting human.

"Well, if you need to, feel free to slap Her Highness around. I'm sure she's used to it," Chalen said. Everyone knew the warrior king was a barbarian. He couldn't help it. Beck Finn lacked half his soul. He and his twin were freaks of nature. The planes would be a better place when they were gone.

The sergeant's eyes narrowed. "I believe I shall forgo torturing Her Highness. I think Beck Finn will turn himself in much more readily if he believes his wife is in good shape. He could be dangerous otherwise. If he believes no harm has come to her yet, he will be more amenable."

Chalen didn't care how it happened. He had no intention of giving up the woman who had tempted his brother. The sergeant could play it any way he wished, but he intended to have that bitch's head.

"Just make sure you keep tabs on her after you let her go," Chalen said with a nod. He didn't betray his true intentions. This was the best team he could buy for the situation. He wasn't going to lose them due to their leader's outmoded morality when it came to consorts. Vampires were taught to treat consorts with gentleness. But he doubted his brother had been shown any. "We wouldn't want her to be left behind with no one to aid her."

The very British mercenary bowed slightly. "I would never leave a woman out in these woods alone, much less a consort. She will bring a mighty price, sir. Her glow is quite strong."

Yes, she would if Chalen intended to sell her. He had no doubt that Megan Finn would be sought after by every available vampire, but that wouldn't be her fate.

Meg Finn was going to pay with her life.

And so would Dante Dellacourt.

"Is he dead?" Chalen asked.

Dante hadn't moved. He lay there like the lazy, good-for-nothing slug he was. Gods, he didn't want the asshole to be dead. There was no way Dante had paid yet. More pain. That was required.

The sergeant shook his head. "I assure you, he's alive. He's merely unconscious. He received a large jolt of electricity. I had to take him down that way. The original plan was to create so much chaos we merely had to pluck our targets from the crowd. The ogre created the chaos needed, but I was rather surprised that Dellacourt was able to bring the bugger down."

Chalen felt his mouth drop open. "What are you talking about? What did Dante do? Fuck the ogre to death? It's about all he's good for."

That bastard had been fucking his mistress for months. That rankled as well. It wasn't fair. Chalen knew it. He'd been the one to put Amanda in Dante's bed, but he couldn't stand the thought of touching her now. At one point, he'd considered offering her a permanent position, but now he had to think about getting rid of her entirely. She knew far too much.

"I'm still not sure how he did it," the sergeant replied. "But he wasn't at all what I expected. From the report you had given me, I rather thought he would be huddling down with the women. Instead, he saved the village. The ogre still did what we needed. The village has been emptied, and my men are going to ensure it stays that way until we can negotiate the terms of Their Highnesses' surrender."

"Torch it when you leave," Chalen said.

The sergeant stopped, his face becoming a blank mask. "As you wish."

"Keep me informed. I want to know the instant you have those twins in custody." Chalen turned off the monitor, and his office sank back into gloom. He didn't bother with the lights nor did he open the blinds. He liked the dark. It suited him.

A wave of stock numbers began to crawl across the bottom of his monitor. The Dellacorp symbol flowed by, along with a ridiculously huge number attached to it. Chalen felt his fists clench. Palgrave Industries was in the toilet stock wise, and it had been since the day his brother had walked into the arena. The press had gotten word that Kinsey Palgrave was fighting Beck Finn and the company's stock had taken a dive because no one believed Kinsey could best the Fae warrior king. The stock dove even further when news of Kinsey's disappearance had made the press.

No one believed he could handle the company the way his brother had.

Well, he would prove them wrong. He would bring Palgrave Industries back to its rightful place, and he would bring Dellacorp to its knees.

Starting with Dante.

* * * *

Dante's head pounded, the pain a sharp hammer beating a rhythm against his skull.

Fuck, he was in trouble. How much Scotch had he had last night? It was pretty much a blank, so it had to have been considerable. *A party?* He remembered climbing a really big tree and thinking that a dog was hot.

Yep, he was going to rehab.

"Dante." An annoyed feminine voice screeched his name.

"Mom?" He tried to focus, but his eyes weren't working. "Don't yell. I know I'm in trouble, but I seriously need something for this hangover."

"I am not your mother, Dante. Wake up!"

He felt something kick him.

"Wake up, or we're going to die!"

Whoever was yelling at him was big on the drama. His whole body ached. "Susie? Susie, don't tell mom. And whatever you do, don't tell Dad. He's pissed enough as it is. Don't tell him I got drunk and blacked out. Fuck, did the paparazzi catch me?"

"Oh, for god's sake, it's Meg."

He forced his eyes open. Meg. His brain started to function again. He'd been with Meg, and there was a tremendously smelly mountain he'd had to climb and shoot through the eye, and he was married. Yes, that last bit sobered him up mightily. He was married.

"Where's Kaja?"

He focused, putting all his will into figuring out how screwed they were. He tried to pull his hands up, but they held tight. His hands were tied behind his back, and his feet were bound as well. He was lying on the floor of a tent. He couldn't see Meg. Where was Meg?

"I don't know where Kaja is."

Dante turned his head up and to the right. Meg had been given the courtesy of a chair. She stared down at him, tension clear in her expression.

"Please tell me they didn't kill her." He couldn't stand the thought. How long had he been out? What terrible things had been done to Meg and his wife while he'd been sleeping?

The flap to the tent opened, and a shadow fell over Dante. Three mercenaries strode into the room.

"Who is this Kaja?" a cultured British voice asked. There was a snap of his fingers, and Dante felt himself being hauled up to seated position.

That was when Dante saw her. A brown wolf poked her nose through the door and glided in on graceful paws. Lovely, undeniably feminine, and way smarter than he'd given her credit for. His Kaja.

"She's just a girl I was fucking," Dante said as though it really didn't matter.

The wolf growled.

"I don't think she likes you," the asshole mercenary said. His hand came up to pet the wolf at his feet.

Dante felt like growling, too. "The feeling isn't mutual. She's

113

gorgeous. Where did you find her?"

Kaja sat back on her haunches. Dante fancied he could feel her satisfaction.

"She was at the marketplace. She was close to you when you took the ogre down," the man explained. "I thought she was yours."

The fuckers had hit him with a Taser. He could use that to his advantage. "I don't really remember much about that fight."

"That's a shame. I would like to hear how you managed to defeat the creature." The mercenary turned to Meg and bowed deeply. "Your Highness. My name is Sergeant Major William Roan. I lead a small group of vampires who take on all sorts of jobs."

"We call them mercenaries where I come from," Meg replied.

"Ah, we have that in common then." The vampire stood in front of Meg. "Are you feeling all right, Your Highness? I deeply apologize for the bindings. They are made from the finest silk, so they shouldn't cut your delicate skin. Are you thirsty? I can have my men bring you anything you like."

"I would like to go home," Meg stated plainly.

"Alas, that is the one thing I cannot give you. I assure you that you will be treated with the utmost respect while we await your husbands." Roan took a long breath. "And after the inevitable happens, please know that I will personally ensure your safety. I believe my employer intends to leave you on your own, but I will not allow that to happen."

"Inevitable?" Meg asked, glancing Dante's way.

Dante shrugged. "When they execute Beck and Ci."

Meg laughed, her chest bouncing a little with the effort. She had tears dripping from the corners of her eyes. Dante had to admit, it was funny. Even if they'd brought a small army with them, he didn't see how this Roan fellow was going to take down Beck Finn.

Dante knew something the rest of the world didn't know yet. Beck and Cian had come into their powers several months ago. Beck Finn had been born the greatest warrior of his generation. Now he was also a Storm Lord. With the flick of his hand, he could call on the power of a hurricane. His cousin didn't have perfect command over his powers yet, but he certainly could handle a band of mercenaries.

Meg bit her bottom lip and nodded. "I'm grateful to you, sir. I would rather not have to watch my beloved husbands being executed, if you don't mind."

Roan stared down at her and seemed to come to some decision. "I can see I've upset you. I apologize, but it is necessary. Trade must flow between our nations."

His hand came out. It almost touched Meg's hair.

"Hey," Dante said. "Her husbands aren't dead yet, Roan. You have no fucking right."

The mercenary pulled his hand back immediately. His face was blankly polite. "Of course. I am terribly sorry."

"Show me your fangs, asshole," Dante said. He had a nasty suspicion. If it was true, it might be bad for Meg—and it might be a tool to use.

Roan growled, baring his teeth. It was exactly as Dante suspected. Roan's fangs were curved and thin. Unlike a peasant's, Roan's fangs were meant to feed but not kill. Those fangs told Dante everything.

"How the hell did a royal end up as a mercenary?"

Now those blank eyes went black and cold. "Even a royal can fall, Mr. Dellacourt. I believe you're about to find that out for yourself. I will protect the consort. She is merely a pawn in this game. But you, I will allow my employer to slaughter as he sees fit. You're everything that is wrong with our system."

The mercenary got to one knee. He patted it, and Kaja walked obediently to him. His hands slipped into the wolf's fur.

Now Dante really wanted to slit the fucker's throat. Even in wolf form, Kaja had a slight glow. In human form, she practically had a halo, but in wolf form it was muted. He doubted that Roan would notice it, though it was likely having an effect on him. It was better that he didn't. The vampire was obviously hungry for a consort.

The mercenary didn't move his hands. "I'll take care of this one, too, Mr. Dellacourt. I have a weakness for the beautiful creatures of this world."

He stood and walked from the tent, Kaja following.

Though it made him crazy, Dante understood. Kaja could learn a lot in this form. She could figure out what they were planning. She could learn what weapons they had. She could get a lay of the land.

She could run away from him. She could decide that he wasn't worth the trouble. She could decide that Roan would take better care of her.

"Dante." Meg pulled him from his fantasy about taking William Roan apart with his bare hands. "What the hell is going on? Why is my captor being nice to me even as he talks about killing my husbands?"

"He's a royal." If William Roan got a look at Kaja in human form, he might fall at her feet. "You haven't spent a lot of time in vampire society. Royals treat consorts like they were made of gold."

"You don't."

He shrugged. "Only with you, sweetheart. You're like my sister now. I don't treat my sister very well."

It was true. Ever since the instant he'd seen Kaja, Meg had kind of faded to the background. She was where she should be, relegated to the role of a loved relative.

Kaja had followed Roan.

"She's playing a game, Dante." Meg was looking at him with sympathetic eyes.

Was he that transparent? "I know that."

"No, you don't. But I know exactly what she's doing. If she'd wanted to run, she'd be long gone. She's going to help us. Is this man working with Torin?"

The fight he'd been so eager for seemed to be coming at him like a steam train. "Yes. There's a faction on the Vampire plane that wants to make a deal with Torin. The royals are desperate for consorts. We age until the moment we take one. You're kind of our version of the fountain of youth. We'll still die one day, but as long as we're taking consort blood, we'll look damn good when we go, if you know what I mean."

Meg let her head fall forward. "What would happen to me if they managed to kill Beck and Ci?"

He didn't even want to think about it. "Right now there would be a riot if you hit the open market. The tournament would be huge and bloody. I don't think Roan intends to allow that to happen. He fully intends to take you when you're available. If he gets his fangs into you, no one will question his claim."

"God, I don't understand any of this. Not really." Meg sounded tired, her voice soft and weary.

Meg hadn't grown up on the linked planes. She'd been born on the Earth plane. It was a difficult plane to travel to. It was very isolated. She didn't have any real comprehension of how special she was.

She needed to understand the power she had over Roan. "Royals are raised to treat a woman like you with great reverence. If you play your cards right, he'll take care of you no matter what happens. But you should understand, he'll have a price for his care. He'll feed off you, and he'll definitely want to fuck you."

Meg shuddered.

"It's going to be okay." If he'd had hands to do it, he would have put them on her shoulders. "They don't understand what Beck is. Roan is a royal. He was raised to be polite around women like you. Just be sweet, and he won't let anything happen to you. It shouldn't be too long before Beck shows up and blows the roof off this place."

But a lot could happen in a short amount of time. Roan was a royal, but Dante would bet the rest were peasants. Peasants didn't have the same worshipful reverence for consorts that royals did. If the rest of Roan's team decided they could make more by selling Meg, they would. If they gave her to Torin—he didn't want to think about what would happen to her.

Beck could handle these guys easily, but Beck wasn't here. Dante was responsible for Meg and for Kaja.

He had to get them away from here.

"Can you move at all?" Dante asked.

He was bound tightly in sonic cuffs. The mercenaries were well equipped. They had all the latest sonic equipment. The swords at their sides could slice through flesh with almost no effort. If they managed to get Beck in hand, they could kill him. Killing Beck would almost certainly kill Cian.

"I have some room, but it could take me a while." Meg's arms moved, struggling against her bonds. They might not be sonic, but the old ways worked, too.

"I can't get out of these." He would need the locking sequence. Even if they could get Meg free, Dante couldn't get out of his cuffs.

His mind raced. "If you could make it over here, I might be able to use my teeth to loosen those ties."

"Or we could wait for Kaja to get me out." Meg nodded toward the front of the tent where Kaja was nosing her way through the flap.

He'd never seen anything as beautiful as that wolf. Kaja would save Meg. There wasn't any hope for him, but maybe the women could get to Beck. He was startled to realize all that mattered was that they were safe. If he could ensure their safety, he would be okay with whatever happened to him.

Kaja shifted, her form moving easily from wolf to one gorgeous, naked woman. She stood, her perfectly shaped breasts bouncing slightly as she walked toward Meg. She really was lovely. He might never get her breasts in his mouth. He really should have sucked her pink nipples last night, but he hadn't quite managed to get his face out of her pussy.

"Kaja, you need to get Meg out of here."

She turned her face to him. Her lips curled up softly. For a woman performing what amounted to grand theft consort, she was remarkably calm. "Yes, that was my plan, Dante."

She moved around to Meg's back.

Dante wondered how much time they had. If she managed to get his cock out, he could probably get off really fast. It might be his last time. Even a hummer would work.

Meg shook her head at him. "Dante, seriously? What is wrong with you?"

Nothing from what he could tell. Meg was staring at his erection. It was pushing his pants up admirably. Nope. Nothing wrong with that. And his fangs were out. He was fully functional. "She's naked. You can't expect me to think about my inevitable death when my wife is walking around with all her pretty pink parts on display. Now, Meg, I really don't care if you watch or not, but Kaja and I need to say good-bye in the nastiest way I can possibly achieve with my hands and feet tied."

Meg flexed her hands. "I don't think I like real, actual bondage. There was nothing fun or sexy about that. At least when Beck and Ci tie me up, I get something out of it. This time, I just got a headache. You don't have time for sex."

"There is always time for sex. Come on, Kaj. I'll be quick." He knew he sounded jokey, but deep down he really wanted her. Without Meg to keep him in check, Roan was likely to take out his frustration on him. There was no way he came out of this whole, if he came out at all. He wanted her. He wanted that moment with her. He couched it in sarcasm, but he wanted to know what it felt like to truly bond with his wife.

"Does the First believe we will flee without him?" Kaja asked, her hands sliding over Meg's, massaging her wrists back to life.

"He's not very smart," Meg replied. "You watched how they put those things on him?"

Kaja smiled brightly. "Of course. Their First did not realize what I am. He allowed me access to many things he should not have. He also fed me a lovely thing called beef jerky. The mercenaries have several pets. They tried to fight me for the jerky, but they fled after I growled. I enjoyed it."

Kaja knew how to get him out of here? His cock could wait. He would rather live. Damn, he'd finally found the thing he'd rather do than have sex. "Oh, lover, I am going to buy you all the jerky you can handle once you get me out of here."

Kaja knelt behind him and with a few twists, his hands came free. Kaja moved in front of him, but before she could reach to his feet, he caught her. He let his hands sink into her silky mass of hair and drew her close. He let her sweet scent fill his senses. He could hear her pulse, feel the softness of her skin against his.

"Thank you, Kaja." He pressed his lips to hers.

The smile on her face lit up his whole fucking world. "You are welcome, Dante."

Kaja knelt back down, and his feet came free. He wasn't bound anymore, but he had to wonder if he hadn't just become her prisoner.

Chapter Nine

Kaja turned her face up to the starlit sky. The black night was illuminated with more stars than any wolf could number. The moon was smaller. A pale silvery presence in the sky, this moon was oddly curved. It wasn't as full and round as the one at home. It did not dominate the sky. The sun, it seemed, held sway here, with the moon only an afterthought.

Kaja heard Meg behind her. She'd been working since the moment that Dante had told them it was safe to stop. Kaja had been staring at the forest in wonder.

Everything was different here. There was no snow, and the stars made different patterns in the sky. Water fell from above in a great sheet that flowed into a crystalline pool. She'd never seen anything like it. Dante had called it a waterfall, but Meg had mentioned something called paradise.

She looked out at Dante, who was bathing in the pool. He'd shed his clothes almost the instant they'd made the decision to stop and walked into the pond. The urge to follow him in had been tempered by the fact that he wasn't using a tub. She'd gotten comfortable in the bathing tub, but the pond was something different. This water was deep. Dante had gone under several times, making her heart skip a beat until he resurfaced.

The sounds were different here, too. There was the whoosh of the water as it hit the pond, and the whisper of the wind in the trees. Beneath it all, she could hear something shuffling under the brush behind her. *Prey.* And yet she found herself more curious than hungry.

Everything about this world made her curious. Especially Dante.

She stared as he emerged from the pool, water dripping from his form. He was so beautiful. His skin was perfect and smooth. Every muscle rippled, from his broad shoulders to his strong thighs. He shook the water off of him. His hair looked different now. It was longer without the "product" he'd spoken of. The water had washed it away leaving only his silky strands behind. It made him look younger, with his gold and red hair brushing his ears. Her eyes drifted down. Kaja couldn't help but look at how his long, thick male part jutted up. Heavy balls swung below. She wondered what it would feel like to cup them, to run her hands along his...cock. He'd called it a cock.

Her eyes met with his. She had the urge to go to him.

"Whoa!" Meg yelled from behind her. "Dante, I did not need to see that!"

Kaja turned, that odd moment gone, and saw that Meg was hiding her eyes.

"Everyone's seen it, Meg. I've been caught naked by every photographer in the States. This body was named 'hottest royal bod' four years in a row. Everyone wants a piece of this." Dante grinned and motioned up and down, indicating his perfect body.

Meg sounded as though she was sick. "Gross."

Kaja bit her lip. Not all things were good in this place. She still didn't understand half the things Meg and Dante said to each other. She knew the words, but not the intentions behind them. Since that moment when the three of them had snuck from the camp, Kaja had been a bit lost. The words they spoke at each other did not match the tone. They did a lot of a thing they called joking. It involved insulting each other in a manner that would have gotten them outcast from the pack had they been pack members speaking to their betters.

Kaja had almost liked it better when they'd been silent, prowling through the forest to get away from the men who had captured them. Dante had ordered her to return to her wolf form after he'd kissed her. That was a moment she'd loved. His mouth had played across hers, lighting up her skin. He'd needed her in that moment.

He did not need her anymore.

They seemed to be safe in this part of the forest. Perhaps the time had come to explore on her own. These woods were deep, she sensed. She could lose herself here and never be found.

"Kaja." Dante's voice had adopted that slightly hard tone he used when he was taking control. That deep tone had Kaja turning her head to focus on him. He was knee-deep in the water. He held his hand out. "Come with me. Take off the shirt, and we'll get you clean before we bed down."

That was not a good idea. Though her heart raced at the sight of him waiting for her, it would be smarter to leave. He was playing some sort of game with her. He wanted to be with her, but not forever. Wolves mated for life. She never expected she would get a true mate, but even a mistress had a role in the pack. She wasn't sure what Dante believed her place to be. He had signed the important things called papers that made her his, but then talked about where he would put her when their mating was done.

She wasn't sure of anything.

She shook her head. "I do not like the water. I am clean enough."

When they bedded down for the night, she would sneak away. He would not hear her. He would not look for her. She would watch over both Dante and Meg. She would stay in wolf form, and they would never know that she followed them. When she was sure they were safe, she would disappear. She would stay in these woods and never leave her wolf form. Her two-legged nature would fade, and the wolf would be all that was left. It would be easier. The wolf felt, but not as much as her woman self. The wolf never cried.

She turned to aid Meg in her preparations. Meg was creating a small nest in which to rest. She had gathered leaves and vines to make a bed. Kaja didn't need it. She would change and be perfectly fine, but Meg obviously wanted a bit of comfort. After the day she'd had, she deserved it.

Kaja was about to lean over and gather leaves from the ground of the forest when a damp hand reached out and grabbed her elbow. She turned and looked up into stern eyes that were the color of the forest. Dante's jaw was set in a firm line as he towered over her. He was so beautiful it hurt her heart to look at him.

"It wasn't a question, Kaja."

She tried to pull her arm away, but he held tight. "I'm tired. I wish to rest."

It would be easy to refuse, to run, if he didn't move her in a way she'd never felt before. She'd been sure he wouldn't come after her when she'd gone to save her gnome captor. She'd stared up at the ogre and realized that death had come for her. She would have gone down fighting, but she would have gone down.

And then he'd been there, yelling at her. His face had been contorted in rage and some strange worry. *For her.* He was so much smaller than the creature, and he'd only had Kaja to distract the ogre, yet Dante had triumphed. The ogre had fallen.

It had taken a piece of magic to force Dante to his knees.

That was the moment—when Dante had been struck with the nightmare magic that caused his big, beautiful body to shake—when Kaja had known she should leave. She'd felt the howl in her throat. It stuck there because she'd forced her jaw to stay closed, but the mating howl was inside her, and it was only for this man.

She could howl all she liked. He would not answer. He would not even understand what it meant, and if she explained it to him, his eyes would get that soft haze that told her she was an object of pity.

"Please, Kaja." His gaze was soft on her. "I'll take care of you. We'll bed down close to Meg, but I want to spend time with my consort. This is our bonding time. I don't care that we're not alone. Meg can ignore it if she doesn't like it."

"There aren't enough earplugs in the world," Meg complained. Her hands went to her hips as she looked at Dante, obviously trying to keep her eyes on his face. "Now isn't the time to bond. Like I don't know what that means. Just lay your ass down and get some sleep. Beck and Cian will be here soon. Then you can paw the poor girl."

The growl that came from Dante's throat did all kinds of things to her woman's parts. *Pussy.* Dante wanted her to call it a pussy. His fangs grew long. He moved toward Meg, never letting go of Kaja's arm.

"And when your husbands return, I will have a long discussion with the warrior half about the way his wife places herself between me and my consort. We will discuss why you think you have rights over my consort and your definition of respect."

Meg's mouth dropped open, and Kaja didn't miss the way Meg's eyes slid away. "Wow, way to Dom a girl, Dante."

Dante relaxed slightly, his arm curling around Kaja's waist. He pulled her into the hard plane of his body. He brushed her hair with his nose, breathing deeply as though her scent brought him comfort. "Vampires get possessive of their consorts. Rather like Fae warriors and their bondmates. You should get used to me being a bit more dominant than I was before. And I'm hungry."

A thrill of fear went through Kaja. Dante was hungry. He needed blood. Her blood.

"Dante, I didn't even think about that," Meg said. "Kaja and I ate, but you don't have any meal pills."

Kaja didn't miss the way his chest hitched or the feel of his cock against her thigh. He'd covered the lower portion of his body with hers when he'd begun to talk to Meg. Now his cock lengthened and hardened and caressed her backside.

"I have a consort. That's all I need." His nose ran along her hair. He spoke to Meg, but all of his attention seemed to be on Kaja. She'd never felt so attended to, so fixated upon. It was like she was his prey, but he wasn't going to kill her. That was not his intent. He didn't want her dead, merely willing to feed his hunger.

He'd saved her life. She did owe him a bit of blood. Without his intervention, she would have stayed in her cage and died when the ogre came. She would never have known what it felt like to be pressed against another body, scents mingling until she couldn't tell where she ended and Dante began.

"I will feed you," Kaja said quietly. She was going back on what she knew was right, but she seemed to take every opportunity to stay close to him. She couldn't seem to help herself. She would pay for this intimacy, but she would have it.

Meg nodded. "There's some space behind the waterfall. It's nice, and the moon filters in so you can see. The grass is soft. I found it when I bathed earlier. I'll stay out here and get some sleep."

"Come, Kaja." The command was still there in Dante's voice, but there was a smoothness now as well.

Still, she hesitated. The pond was so much bigger than the tub. "I can feed you here on land."

"That's not what I want, Kaja," he growled. He placed his forehead to hers and took a long breath. "I'm on edge, sweetheart. Please forgive me. It's been a long day. I'll try to explain it to you. This first time is important. I've never fed from a woman before. I want it to be special."

Special. She understood the word, but now she felt it. He'd never fed from a woman before. She'd never been so close to a man before. He'd given her that. He'd been the one to make her feel included. When he commanded her, it made her feel safe and wanted. He seemed to know all of her weaknesses.

Now he said a word that tugged at her.

"Please, Kaja. Come with me. Trust me. I'll take care of you."

No one had ever said *please* to her before. Kaja placed her hand in his.

"I don't understand your preoccupation with water," Kaja said, her hand shaking as she pulled the shirt over her head and let it fall to the ground. She hadn't drowned in the tub, but she still would prefer to not go into the pond. Her feet hit the water. It was slightly cool. The ground under her was a soft sand. Yes. She sought that magic memory Dante had given her. Sand was the word for this ground. She sank slightly, her toes wiggling around in the soft stuff. It felt nice.

"The water feels good." Dante drew her out, taking both of her hands in his. "I'll hire the best swimming coach we can find once we get back to my plane. When you're comfy, we'll go to Hawaii. It's beautiful there, Kaj. We'll swim and drink and fuck to our hearts' content. I can show you so many things."

Tears pricked at her eyes. She wanted so badly to believe him, but he said two different things. There was a part of her that was still waiting for him to hurt her. He could pull her out into the deep part of the water and hold her down. He could kill her.

She might let him, because she didn't want to live in a world where no one could love her.

"Kaja." He said her name on a sigh and pulled her close. His hands came up to wipe away her tears. "Don't cry, Kaj. Please. It kills me. If you don't want me, I'll let you go to sleep. I can go hungry for one night. I'll find something to eat, I promise."

She wrapped her arms around him, reveling in his feel and his scent. He was a magician. He always knew what to say to her. She sighed and gave up any thought of leaving him. She didn't really want to. She was stupid. What the pack had said about her was true. She knew her heart would be broken in the end, and she couldn't walk away. She simply opened herself and practically begged him to love her.

But how could he say yes if she said no?

"I want you, Dante."

The smile that broke over his face showed off his delicious fangs. They were beautiful, like the rest of the man.

"Oh, baby, you have no idea how glad I am to hear that." His face turned to granite. "But we have a few things to discuss first. I've thought a lot about this, Kaja. Beck is right. I need to put this marriage on a firm footing. You need to understand that you cannot do what you did today."

"Save you? You do not wish me to save you when…assholes take you and bind you down?" She was proud of herself. Anuses were very important to the Vampire plane. They seemed to speak of them often.

His head shook even as he pulled her close. "That's not what I mean, love, and you know it. I'm talking about the way you ran away from me when the ogre was attacking. You didn't bother to tell me what you were doing."

"I was in my four-legged form," Kaja said, enjoying deeply the way his flesh slid against hers. "Would you have understood growls and barks? Does your magic cover that?"

She was beginning to understand that magic was created by smart people, but it still seemed to be the right word. Dante had called it technology, but it was magical. Dante's people were magical.

His hand buried itself in her hair. "You know you could have spoken to me before you changed. You made a choice to put yourself in danger. You made a choice to leave me. It is not acceptable."

She frowned. She'd known he might be upset, but she'd had her reasons. "Cara was in danger."

"So were you." He kept pulling her further in. The water covered her hips now. It was nice and cool. It felt like silk gliding against her skin. "You're my primary concern. You can't run off on your own. That's not the way this marriage is going to work."

She hadn't been certain the marriage was going to work at all. "I do not understand what you require of me."

"I intend to make that clear, love. Put your legs around my waist. Don't let go." Dante began to walk with purpose toward the waterfall. Kaja wound her arms around Dante's neck and her legs found his waist, locking her ankles behind his back. Her heart trilled in her chest as the water hit her hair. The sound filled her ears, a roar that couldn't be denied.

In an instant, it was over. She was on the other side. The moonlight filtered through the fall of water. She found herself in a silvery alcove with only Dante for companionship. It seemed utterly perfect.

"Do you understand what punishment means, Kaja?" Dante asked, his face perfectly serious.

Yes, she knew that word. She did not particularly like that word. "You will punish me because I tried to save my friend?"

He didn't seem interested in hurting her. He seemed far more interested in inhaling her. She didn't move to get away from him because his hands held her tenderly and his nose ran all along her neck. If this was his version of punishment, she might have to be bad more often. He kept one hand around her waist, and the other gripped her backside. She liked the way he cupped her rear. It made her pussy feel achy and wanting. Oh, he worked some magic on her.

"Not for saving your friend, love," Dante murmured into the flesh of her neck. His tongue came out and licked a line from her collarbone to her earlobe. "I'm going to punish you for not discussing it with me. But first, I'm going to explain how this relationship is going to work. You're going to obey me in the important things, Kaja. I'm not going to tell you what to do every minute of the day, but when your life is on the line, you will mind me, or this will happen."

Dante picked her up, his arms going under her knees and around her back, and began walking to the shore. Kaja held on and shivered as the cool night air hit her skin. She wasn't sure what was happening, but he'd been nothing but tender so far. She was willing to give him the benefit of the doubt.

And she liked the way he carried her. She felt small and light when he held her in his strong arms. She let her head drift to his shoulder. His skin was on the cool side, but still felt smooth and comforting to her.

The small cave seemed intimate and a bit romantic to Kaja. It was like the rest of the world had fallen away and left behind only her and Dante. They were the only ones in this small world.

Dante walked with purpose toward a large rock that jutted from the side of the cave. He sat down and tipped her face up to look at his. His eyes had taken on a glow. He looked alien in the silvery light. She was beginning to understand that he was two-natured as well. There was the happy, funny Dante, and this man, the powerful First. The First lay buried until he showed himself with fangs and claws and these eyes. The color bled, leaving no white behind. His eyes glowed a bit and threatened to pull her in. Kaja felt herself get caught by his stare.

"I won't allow you to put yourself in danger." His voice had taken on that deep tone she associated with the First. "Place yourself across my lap with your ass in the air."

Now she hesitated. "I do not understand."

"Then let me explain, sweetheart." He picked her up, his hands circling her waist. He proved his strength and agility by neatly flipping her over.

Kaja found the world upended. She was staring at the ground, her naked ass high in the air. She felt vulnerable, her body completely under his control. She shivered in the slight chill. And then she was howling because something sharp slapped the tender flesh of her backside. It lit her ass like lightning. Kaja kicked, trying to get away.

Dante used one big hand to hold her down. "No. You're not getting away from me. You're going to accept your punishment."

She did not like this punishment at all. Dante's hand rained down on her. Over and over he smacked at her flesh. Tears pricked at Kaja's eyes. She thought about changing. If she changed forms, he would not be able to hold her. She thought about running, but something was happening to her. Her flesh sparked when he struck her, but then he slowed his slaps. In between, Kaja began to feel a sweet heat invading her flesh, as though the very cessation of pain turned into a sharp, aching pleasure.

It was not so bad. It was starting to feel like something good.

"That's right, love." Dante's voice was rich like the honey that sometimes dripped from beehives in summertime. "Relax. Take what I give you."

His hand came down again, slapping a fleshy part of her ass. This time his hand stayed there, smoothing the hurt. The pain sank in, and she felt a different ache begin.

"Shit, Kaja, baby, I can smell you. You're getting wet." His fingers delved into the crease of her ass. Kaja moaned at the touch. "You're getting wet and ready to get fucked."

It did seem that way. She couldn't control her response.

Dante slapped at her ass, harder this time. "You're not getting it right now. Not until you apologize sweetly and promise to never do it again."

His fingers ran down the seam of her ass, and she felt a gentle touch to her pussy. It made her wiggle and writhe.

Another smack. This one echoed through the small cave. "No moving. This is my time."

His time? It felt like her time. She struggled to breathe as he played with her. His fingers burrowed into her pussy, first one, and then two. He traced all of her female parts. Kaja could feel herself getting wet. The juice seemed to come from somewhere deep inside. That place inside was demanding more, but Kaja held still. The First wanted her to remain still, to let him…play.

She liked to play.

"Fuck, you're so creamy and ready." Dante groaned as he slid a finger inside her. *Fucking*. He'd called it fucking. He was doing it with his finger, but she could feel the hard line of his cock poking at her belly. It throbbed beneath her, yet still he played. "Tell me you want this, Kaj."

She liked when he called her Kaj. It seemed so sweet and

familiar. It was something no one else had ever called her. No one had ever said her name, much less given her a sweet, secret name. "I want this."

She wasn't sure she wanted to want it, though. It would only make things harder, but she couldn't deny herself this pleasure. Her heart, it seemed, was as foolish as the pack had said she herself was. Her heart simply wanted. Her mind could see the ache coming, but her heart demanded what would surely hurt her in the end.

But at least, just once, she would pretend to be loved.

Dante spread his knees apart and moved her between his legs. She found herself kneeling on the sand beneath him, looking up into his eyes. She held on to his knees to find her balance.

"Kaja, you know how I put my mouth on your pussy?" Dante's hands were restlessly stirring up her hair.

She glanced down. His cock was thick and almost purple in the dim light. She stared at it, struck by its odd beauty. She had seen male parts before, but Dante's seemed lovely and graceful, where the others had been blunt and ugly to her. She tentatively brought her hand up to touch it.

"That's right, sweetheart," Dante murmured. "Touch me."

She let her fingers trace the line of his cock. It was soft. She'd expected roughness, but the skin was silky and smooth. Her hand played around the stalk. She could get her hand to close around it, but barely. She could put both hands around it, but the head still rose well above her fists. The smooth stalk bulged into a thick, bulbous head. She watched, utterly fascinated, as a drop of white, thick fluid seeped from the head.

He wanted her to taste him. He'd tasted her over and over the night before. Now he wanted to share that piece of himself with her. Emotion threatened to choke her. No wolf would ever allow her to do this. They would never offer. They would know she would bite them, but Dante asked her to take his essence deep inside her—into her pussy and her mouth.

She leaned forward and breathed in his scent. He smelled clean, but there was a divine musky scent that made her want to huddle close to him. She allowed her tongue to come out, and she gently licked the drop seeping from his cock.

He tasted salty. It coated her tongue, and the minute she'd lapped the first drop up, another had taken its place.

Dante stared down at her, his face tight. "Stop playing with me. I want your mouth on my cock. I want you to take it in your mouth."

It did not look like it would fit into her mouth.

"Kaja," Dante said, impatience dripping. "It would please me if you would try to take me into your mouth."

And she could not refuse that. She wanted to please him so badly.

She put her lips on that big cock and opened her mouth. Dante's fingers wound into her hair, and he pulled her forward.

"Follow my lead. I'll teach you how to suck my cock." His words had lost their smoothness. He seemed to be grinding them out of his mouth now. "Use your tongue to lick me all over."

That wasn't easy. He filled Kaja's mouth. He kept pressing in. She had to fight to breathe for a minute, but then calmed and let herself relax. She breathed in through her nose and let Dante sink into her open mouth. She rubbed her tongue along the underside of his cock. He felt silky, and she could taste his salty arousal dripping into her mouth.

"That's right. That's what I want."

Guided by instinct, she pulled back a bit and whirled her tongue around the head. She loved the feel of the skin and the small indentation on the backside of his cockhead. The muscles of Dante's thighs tightened and became hard as rocks. Everything about the man seemed hard.

It struck her suddenly that she was in control. She had this man in the palm of her hand, and he trusted her. The hand in her hair wasn't there to pull her back. It was there to keep her in place and encourage her.

"Take more, Kaja," Dante said. It wasn't a request. It was a harsh demand.

There was a piece of her that deeply responded to his dominance. He'd earned it. He'd saved her. He'd proven stronger than she was. In her world, it gave him the right to dominate her. He was the alpha, the First. And she was his mate.

There it was again—that howl that meant she claimed him. She forced it back. It would do nothing but prove she was a barbarian. The more she spoke to Meg and watched Dante, the more she realized she would not fit into his world. The buildings were made of materials she couldn't conceive of, and they rose into the sky like mountains. She didn't belong there.

But she was going to try. She'd never given up, even when she'd had absolutely nothing to gain. She wasn't about to stop trying now that Valhalla was close. Perhaps she could become what Dante needed. But her mating howl would never be voiced. It would be more than he could handle.

She swallowed it down even as she wrapped her mouth around his cock. She sucked and licked, his throaty moans leading the way. She whirled her tongue around it, moving her mouth up and down. Her hands found their way below to cup the heavy sac that hung under his cock. The skin here felt different, but every bit as intriguing. She wondered what it would feel like to lap all around the round balls.

"Just relax, sweetheart." Dante's voice had gone to a guttural place. His hands tightened in her hair. "I'm almost there. Let me fuck your mouth, and then I'll see to you. I want you to swallow me down. I want you to take what I give you."

Dante picked up the pace. He pushed and pulled at her hair, forcing that big cock into her mouth and then dragging it out. Over and over, he fucked between her lips. She tried to keep up, her tongue licking all around. There was a rhythm to his thrusts, and she found herself relaxing and finding the beat. She let her mind drift. It was instinct that led her. It seemed right to open herself to him.

"What the hell?" Dante's rhythm was blown, and Kaja felt something amazing roll over her body. Heat and a wet, delicious pleasure took over her lower body as though she was the one receiving pleasure. She shivered as a salty taste filled her mouth. Dante's cock swelled, and Kaja could feel him come. Pleasure, so much pleasure. It went beyond the mere feeling. The connection that had opened between them was beyond anything she'd ever dreamed of. She felt his pleasure, and for the briefest moment, she could have sworn she felt him—the real Dante.

The connection had been strongest at the moment of his orgasm. Yes, she knew that word. She'd brought him to orgasm. As he'd reached the pinnacle, she'd share a piece of his soul.

Kaja kissed his cock one last time and leaned back, ready to accept his praise.

Dante stared down at her. His eyes glowed in the darkness, and Kaja knew what it meant to be prey.

Chapter Ten

Dante felt like the whole world had turned on its head. One minute he'd been perfectly happy having his cock attended to by his consort, and the next she'd been deep inside his mind, invading with a sweet sense of intimacy that he'd never felt before. He was a man who'd never felt alone once in his life, but when he'd touched Kaja's mind with his own, he'd realized that he'd never really known what it meant to be together with someone. He'd understood Kaja in that one instant more than he'd ever known another being.

That had to stop.

When the hunger had come, he'd been more than happy to give in to it.

"What's wrong?" Kaja asked.

He could sense her fear. There was the smallest part of him that reveled in it. Kaja was powerful on her own. The fact that she was frightened spoke to the beast that obviously lived inside him. He had ignored this primal side of himself for far too long. Now, with a consort so close, he couldn't ignore the part of him that needed blood—real blood.

Her blood.

"Nothing is wrong, consort." His voice sounded odd to his own ears. It was deeper and more demanding than it had ever been before. The world looked different with his eyes fully opened, his senses on alert. Kaja glowed, the halo that surrounded her so fucking gorgeous to his eyes.

Her blood would be the best he'd ever tasted.

He felt his dick get hard again at the thought of having her in his arms. This time he would pull her close. He would get his fangs in her neck and drink his fill.

"Come to me."

Her beautiful, graceful form backed away.

"Do not run from me, consort." His fangs had popped out, filling his mouth and forcing him to speak around them. "I am only barely in control now. If you try to flee, I think I'll lose it, and I'll take you without any kindness. I don't want that between us."

Oh, but it was there. The desire to take her because she belonged to him was right there beneath the surface. His senses were filled with her. Her skin glowed, and he could smell the soft, musky scent of her desire. Her lips were full, swollen from the way he'd shoved his cock in between them. He'd shove his cock into her pussy, too. She was his. He'd bought her, fought for her. It was only right that he take her.

Kaja swallowed and got to her knees. "I do not want that between us, either."

It was the gentle hitch in her voice that pulled him from the edge. She'd seen so much violence, known so little kindness. He'd closed that odd connection between them before he'd seen too much, but he'd caught the edge of Kaja's reality. The last thing he wanted was to be another person who used her.

But that's what you're doing. That voice in his head didn't seem to care about his hunger. He wasn't using her. He was saving her. If he hadn't bought her, Beck would have been forced to kill her, or she would have spent a lifetime alone, wandering the forests. He'd done her a favor. And when she'd paid him back by convincing his father he had settled down, Dante would find her a nice home. She would have luxury like she'd never imagined.

"What should I do?" Kaja asked.

He could think of a million things she should do. She should run because he wasn't worthy of her. He was a selfish bastard, and he always would be. He couldn't commit. It was simply impossible. This raging passion he felt for her would fade. It was inevitable, so if he

135

had a heart in his body, he would save her the pain.

"Come to me." He held out his hand and indicated that she should sit on his lap.

She got to her feet and stepped forward, placing herself on his lap, the soft flesh of her ass kissing his thighs. The minute her skin touched his, he felt something ease deep inside him. That nagging beast that raged below the surface let up the tiniest bit.

"Put your arms around me." He let his hands drift to her waist as he breathed her in. Her hair was mostly dry, and it bloomed around her delicate face like a halo of softness. He let his nose run through it. Kaja's hands found their way around his neck, and he could hear the way her heart sped up. She might be frightened, but there was obviously a part of her that wanted, too. She knew what he was going to do, and yet she wrapped her body around his, allowing him to fill his every sense with her.

His heart began to pound in time to the rhythm he heard. Kaja's chest thudded as he ran his nose along the line of her neck. He could hear the blood running through her body like a river of life. His fangs scraped her skin, and she trembled.

"Don't be afraid." He couldn't stand the thought now. Her arms were around him, circling him in her light. Her very touch had softened his predatory instincts and brought out a need to please her. A consort had her power, too.

"Will it hurt?" The words came out on a breathless whisper.

He kept his mouth close to her neck. He couldn't seem to move it. It was far too tempting. But he soothed a hand down her back. "I don't know, love. I don't think so. Consorts seem to love the bite, and it's always followed by some righteously nasty sex."

He felt her chuckle, and something eased inside him. "You sound like Dante again."

He felt more in control. Her very nearness allowed him to push the beast back. It was still there, simmering below the surface, but he felt more like himself.

And he was hungry. So fucking hungry.

It gnawed at his gut, but it was so much more than physical. He hungered for her. If someone had offered him a pill at that moment, he would have smacked them down. He didn't need fucking nutrition.

He needed her.

But there was a process. Every royal knew it. Every royal was forced to study it right along with an embarrassing course in sex education. Dante had laughed his way through it, from the talk on safe feeding to the teaching plastic model every student had been forced to "feed" from to prove he wouldn't rip its throat out. Delicacy was given high marks. If he simply bit down, she would be in agony. Persuasion was the key.

"Look at me, Kaja." He looked into her eyes, not allowing himself a moment to blink.

"They're so beautiful. So green. Like the forest in high summer before the winter takes everything away." Kaja stared at his eyes, not fighting him at all. Her mouth was slightly open. This was what the class had talked about. Persuasion. It felt good to pull her in and know she was his for the taking. She wouldn't feel the pain of his fangs penetrating that smooth, white neck. All she would feel would be pleasure with every drag he took from her.

"You're the beautiful one, Kaj." He smoothed back her hair. Her crystal-blue eyes were a bit cloudy, but he couldn't mistake the affection there. She was fully in the moment with him.

And this was more than a feed. He pulled her close, her nipples brushing against his chest. They were hard little points. He could feel her wet pussy rubbing against his thigh. Kaja was ready for a long, hard fucking, and he would give it to her. After.

Instinct led him. He forgot about the class and everything he'd ever heard about this act. This was between him and Kaja, and no one else in all the planes of existence could know what it felt like. The world had narrowed down, and Kaja filled it. There was only the scent of her, and the pearly glow of her skin, and the sound of her heart.

He gently grabbed a handful of silky hair and pulled her head back, exposing the long line of her neck. A single vein seemed to pulse and tempt him. He licked from her collarbone to below her earlobe, following that sweet river that would feed his hunger.

"Please, Dante." She squirmed.

Dante chuckled. There was no fear in her voice now. She wanted it. She was ready to beg for it. And he was done playing. His cock ached and every muscle in his body screamed to take her.

"Yes. Yes, it's time." It was time to join with her. The phrase stuck in his head like a song he couldn't get rid of. *Joining. Being. Kaja.*

Dante struck. He didn't question how he knew where to strike. He simply let that primal piece of himself take over, and his fangs pierced the vein with flawless accuracy. Not too deep. He felt the small hollow in his fangs fill for the first time with sweet, living blood. *So warm and rich.* He hadn't realized how cold he'd been before, but as Kaja's blood began to flow through his system, he knew he'd never look at a meal pill again. This was what it meant to be full and complete. Her blood invaded him like the sweetest drug he'd ever known. She was better than alcohol, better than anything.

He dragged blood into his body as Kaja moaned in his arms. She clung to him, her hands clutching as though she never wanted him to stop.

And that was the danger. She didn't want to stop. He didn't want to stop. He could drink until she was dry and still want more. Just another minute and he would stop.

Then there was something beneath the taste. Dante felt something skittering on the edge of his consciousness. It was a single vision.

The world was white and cold. All around him was snow. It coated the ground and filled the air. White flakes danced through the wind and played on his snout.

He had a snout. He had four feet and a strong body. He could feel the long line of his spine. He scented the air. It was like the layers of an onion. There were surface smells—his own body, the scent of pine trees, the clean smell of snow. But there was more. He breathed it in, peeling back the layers. There was dirt under the snow. It had a loamy smell. To his right, he scented blood and the smell of the pack. That was his pack. He turned toward them. They had a huge buck down, its tan hide opened, and the blood made a stark contrast against the snow.

His heart constricted. There was a reason he stood behind. His stomach gnawed in hunger. It felt like his stomach was trying to turn in on itself. He wanted that flesh. He needed it, but he wasn't welcome. He would have to wait until the pack was done and hope that there was something left. He would munch on the bones and try to tear the bits of meat that would cling to the hide.

He stood apart and watched them.

He was Kaja. Dante's eyes flew open, and he released the vein.

What the hell had happened?

Kaja slumped back in his arms. He tightened his hands on her so she didn't fall. Had he taken too much? He forced the odd vision out of his brain as panic took over for a moment. He couldn't have hurt her. He wouldn't want to live if he'd hurt her.

Kaja's eyes came open. A dreamy look crossed her face. She lifted a hand to his cheek. "That did not hurt."

Relief swept over him. She didn't look anything like a woman he'd abused. She looked like a woman who'd had a good time. She looked like a woman who was satisfied.

His eyes strayed to the twin marks on her neck, and he felt his cock swell again. Those small holes marked her as his. She belonged to him. More than any piece of paper or monetary exchange, the fact that her blood was in his body, sustaining him and making him warm and alive, was proof that he owned this woman. The worries fell away, and he began to hunger again.

He wasn't going to hold back this time. She'd agreed to mate with him before. That would have to do.

He let his hands drift to her breasts. He would be able to sleep with his head pillowed on them. They molded to fit his hand. The nipples were already hard before he ever touched them. He rolled them between his thumb and forefinger while Kaja made that soft whimpering sound that always made his dick strain to get inside her.

"I want to fuck, Kaj." He should warn her before he rammed his cock into her.

She nodded and scrambled off his lap. Dante was about to chase her down when she got to her knees in the soft sand and dropped to all fours. Her round ass was presented to him, and he couldn't resist. He fell to his knees behind her feeling more powerful than he'd ever felt before. He wasn't sure if it was her blood singing inside him or the fact that she was so submissive. He'd never wanted it before. He never wanted a female on her knees waiting for him to take his pleasure. It made him responsible for her, but he couldn't resist Kaja. He traced the line of her spine with his hand, inspecting the bounty placed before him. Her ass cheeks were round and formed a sweet upside-down heart.

"Spread your knees apart." He wanted to see her asshole. His cock twitched against his abdomen. The fucking thing was standing straight up.

Kaja was obedient. She spread her legs further, giving him full access to all those holes Dante was thinking about fucking. He could see her pussy glistening with moisture and her little anus peeking from between her cheeks. It was a pale pink, almost a rosy brown, and it looked so tight.

"Did that lame-ass Second of yours ever fuck this pretty asshole, love?" His fangs were back out. It wasn't entirely about the sex that was about to happen. There was an edge of violence to his mood as well. He didn't like to think about the fucker who had raped his wife. That was what it had been. This Second of hers had shown her no pleasure, no kindness. He'd held her down and tossed her aside. He'd taken something that belonged to Dante, and if Dante ever met up with him, there would be a reckoning.

Kaja's sweet face turned, her eyes wide with obvious confusion. "No. Why would he do such a thing?"

Dante almost laughed. He was glad that asshole hadn't taken hers. "I'll do it because it's mine. You should get used to me. I'll be on you all the time now. I'll fuck any hole that's big enough to fit my cock into because you're my wife."

A smile curled her lips up, and it did odd things to his heart to see her smile. "I am glad my ears are small then."

He laughed while he moved between her legs. "I think your ears are safe, love. But I assure you once we get home and I have you properly prepared, you will accept my cock in your ass."

"Or you will spank me." It was said with a breathless sigh.

Fuck, she was so submissive when it came to sex. She might fight him elsewhere, but she submitted where it counted. He smacked that gorgeous ass and felt her tremble. "That's right. Don't forget it. I'll spank you and that won't be the worst of it. I'll have you tied up and tied down, and you'll be utterly at my mercy. But for now, I'll settle for this."

Dante lined his cock up and pushed his way in.

Heat and tight pleasure threatened to swamp him. He pushed his cock inside, gripping her hips and forcing himself into her. A savage joy overtook him. She was so snug around him that Dante had to breathe to control himself. He wanted this to last. He pulled out and thrust back in, not missing the way her pussy sucked at him. He thrust until he was flush against her, his thighs pressed to the backs of her own. Her head had fallen forward in complete submission. Her body was his to do with as he pleased.

He dragged his cock out again and then set a brutal pace. He fucked her like a jackhammer, using her body with ruthless precision. He controlled the movement by tightening his hands on her hips and forcing her body to accept his dick.

He was just about to let out a roar and fill her when it happened again. It was a flash of Kaja. This was how the Second had taken her, though he'd had a friend hold her down by the neck while another had forced her legs apart. She'd gritted her teeth and endured as the Second had used her. It was all Kaja knew. It was why she'd gotten into this position. Kaja didn't understand that there was more than one way to make love. She only knew how to be raped.

Dante fell back, tears coating his eyes and making the world seem like a watery mess. What was he doing? He was treating Kaja like a possession, not something precious and valuable. He was behaving as all the men who Kaja had known before had behaved. She was his wife. Her blood was in his body. She was worth more than this.

"Did I displease you?" Kaja was on her knees, her arms covering her breasts. She'd turned in on herself. He could see that now. Her face went blank when she retreated.

No. She hadn't displeased him in the least, but he couldn't say the same for himself. The urge to walk away was right there like a knot in his chest that wouldn't let him breathe. He didn't want to feel this way. He didn't want to be responsible for her. He wanted to be the man he'd always been before—the good-time guy. He wanted to party and fuck pretty women and send them on their way. He didn't want to have his heart ripped out every time Kaja turned those gorgeous eyes on him. He didn't fucking want to care.

"I should leave then." Kaja's eyes turned down, but not before he

141

caught the sheen of unshed tears. "I will find a place to sleep, but I won't go far."

She would curl up and cry and wonder how she'd failed him. He knew exactly what she would do. He could tell her it wasn't her fault, but she wouldn't believe it. She would only believe it if he showed her.

He couldn't let her leave. "Kaja, I'm not done."

She bit at her bottom lip. "But you pushed me away. Perhaps if you told me what I did wrong, I could learn how to please you."

He reached out and pulled her close. Only when her arms went around him did he relax again. He'd fucked up, but he could fix it. "You didn't do anything wrong. I didn't want to make love that way. I want to see your pretty face when you come for me."

"But the mating..." she began.

He shook his head and forced her to look him in the eyes. "No mating. Mating is for assholes who want to use you and give you nothing in return. Put that word out of your mind." He let his hands roam as he eased her onto her back and got between her legs. He covered her body with his. Yes, this was what he'd missed. He was wrapped in her softness. "We're going to make love, you and I. We're going to fuck, but in the sweetest way possible. Do you understand?"

"No, but I already like it. I like being close to you." Her legs moved against his hips. She was already accepting him in a way she hadn't before. She hadn't moved when he'd mounted her from behind. Now she was participating. Her hands ran down his back to the muscles of his ass.

"And I like your hands on me. Oh, touch me everywhere. I want to feel you all around me." He was right there again, with his cock at her pussy, but this time she was the one who pulled him inside. Her hands gripped his ass, and she spread her legs.

"I like this making love, Dante," she said. "I like this so much more."

So did he. She was with him this time. He took over, thrusting in gently and pulling out, simply enjoying the feel of being inside her. He let his head drift to her neck. He could hear the soothing sound of her heart racing and feel her warmth surrounding him. He fucked his wife for the longest time. She came over and over, her mouth opening and crying out his name as her legs tightened around him. Five times she shuddered and came beneath him before her arms fell away.

"Dante, I can't." Her head had fallen back, and though she begged for mercy, there was a smile on her face.

"One more. I want one more, and then we can be done. For now." He didn't want her to get it into her head that she would be allowed more than a night's rest. He intended to be inside her again before she fully awoke the next morning. He intended to fuck her until she forgot there had ever been a man there before him.

"I can't," she whispered.

But she could. He pushed himself up and ground his pelvis against her clit as he fucked his cock as deeply into her as he could go, and she lit up around him.

Then it was finally his turn. He let go, and the pleasure made his body jerk as he came.

Another feeling flowed through him. Utter satisfaction. He was satisfied because he was complete in that moment. And then he realized the feeling wasn't his. It was Kaja's. Her heart, her sweet, brave, loyal heart, was at peace for the first time as he came inside her. She held him, clinging to him. So much of her pleasure came from pleasing him.

Dante shuddered one last time and let himself fall on her. Her breath came out in a happy sigh, and she squeezed her arms around him.

He should roll off her. Some voice deep inside him told him to run, but it was a distant thing now. There was another voice that told him to revel in her. She was his, but this voice didn't tell him to take her because she belonged to him. This voice urged him to take care of her, to cling to her as she was clinging to him, because they belonged to each other.

After the longest time, he rose to his feet. They needed to bed down for the night. Kaja didn't protest when he lifted her into his arms and cradled her to his chest. Her arms drifted around his neck.

When he took her into the water this time, she didn't flinch. She simply trusted him.

Dante knew he was in way, way over his head, and there might not be any way out.

Chapter Eleven

Chalen Palgrave felt his blood pressure rise as he attempted to process the words his employee was saying. It had been a rude awakening from a sound sleep. "What exactly are you trying to say to me, Roan?"

Roan's expression never changed. His face was utterly blank. From what Chalen could tell, the damn Brit never had an emotion at all. "Dellacourt got away."

Yes. That was what he thought the fucker had said. Chalen forced himself to lean forward when all he really wanted to do was to take his tablet and throw it off his balcony. *Hell*. That was wrong. What he really wanted to do was wrap his claws around Roan's throat and squeeze until the Brit died. "What do you mean he got away? Dellacourt's an idiot. You're the best mercenary money can buy, or at least that's your reputation."

He hadn't been able to hire a truly reputable firm. On the Vampire plane security was always handled by private firms, but they tended to be touchy when it came to potentially breaking the law. Roan and his men were outside that circle, but they were damn expensive. Of course, Chalen never actually meant to pay them, but

Roan didn't need to know that.

"He proved himself to be quite cunning." Roan's face turned thoughtful as though he was trying to solve a puzzle. "I had him in sonic cuffs. They were behind his back, and it was only myself and my second-in-command who knew the code to release him."

Excellent. "Then your second-in-command is a fucking traitor. You should execute his ass now."

Roan sighed in a way that set Chalen's fangs on edge. It was condescending, that sigh. "Harry has been with me for ten years. I assure you he wouldn't help another royal, certainly not one like Dante Dellacourt."

Chalen knew all about Roan's team. They were all disenfranchised royals who'd turned their backs on their people. It wasn't at all surprising for impoverished royals to go into the military. They did it so they could come out and work for the big corporations. Roan had gone out on his own and taken a bunch of his former team with him. He claimed he didn't want to work for anyone but himself. None of them could be trusted. He wondered if Dellacourt had offered them more money. "None of you are above turning on each other for cash."

Now Roan's eyes narrowed. His lip curled back to bare perfectly sharp fangs. "Are you accusing me and my men of failing to honor the contract I signed?"

Chalen backed off. He still needed the mercenary. Oh, he wouldn't for long, but if he gave any indication that he was turning on Roan, things might get dicey. Roan was known as a man who honored his obligations, but he was also said to be a man who believed in revenge. Until he was ready to get rid of his mercenary, Chalen would have to deal with him. "Not at all. I'm frustrated at your lack of progress. If no one turned traitor, then do you have a theory on how Dellacourt and the consort got away? I assume you lost Meg Finn as well, or you would have led off with that news."

That bland professional expression was back. "He fled with his cousins' wife. I do have a theory, but you might think I'm crazy. I believe he has a well-trained dog."

"A dog? A fucking dog got him out? You let a dog outsmart you?"

"Well, I admit, I didn't think she was anything beyond a very lovely bitch. Nothing about this job has gone the way I thought it would. When I set up the distraction, I assumed I would catch him as he fled the marketplace. I was rather surprised when he managed to kill the ogre."

Chalen was surprised at that himself, but Dellacourt had always had all the luck. "None of this explains how his dog managed to get him out of sonic cuffs."

"Harry was close when Dellacourt took down the ogre. He said Dellacourt seemed to be trying to save the dog, and he called the dog Kaja. Odd name for a dog, especially one he refused to acknowledge as his. He tried to tell me that this Kaja he referred to was some random woman. I didn't think anything of it at the time. I thought he was just trying to protect the dog. He might have thought I would hurt it if I knew it was his. Foolish, but it makes sense. The dog was with me when I put the cuffs on Dellacourt."

Chalen was seriously beginning to question the mercenary's intelligence. "You do realize a dog doesn't have opposable thumbs, right? It's sort of a requirement to work the cuffs."

"Well, she didn't have them in dog form. Or maybe she was more of a wolf. But what if she was able to shift? Also, I swear that wolf had the faintest glow. It reminded me of a consort's glow."

Chalen's mind was working overtime. "The Planeswalkers have been venturing further and further out to find consorts and bondmates. I'm curious about the wolf."

If Dellacourt had found an exotic consort, he wanted to know about it. If she was powerful and rare, then he really wanted to know about her. She could prove to be valuable. And if not, then killing her might upset Dellacourt, and that would be one more way to make that asshole pay.

"I'm sure you're upset by this setback, Mr. Palgrave. If you wish, I can take my men and leave. I'm sure you can find another squad to do the job." Roan straightened his flak jacket. "They left by foot with no technology. Dellacourt had a weapon, but I believe his dog ran off with it. He might have it. It seems to be some sort of projectile weapon. Good luck, sir."

"Wait." He hated it, but he couldn't find anyone else quickly.

And there was the small matter of dealing with Roan himself. It would be easier to deal with the man if he was close. "Just get the job done. Find Dellacourt and the consort, and get me the twins."

He cut off the connection and sat back on the bed as the tablet chimed again. He closed his eyes. Another snake to deal with. This particular snake was Fae royal, however.

"King Torin," Chalen said with a deferential bow of his head.

Torin Finn was a man in his prime. He looked somewhat like his nephews. The coloring was the same, but there was a thinness to his frame that gave him an air of miserliness. "Chalen. I called to get an update on your progress."

"Make him tell us, My Liege," a nasty voice said.

Torin's hags. Chalen's stomach turned. He'd only seen their true forms once, but it was enough. There were two, and they stood behind the king. They looked lovely in this form, but he couldn't help but see their true faces. Just a glimpse was all it had taken.

"Down, woman," Torin said with a snarl. He turned back to Chalen. "Do you have the twins?"

The hags retreated, but only slightly. They were always present, a prop to hold up Torin. He'd heard rumors that the hags had been effective in putting down the rebellions that had popped up. Blood ran wherever they showed their faces.

"Not yet, Sire, but I have a plan to ensnare them." Chalen tried to take a page from Roan's book. He carefully schooled himself to look as confident as he could. "I'm going to use their bondmate to bring them out."

Torin's green eyes narrowed. "Yes, I heard they bonded. I rather thought I had ensured they could not. Damn Planeswalker demons."

The new king of the Seelie Fae hadn't been able to make a deal with the demons. He didn't have anything to offer them, and he wouldn't until he could open the borders again. He wouldn't do that as long as his nephews were out there waiting to get back in. He had to wonder how bad the situation was in Tír na nÓg, cut off from all the planes they used to do business with. If this particular mission hadn't been about revenge, he would have looked to make a profit. He was certain bootleggers were making a killing. But he had other things to think about.

"They will come for their mate. I'll have their cousin as well."

Torin nodded. "Young Mister Dellacourt. His family is giving me hell with the Vampire government. I think they would have formally recognized me if it hadn't been for Donald Dellacourt. He's kept me out for years. I won't accept it any longer."

"When his son is dead, he'll turn his attentions elsewhere." Chalen intended for Donald Dellacourt to turn his attentions back on Torin. No one could ever know that Chalen had a hand in Dante Dellacourt's death.

The hags behind Torin stared through the tablet screen, their dark eyes glittering as though they could see through him. Torin turned to the one on the left. He lifted a brow.

"He will do as he says. He believes this will satisfy that dark place in his soul. It thirsts for blood. He believes the twins took something from him," the hag said.

He hadn't mentioned why he was willing to help Torin to the hags. He wished Torin hadn't told them. He didn't like them knowing something so personal about him. It was to keep as much distance as possible, but there was no reason not to speak now. "They killed my brother."

The hag on the right giggled. It was a terrible sound. "Yes, you're a smart one to have figured that out. So smart."

He had the distinct impression he was being taunted. "What do you know, hag?"

Torin reached around and slapped the female. Her head snapped back with a vicious crack. A thin line of blood ran down her chin, but there was a smile on her face. Her sister got to her knees and rubbed her head on the king's lap. Chalen was nauseated at the sight.

"Don't mind them," Torin said, dismissing the hags. "They're useful, but they enjoy causing chaos. We have excellent intelligence that it was the warrior half of the twins who slaughtered your brother. Your brother was a threat to them somehow. I had a spy there. They killed her as well."

The hag with blood on her mouth leaned in. "Our sister."

The other smiled a vicious grin that showed shiny teeth. She looked vaguely reptilian. "The twins will pay, and so will their bitch. They think we don't see. We see everything."

"Then you saw how my brother died." He had to know.

"Oh, yes, dear," the hag on the left said with her hollow laugh. "We saw the whole thing. Such a messy thing when a vampire dies."

His fists clenched, and he vowed to kill Beckett Finn slowly. If Kinsey had exploded, then the bastard had caught his heart. It was the only time a vampire exploded. It was said to be a horrific, barbaric death, and one not fitting his brother. Yes, the twins would pay, and their bitch and their bastard cousin. "I'll get you their heads."

"And I'll reward you," Torin said in a soothing voice. "All of the Seelie Fae will bless your name. Trade will flow through our people. You'll be a hero, Chalen Palgrave. Now, is there any way I can help? Did the ogre do its job?"

The ogre had been a gift from the king. Apparently Torin had made deals with certain factions in the Unseelie plane. "Currently the renegades are on the Refugee plane in the forests. Those forests are vast, Your Highness. If you could, perhaps, spare a search party? My mercenaries will have trouble tracking them."

"I have a few friends who might be willing to help. They aren't really friends, of course. They're stinking Unseelie, but they'll do anything for gold. Tell your mercenaries to expect a group of goblins. They can be quite devious. And, Chalen..."

"Yes?"

"I don't expect to see my friends again. Do you understand?"

He would have to tell Roan to kill the goblins when the mission was done. Of course, perhaps the goblins could kill Roan. He would have to think on it. Treachery was a difficult business. "Absolutely, Your Highness."

When the tablet blinked off, Chalen lay back down in his bed, his dreams filled with blood.

* * * *

"Dante, get off the poor girl." Meg stood over Kaja, her eyes rolling as she looked at Dante.

Kaja smiled up at her. It was easy since Meg was her friend. Her first friend.

"I do not mind." She liked how Dante laid his head in her lap.

She let her hand drift down to rub his scalp. The clothing she was wearing felt odd, but he'd assured her she needed it. He'd given her some of his clothing. Like magic it had become a skirt and shirt for her to wear, and Dante's own clothing had grown, manufacturing more so he lost nothing by giving to her.

His eyes drifted closed. "That's nice, Kaj. As for you, Meg, don't you have something to do?"

Meg's hands were on her hips. "Well, I thought the point of this exercise was to flee and attempt to survive. You're the one who's turning it into a honeymoon."

She was mightily confused. "Why does the moon need to be sweetened?"

Meg gave up and sat down beside her with a laugh. "I don't guess the translators are completely up on all the Earth lingo. You see, on the plane I was born on, when a couple gets married, they take a trip together. It's time for the couple to celebrate their union."

Dante yawned, his arms stretching and then wrapping around Kaja's hips. "We call it bonding time. It's a special and sacred time between a vampire and his consort. It shouldn't be interrupted by a harpy."

Meg's eyes narrowed. "Harpy? Have you forgotten that we were taken prisoner yesterday? I am not over reacting. Torin is making his move."

She'd learned a bit listening to Meg and Dante argue all morning. Meg was a queen. It was something like being the First among women. Her husbands were the kings of their plane. There were many planes and many doorways. She'd been taken through one of those doorways by a creature called a demon. Dante was going to take her to his plane to meet his pack—family.

She was going to meet Dante's family.

Her heart sped up at the thought. What if they did not like her?

"Well, Torin could have picked a better time," Dante complained. They had stopped by a lovely brook to rest for a bit before moving on. The sun was warm on Kaja's face, and she let her worries drift away. Her skin was still singing from the morning session with Dante. He'd proven true to his word, waking her up by rolling his body on top of hers. He'd kissed her and played with her breasts. By the time he'd thrust his cock deep inside her body, she was begging him to take her.

They'd stopped twice since they had left camp this morning. Each time he'd pulled her off into the woods and had what he called his "wicked way" with her. Once, he'd fed from her.

Oh, she loved when he was hungry. When he'd first caught her with his eyes, she'd lost her fear. After that first time, she'd been happy to submit. The pleasure that coursed through her when he fed was like nothing she'd felt before. For the time he drank from her, she felt connected to him. She felt warm and safe and loved.

But she no longer could see his soul. The first time he'd fed from her, she'd seen pieces of his childhood. It had been a flash of Dante and his family. There was a bowl of something called punch and candles had floated on top. He'd been a boy trying to blow out eight candles so he could have his toys. When she'd been in the moment with him, she'd felt like she belonged. Dante's parents had loved him.

But then the vision had closed, and though she'd tried to get it to come back, she couldn't see it again. There had been only pleasure, but none of the spine-melting intimacy of the first time.

Meg shook her head and relaxed back on the grass. "If I get murdered, it's going to be all your fault."

Dante's eyes opened. "Kaj, love, do you sense an army coming after us?"

She took the question seriously. She closed her eyes because they often lied. Her nose didn't. She breathed in the world around her. Dante's signature was the strongest. She loved the way their scents mingled. He was on her and she on him. She could still smell their lovemaking. It was comforting. She sensed Meg. Beyond that there was only the forest and the clean smell of the water.

"No. Though there are several small creatures near." Her stomach growled. She glanced back around at the brush behind her. There was a slender tree standing right in front of the bush.

She straightened up because she was absolutely certain it had not been there before. She remembered staring at the bushes, thick with brambles, and knowing she could find her meal there. There had been no tree in front of it. She studied the one there now. It was slender. A mere babe compared to the giants around it. The trunk was an ashen gray, and there were lovely, graceful branches sprouting from its top.

She noted that the dirt around it was disturbed. It formed a near perfect circle around the tree's base, as though it had been planted by two hands rather than growing in a natural way.

Gently, she eased Dante's head from her lap.

"Kaja?" Dante sat up, but she was working on the problem. Her brain raced. There was something about that tree. She searched her memory. Trees looked alike. But smell didn't lie.

She got to her feet and approached the tree in question. She touched it, feeling the bark. It was a youngling. The bark wasn't rough yet. It was soft against her hand. She sniffed at the limbs. They smelled like another part of the forest. She remembered it from the night before.

"This tree is following us."

Dante was on his feet beside her. "Maybe you don't understand things on this plane. Trees tend to stay planted in the ground. You see, they have these things called roots."

Dante continued on, but Kaja smiled. The little tree shook its branches. It was as though it knew it had been caught and gave up the game. One limb came out and patted her cheek with playful affection before turning its attention to Meg.

Dante threw his hands up. "See, that's weird. What the hell is that? Is it a weird Fae thing? Maybe we should chop it down."

A single branch extended, and the leaves formed something like a human hand. She thought the tree was going to wave, but it merely closed its "fist," leaving only the middle "finger" extended.

"Now that's just rude." Dante stared the tree down. "Since when do saplings give me the finger?"

Meg walked forward, tears in her eyes. "Cian."

"Since when did Cian become a tree?" Dante reached out to Kaja, his hand finding hers. He pulled her behind him.

She wasn't sure what he was trying to protect her from. The tree didn't seem to be hostile. And the tree seemed far more interested in Meg.

The tree reached a branch out and touched Meg's hair. There was no way to mistake the tenderness of the gesture.

"It's Ci," Meg said, her breath hitching. "He found me." Meg touched the slender trunk, and her eyes closed.

Dante's hold loosened as he relaxed, but he kept a hand around her waist. "Cian came into his powers a few months back. He's a Green Man. Do you know what that means?"

She didn't, but she could infer a few things. "He has power over plants."

Meg's mouth curled in a secret smile. Her eyes remained closed as she placed both hands on the tree. "He has power over all things green and vital. He used the trees to track us. He's coming for me. Always."

Her face turned up as a light rain started.

"Beck is here, too." Dante had a smile on his face. "Beck controls storms."

Kaja knew she should be afraid. Beings that controlled the elements were witches, and the pack killed them. But the pack had been wrong about so many things. Beck and Cian had been nothing but kind to her. She would not let old fears lead her.

"They know where we are?" Kaja asked.

"So it seems," Dante replied. "Meg, the tree or the rain wouldn't happen to be able to give you an estimated time of arrival? And tell them to bring my freaking bikes back. It's a trudge to the Vampire plane, and I've been taking us in the opposite direction in order to fool the fuckers who tried to kill me. And they better have charged the batteries."

Meg's eyes opened. She seemed so vibrant with evidence of her husbands' love and care all around her. "Cian is coming. Beck has to deal with things at the village, but Cian will find us. He should be here this afternoon. We're to wait for him."

Dante's arms wrapped around Kaja's waist, pulling her in front of him now. The danger had obviously passed. His hands slipped over her hips. "Well, if we're supposed to wait and we have a little time, I can think of a few things to do."

He was constant in his affection. She let her hands drift over his. If she ran away, would he come for her? She watched Meg smile up at the rain caressing her and wanted so badly what she had. Her men had done amazing things to find her. Their love for each other was palpable.

Dante wanted her. He wanted her often, but what did it mean?

153

Sven had wanted her, too. The feeling had obviously passed. Would Dante's passion pass?

"And, Dante, Ci says he's happy you and Kaja seem to be bonding." Meg smiled at them. Kaja reveled in her approval.

Dante kissed her hair. "Not as much as I'd like, thanks to Meg's insistence on running. But now I can relax because there's a tree and a rain cloud to guard her. Now I can get in some serious bonding time with my consort. Tell Ci to hurry. I want to get home to my nice comfy bed and other things that make bonding time special. I hope I'm stocked up on double-A batteries."

Dante took her hand and started to lead her away. "And Meg, I would be careful with the tree. It looks like it has thorns. I would watch for those branches. You might be better off playing in the rain, if you know what I mean."

She took one last look at Meg, her smiling face turned upward as gentle rain kissed her skin. If she heard Dante, she didn't show it. She was lost in her husbands' love.

Kaja followed Dante, her feet shuffling behind him. The grass beneath was soft on her bare feet, but her mind was in a different place. Meg was so loved.

It was easy to lose herself out here. The intimacy of the woods made Dante feel like the only person in the world. And she'd been the only female available to him. He was young and in his prime. He was male. She'd heard about young males. They mated at every given opportunity.

Was that all she was to him? An opportunity to mate—to fuck? What did any of it mean? Did he feel even the smallest bit for her that she felt for him?

Dante stopped once they were completely surrounded by thick trees. It was isolated, though they would be able to hear Meg if she needed them. Dante immediately pulled her into his arms. She could feel the line of his erection nudging her. "Alone at last."

Would she be alone again once Dante's passion was expended?

His lips pressed against hers, his tongue languidly invading her mouth. He kissed her, his hands pushing at the clothes she wore. "Baby, I promise I won't let you out of bed for a week once we get home. I'm going to fuck you six ways from Sunday."

154

Her body was already responding to him. He'd taught her so much in the days they'd been together, but almost all of it was about how to receive and give pleasure. Kaja wanted more.

"What does it mean?"

Dante chuckled. His hands clutched at the globes of her ass, pulling her into the cradle of his thighs. "It means I'm going to be all over you, consort. We'll say a quick hello to the family. I'll receive praise for finding a gorgeous consort, and we'll disappear for a week or two. I'll have the staff bring you food, and I'll take my every meal from this lovely neck of yours. Although, there is a nice vein that runs close to your pussy. Damn, I need to try that one. I'll be able to smell it when you come. You always come when I feed."

"That is not what I meant." She pushed at his chest, trying to get his attention on something other than her breasts.

Dante stopped as though he finally figured out that she was serious. "What the hell is going on?"

She bit at her bottom lip. "I do not understand what I mean to you."

His eyes rolled, and a long-suffering sigh heaved from his chest. "Women. Kaja, do we have to do this now?"

She wasn't sure what "this" was. "When would we do this?"

His shoulders came up, bunching in frustration. "I don't know. If I had my way, we wouldn't do it at all. Can't we just have a good time?"

Kaja thought about Meg. She hadn't been having a good time. When she'd realized her husbands were with her, seeking her, she'd looked blissful. She'd looked transcendent. Kaja would bet that Beck and Cian had never told Meg that their relationship didn't have to last forever. They had never offered to buy her a nice house when they were finished with her because they would never be finished with her.

"I do not think this will be a good time." Her heart was starting to hurt.

His face became hard, his jawline a razor's edge. "Don't try to tell me you don't enjoy fucking me. I know that's a lie. I can still feel your pussy squeezing me."

And she could still feel his arms around her. They still spoke two different languages, wanted two very different things. It was easier when she could feel his mind, but he'd shut that down. The last time they'd made love, she'd felt the wall come down between them as though he'd slammed a door in her face. "I like the mating. But I don't like the way I feel when I know it's only for now."

His body relaxed, his arms coming out, coaxing. "Is that all? Baby, don't worry about that. I promise the future is going to sort itself out."

Perhaps. Perhaps not. "I have lived my whole life hoping things would work out. They never have. Things do not simply work out."

He smiled down at her, smoothing back her hair. "Of course they do. They work out all the time. Relax, and it's going to be fine. One way or another, you'll be taken care of."

But she didn't want to be taken care of. She wanted to be loved. Perhaps he had taught her more than pleasure. If someone had asked her what she wanted weeks ago, she would have told them she wanted a warm bed, enough food to fill her belly, and peace. Dante was offering her all of that, and now she wanted more. She was worth more.

His hands moved to her shoulders, gentling her. "Look, the future might have already been decided for us, you know. The way we've been going at it, you might be pregnant."

A pup. Baby. Dante's people called them babies. She might be pregnant, a baby growing in her belly. The idea had panicked her before, but now a strange tenderness filled her. She'd worried that the pack wouldn't accept a child from her belly any more than they had accepted her, but the world was so much bigger now. She herself was bigger than she'd been before. She could make her way in this world.

And if she could not, then she would find another. She would never stop searching. She would walk the planes until she found the place where she belonged.

She loved Dante.

"Kaj, don't cry." His face had fallen.

She felt the tears coursing down her cheeks, but he didn't understand. She wasn't sad, not exactly. There was a certain joy to her tears. She was stronger, and it was because she loved Dante. It didn't matter that he couldn't love her back. Her love for him made her better.

A baby. She could have his baby. She could have a child to hold and love and show the world to. The thought blanketed her heart in warmth. It scared her before. Now it was something to long for. A child with Dante's green eyes. A child to pour her love into.

"Kaja," Dante said, his voice achingly quiet. "I'll stop. We don't have to make love again until I can get you on birth control. If you really don't want to risk it, I can get you some medicine that will take care of it."

She shook her head. That was the last thing she wanted. "I don't want medicine."

The wolf she'd been still wanted to run from him. He could break her so easily, probably would, but the woman she was becoming stood her ground. If she didn't fight, would she always regret it? How did one fight for a man? Would it even work if he didn't want to be with her?

She wrapped her arms around Dante, her decision made. She would spend this time with him. She would make all the memories her heart could hold. When the time came to leave, she would do it with dignity. And she wouldn't slink away to the woods. She would find a home. She would build a life.

"Kiss me." She turned her face up as Meg had done to the sun when she'd realized her husbands were there. Dante was Kaja's sun for now.

Dante gazed down at her, his eyes searching hers. "Are you sure? I really don't want to hurt you. That was never, ever my intention."

"Why did you buy me?" She needed to know the truth.

His face flushed slightly, but his hands tightened around her waist. "I needed a wife. You were the first one I found."

She'd been convenient. She could accept that. She'd gotten something from the deal, as well. Her life. "But you don't need a forever wife."

He brought their bodies together with a little bang. "Damn it. I explained this to you. I'm crazy about you. I just don't think I'm going to be good at the whole marriage thing. Look, it's not like I'm going to toss you aside. We're married forever. There's no going back, but one day we might want to go our separate ways. I don't want to lie to you. I want to be happy for now. Now is all we have."

Yes, it was. The present was certainly all they would ever have if Dante wanted it that way. She couldn't force him to feel for her what she felt for him. She couldn't make him accept her forever. She could only control what was in her heart. She could only want what she wanted—and she wanted him. For as long as she could have him.

"Then kiss me."

His face bunched up, his forehead wrinkling. "I really am crazy about you."

Crazy wasn't love. Even she knew that. "Kiss me."

He lowered his head, his lips brushing hers. "I know you don't believe me. I'll show you."

His hands gripped the cheeks of her ass and hauled her up. She wrapped her legs around his body as he walked her to the nearest tree and placed her back against the huge trunk.

"Gods, I really hope my cousin isn't hanging around in this one," Dante muttered as he took her mouth again.

She loved the way he kissed her. No one had kissed on her plane. She allowed her mouth to flower open under his. His tongue caressed her own, and she sighed. She was pressed between the hard bark of the tree and his body, but she didn't want to be anywhere else. When he kissed her, they were the only two people in the world.

Of course, when he bit her, when her blood flowed into his body, it felt as if they were one person. She loved that above all else.

He pressed in, his erection shoving against her pussy. His hips moved as though they couldn't help themselves. "Gods, I want you. I want you all the fucking time. How can I want you so much?"

He kissed her, his mouth dominating hers. One hand found her breast, and he cupped her, playing with her nipples. His mouth ran down the side of her neck. There were still tiny holes from where he'd fed this morning. They seemed to close quickly, but the healing bumps were still there. He licked at them, seeming to find them endlessly fascinating.

Her whole body threatened to light up when he touched her neck. She'd never thought of her neck as being particularly sensitive, but now she squirmed every time he touched her there. When he licked her neck, she felt it in her pussy.

"Please." She was well aware she was begging. She wanted that bite. She wanted to feel him. "Please don't shut the door between us. Please."

His head came up. "You feel it, too?"

She clutched his shoulder, staring into his eyes. The irises were wider, but the green hadn't totally taken over. "I need it. I need to feel it. I've never felt so good as when I feel those flashes of you. I don't know what it is, but I need it, Dante."

"It scares the fuck out of me," he muttered.

Maybe her soul wasn't as nice as his. If she caught glimpses of him, then he most likely saw her. It wasn't nice to be her. It was ugly and lonely. She was being selfish.

She let her legs drop.

"Kaja?"

"Just kiss me. You can teach me later how to keep our minds apart."

His hands softened, cupping her cheeks. "What's wrong? Why did you shut down?"

"I wasn't thinking," she admitted. "I believed I was the only one who felt our joining in my mind. I understand. I don't want you to see those parts of me. I am so sorry."

His fangs suddenly seemed larger than before. "You want to hide yourself from me, consort?"

Yep, that other part of Dante had come out. His eyes were huge green orbs now. "You cannot wish to see me. It's ugly. I didn't understand. I will learn to shut it off, as you do. You can teach me."

His hands tightened around her arms. "I will not teach you to hide yourself from me. You'll be open. You'll give me everything. You look at me."

She got caught in those eyes. She felt her whole body relax. She knew she should fight him, but it felt far too good to let Dante take control. She trusted him not to harm her physically. Her heart was another manner entirely.

"It makes no sense, Kaj." He sounded more like Dante now. "It scares the crap out of me, but the minute you start talking about putting up barriers and walls between us, I go a little crazy. Baby, you're making me so crazy, but I can't help myself. I fucking need you, too. Gods, you taste like sunshine."

He gripped her hair and pulled her head back, exposing the line of her throat. Her heart skipped as he struck.

And there it was. She felt him, his soul and being brushing and mingling with hers. They tangled together.

He was beloved. His parents, his sister, his teachers. No one had been able to resist him as a child or even a teen. He'd been smart, so smart. He'd been like a magnet. Popular with everyone because everyone wanted to be near him.

When had it changed? When had his boyish charm become mere childishness?

He had his insecurities, too. What was he worth? Money? That could go away. He'd seen it a million times. What would he be left with? His intellect hadn't gotten him far. He was lost, adrift without any real thing that mattered.

Her mind was assaulted with sex. Dante had begun young and hadn't ever stopped. He loved to fuck, and he was good at it. But he didn't take it seriously. He made sure that none of the women he took to bed were serious either, until he'd met a wolf.

She reached for those feelings. She was there in his soul, but her place was so uncertain. He wanted her, but he didn't want to want her.

She was beautiful to him.

She felt his fangs in her neck, her body going languid under his, and she was assaulted with a single memory.

"What do you mean she's dead?" Kaja spoke the words, but it was Dante's voice that came from her mouth. She was inside his body looking at his cousin. Cian. It was Cian, and he was so pale and thin. Her heart, Dante's heart, was sick at the sight of his cousin.

"Torin's men killed her," Cian said, his voice a flat monotone. "Bronwyn died in my arms. I couldn't even get her body out. I had to leave her behind. That bastard probably burned her."

She felt sick. Bronwyn, sweet, mischievous Bron, couldn't be dead. Dante loved Bron. He'd spent so much time at the White Palace playing with his cousins, Cian and Bronwyn.

Torin had taken that from him. He'd taken his uncle and his aunt and his sweet cos.

He would try to take Beck and Ci.

A fire was in Dante's belly. She could feel it. He'd buried it because he didn't believe he could help, but this was Dante's passion. Seeing his cousins returned to their throne.

This was the cause he was willing to die for—if only he had the courage to admit it.

She came out of the memory, her back against the soft grass and Dante thrusting gently between her legs.

"Welcome back," he said with the sweetest smile on his face. "I thought all this work would be for nothing. Not that I was going to stop or anything."

He pushed his cock deep inside. Kaja let herself sigh. It felt so good.

"If I ever meet your pack, you should know I'm going to kill all of them, love. I'll eviscerate the whole lot." He leaned his body down, never letting up on the slow slide of his cock. Where had her clothes gone? She was utterly naked and skin to skin with Dante. His flesh pressed to hers, surrounding her with his scent and feel.

What had he seen? Had he touched her soul the way she'd touched his? Did he know how empty she'd been before she'd been filled with him?

"Don't you pull away from me now," Dante said with a growl. "I got through the bad part. Now I want the fun part. The connection is weird and disconcerting, but I have to admit, this part feels good."

He pushed himself at her. Kaja gasped as she felt his pleasure. Their minds met once more, and she could feel the joy Dante took in their mating.

He loved her tight pussy. It felt so small, closing around him and claiming his cock. He could feel her muscles milking him. It was such intense pleasure, and she knew he'd never felt it quite like this before. He loved the way she held him tight. Even her nails biting into the flesh of his back felt good to him. He reveled in her.

Light. She was surrounded by it. She could see through Dante's eyes. She was beautiful to him. There was a gorgeous golden glow surrounding her. This was how a vampire identified a consort. He thought she looked like an angel from something called the Heaven plane. She was his angel.

Her heart felt so full. She could see herself through his eyes, and she would never be able to feel ugly again. He was her warrior, even

161

if he didn't know it.

She opened herself and let everything out. Her pleasure, her love, her joy.

"Oh, baby, oh, baby, Kaja," Dante said, losing his rhythm. He picked up the pace as though he could deny it no longer. His heart was racing. She could feel it. Her own started to pound in time to his. She pressed her hips up, allowed her hands to cup his ass. She loved the feel of his muscled ass pumping into her pussy. She could feel him rushing toward orgasm.

His balls drew up. There was a tingle at the base of his spine, and it started. His essence shot from him. It flowed out of his body making him twist and turn with pleasure. She was overwhelmed with Dante's feelings and emotions. She could feel her own muscles squeezing around Dante's cock. It was so tight. It felt so good to give her everything he had. It felt different and right. He wanted to give her all of it. He wanted to fill her up.

He ground out the last and fell on her.

Kaja could feel the door between them closing as she came back to herself, but before it winked out of existence, she felt one last thing from Dante.

Peace.

She'd brought him that.

Chapter Twelve

Dante glanced back at Kaja one last time before pushing through the bushes. He wanted to stay with her, to cuddle her and fall asleep, but he needed to check in with Meg. Despite the tree and rain cloud, she was still his responsibility until one of her husbands actually showed up in person.

And he could do with a bit of time away from Kaja. His instinct was to stay close to her every minute of the day. It was disconcerting. What the hell was happening to him? None of this was going the way he planned.

But he wouldn't change it. He wouldn't take it back. That kind of scared him, too.

He brushed the leaves from his clothes. The light was brighter here, so his sunglass implants flowed to cover his eyes. The world came into sharp focus, and he could hear Meg. She sat beside the river, and his heart fell when he realized she was crying. The rain cloud was gone, and the tree seemed to be just a tree again.

He rushed to her, kneeling down. "Meg? Are you all right? What's wrong?"

She glanced up at him, her face streaked with tears. She brushed them away with the back of her hand. "I'm fine. It's been a rough couple of days."

He settled in beside her. "Talk to me. You can talk to me."

She stared at her lap and took a deep breath. "It's really happening."

Torin. Yes, he was feeling that, too. "It's going to be all right. Beck can handle anything Torin throws at him."

"He sent a group of goblins to attack our village. Beck said it was horrible. We lost some of our people, and they burned down our farm. Our home is gone."

Dante reached for her hand. He felt a strange mix of rage and sorrow. He loved that village. Beck and Ci had built it with their own hands. Dante had been there, too. They had been kids when Beck and Ci lost their throne. Dante had just started college. Dante's father had offered them asylum, but the kings had chosen to stay with their people on the Refugee plane and build a world for themselves.

Beck and Ci had been forced to grow up fast.

"I don't want you to worry about a thing, Meg. You and Beck and Ci can come home with me and Kaja."

"That won't solve anything. It will only make things worse in the end. There was a reason Beck and Ci didn't go down that road the first time. They have people depending on them." Her hand tightened in his. "Torin isn't going to leave us be, is he? He'll try again."

"Yes," Dante replied. It was a hard truth. No matter how much Beck and Cian wanted a peaceful existence, it wasn't going to happen. Torin had to kill the twins or he would never feel safe. He would never be able to open the plane again. Torin had been patient, but it appeared his patience was at an end.

"Dante, I'm scared."

He put an arm around her shoulders and held her close. They had been through a lot together, he and Meg. It looked as though they would go through much more. "Beck needs to get serious about alliances. My father has been working to move the Council toward repudiating Torin."

"It hasn't worked in thirteen years. The Council is closer to acknowledging Torin than they are to repudiating him."

"Only because we need the trade. Royal vampires need consorts.

If the Council realized Beck and Ci were serious about taking the throne back, I think they would change their minds. We need to talk to the Unseelie. King Fergus will never acknowledge Torin."

"He's heard the rumors," Meg muttered. "Torin is enslaving the *non-sidhe* on the Seelie plane. He believes the Unseelie are impure. If Torin gets strong, he will go after the Unseelie on their own plane. Fergus doesn't want that. But you know Fergus has sons, too."

"I've heard the rumors," Dante replied carefully.

"They aren't rumors."

Prickles of trepidation rode his arms. The Unseelie kept to themselves for the most part. Their borders were heavily guarded. Trade flowed, but the king of the Unseelie never left the plane. It was said that he had sons. Twin sons. "Are they symbiotic?"

Say no. Say no. He didn't want to think of super-powerful Unseelie twins. Beck and Cian had been raised in the light court. He couldn't imagine twins with their power who had been raised by monsters.

Though Dante was rapidly realizing sometimes monsters came in many forms.

"Yes. Their names are Lachlan and Shim," Meg explained. "They need a bondmate. They aren't as far gone as Beck and Ci were when they found me, but it's getting bad. It's why Fergus reached out to us. He believes placing Beck and Ci on the throne is the best shot he has at saving his sons."

Dante's mind was racing. Fergus would have to be dealt with carefully. The Seelie and the Unseelie had never exactly gotten along. The Unseelie had sent an emissary thirteen years before, Fergus's daughter, Gillian. She'd died when Torin had slaughtered the royal family. Fergus had sent assassins after Torin but hadn't had any luck getting to him. It was said he wouldn't risk his sons in a war.

But what if Fergus blamed all the Seelie? Would Beck and Ci be in danger if they walked into the Unseelie *sithein*? His head was spinning. After so much waiting, it was all happening fast. There was a lot to consider. He should sit down and strategize with Cian. If Torin was making his move, it was time to get serious. Beck and Ci wouldn't be allowed to hide anymore. They would win or they would die.

Dante meant to make certain they did not die.

And how would he do that from the desk of his lovely office? Who was he kidding? He'd gotten married to preserve his cushy future. He wasn't about to throw it all away to go to war. He would make certain that his cousins had all the money he could throw at them, but he wasn't a warrior.

Some odd emotion made his chest feel far too tight. That beast that Kaja always seemed to bring out in him was right there, pounding at him. He wasn't a warrior.

But he could be.

"Dante, don't worry about it," Meg said with a sad smile, as though she could read his thoughts. "You need to worry about Kaja right now. We'll figure all this out."

Gods, he was sick of being treated like a kid. He was thirty years old, and everyone acted like he was a fucking teenage boy who didn't need the stress of real life.

Maybe if you started acting like an adult, they would treat you like one.

That beast inside was starting to annoy him. If only the beast didn't make so much sense. "I want to help. This is my family, too."

"Well, I thank you for that," Meg replied. "We need all the friends we can get. I can't tell you how much it terrifies me. We don't have an army."

Oh, but they would. If rumors were correct, they would have an army of peasants waiting for their return to Tír na nÓg. Peasants could be dangerous. Dante couldn't help but think of his plane's own history. "We need to find Torin's weaknesses. We need to get on that plane and start getting the people ready for the true kings' return."

"He has it guarded," Meg said with a helpless shake of her head.

"We'll find a way." His mind was filled with possibilities.

Meg patted his leg. "I don't want to think about this now. It's coming for me soon enough. Tell me about Kaja. You two seem to be getting along."

"Yes, she's a lovely woman." His chest felt too tight for another reason now. Kaja was so much deeper, smarter, more complex than he'd thought. He'd thought he could make a deal with her, but he didn't have anything Kaja would want. She didn't even really understand the concept of money. What did he have to offer her except money she didn't need and an impressive cock?

And yet she wants you. She wants something deep inside you, something money and fame and privilege can't touch.

"When I make love to Kaja, I can feel her," Dante said quietly. It wasn't something he had expected. No one had warned him in sex ed class about some mystical connection that would form when he made love to his consort.

"Well, I would hope so," Meg said.

He didn't want to exchange sarcastic remarks with her. "I mean I can feel her past or her soul or something. Sometimes it's flashes of her history, like a movie in my head, except that I am her and I feel what she felt. I know what it was like to be Kaja, and it sucked before, but she's still here and still trying. I don't know if I would still be trying."

Meg's face was bunched in concern. "I didn't think that happened between vampires and consorts. I thought that was something that only happened between bondmates and psychic Fae."

Bondmates tended to boost the powers of psychic Fae, and in Meg's case, she actually bridged her husbands' shared soul so they each had access to the other half. "I don't know why. I only know it's happening and it's gotten harder to shut it down. Every time I feed, it gets harder and harder to put a wall between us."

Meg studied him for a moment. "Kaja isn't from a plane we know a lot about. Maybe her bonding powers are different from others. Maybe that's why the connection is different. Why would you try to shut it down?"

He didn't even like to admit that to himself. "I didn't marry Kaja because I wanted to. My father forced me to. I had to get married or he was going to kick me out of the business."

"Well, I suppose lots of marriages start off as marriages of convenience. So you explained all this to Kaja?"

Not exactly. "I told her that we would be married for a while and then she could have her freedom back."

There it was. He could say the words, but there was something inside him that knew he wasn't going to let her go. He was really only fighting himself now.

Meg pulled her hand back, and he could see her withdraw. "Well, that's disappointing. I thought there wasn't a whole lot of divorce outside the Earth plane."

"I wasn't planning on divorcing her. I was planning on going my own way and letting Kaja go hers."

Meg's head shook slightly, but he could feel her derision. "After you slept with her and fed from her. And does Kaja understand this?"

Dante thought about Kaja's eyes. When he made love to her they were lit with desire and life. But then he would catch her when she thought no one was looking, and there was resignation there, as though she knew it wouldn't work out. "I think she understands far too well."

"So, you're going to use her."

Yes, that had been the plan. "I don't know anymore."

"Really?" Meg looked at him again, her right brow rising in question.

"Yeah. I don't know what I'm doing, but I know I feel more for her than I've ever felt for anyone in my life. I don't know if it's going to last." He didn't even know if he wanted it to. Kaja seemed to be all he could think about. She was rapidly becoming an obsession. Even now, he could see her lying in the grass, her pearly skin in sharp contrast to the green around her, the twin holes in her neck on full display. When he got her back to his home, he would have to give her some of his own blood. It would heal the marks, but damn, he liked looking at them. It was barbaric. It was fucking hot.

"Uh, Dante, you having some trouble there?" Meg asked, her eyes on his mouth.

Fuck. His fangs were out again. This was why he didn't want this passion to last. He couldn't walk around the rest of his life with a hard-on and full fangs—and this weird, soft place in his heart that clenched every time he looked at her or thought about all she'd been through.

She was so strong. "She deserves more than me."

Meg shook her head, her hand back on his knee. "No. She deserves you, but she deserves the best you. Don't you see? This is what happens. I've been where you are. I fell in love, and it changed me for the better. It forced me to grow up. It made me a better person.

This is wonderful, Dante."

It didn't feel wonderful. It felt terrifying. He should have found another way. He should have paid some fallen royal to marry him. She would have been reasonable. He wouldn't have been desperate for some random royal's blood and body. He wouldn't have formed this weird connection to some sad-sack royal. It would have been a neat exchange of money for a convenient, no-emotions-involved marriage. He wouldn't feel all twisted inside.

"I don't know how wonderful it's going to be. I'm worried that she won't fit in." It had been the chief thing to recommend her in the beginning. He'd wanted to find a consort who would send his father running for the lawyers, but now he couldn't stand the idea that his father wouldn't like her.

"I think you'll be surprised," Meg said. "I think she's smart and adaptable. And, if you're worried about your family accepting her, I wouldn't. She's different, but there's a sweetness to Kaja that I think your family is going to find irresistible."

The idea played around in his brain. What if it could work? The thought of loving Kaja terrified him, but the idea of not having her around caused his heart to knot. He was a mess. He wanted her. He simply needed to accept it.

He couldn't help the smile that had his lips curling up. Meg was right. Kaja was sweet, and she tried so hard. Perhaps it would make up for her lack of proper manners. It could work.

His mother would view Kaja as a challenge, a sweet baby bird to take under her wing. Susan had always appreciated the odd creatures of the planes. Despite her ridiculous adherence to parliamentary procedure in the boardroom, his sister was actually quite open-minded.

But the rest of society would be hard on her. The press would freak when they found out Kaja spent time on four legs.

How was he going to protect her?

"Don't worry," Meg said. "It really will work out. And it will work out for me and Beck and Ci, too. I have to have faith."

He hoped faith was all they needed.

* * * *

Kaja came awake slowly, brushing away the small bug that seemed to be intent on biting her. Her nose tickled. She wriggled it, trying to hold on to sleep. She was warm and happy. With Dante wrapped around her body, she'd slept better than she had her whole life. Her dreams had been sweet. She did not wish to leave them.

But the small buzzing creature was insistent, and it seemed that it had brought some friends.

She opened her eyes and focused on the small thing that had landed on her nose.

Bright blue wings fluttered, and Kaja was shocked to find it had a face. Her first instinct was to eat the little thing. It wouldn't be much of a meal, but it might be tasty. And then she remembered Dante's words. She could not eat things that talked back.

"Hello," she said, hoping the bug wouldn't talk back.

Its tiny hands flew up, and Kaja would have sworn that the thing looked grateful. Its mouth opened and a rush of beeps and light, tinkling words rushed from its mouth.

No meal for Kaja.

She forced herself to sit up. The creature took flight briefly before landing on Kaja's knee. The winged insect once again began speaking.

"Slowly, little one," Kaja said, remembering what Dante had told her about the magic.

The insect shook its head, words spewing from her mouth, but Kaja was beginning to catch pieces of them now. "Save...family...bad Fae...eat."

Kaja looked around. She was alone, but Dante's shirt was folded beside her on the ground they had slept on. Kaja breathed deeply. She could smell Dante and Meg. She opened her senses. They weren't far away, and they seemed to be speaking quietly.

"Please to help. My babies. The pixies will be grateful always."

She couldn't turn that request down. There was a family in need, a mother who could lose her pups. She nodded at the blue creature, the pixie. "Where are your babies?"

The pixie took off, her wings flapping faster than Kaja's eyes could track. She darted away from the camp. Kaja thought about finding Dante, but then she would lose the pixie and the pixie babies could be eaten. She raced to follow the flying pixie as she moved through the forest. In and out of trees and bushes, the pixie darted. Kaja leapt and feinted around a bramble brush. She could feel her feet being cut, but she feared the pixie would not allow her to help if Kaja showed her the wolf.

Then she stopped. There it was. It was soft at first. If she hadn't been listening for it, she would have thought that it was only the play of the wind on the trees. A mewling cry, so soft. She moved forward, keeping her steps light. She didn't even think about the fact that she was naked. Clothes were something she'd recently been introduced to, and Dante seemed to shed his often enough.

The pixie landed on her shoulder. "There. There."

Kaja carefully pushed back a branch and took in the sight in front of her. Strange green men stood around a big, black cooking pot. The water appeared to be just beginning to boil. There were two of the creatures, both with squat bodies covered in corded muscle. Very little hair covered their heads. What they had was black and wiry, and these men did not smell at all good.

One stood by the fire. "Almost ready now."

The second grinned, showing sharp teeth. "Yes, I can tell that it is. These pretties will make an excellent soup. Sorry we didn't catch the mum. She was a nice, fat one."

Kaja felt a tiny foot stamp on her shoulder. Apparently fat was not a good thing to be. For a wolf, it was nice. It tended to mean a wolf could survive the harsh winters, but the pixie seemed to take offense.

"All right, then," the First said. "We've waited longer than we promised. It ain't our fault they aren't out here. If those buggers have a lick of sense, they found another plane to hide on."

She wasn't sure which bugs the being was talking about, but she felt a need to save these. The mother was upset, and no wonder. Kaja could see the small pixies with their gossamer wings being held in the cage. Her babies. The mother couldn't allow her babies to be turned into some form of food for smelly male creatures.

She turned her head, careful not to dislodge the pixie. She put her finger to her mouth to let her new friend know not to shout out. The pixie nodded and her wings moved as she left her perch.

In a blink, Kaja changed, her world moving from two-legged to four. The pixie landed on her snout, looking seriously into Kaja's eyes. If the pixie was frightened of Kaja's wolf, she didn't show it.

"Please." The pixie repeated her refrain.

Kaja nodded, and the pixie took off, her wings flapping.

On soft feet, Kaja burst through the bushes and attacked the first green thing.

"Get the wolf!" a man's voice shouted, and Kaja could feel what she should have sensed all along. She was surrounded, but they had masked their scents or stayed downwind. The soldiers from the marketplace were all around, and more green beings leapt from their hiding places.

Too late. She realized the trap had been laid and baited.

"Don't hurt her," the leader said. He was the tall vampire who had been kind to her and fed her treats. He seemed to only have a real problem with Dante.

Dante. He was going to be so angry with her. He was going to punish her, and maybe not in a nice way this time. Dante did not like it when she risked her life. She turned and sought a way out. The pixie was trying so hard to get the cage open and let her babies free. It appeared the pixie hadn't betrayed her.

There was nowhere to run, but she could do what she set out to do. Kaja leapt and pulled down the cage. It clattered to the ground, and the door flew open. Pixie wings fluttered as they all got away.

"Saved them, did you, pet?"

Kaja looked up at the man who had caught them before.

"I rather thought you would," he said, not unkindly. He turned to his men. "I know it doesn't make a lick of sense, but that wolf is a consort. She is to be taken care of and protected. I'm sorry, consort. It will only hurt for a moment."

He held the magic box in his hand. Light flowed from it and into her.

She felt fire in her veins, and Kaja fell.

Chapter Thirteen

Dante felt her fall. It was like some invisible connection that was always there in the back of his mind had been cut off abruptly. As though Kaja was there in his brain, a low soothing hum, and now it was silent.

"Something's wrong with Kaja," he said, getting to his feet.

His heart was racing, panic threatening to overtake him. Maybe he'd fed too much. Gods, if he'd hurt her, he would die himself. *Please, please.* He sent out silent pleas. *Let her be all right. Let it be a mistake.*

But he knew it wasn't true. Something was wrong. The connection between them had been cut. Kaja wouldn't do it. She didn't even know how to. He pushed through the brush and into the small copse where he'd left her sleeping.

Why had he left her at all? He knew how dangerous it was. He was an asshole who couldn't even take care of his wife. He'd left her here alone and vulnerable because he couldn't deal with how she made him feel. He was as irresponsible as everyone made him out to be.

She was gone. Her clothes had been left behind in a neatly folded pile. The grass around them was a mess, but he couldn't count that as evidence that she'd been dragged away. He'd fucked her on this grass. He'd rolled with her and played and screwed. He'd let her fall asleep in his arms.

Where the hell had she gone?

"Dante?" Meg's soft voice reminded him that Kaja wasn't the only female he was responsible for.

He turned and felt his eyes widen. Meg was covered in butterflies. They clung to her hair and perched on her shoulder. Beautiful, winged jewels that glistened in the sunlight. Meg was a lovely picture standing there with butterflies creating a halo around her head.

"She says she knows where they took the wolf," Meg said.

"The butterfly?" There was a reason he didn't spend a lot of time in faery forests. The animals knew better than to talk back on his plane.

"They're pixies. Calm down and you'll be able to hear them."

He didn't want to listen to insects, but if they knew where Kaja was, then he would do it. He moved close to Meg, and sure enough, there was a small cacophony of tiny, musical voices.

"The wolf tried to save us."

"Pretty wolf."

"Bad goblins. Mira hates goblins. They smell bad, and they tried to make Mira into soup. I don't want to be soup."

"I want my papa."

Kids. They were only kids. Well, naturally his Kaja had tried to save a bunch of lesser Fae from getting put in a pot. "Where is Kaja?"

"In the woods."

"They took her. They put lightning in her belly and took her."

They went on and on, their wings fluttering as they all spoke at once.

"Please, younglings, one at a time," Meg said, her voice pleading.

And then a larger butterfly swooped by Dante's head. Larger than the younglings, she would still fit in the palm of his hand with room left over. But there was no doubt this one was in charge.

"Stop. The queen is right. We must remain calm." Her voice was tinny, but his ears were damn good. He stared down at the pixies.

He'd never seen one up close. Lesser Fae. It didn't mean that they were truly less important, merely smaller. The brilliant blue pixie landed on the hand Meg held up. "Your Gracious Highness. I must ask for your help. There was a young woman who came to my aid. She saved my babes, but it was a trap. The goblins captured her."

"Goblins?" Bile rose in his throat. Goblins could do just about anything to her. And they would, unless they realized they could make a profit from her. "Where is the chieftain?"

The pixie shook her head. "It's not a tribe. It's only a handful of goblins. I thought there were only two of them, but once the nice lady had turned into a wolf, they leapt from the bushes and grabbed her. They had magic."

No, they had technology. "The vampires caught up with us, and they brought friends. Why the hell would they bring in goblins?"

Meg shrugged. She'd paled, as though she couldn't stand the thought of Kaja being caught, either. "It's Torin. We've heard he's made some deals with disloyal Unseelie. They don't seem to realize that he intends to kill anyone who isn't *sidhe.*"

The pixie's wings fluttered. "Please help her, Your Majesty. She was so kind. I can't stand the thought of her being harmed for helping me."

"Where are they?" His voice came out in a harsh rasp, and he noticed his claws had popped out. Rage was beginning to build, shoving the panic and fear to the side. Another fucking vampire had taken his consort. If that mercenary had laid a hand on his consort, he was going to tear it off his body and shove it down his throat.

The pixie turned from Meg. She then flew back behind Meg's head as though begging for protection.

"He's not going to hurt you, little one. You're not the one he's angry with," Meg said. "Dante, you have to be careful. You're obviously upset. Damn, you look scary."

Meg had never seen him in this state. She'd seen his fangs and claws, but even when they had killed the hag, he'd remained in control. Now, the thought of someone touching his Kaja was making his eyes bleed out. It was something that opened his senses and prepared him to fight.

And he would fight. He would kill, because no one was touching his consort. "Where is Kaja?"

Meg held her hand out, and the big blue pixie landed gracefully. "Take us there. The wolf is the vampire's mate. He will be grateful to you, and so will I."

"Meg, you can't come with me." He'd lost Kaja. He wasn't about to lose Meg, too.

Her face hardened, and Dante could believe she was a queen. "If you leave me here, I'll follow and probably cause trouble. Kaja is my friend. She saved me too, you know."

There wouldn't be any moving her. And she truly knew how to cause trouble. "Fine, but you hide when we get there."

The small pixies fluttered off Meg's hair and seemed to be talking to the mother. They flew off, more than likely in search of sanctuary, but the mother stayed behind. She flew in front of them, leading them through the woods.

Dante ran to keep up. The pixie was a tiny dart flying through the woods toward the target. He longed for a weapon—any weapon. They'd been forced to leave the gun behind. Kaja had buried it. He didn't even have his tablet. All he had were his claws and fangs, but he charged through the woods like a man with an army behind him.

He could feel Meg running to keep up. When the pixie stopped, he turned to Meg.

"You hide. You watch. You wait for Cian. He can get Beck, and he can save Kaja if I can't." Dante stared at her, letting her feel his will.

Meg frowned but did as he asked. She placed herself behind an enormous oak tree. Dante felt better when the tree's branches seemed to move to conceal her. She disappeared, masked by green vines and leaves.

Cian was here, even if he wasn't a physical presence. He would watch after his wife. It was time for Dante to take care of his.

There was nothing for it. He was alone. He had no weapon but one. He had to turn himself in and hope they would let Kaja go.

They wanted him.

Dante walked into the open and was immediately surrounded by soldiers.

"Mr. Dellacourt," a very upper-crust voice said. "How nice of you to join us."

He was surrounded. They moved quickly to encircle him, the vampire mercenary unit proving how well trained it was. Discipline marked their every move.

The impulse was there. He wanted to fight. He wanted to tear into these men and feel his claws rip through flesh. He would feast on their blood. It would fill his belly when he took his consort back. What had happened to him? That was barbaric. Only primitives fed on their enemies. But he wanted to.

One thing held him back. The sight of Kaja in Roan's arms. The soldier held her, her human body naked and limp. Her beautiful brown hair trailed down toward the ground. Her skin was pale, but her chest rose and fell with her breath. A strange feeling gripped his heart. Kaja. She was alive. That was what mattered.

"Let her go," Dante said.

The man who held her tightened his arms around her body. There was a distinctly possessive stance to his hold. "I think I have the upper hand, Mr. Dellacourt."

He really hated this guy. "I can cause a lot of trouble."

The mercenary looked down at Kaja. Dante couldn't miss the way his eyes softened. William Roan didn't even try to hide the soft spot he had for Kaja. Of course, now that she was in her human form, she couldn't hide her glow. Any royal with a soul would be soft toward her. He might be able to play on that.

"She might be worth a bit of trouble," Roan said. "I was rather surprised. When I hit her with the Taser, she changed forms and became one of the loveliest females I've ever seen. Look at that glow. She would have every vampire with the money to enter a tournament after her. In the old days, we would have fought wars over her. How did you end up with such a gorgeous consort?"

Because other people were too stupid to see how amazing she was. "Just lucky, I guess. I won't let you have her."

"No, I suppose you won't. It's going to tear apart our plane, you know that, right?" He pulled Kaja close to his chest. His fucking head rubbed against hers as though he enjoyed the contact. "I'm one of the greatest warriors of my time. I can't find a consort. I'm aging. It isn't right. I could kill anyone in battle, but there are no battles to be had. I have to steal one if I want a consort."

The fucker wasn't going to steal his consort. "She won't go with you. We're bonded."

Roan shrugged. "Perhaps she can bond again. The bond she shares with you would be broken with your death. Someone wants you dead, Mr. Dellacourt. Someone wants your cousins dead so trade can flow and we don't have to tear each other apart over what should be our right."

"She doesn't belong to you." Dante had to force the words from his mouth. His fangs seemed far too large for his head. "She's mine."

Roan sneered at him. "You didn't fight for her. I saw the records. There was no tourney. Just a simple sale. How much can you buy with money? When do you have to prove yourself?"

He'd been asking himself that question a lot lately. His blood was up. If Roan wanted a fight, he would provide it. "Is that all you want? You and me, asshole. Let's go now."

Roan's fangs were out. "If only it were that simple. I would love to kill you and properly claim the consort, but I can't let you go so easily. I signed a contract to bring you in alive. Your death will have to wait."

Torin. It had to be Torin. "What about my Kaja?"

Roan's eyes became hooded with suspicion. "I believe my employer might be somewhat cruel toward her. It's better I keep her."

"Or, you could let her go. I won't fight if you let her go."

But the beast inside was desperate to fight. It wanted to kill. Dante was stronger. If he could save Kaja, it would be worth it. He hadn't done much with his life anyway.

Kaja was the best thing he'd done.

Roan looked down at her as though considering it. "I might be persuaded, but you have to tell me where the queen is."

His gut hurt. He couldn't give up Meg.

"I'm here."

Damn it. Meg walked into the circle.

"Your Highness." Roan nodded. "I promise, I will see to your safety. I had it written into my contract that you were to come to no harm."

"Very nice of you," Meg said with a wry smile. Dante wanted to shake her. She really should be more afraid. "So, you're going to kill my husbands and I'm supposed to thank you for leaving me alone in a faery forest? Let me tell you, buddy, no one would thank you for that. Faery forests are freaky. There's a ton of shit out there, and it's all waiting to eat you."

Yep. Meg had lost her damn mind. "Meg, get behind me."

She shook her head. "So they can kill you first?"

Roan gently laid Kaja on the ground. "Your Highness, this isn't necessary. I have no intentions of leaving you to fend for yourself. Once the renegade kings have been captured, my men will be more than willing to see to your every comfort. We'll take care of both you and Kaja."

Meg's eyes rolled. "Yeah, I'll bet you'll take care of us. I can imagine what kind of care we'll get. Don't worry about it. I think Cian will be here soon, and he'll have a few things to say."

Roan frowned. "What about the warrior king?"

Meg shrugged. "He was busy. That or Ci drew the short straw. I know they weren't playing Rock, Paper, Scissors. Cian always wins that because Beck always picks rock. There's a reason Cian's the intellectual half, if you know what I mean."

Roan laughed. "Well, I suppose then I shall have double the reason for the warrior king to come to me. This is good. We can easily kill the intellectual half, and then the warrior will be vulnerable."

It was Meg's turn to smile. "You go on and try that, buddy. You just try to kill my Ci."

Dante kind of wished they were both on their way. And he didn't see what Cian was going to do. Cian was good with plants. Was he going to have the flowers attack or something?

"Don't worry yourself, Your Highness," Roan promised, his men standing stalwartly behind him. Dante tried to do a quick count. It looked like he had ten well-armed vampires with him. "As I told you, I will make sure you are unharmed."

One of the goblins moved toward Meg, yellow teeth gleaming. "I won't. I'm being paid double to take you down, Your Highness."

Dante took off, his feet moving faster than ever. He wouldn't let them take Meg. He couldn't. He attacked, letting his claws sink into the goblin's flesh.

"Dante, don't," Meg called out.

Two other goblins jumped him. He roared as he felt goblin teeth bite at the flesh of his shoulder. He winced and tried not to think about how nasty a goblin mouth was. Dude probably didn't floss. He simply threw his elbow out and caught the fucker in the chin. The goblin fell off his back with a thud.

Meg was busy slapping at goblin hands as the vampires surrounded her, pulling the goblins off. All the soldiers concentrated on saving the consort. No one seemed eager to help him. He hit the grass as a goblin shoved a fist in his belly. Goblins were squat but so strong. The goblin was on him in an instant. Dante put his hands up, shoulder aching, but he managed to keep the goblin from tearing out his neck.

Black eyes stared down at him, and sharp teeth gnashed. "Torin will have your head."

"Yeah, well, I'll have your balls, asshole." He brought his knee up, viciously catching the fucker's balls. Goblin, *sidhe*, vamp, or human. It didn't matter. If it was male, it didn't like having its balls busted.

The goblin howled, and Dante was able to roll him off. He sprang to his feet. Meg was surrounded by vampires now. They formed a phalanx around her, keeping the goblins at bay.

Dante punched out at the goblin who came at him. He looked back at Roan. "You're trustworthy."

Roan Tasered one of the goblins. The sickening smell of burning flesh hit the air. Cold iron. The mercenaries had tipped the darts with cold iron. They were prepared to kill Beck and Cian.

Roan turned to Dante. "This was not my plan. Bloody hell! You better get your consort, Dellacourt. I don't dare leave the queen unguarded."

Dante turned, and Kaja was getting to her feet. She was unsteady, but she reached for a rock. There was a goblin running straight for Dante, a wicked, curved blade in his hand. Kaja was weak and obviously disoriented, but she threw the rock at the goblin's head. It hit him, and he turned, growling at his new prey.

Not going to happen. With a burst of speed he didn't think himself capable of, he crossed the distance between him and Kaja as the goblin lashed out. It caught him across the chest, opening a gash in his skin. Dante hissed at the pain. That blade had gone deep. He heard Kaja scream as the goblin raised the blade again. Her hands pulled at him, as though she would take his place and the blade for him.

His brave, sweet Kaja.

He didn't have time to avoid the blade. He shoved Kaja back and took it straight to his gut. The pain burned, an agonizing fire in his flesh. He was close, so close to the goblin.

"Enjoy that, vampire." He shoved the blade in further, twisting it.

Dante stumbled back, the blade coming out of his gut. Blood. So much fucking blood. The world seemed to slow down. It got louder. Meg was screaming. Kaja called his name. The goblins began to circle, sensing blood.

He needed a fucking weapon.

"Kaja, run." He held his hand to his gut, trying to keep himself together. The goblins would tear him apart, but they would take their time. Their bloodlust was up. They would ignore Kaja until they'd finished with him. "You have to run, baby."

It would be all right as long as Kaja got away. He could take the pain. His hands shook, but he could stay alive long enough to let Kaja get away.

The ground underneath him shifted. *Fuck.* Why was the ground shaking?

Dante fell as vines burst from the ground, sending dirt flying. Kaja was suddenly kneeling beside him, her hands covering his, trying to keep his guts on the right side of his skin.

"I told you to run," he growled her way. Even as he roughed up his voice, something inside him calmed as her scent, the touch of her skin, her nearness washed over him.

She shook her head. "I cannot."

"This is going to cost you a nasty spanking, Kaj."

"Survive, Dante," she replied, tears coursing down her cheeks. "Survive and I'll lay over your lap."

Her arms wrapped around him. The ground seemed ready to swallow them whole. Vines and roots spat from the dirt.

"Retreat!" Roan shouted, his eyes wide as he seemed to catch sight of something terrifying.

"Baby." He forced himself to talk when it hurt to even move. "You have to go. Something bad's happening."

Kaja's arms tightened.

Roan was suddenly in front of him. "Feed. No one likes to talk about it, but your consort can save you. Her blood can heal you, Dellacourt. I never meant to hurt the women. If I've been betrayed, then I assure you I'll take care of it. Feed and live."

Roan took off, and Dante finally got a good look at what had sent the mercenary running.

Cian.

He strode forward, the trees and bushes bending around him to give him access. Cian Finn's hands were stretched out as though he embraced the world around him and it embraced him in return.

Dante watched as the goblins were caught by vines. They snaked across the field and caught their fleeing prey. The vines wrapped around their ankles and pulled the goblins screaming into the ground. It was as though they were being swallowed feetfirst. The goblins clawed and fought, but they went down screaming, the earth sucking them into the dirt.

"What is happening?" Kaja asked, her voice tiny and frightened.

"Cian is happening, love. He won't hurt you."

His cousin was utterly transformed. The Green Man walked toward them now, and he was pissed off.

The vampires were fleeing, but some of them got caught by the trees. The mighty oaks leaned over, and their heavy branches became wooden swords.

Kaja's arms tightened around him, one hand covering his heart as though she could stop the trees.

Smart trees. And they had damn fine aim. A vampire screamed and exploded as a tree branch caught him straight through the heart.

Chaos reigned. Blood flowed. Weariness flooded Dante's system. Kaja would live. Cian would see to it. Cian would take her to Dante's family, and his father would take care of Kaja. His father. Anger fled. He loved his dad. And his mother. And his annoying sister.

The world was loud with the business of dying, but Dante still spoke to Kaja. "Baby, tell my family I love them. Can you do that? You go to them. They'll take care of you."

Dante saw Meg run to her husband. She leapt into his arms and wrapped herself around him. The goblins were gone, taken deep into the ground. The vampires had fled, and those who weren't fast enough were puddles of blood. Cian kissed Meg. It was a beautiful sight. The tiny pixies clung to Cian's hair.

They had gone to find the Green Man. *Clever pixies.*

"Please, Dante," Kaja begged. She put her wrist to his mouth.

Oh, he wanted to, but he wasn't sure he was strong enough to stop. Instinct told him that Roan was right. Kaja's blood could save him. *Fuck.* He couldn't risk her. It was better to die than to live without his Kaja.

He leaned back against her. "No, baby. I could hurt you."

Cian and Meg were suddenly in front of him. Cian looked down at him.

"You're worse for the wear, cos."

Ci was good at stating the obvious. "Yep. You suck, man. Next time, give me the heads-up that you're leaving."

"Will do." Cian's gaze turned to Kaja. "I heard the asshole who I intend to kill say that you could save Dante."

"Don't," Dante warned.

"Yes, but he needs to feed. He won't feed." Kaja's voice was pleading.

Cian smiled. "I think I can fix that."

"Don't you fucking dare, Ci." There was a knife in Cian's hand.

Cian Finn neatly sliced a small hole in Kaja's wrist. Not much, but enough to get the blood flowing, and Dante's instinct took over when she pressed it to his mouth. Sweet, rich blood flowed and he couldn't help it. His fangs sank in, and he drank.

Velvety warmth flowed into his mouth, and he could feel himself healing.

She invaded his system. Her memories, her hopes, her dreams assailed him. She was so sweet, so strong. She'd been battered, but her heart was whole, and she offered it up.

"That's unbelievable," Cian breathed.

"It's working," Meg said, relief obvious in her voice.

But Dante was concentrating on Kaja. His defenses were down, and he let her flood him. He was battered with her emotions. She'd wanted to die when she'd seen him gutted. She'd wanted to lie down beside him and never get up. She wanted to bear his child. She wanted it so much.

She loved him.

He saw himself as Kaja saw him.

Dante felt his skin knit together and forced himself to stop.

Kaja slumped to the ground.

Dante touched her hair. She was utterly exhausted, nothing more. He'd taken a bit too much, but he could sense she would be all right with rest and care. He stood and hauled his lovely, brave bride into his arms. She curled against him.

Cian looked at him. "Still thinking about setting her aside?"

"Never," Dante said, and he walked from the forest.

He might not understand what had happened, but he knew one thing.

He would never let her go.

Chapter Fourteen

Dante walked into his father's office freshly showered, shaved, and utterly presentable.

So why did he feel like he didn't belong here? Everything about the office was perfectly normal. He knew every nook and cranny of this space. He'd spent great portions of his childhood in this office. Now it felt foreign. Everything felt alien and odd, even the clothes on his back.

"Son, I will say, I never expected that you would find a consort so quickly," his dad said, a smile on his face. He was a familiar figure in an expensive suit and worn boots. "You always were the smartest kid I knew."

Dante thought about Kaja, asleep in his room. She was cuddled up in his big bed where no woman had slept before. He'd always taken them to hotels or gone to their places. His wife was asleep in his bed—their bed. And he wanted to be next to her, watching her breathe. She looked right in his bed.

He'd nearly killed her.

Damn. That was a bit overdramatic. He knew she was going to be okay, but he hadn't really calmed until he'd made it to his cousins' village and Flanna had pronounced Kaja perfectly fine, merely tired from blood loss. She'd been sleeping for almost twenty-four hours, but she had opened her eyes and responded with the sweetest smile before sinking back into healing sleep. He'd carried her all day, placing her across his lap when he got his bike back and taken them home. She'd cuddled against him the whole way here.

"Dante? Have you heard a word I've said?"

He turned to his father. "Sorry, I was thinking about something else."

His father grinned. "You were thinking about her, weren't you?"

He nodded. It seemed foolish to try to hide it. "Yes."

He seemed to always be thinking about her these days. Kaja was becoming an obsession.

His father came and stood beside him. They stared at the city. From Donald Dellacourt's office, Dallas spread out like a sea of buildings resting on clouds. From this far up, Dante couldn't even see the ground. He rather thought that was the way his father liked it. His father had come from a ranch in West Texas, an impoverished royal, all the way to the heights of society. Dante hadn't seen the ground as a small child unless he was being taken by hovercar to the door that led to the Seelie plane. That door was guarded now, and no one had been through it in years beyond the occasional political emissary.

"It's only right, son," his father was saying as he put an arm around Dante's shoulder. "She's your consort. I can't wait to welcome her into our family. The housekeeper said something was wrong with her."

"She lost a lot of blood."

"She's hurt? What happened to her?"

"I did," Dante replied. There was on odd mixture of guilt and pride that came with the memory, as though the two pieces of Dante's soul were at odds over the incident. "I was the one who was injured. Kaja healed me."

His father's arm dropped. "Why? What the hell happened? Did you get in a fight? Was it a tourney?"

Dante held his hands up. If he didn't stop his father, there would be doctors all over the place. "I'm fine. Kaja's fine. We got attacked in the marketplace, that's all. Torin is finally making his move. I guess the asshole realized Beck and Ci aren't going to conveniently die."

His father had turned a little pale. "Torin attacked the marketplace?"

"He sent mercenaries to attack the Refugee plane, as far as I can tell. Some asshole impoverished royals have formed their own army, and they are all about letting trade flow."

There was a tight set to his father's eyes that told Dante he didn't like this subject. "They want consorts. It's all the government can talk about these days. There are so few to be had. There's an entire generation of royals who can't find consorts. They're aging, and they don't like it. You have to understand, Dante. A royal is brought up to believe that finding a consort is his or her right. We live longer with a consort. Without a consort, we might as well be peasants."

It was a hard truth to swallow, but he knew his father was only laying it on the line. "Now that Beck and Cian have come into their powers, maybe things can change."

The look in his father's eyes was grim. "I don't know. I think it might be too late for that."

He turned and looked his father straight in the eyes. "What do you mean?"

"I mean that when your cousins come to visit next week, I'm going to try to convince them to run."

"What are you talking about? Where the hell would they go? Torin decimated their village." It had been a terrible thing. Beck and Cian had built the village up over the years, and it had taken a single afternoon and some well-placed sonic charges to bring it all down. He'd mourned with his cousins the loss of their home.

"I think it's time they went to the Earth plane, son."

The words hit Dante like a grenade threatening to explode. "Why the hell would they go to some backwater plane that isn't connected to anywhere else?"

There were a few doors to the Earth plane scattered around, but they were very difficult to access and few braved them. The Earth plane was almost entirely cut off. In Dante's mind, if his cousins fled to the Earth plane, it was an admission of defeat.

"Because the tide is turning. If our government decides to recognize Torin's claim to the throne, they have to acknowledge that Beckett and Cian are renegades. Those mercenaries who are after them now, they'll be joined by every soldier on every plane who hears the news."

Dante's stomach turned. How was this happening? "Beck and Ci won't go."

They would stay and fight. They wouldn't leave their people behind.

His father simply shook his head and sat down behind his desk. "Let's talk about something more pleasant. We'll deal with your cousins' situation when the time comes. Now, I know you need your bonding time, but the sunscreen project is at a critical state. I want you to get to work. The chemists have the formula down, and we'll be ready for testing soon."

He knew he should be excited. This was the very reason he had gotten married. He'd changed his entire life to stay on this one project. Now all he could think of was how to keep his cousins alive.

"Dante?" His father leaned forward. "Are you all right?"

No. He wasn't all right. He was changed, and he wasn't sure he liked it. This was his home and somehow he felt out of place. It would be all right. He'd been through a lot. He needed time and space to forget what had happened in the woods. It was just a little post-traumatic stress disorder.

He would be fine. He would get back to normal.

He wanted to see Kaja.

"I'm good," Dante said, forcing a smile on his face. "A bit tired though."

Yeah, almost dying would do that.

His father got back up and walked around the desk. He enveloped him in a bear hug. Love for his father rushed over him. Dante hugged him back. Despite their differences, he loved the old man.

"I was wrong to say what I did to you, Dante. You're my boy, and I would never kick you out," his father said, emotion choking him. "You'll always be my boy."

Now the emotion that flowed over him turned bittersweet as he realized he was leaving something behind. He might live in this mansion forever, but he was changed, and his childhood was irrevocably over. He had been Donald Dellacourt's boy for thirty years.

But now he was Kaja's man.

"I love you, too, Dad."

* * * *

Kaja came awake slowly, her brain opening in layers. She'd slept so deeply that no dreams had jarred her. Just sweet sleep. Each time she'd awakened, her eyes would open and she would see Dante's face hovering over hers, protecting her, and she had known she could sink back into sleep.

This time, however, he was not there. She opened her eyes, and Dante was not holding her or standing watch over her.

She sat up in bed, feeling stronger, but there was still a delicious weakness to her system. She had saved him. Dante was alive because her blood sustained him.

All of her life, she had allowed things to happen to her because she knew no other way. Until she had been kicked out of the pack, she had not known that she could change things. She had saved Dante. She was strong.

She pushed back at the blankets that covered her. They were rich and soft, made of some material she'd never felt before. She touched the gown covering her body. She vaguely remembered Dante slipping it over her head and calling her a princess as he tucked her in.

Where had he gone?

She looked around the room, her memories surfacing. Dante's room. It seemed larger than her pack's long house. Dante's memories of this room were strong. She'd seen it when he fed. She could see it as it had been when he was a child. He'd loved hovercars and bikes. He'd followed racing circuits, and he'd been past disappointed when his father wouldn't let him enter something called the BMX Sky Racers. She found the desk where he'd sat and worked on homework when absolutely forced to. He preferred to play with his tablet. It still sat on the desk.

Kaja touched it and was startled when a woman popped up. She was small but lifelike. How had she fit inside the thin tablet? Why was she half-naked? If she'd learned one thing about Dante's people, it was that they preferred to be fully clothed. Not this woman.

"Hello, Master. What can I search for tonight? I've found some amateur pornography guaranteed to shock and arouse you."

Kaja took a step back. "I do not think I wish to be shocked."

She was already shocked by the small woman who hovered above the tablet wearing what appeared to be strips of leather that did not cover her incredibly large breasts. And the minute Kaja spoke, the woman changed, morphing into a much older woman in a business suit.

"Apologies, ma'am. I'll go into 'mom mode.' Now, would you like a rundown of stock quotes?"

Kaja turned away, a bit frightened. She looked around, seeking the doorway out. There were double doors with filmy curtains covering them. She strode over and threw them open and gasped. She was no longer in a building, but outside and so close to the sky. Lights twinkled all around her, like fireflies in odd colors. Yellows, pinks, blues, and purples lit up the sky in the distance.

She held on to the doorframe. There was ground beneath her, but she could tell she was high. Very high.

"Kaja, you're awake."

She turned her head, and Dante stood at the edge of the railing. *Balcony*. This was a balcony.

Dante had turned toward her, his handsome face soft in the moonlight. The moon was so big. It was almost as though she could touch it.

"Come here, sweetheart," he said, holding a hand out. "I want to show you something."

She bit her bottom lip and forced herself to be brave. She stepped onto the balcony. It felt solid under her feet. She walked toward Dante. He was dressed in a suit, the tie loosened and jacket discarded. His hair was back to perfection, and she missed the messiness of before. He looked unattainable again, like a man who had never fought with claws and fangs. But he was still so beautiful to her.

"Look at it, Kaj." He pulled her to the railing when she placed her hand in his.

She felt her breath blow out of her body. It was stunning. Dante's arms wrapped around her waist, anchoring her. "It's so high. Should we be so high?"

He chuckled, his breath warm against her head. "It's the only way to avoid the pollution. You can't see it at night, but there's a cloud of bad air that hangs over the surface. Instead of solving the problem, we built higher. Don't worry, you'll never go to the surface in the city. We have walkways and hovercars to take you from building to building."

"You never touch the ground?"

She felt him shrug behind her. "On vacation, perhaps. There are places that have been kept clean. The further you get out of the cities, the more likely you are to be able to comfortably dirt walk. But this is our home. This city is called Dallas."

Dallas. She tasted it on her tongue. Odd-sounding name. And no forests. The balcony had a few trees, but they were rooted in pots, not the earth. The whole world around her looked foreign and alien. Beautiful, but beautiful things could be deadly.

"I'll show you everything tomorrow," Dante murmured. He turned her around so she was facing him. "But for now, I don't think we need to leave our rooms. Are you feeling better?"

She nodded and buried her face in his chest. She felt better here, surrounded by his scent. She felt safer.

"Excellent." His hands reached down and hooked beneath her knees as he hauled her against his chest. "I have a few things I've wanted to do to you."

She shivered in his arms. "You're going to spank me?"

It was what he'd promised. She'd violated direct orders. She wasn't afraid of Dante's version of punishment.

He smiled down at her, but she didn't catch that hint of fangs she loved. "Not tonight. I think I would be a bit of an ass if I spanked you when you're still tired due to blood loss. No, I'm going to take care of you tonight. But don't think for an instant I've forgotten what happened out there. You will answer for your disobedience. I'm actually having a room renovated for that very occasion."

"There are more rooms?" This one seemed so large. Far too large for the two of them.

"Yes," Dante replied as the door on the far end of the room swung open. "Susie and Colin are moving to the east wing. We're taking over this whole wing of the penthouse. We have ten rooms all to ourselves over three floors. Of course, there are also common rooms."

Well, of course.

"But I don't want you to worry about any of it." Dante set her on her feet. She was in a plush room that seemed to be made from smooth stone. She recognized one fixture. A huge bathtub dominated the room, but Dante walked to a glass enclosure. He was unbuttoning his shirt as he stood next to it. "Shower. Thirty-eight degrees Celsius."

A waterfall poured from a fixture in the ceiling. Dante shucked the rest of his clothes. With each piece he tossed aside, he shed the civilized man she didn't understand. Somehow he became something different without the trappings of his culture on his body. He turned to her, and her heart raced. There they were—the fangs she loved. She loved how savage they made him look, how strong and powerful. She loved the way they felt when he drank from her. Without thought, she allowed her neck to roll back.

He was on her before she could breathe, his hand tugging at her hair. "Don't you dare, consort. Don't you tempt me. I can see you want it, but there will be none of that."

Even as he said the words, his head leaned down, and he ran his nose along her neck.

"I am fine." Kaja felt strong.

He growled. "No, Kaja. I'm beginning to think I should spank you. I ate two meal pills so I wouldn't feed from you. They taste like ass now. I only want you. You're a fucking addiction. You're also still recovering."

She pressed her neck to his mouth. If he was addicted, then so was she. She never felt closer to him than she did when they were connected like that. "I am fine."

He gently shoved her away. "Damn it. You are pushing me. I've had a rough couple of days. I want to be gentle with you. Fuck that. I want to tear into you, but not tonight. You mind me."

She softened against him. This wasn't about her. This was about him. He would feel bad if he was rough with her. She could give him that. She let her arms wind around his waist. His cock was already pressing against her belly. She hoped he didn't intend to be too gentle with her. She could handle the fact that he wouldn't bite her, but she needed him to make love to her.

She pressed her mouth to his chest. "I'll behave."

He lifted her head up. "No, you won't. But then that's one of the things I lo—like about you. And you're not completely off the hook, love. I need to explain the way relationships work here. I'm in charge of us, especially in the bedroom. I'm the one with the fangs. I'm the one who could hurt you, so by the gods, you will listen to me."

She wanted to roll her eyes. He hadn't hurt her. He hadn't even come close. Still, she was learning how to handle her husband. When his voice got rough and hard, she softened. "Yes, Dante."

It wasn't as if she were giving up the battle, merely pleasing him. And she'd learned that no matter what he said, he was indulgent with her.

"Oh, like I believe that," he laughed. "But I'll take it tonight. Now, this isn't about punishment. This is about getting you ready for some of the things I want to do to you. I don't know what marriages are like on your plane. I know Fae marriages can be all about respect and treating your wife like a lady. That's crap, love. You're my wife. I'm going to do all sorts of filthy things to you because you belong to me. You're my little toy. I'm going to fuck you as often as I can and in as many ways as my filthy mind can come up with. That's a strong marriage."

She had no idea what he was talking about beyond the fact that he was going to fuck her. Yes, she wanted that. Dante's version of mating was an amazing thing.

His eyes went hard, the irises enlarging. He tugged the nightgown off her body and let it pool on the floor. He stared at her for a moment. Her nipples hardened under his gaze, and she could feel her pussy already getting warm and wet. How did he do this to her?

"Turn around, Kaja. Put your hands on the sink and spread your legs. You're going to mind me or I won't fuck you. Do you understand me? I've gone without before, and I can do it again. I'll get you crazy for it and then I'll tuck you in bed and we'll cuddle."

She turned to him, sure there was an outraged look on her face. "I do not wish to cuddle."

He slapped her ass. "Then do as I tell you."

There was a smile on his face that let her know this wasn't as serious as he made it out to be. He liked his games. She turned back and did as he asked, the surface cool under her fingers. Marble. The word floated into her brain. She stared down at it. It was lovely and totally foreign. So many new things.

Like the mirror. She could see herself in it. She would never get used to it. She wasn't sure how much she liked seeing herself, but she loved watching Dante with her. She watched as he opened a drawer and pulled something out of it.

"Do you want to know what I'm about to do?"

She did and she didn't. The thing he held in his hand looked like a cock. It was big, with a purple head and a thick stalk. "What is it?"

"This is a training plug. It's set to expert level. I'll tone it down." He pressed something and the cock seemed to shrink. "See? A bit more manageable. I bought this for you. Normally I would have brought you to the shop with me, but you were in bed. I think I described your ass perfectly though. Tight as a virgin."

"You spoke of my anus to people?"

He shrugged. "Of course. I have no discretion at all, lover. I'll talk about how fuckable you are to everyone willing to listen. And when I've had a bit too much Scotch, I might put on a show. There's a club I want to take you to once you settle in a bit. You'll like it. I'll spank you, and everyone will see what a gorgeous consort I have."

His hand was caressing her ass. She didn't mind the thought of nudity. She rather thought vampires wore clothes far too often. Nor did she have a problem with showing her love for her husband in a public way. He was beautiful. She was smart for having him.

"Though we'll have to make sure it's not a night when Susie is there. Gods, I walked into The Club one night and Susie was there with Colin. I swear I went blind for a week. I promptly told the man who owns The Club that he needed to inform me if I was going to run into my sister. Now there's a scary vampire. I'll introduce you to Julian someday. He's fairly terrifying, in a perfectly polite way, of course."

She wasn't sure she wanted to meet this Julian person, but she was happy that Dante had settled down. He was talking a mile a minute, which meant he was comfortable. And his hands were doing amazing things. He got down on his knees, his body disappearing from sight.

She gasped as she felt his hands on the cheeks of her ass. What was he going to do? He'd said he was preparing her. She had a suspicion.

"See, look at that sweet asshole. Yeah. I'm going to get here and fuck this asshole. We're going to be friends, you and I."

Her husband was crazy. He was talking to her anus. Then he was doing more than talking to it. She shivered as he touched it. A dark, jittery feeling danced all the way up her spine.

"Kaja, I'm going to become acquainted with your pretty anus, and you're going to let me. You're going to stay still while I play with you. Is that understood?"

She knew what he wanted. "Yes, Dante."

She stopped, catching a glance of herself in the mirror. She had a content look on her face. Despite her mild discomfort, she was happy here. It felt right to be alone with Dante, to submit to him. She was actually pretty. Her mouth was not downcast, and her eyes sparkled.

"Move into the shower," Dante ordered.

She straightened up and walked to the glass room. Dante had called it a shower. It reminded her of the waterfall where they had first made love. She stepped underneath the clean, warm water and let it flow over her.

Dante crowded her, his hands running up her body. "Such a sleek thing. Do you have any idea how much I love your breasts?"

He showed her, his hands cupping and playing with her nipples. She wanted to touch him back. "Dante, please."

"Not so fast. Assume the position again and lean over. I want your ass in the air. You couldn't possibly think I would settle for a little fingerplay. I'm going to work the dildo into your ass, and you're going to wear it. It's going to stretch you so you can handle my cock. You want to take my cock, don't you?"

"Yes, but not there," she replied honestly. "I do not think it will fit there."

He laughed, his hand tracing her spine. "That's what the dildo is for. It's a training tool. It's very high tech. You'll see. Now, do I have to spank you?"

She leaned over and placed her hands flat against the wall of the shower. Warm water beat against her back. She felt Dante between her legs, opening her cheeks.

"I want you to relax. This is some lube to help ease the dildo inside. The training device is made to mimic flesh, so it won't be cold, though it will be hard. Fuck, I'm hard."

She bet he was. She could tell from the way he was talking that he was terribly aroused. She wasn't sure about taking this dildo thing, but he seemed so aroused by it that she was willing to give it a try.

A warm liquid that felt different from the water had her asshole puckering.

"That's the lube, and I would watch the way you clench this sweet hole, if I were you. I'll get in no matter how hard you try to keep me out, and there might be punishment when you clench."

Something hard pressed against her asshole. She whimpered, but Dante was unrelenting. He pressed the dildo in and pulled it back, rotating it around and gaining ground.

The feeling was foreign, and it made her ache. She wasn't at all sure that she liked it.

"You're fighting me. Stop. Press out against the dildo."

Kaja wanted to get it over with. She would take the dildo, and then they could move on. She would prove that she could do it, and then he would be satisfied. She flattened her back and the thing slid in.

"Perfect," he said.

Now that it was inside her, it wasn't so bad. It felt tight, but it wasn't painful. She clenched around it, trying to decide if she liked the sensation or not, and then the burning began.

"Dante. Something is wrong."

He stood up and turned her around. "Nope. It's working perfectly. Does it burn?"

Tears filled her eyes. It burned, and it made her ache. It wasn't pleasure, and it wasn't pain. It was an oddly erotic awareness of a part of her body she'd never paid attention to before. "Yes. It burns."

"Stop clenching. Relax. The dildo is in training mode. When you clench your ass, it secretes an oil found in a root called ginger. It won't hurt you. It just burns a bit." He seemed perfectly unconcerned with her discomfort. His eyes trailed down to her breasts. "I want to eat you up."

He lowered his mouth to hers, and his tongue invaded. He kissed her again and again, his hands dragging her against his body. His cock pulsed against her stomach. She lost herself in the demands of his mouth and relaxed.

A low hum started in her ass. She gasped at the sensation. Now that was pleasure. It started deep inside and radiated out.

Dante's lips curled up as he looked down at her. "Ah, see what a good girl gets? It will pleasure you when you behave and make you feel the burn when you try to keep it out. Don't keep me out."

He pushed her against the wall of the shower, and she found herself dangling as he used his strength to hold her up. She wrapped her legs around his lean waist and nearly screamed when that big cock of his started to push into her pussy.

"Fuck, I can feel it, too. Oh, fuck, that feels so good." He widened his stance, and his cock slipped in another few inches. His hips flexed up. "It's good, Kaja, baby."

She groaned as he seated himself in her pussy. Between the dildo and Dante's monster, she was so full. She thought she might burst, but the vibrations of the dildo and the silky slide of Dante's cock had her panting and begging. She was on the verge, and he'd just started. She opened all her senses, practically begging him to join with her.

She was surprised when he tentatively opened up. The door between them cracked.

He thrust into her. "Don't kill me, Kaj. Send me something nice."

The door swung open, and she thought about what to send Dante. She thought of being free and running. She thought of summer when the fjord was crisp and flowed and flowers sparkled everywhere.

She opened herself and was flooded with Dante's desire. He wanted her. He loved how packed with cock she was. He'd done that. He'd filled her holes and taken her. He was a marauder, and she was the sweetest booty he could steal.

He hit that perfect spot, and she went off, her eyes closing as she felt Dante's orgasm. His cock exploded, bathing her womb. He wanted to cover her in it. He wanted to know that she had pieces of him inside her.

Even as she came down from the heights of the orgasm, the dildo in her ass sang, and she wondered if one could die of pleasure.

Chapter Fifteen

Two weeks later, Dante stared down at a marketing spreadsheet, the numbers swimming in front of his eyes. He was knee-deep in reports. They came in from everywhere. Everyone in Dellacorp it seemed had a fucking report. Marketing. Financial. Business Management. Project Management. Human Resources had to chime in. They were all placed on his desk by his lovely, somewhat airheaded assistant, and then, he would swear to the gods that the fuckers bred and made more reports with more numbers.

His head was going to pound if he spent another second behind his desk.

The door to his office opened, and Sandy, the hot blonde, stuck her head in with a grin. Dante wanted to groan but managed to keep himself professional. Sandy had been his "assistant" for over a year now. He'd hired her when he was head of Dellacorp's Green Division. He'd hired her because she had nice tits and didn't mind screwing her boss.

"Hey, boss man, your sister's here," she said with a wink. "You want me to tell her you're out or something?"

Susan pushed past her with a frown on her face. "I'll let myself in. You—go do something."

His big sister, the CEO of the company, stood in front of his desk. She wore a designer suit, killer heels, and a frown that would chill the warmest heart. Her green eyes narrowed as she gestured toward the now closed door. "Is she capable of doing anything besides her nails?"

He declined to tell his sister that Sandy was double-jointed and that made her capable of a lot of things, none of which helped him out now that he was serious. At the time, Sandy had been practically perfect. Now, he constantly worried that he was missing something important. But his sister might be able to help him with that. "How much do you love me, Susie?"

Her eyes narrowed suspiciously. "More since you brought Kaja home."

Susan had adored Kaja on sight. They'd spent a lot of time together in the last few weeks. Dante had been grateful for it. He'd had very little time to spend with his bride, and it showed in their intimacy. Kaja needed him, and he was hiding in his office behind a mountain of paperwork. He was fucking everything up, but he didn't know how to stop. He had the job he wanted and people were finally taking him seriously. He was more miserable than he'd ever been in his life because he had no idea what to do with his wife.

She should be attending charity functions and having teas with other consorts, but that wasn't Kaja, and he wasn't sure how she was ever going to fit. He thought about it all the time, and it was driving him crazy.

Kaja scared him. Kaja tempted him. If he didn't watch it, Kaja would become his whole world.

And he didn't want that. This was what he wanted. He wanted his big corner office and his enormous paycheck and the respect of those around him. It was what he'd trained for. He'd spent years in school so he could take over a big part of the family business. It was the very reason he'd gotten married. It had to be his focus now.

Fucking coward.

He ignored that voice in his head and dealt with the problem at hand. "I need a real admin. I need someone who understands the company. Don't we have a beauty division Sandy would fit into?"

Susan crossed her arms over her chest and stared down at him. "We have a consumer product panel that she would love. Why? Do you have someone in mind, and please tell me she's at least of age?"

He didn't give in to the urge to needle his sister. "Yes, I was thinking about bringing in Mack. He's smart and organized, and he knows this company like the back of his hand. He's being wasted in reception."

His sister's eyes got wide. "You want a male secretary? A fifty-year-old male secretary?"

He couldn't argue with her. He'd made that bed. "Admin. Secretary is a little dismissive. And yes, I would like to hire Mack. Mack's been around forever. He knows what he's doing. Hell, he can do half this paperwork himself."

His sister's mouth hung open for a moment. "Holy shit, you're serious about this. You're really serious. I was coming in here to bitch at you about ignoring your wife, but you're actually working."

Yeah, he deserved that, too. All of it. "I'm not a kid anymore. I have a consort. I have to take care of her."

"I can see that," Susan said, her voice softer than before. She walked to his ultraexpensive leather sofa and sat down. "Come and sit with me, Dante."

He got up because she was his sister and his boss. And because it had been a long time since he'd simply sat and talked with her. It was so obvious now that he'd been drifting. He could remember with crystal clarity that moment in the forest when he'd been sure he was going to die. The fact that his sister could be a ball-busting boss hadn't mattered then. The fact that she'd been a damn good sister to him had.

"The sunscreen project is showing some remarkable results," he began. "We should be ready to take it to the FDA in a week or two."

She held up a perfectly manicured hand. "I don't want to talk business. You're doing a great job. I can tell from the reports. I want to talk about Kaja."

His stomach took a turn. Kaja. Guilt gnawed at him. He couldn't even pretend to not have noticed her unhappiness. He felt it every time they made love. She longed for a forest, for grass beneath her feet. She felt trapped here.

Wasn't that what he'd wanted? She wasn't suited for life in a high-rise penthouse. He could find someplace nice for her and keep his cushy job and get on with his life. Except it would seem empty without Kaja in it.

"What about her?" Dante asked, trying to sound unconcerned.

Susan smiled, her eyes lighting up. "She's a sweetheart. I don't think you could have found a better consort, but I have my concerns. She's never lived in a society like this."

"She's smart," he said before thinking it. "She'll adapt. We have to give her time."

Time to forget that she was connected to nature and now all she had were vampire-made structures around her? Everything was fake. Even the trees on the balcony were fake. They even faked photosynthesis.

"Of course," Susan said, putting a hand on his shoulder. "She is very smart and quick. She's funny, too. I enjoy having her in our family. I'm not worried about that at all. I'm worried about the press. My office has fielded over a hundred calls about your new consort."

He'd known that would happen. At the time he'd come up with what he now thought of as the stupidest plan ever, he'd counted on it. The press would be the thing that pushed his father to allow him to live apart from her. Now he would do anything to keep the vultures off his consort. He couldn't stand the thought that people were talking about her, judging her. "Tell them to mind their own business. I've been saying *no comment* to every single one of them."

"Yes, I know, and that's a problem," Susan replied. "It's making them curious. There are some reporters saying there's something wrong with her. They're wondering if she isn't a bit slow, if you know what I mean. It's come up that if someone like Dante Dellacourt had to settle for a damaged consort, we should consider making a deal with Torin."

He felt his fangs come out. "She isn't damaged."

Susan held her hands up in a conciliatory fashion. "I know that. She's wonderful. But she is outside the norm. She changes into a wolf, for gods' sakes. We have to reconsider the hardwoods in the penthouse because her paws go four different directions when she tries to walk on them in her wolf form. And we need to talk to her about hanging her head out of the window in the hovercar."

"She says it feels nice." Kaja liked the wind in her hair. It was the only thing she liked about being up so high. He'd caught her trying to see the ground more than once. If she made it to the ground, she would be terribly disappointed. It was noxious down there.

"And I think it's charming, but the press is going to eat her alive over it. I hate it, but we're a society that thrives on conformity. The occasional oddball can be celebrated, but only when said oddball makes a ton of money. Kaja is going to be seen as a cautionary tale if we don't fix her."

"She doesn't need to be fixed." This was exactly what he'd been avoiding. This confrontation. He knew Kaja didn't fit in. He knew she was miserable.

Not always, that inner voice said. *When you're inside her and you open up, she's happy.*

But it wasn't enough.

Susan stared out the window. It was a rainy day. Gray clouds rolled by, making the world seem foggy. "Mom thinks bringing in a tutor would help. Kaja can learn to read and how our society works. I've already ordered a wardrobe fit for a princess, and I can have Dellacorp's media advisor train her on how to deal with the press."

"No," he said as fast as he could get the word out of his mouth. He wasn't about to let the media advisor anywhere near Kaja. Jana was a shark. She'd eat Kaja up and spit her out. And he'd slept with Jana. She was such a bitch she would probably throw it in Kaja's face just to spite her.

Susan rolled her eyes. "Fine. I'll try to find someone you didn't sleep with, though that makes my job hard."

Maybe Susan was right. Maybe all Kaja needed was time and some training to adjust to her new home. *A little kindness from you wouldn't hurt, asshole.* He ignored that increasingly loud voice. A present. He'd get her a present, and that would pacify her.

He had work to do. Work he didn't care about.

"Do what you need to do, Susie. I'm up to my eyeballs in this sunscreen project." His eyes trailed back to the desk and his mountain of paperwork, but his brain went to a different place. His mind thought about the forest and how Kaja looked naked on the grass.

Susan considered him carefully. "Yes, I can see that. It surprises me."

"Because you're shocked I can be professional?" There was the bitterness that always lurked under the surface.

"No," Susan replied with a tired smile. "That's not what surprises me. I'm a little anxious about this turn in your behavior because I always believed you would leave this plane entirely and join Beck and Ci and fight for their cause. I don't know how I feel about it. Part of me is utterly thrilled that I don't have to worry about you dying in their war. And part of me aches because I don't think this is who you are."

Tears threatened. He bit them back. He'd never once imagined his sister knew him so well. He would have told anyone who asked that his sister rarely thought of him at all outside of how obnoxious he could be. Had that all been his perception? "This is who I was raised to be."

She shook her head. "Oh, you're more, little brother. I always knew that. You're the kid who took on the older, bigger boys because they made fun of a girl you liked."

He remembered her. Fourth grade. Trista. A very nice peasant girl on scholarship. He'd had no intentions toward her. She was funny and sweet. She didn't deserve to be picked on by sixth graders. He'd nearly gotten suspended for the fight he'd started. "I was young then."

Susan's hair shook as she leaned forward. "You think I don't know some of the things you've done? How about paying for our old nanny's nursing home? You did that out of your own pocket."

"The state-run places are terrible. I couldn't send her there. You would have done the same thing."

She sighed. "I didn't keep in touch with her. You give a damn, Dante. You just don't like to show it. You're a crusader who's hidden himself away as a playboy. I've always thought of it as you trying to reconcile Dad's world with the one in your heart."

"That's a bit dramatic. I think I've always been trying to live up to Dad's expectations and failing spectacularly."

"Only because you never understood what Dad really wanted. He wanted you to find something you were passionate about. He wanted you to be happy. I don't think you're happy, Dante. I don't think you were happy when you were partying, and I don't think you're happy behind a desk."

He wasn't. And it was awful that someone saw it. He had everything a person could want, and he wasn't happy. *But you were. You were happy with Kaja in the woods. You were complete.* "Maybe some people aren't smart enough to be happy."

She huffed, a frustrated sound. "You are so slow sometimes. You're happy when you're fighting for Beck and Ci. When you're talking politics and how to help the masses, your eyes light up and you become this different person altogether. That's your passion. Not numbers and spreadsheets. And I saw you the other night with Kaja. When you thought no one was looking, I saw your fangs and your eyes bleeding out. It was primal, something we try to hide. But you were happy, brother. And that made me happy."

He tried to hide that. "If the press caught me like that, we would all be in trouble."

"You think I don't go a little crazy around Colin?" Susan asked. "I know royals try to hide the way consorts make them feel, but it's stupid. It's love. It's how we love. The sharing of emotions and sensations is how we love. They don't prepare you for it."

Dante let a beat of silence slip by before he said, "I can see Kaja's memories."

Susan leaned forward, surprise clear on her face. "Seriously?"

He'd known he shouldn't talk about it, but the temptation was too great. He didn't have Beck and Ci to talk to. And he didn't trust anyone else. "It's like I'm there. It's like I'm her. I live out her memories when we're connected."

"Wow. That must be her power." Susan contemplated the situation for a moment. "It must be because she's different. I don't get anything like that from Colin. I get a lot of thoughts about how hot I am and how much he loves me, but I don't ever become him. I'm kind of glad about that. I don't think working on a farm would be an experience I'd look forward to reliving."

He sat back, inexplicably tired. "Yeah, well, being an outcast in a wolf pack hasn't been awesome."

"Outcast?"

He hoped he wasn't telling his sister something Kaja wouldn't share, but he felt like Susan should know. They were getting close. "Her parents are dead. Her siblings were killed because her father tried and failed to be the leader of the pack. She was spared because she was a baby, but they treated her like shit. The pack leader's son raped her and then threw her out of the pack when he was done with her. They expected her to die."

"Gods, I had no idea. She's so open and loving." His sister's hand was over her heart. She wouldn't think less of Kaja. Susan would love her all the more for how resilient she was.

"Yes, she's strong," he said. "She didn't let it kill her heart. That's why I cringe at the thought that she needs to be fixed. She could teach the people of this plane a thing or two."

Susan nodded. "I understand. Let me work with her. You'll see. She'll settle in. She'll learn our ways."

He had to hope so. "Please make sure the tutor is a kind woman."

"I actually was thinking about a man," Susan began.

"No." He wasn't leaving his lovely, strong, interesting consort alone with some man.

Susan smiled as though she'd been testing him and he'd passed. "Fine. I'll find a very nice woman to teach our Kaja. Colin can help, too. He likes her. And mother wants to throw a big party for her next month. She's inviting everyone, including the press. We'll polish her up, show her off, and then she can go back to being herself." Susan leaned over and hugged him. "But you should think about slowing down and giving a lot of consideration about what you want. Dad talked to me about what he thinks is going on with our government. You know damn well Beck and Ci won't run. I'll do anything I can to help, but I'm strictly financial. You could help them in other ways. Mom and Dad will try to tell you to be safe, but you've never been safe. It's who you are. It's why I love you."

He was shocked at the tears in his sister's eyes when she kissed his cheek and stood to go.

"And I need those reports tonight, Dante."

The doors closed behind her, and Dante knew he had a lot to think about.

Chapter Sixteen

Kaja stared at the machine in front of her. Like everything else on this plane, she found it confusing and difficult.

"What would you like to drink, mistress?"

Though the machine had no face, it still spoke. It still asked her questions she wasn't sure of how to answer. Everyone did that here. Everyone had questions. She could still feel the press of the people called reporters from earlier in the day. She'd been out with her mother-in-law shopping, and the reporters had found their car. When she and Alana had gotten out, there had been a rush to surround them. Kaja had changed out of sheer fear.

She could still hear the shocked shouts and see the flashes as the reporters took pictures and video.

Dante's mother had been horrified. Oh, she'd pretended to be angry with the reporters, but Kaja had heard her calling someone known as a lawyer.

She had caused this family an enormous amount of trouble. It was time to seriously consider moving on.

"Mistress? Have you changed your mind?"

No. She was still thirsty. She simply didn't know what she

wanted. It was very much how the last few weeks had gone. She was stuck in limbo, trapped between loving Dante and facing the knowledge that she did not fit in to his world and never would.

"Tea." Alana often had tea. She'd watched Dante's mother speak to the machine.

There was a short hiss, and the machine went into motion. She stared at it, but she didn't really see it. She saw Dante in his perfect suit as he came home from work each night. He would come in and try to talk to her, but she didn't understand half of what he said. He asked about her tutors and her classes and seemed very pleased that she was rapidly learning what he called academics. But the rest seemed to elude her.

Now, she'd utterly humiliated her new family. She'd heard the news of her failure reported on the DLs that everyone here seemed to watch. She was being called the Dellacourt Beast.

And Dante was further away than ever. He still made love to her, but he was always working. He didn't have time for her anymore. Now that they were back in his home, he seemed to understand that he'd made a mistake.

She wanted to talk to Meg.

The machine finished. There was a lovely teacup with a saucer and steaming liquid sitting in the center of the machine. "Does my mistress wish for cream and sugar?"

"Yes." She'd never had cream and sugar, but it seemed like something interesting to try.

"And where should I put it? Directly on your thighs and buttocks?" The machine's voice became distinctly nasty.

"No." Kaja took a step back and heard a chuckle.

Dante stood in the doorway, his jacket gone. He still wore his tie, but his hair was utterly perfect. He was cool and collected, and the very image of the modern vampire. He was a man who should be married to the perfect consort, not one the press reviled.

"Mom put the beverage dispenser on 'weight management' mode. It gets bitchy. You have to learn how to talk to it. You're the boss." He got down on the machine's level. "Look here, you piece-of-shit machine. She said she wanted cream and sugar, and if you don't give it to her, I will pull your plug, shove you into the recycling bin, and you'll come back a toaster. Do you want that?"

Immediately a stream of white came from the machine's dispenser followed by a cube of sugar. "I hope you enjoy your beverage. Please let me know if I can help you further."

Dante reached in and grabbed the delicate cup and saucer. He indicated that she should sit at the table and placed it in front of her before turning back to the machine. "Give me three fingers of Scotch. Single malt. Fifteen years."

The machine seemed to race to do his bidding. In no time at all, he was picking up the glass and sighing as he sipped the Scotch. He'd been drinking a lot of Scotch lately. Still, he turned and sat down at the table in front of her. "I heard you had a rough day."

The tea smelled lovely, but she suddenly knew her stomach wouldn't accept it. She pushed it away. "I made a mistake."

She waited for him to berate her. She would take it. She knew she shouldn't have allowed her four-legged form to be seen.

Dante's lips quirked up. "Not a mistake, Kaja, baby. You were beautiful. I told you, I think you're gorgeous any way you are."

The doors to the small kitchen opened, and Alana Dellacourt walked in. Her face was lined with worry, but when she realized she wasn't alone, she seemed to force a smile on her lips. "Oh, hello, Dante, Kaja."

Kaja wanted to hide. She'd put Dante's mother in a terrible position. She'd embarrassed the poor woman. She started to get up, to excuse herself like the etiquette tutor had taught her, but Dante's hand came out and covered her own.

He grinned up at his mother. "I saw the DL story about your brush with the paparazzi today. Nice use of four-letter words, Mom."

Alana actually laughed. "I also used my four-inch Louboutin stilettos on one of those jerks. He tried to touch Kaja's fur."

Dante's fangs popped out. "Who?"

His mother waved him off. "I'm not telling you because I don't want to bail you out of jail. I took care of it. He won't be walking for a bit. Calm down. It was only natural. No one has ever seen a shanimal before."

Dante's hand slapped at the table. "Motherfuckers! I told Meg. I came up with that. I totally came up with that."

Alana shrugged and ordered a wine from the beverage dispenser. She smacked it when it asked if she really wanted the calories. "Well, CVN news is claiming to have named the new species. And more."

Dante's eyes lit up. "Was bestiality mentioned?"

His mother sighed but ruffled the top of his head as though she'd known he would ask. "Yes. You're being called a pervert of the first order."

"Nice."

Now his mother slapped his perfectly coifed head. "It isn't nice for Kaja."

Kaja watched their byplay with growing curiosity.

Dante shrugged. "I'm not worried about it. Something new will happen, and the fact that Kaja's also a wolf will totally blow over. Maybe I should give them a photo op of me and Kaj playing with a Frisbee in a park."

"You will not," Alana said, giving her son a stern look.

"I am very good with a Frisbee. I catch it every time. I am also good with rubber balls," Kaja added. Dante had taught her several games. She liked them. They were fun. And they allowed her to run when every other time she seemed to be forced to walk.

"Dante! Don't you dare do that with her," Alana nearly shouted. "What are you trying to do?"

Dante's eyes narrowed, and he sat back. "I'm trying to find our way. She isn't a properly bred Fae consort. She's different. I won't force her into some mold because that would make it easy. I like Kaja the way she is."

But the way she was would get them all in trouble. Even she could see that. She'd learned enough about Dante's home to know that personal lives affected the stock market, and the stock market was the most important thing on this plane. She still didn't quite grasp how a list of valuations made the world go around, but it seemed to be the way here. She was going to cause Dante's company trouble.

"I will try harder."

Dante held out a hand. "Kaja, don't listen to them. You're fine. And I won't allow the press to define our marriage. Now, I got a call from Julian Lodge. I'm supposed to meet with him in an hour. It's something supersecret."

Alana went very still. "Have you done something you shouldn't? Maybe we should send you in with a guard."

Dante frowned. "Julian Lodge isn't calling me in to have me killed. He sends that Taggart fellow out for that sort of work. I have a suspicion it's about Beck and Cian."

"You're leaving?" She only saw him at night, and now she wouldn't even get that?

Dante's expression shuttered. "I won't be gone for long. Well, I don't know how long I'll be gone. And I should tell you now that I have to leave for DC in a couple of days. It's a business trip. A week or so."

Her heart felt too small for her chest. "I will go with you."

She didn't fit in here. She'd fit in even less if Dante wasn't around at all.

"I don't think that's a good idea," Dante said, his voice tight.

Alana patted her hand, a sympathetic look on her face. "You don't want to go to stuffy old Washington. We'll have fun, dear. We'll go shopping and see a show. But for tonight, I'll keep you company. Colin should be here soon, and we can all have a nice dinner."

More shopping. Less Dante.

She'd become an inconvenience. Like she'd been with the pack. These people might be nicer about it, but she was being relegated to the back of the room again. It hurt even more this time since, for a while, she'd believed she might belong.

She would never belong here.

Kaja stood. "Thank you, Alana. I believe I will skip dinner this evening. I would rather go to my room."

And figure out a way to contact Meg. Meg would be able to tell her how to leave this place.

Dante was on her heels as she walked from the room. "You need to eat."

She continued on her path. "I am fine."

He grabbed her elbow. "Kaja, go back to the dining room and eat your supper."

He was using that voice on her, the one that usually had her panting after him. Now it simply made her a bit angry. He was pushing her aside. He'd brought her here to this place where she didn't belong, and now he was leaving her to languish. He'd taught her what she wanted and then took it all away.

"I am going to my room. I will stay there. I will not leave the house again. Now, let me go." If he wanted to leave her, then she didn't have to obey his commands. That was another thing she'd learned. She wouldn't mindlessly follow someone else's commands. She was the only one who would ever truly look out for her, so she was done being meek.

He took her by the elbow and began to walk with her. "Fine. We'll go to our room. You seem to want a fight. We can do that in private."

She dug her heels in, but he was so much bigger than she was. He simply hauled her along. "I'm not trying to fight. I'm trying to be alone. I want my own room. You have enough rooms that I should be able to have my own."

He turned on her, his face a mask of irritation. "Now you want your own room? Really? Just a couple of weeks ago we had far too much space. Now I'm encroaching on yours?"

A few weeks ago she'd thought life would be different. "It's only for a little while."

His brows made a curious *V* on his forehead. "What is that supposed to mean? Is this some shanimal thing?"

And she hated that. She pushed away from him. "I am not a shanimal. I am Kaja. If you can't use my fucking name, then don't talk to me."

Yeah, she'd learned how to curse, too. And it felt good.

His jaw hardened. "Kaja, do you want to explain what this is about?"

"I want to leave this place."

He crowded her until her back was against the wall. The door to their room was so close. If she could reach it, perhaps she could bar his entry.

"Really? And where do you plan to go, consort? You don't know how to drive. I doubt you could find your way around the house, much less the city. So, I have to assume you have a place in mind. Did I turn my back too soon? How have you been spending your days? Or, should I ask who you are spending your days with?"

He ground the questions out of his mouth as though each word hurt to say it. Kaja was very confused. "I have spent the days with your mother or Susan."

"Yeah, that's what I thought, but now I have to wonder if you've met another vampire." His eyes deepened to the rich green of the forest. She could feel his persuasion creeping in. He wanted her. It rushed against her skin like a wave, but she wasn't buying it. He wanted to fuck. It didn't mean he wanted her.

"I'm not meeting some other vampire." Kaja nearly spat the words at him. "I don't know if you've noticed, but they don't exactly want to welcome me. I'm the Beast, remember."

It was what they had called her when they weren't laughing. They had called her a beast, and humiliation had washed over her. All she'd thought about as they had taken her picture was getting back into Dante's arms.

It was dangerous to forget he didn't really love her.

His face softened. "Kaja, they're stupid. Is that what has you so prickly? It will be yesterday's news in an hour or so. They'll find someone else to pick on. In a few weeks, things will calm down, and we can take that trip we talked about."

That was what he'd said weeks before. Their "trip" kept getting put off. And she knew her status as an outcast and a beast wouldn't blow over. "No. I want to leave. I wish to leave this plane. I want to go back to the forests."

"No." He turned and walked into the front room of their apartment.

"What do you mean *no*?"

He walked toward the bedroom. "It means what I said. You're not going anywhere. You're my wife. You'll stay with me. Now I'm done arguing with you. You can eat supper or go hungry, but you're not going to leave."

He dismissed her so utterly that she felt something nasty start to kick around her brain. She looked around the apartment. It was so perfect. Perfect art. Perfect furniture. Perfect rug. Everything was in its place, and that was what Dante was trying to do with her. She had her place, and she wasn't to leave it.

She picked up the glass vase Dante claimed was a masterwork and threw it across the room. It shattered when it hit the wall. Something about the destruction made Kaja feel satisfied. And it did what she'd intended. Dante turned, his eyes wide.

"What the fuck was that about?"

"You cannot keep me in a cage." She could see plainly now that this grand place was exactly that—her new cage. This whole plane was a cage. Perhaps she could have handled it if he was here with her, but she'd been forgotten. It was better to be alone than to languish here.

His hands clenched into fists. "I have papers that say I can do anything I want with you, Kaja."

And he thought she was stupid. "I know all about your laws. You cannot keep me. You cannot make me your slave."

"You've been talking to your tutor, love? Well, she's a very smart vampire, but she is a peasant. The laws we have are there so we don't look like barbarians, but I assure you no one is going to come between a royal and his consort. I haven't been abusing you. No one is going to question my rights. Try going to the police. They'll pat your head and bring you home to your...cage."

Weeks of tension had built inside her, and now it came rushing out like a volcano finally erupting. She wanted to hurt him the way he'd hurt her. "Then maybe I will take your advice. I'll find another royal. All of you royal vampires seem to sniff around consorts. I've heard royals aren't very picky these days. They'll even fuck a beast. Well, when they think to. Maybe I can find a royal with a bit more of a sex drive."

"You are pushing me," Dante said, his voice a low snarl. "I don't know why. I've done nothing for the last few weeks but work for our future."

"I don't want this future." Frustrated tears filled her eyes. How could she make him understand? How could she tell him she felt smothered here? "I want to call Meg and go to the Faery plane."

He moved faster than her eye could track. She'd noticed since he'd started taking her blood that he seemed stronger, faster than he was before. "You are not going anywhere. I am on the edge. Don't do this. I can't promise you that I won't do something I'll regret. Back down now, consort."

She knew what she should do. It was there in his stance and his voice. She was "pushing his buttons," as they said on this plane. She'd been studying. Vampires were ridiculously possessive of their consorts, and they could be very domineering. It was one of the things she'd missed over the last few weeks. Even their sex had been bland.

"No. You don't own me."

His fangs seemed larger than ever before. "I thought to let them finish our playroom before we used it, but you made that choice, love. If you're leaving then I should at least get what I can now."

He picked her up, cradling her to his chest.

"Dante, put me down."

He didn't bother to reply, simply carried her down the hall to the second bedroom. All the last week, deliveries had come and workers had been walking in and out of the room. She'd been told not to take a peek. It was supposed to be a surprise. Now her heart raced as she realized she was going into the room he said was for play. Sex. That was what he meant by play. He meant sex, and Kaja got the feeling it wouldn't be easy, lazy sex. It would be rough.

He was right. If she was going to leave, she wanted a last time with him. She would never forget him, and she could hold the memory in her heart.

He kicked open the door. It flew back and slammed into the wall.

She struggled to see. The room was utterly transformed from a nice bedroom into something dark and exotic. Dante didn't bother to explain the strange cross on the wall or why there were so many hooks in the ceiling. He simply walked to the center of the room and set her on a plush ottoman. It was circular and large.

Before she could move, he had her hands in his. He dragged them behind her back, and cold metal snapped around her wrists. She tugged, but her hands were locked together.

"Clothes, off. Command 125." With his words, her clothes receded around her body, shrinking to a neat pile at her knees. Dante smiled, but it was a harsh thing without an ounce of humor. "I programmed your clothes, love. I could have had you naked at any time."

Her eyes slid from his. "Well, you did not want to."

He tugged her head up. "Is that what this is about? Baby, I'm trying to figure this out. You think I don't want you?"

It was so much more than that, but it was something she could answer. "I think you like sex, but I'm just a body."

He groaned and hauled her against his. "So untrue. Gods, if you could sneak a peek into my brain during the day you would know it's always Kaja—all the time. I have to concentrate to not think of you. You invade my thoughts all day. I sit in meetings and all I can think of is you riding my cock. It plays hell with me. I can't properly explain why talking about marketing gives me a hard-on."

She didn't understand him at all. "But you are never with me."

His eyes had softened now that he had her naked. "It's work. You don't get it. This is the way my plane runs. You'll settle in."

She wouldn't, but she wasn't sure how to make him see it. How could she make him understand that her heart hurt every time he walked out the door? "I won't. No one will accept me."

His hands cupped her shoulders. "I accept you. You have to understand. I can't let you go. I won't let you go."

She felt deliciously vulnerable. She was naked, her nipples puckering in the chilly air. She couldn't move her hands. The way they were chained behind her back thrust her chest out. Dante couldn't seem to take his eyes off her breasts. It was so odd. She was naked, and he was clothed. He looked like a perfectly powerful vampire, proper even in his business suit, though his erection was tenting those expensive pants of his. She would still call Meg when this was over, but she wanted this time with him.

He ran his fingertips over her nipples. "I have responsibilities. Can't you see that? I have to provide for you. I have to not be a fuckup."

It was important to him. He took his work seriously, and she understood he needed to have a place in this society. Appearances were very important on this plane. She was going to ruin his. She was never going to be the lady consort he needed, but for tonight she could be his comfort, and he could be hers.

She lowered her head. He sighed, and she could feel him open to her. His relief at the fact that she was submitting practically poured across her skin. He didn't want to fight—not her. There was a fight building in her Dante, but she didn't sense that it was a fight with her. He'd been genuinely surprised at her anger.

Oh, it was getting so easy to read him when they were truly intimate. When they were together and open, she didn't want to run. When she could feel his soul brush hers, nothing could keep her away. But the times when he held it back from her, those times caused an aching chasm to open inside.

He pulled away, his hand running through his hair. "Sorry. I was pushing myself at you, wasn't I?"

She bit back a sob. "I didn't mind."

"I don't understand this connection thing. I wasn't raised to expect it the way Beck and Ci were."

Mates on her plane, true mates, could speak without talking. She would never have that because Dante feared the binding. She would always be alone. It wouldn't work if he never wanted it. None of this would work. She should have remembered that. When he found a place for himself inside her brain, she was in his. It couldn't be nice to be her. She wouldn't force that on him. "I will behave. I will go and have my supper and cause no trouble."

He cursed and pulled her hair back. "See, I'm fucking up again, and I don't want to. I want to do what's right. I just haven't figured out what that is yet. You want this? You want me to flood you with myself?"

She looked at him through a veil of tears. "I think you're so beautiful, but it does not mean anything if it isn't shared. You do not want to see me. My essence is not lovely. I understand."

He growled at her. "You don't understand a thing, but I am beginning to."

He kissed her, his mouth covering her own, his tongue plundering. He hauled her against his body. His erection prodded at her belly.

"I'll give you what you want, Kaja. You give me what I need first."

She gasped. His desire sparked across her skin and into her brain like lightning striking. He wanted so much, all of it from her. He wanted her soft and willing. He wanted her trust and her submission. He wanted to be in charge of her because no one thought he could handle anything. She was important to him. She could feel it.

"You threw a priceless vase at my head," Dante said, his voice deepening.

Yes. She had done that. At the time, it had seemed like a good thing to do. Not so much now. She glanced around the room. There were some very odd toys lying about. She bit her bottom lip. "I'm sorry."

His fangs gleamed in the low light. "Not going to do it, sweetheart. You're in for some serious punishment."

There was that word again. *Punishment.* It made her nervous and excited all at the same time. He hadn't punished her since that day under the waterfall. He had mentioned that he'd gone easy on her then. "You said you had a meeting with the scary vampire. You do not want to be late."

He laughed outright. "Nice try, Kaj. Trust me, when Julian Lodge finds out I'm late because I was disciplining a bratty young lady, he'll forgive me. Nothing is more important to that man than discipline. Show me your ass and be glad I don't use a ball gag on you. The next spiteful words out of your mouth will cause me to stuff something in there. Do you understand?"

She understood the desire that came off him in waves. It was easy to submit when she could feel how much Dante craved this. Just talking the way he was got him hard. Every word pulsed in his cock. Gods, she could feel it in her pussy. He wasn't hiding, and the connection between them sparked and crackled. She did as he asked. She turned awkwardly on her pedestal and kneeled over, leaving her ass exposed. Her hands were chained together behind her back, so she rested her cheek against the soft velvet of the ottoman.

"Yeah, that's what I want. Look at that. Such a pretty ass. What should I use on this pretty ass? I'll be honest, love. I'm surprised that a bad girl has such a gorgeous ass."

His hand slapped at the fleshy part of her buttocks. He didn't hold back. The pain bit into her skin and had her eyes tearing up. He smacked her ten times in rapid succession, the blows raining down. She cried out. It hurt and yet she felt the intent behind it. He enjoyed watching her skin redden, knew that it would make what he did later even sweeter.

She was beginning to hear his thoughts.

Such a sweet ass. It's going to feel like heaven to fuck that ass. Mine. Mine. Mine.

He spanked her. She counted. Twenty. Twenty-five. Pain morphed into a pleasant feeling that had her almost floating outside her body. Thirty. He was calming now. She could feel it.

He stopped briefly. "Don't think I'm done. That vase really was priceless, and I still owe you for not running from the goblins when I ordered you to."

She felt something slightly cold dribble between the cheeks of her ass and clenched her teeth. She knew what was coming. He'd made her wear the training plug several nights over the last few weeks. Each time the plug got larger, filling her with what felt like warm flesh. When she tightened around it, it delivered the hated ginger oil and made her tight ring feel like it was on fire. And she'd taken a strange pleasure from that as well. She'd enjoyed that moment when he would work the plug in. She'd come to crave it.

"That's right," he said, fitting the plug to her. "See, it's opening for me. So much easier than a week ago."

He rimmed her asshole. She whimpered a bit as he began working it in. He loved to hear her cries. It made his dick twitch. The connection was easy to hold on to now that he'd stopped fighting it. When his cock pulsed with desire, she felt it. Gods, he loved dominating her. There was nothing in Dante that wasn't focused on her, and she got a glimpse of what sex had meant to him before he'd met her.

Fun. Playful. He'd had a lot of women, and not a one had touched him past his cock. He'd been entertained. Not once had he wanted this.

Responsibility. He was responsible for her. It had been scary in the beginning, and now he longed for it.

He used to lie back and enjoy the sex. A blonde with large breasts flashed through her brain. She would ride Dante, and he liked it. He would sit back and let her have her way with his cock. He would never have shoved the busty blonde across his lap to spank her ass.

The plug slid home, and Kaja felt something settle deep inside her. She was different for Dante. She was something more.

"See, that is really amazing," Dante said, his breath harsh. "I can feel it. I feel that fucking thing." He pulled on the plug. "Wow. I can feel the plug in your ass. Why did you complain about this?"

Kaja smiled. She loved the connection now more than ever. She clenched hard around the plug and winced as the burn began.

"Damn it, Kaja. That is not fair. Holy hell." But he pushed the plug in further. "It's not going to save you. I felt every smack on your ass. I also felt your pussy begging for more. I won't back away from the connection between us, love. I will never back away from this again."

He fucked her ass with the plug. The oil burned for a moment, stimulating and making her ultra-aware of what was happening to her. She relaxed and allowed the plug to start vibrating.

"So much better," Dante said with a sigh.

He hadn't had their connection open when her poor asshole was first getting used to the plug. He might have rethought it then. She bit back a grin at the thought. He seemed to like how it felt now. He pressed the plug in, and she felt him step around to the front.

He took her by the shoulders, lifting her to a kneeling position. He'd unbuttoned his shirt and she could see his sculpted stomach muscles. She loved how lean and strong he was. The plug whirred in her ass, pleasure and jangling discomfort mixing in a concoction that had her off-kilter and waiting for more.

Slowly, Dante lowered the zipper of his trousers. His cock sprang free. He looked powerful and decadent with his huge cock thrusting toward her. His hand tangled in her hair.

"Take me deep. Get me hard."

He shoved his cock into her mouth. She struggled to take it all because, despite his words, he was already as hard as any stone. She gagged but opened her mind and let herself feel him.

So good. It was so good to fuck her mouth. It was savage and primal and perfect.

It felt good to Dante, but more than simple pleasure invaded Kaja's brain. He needed this. He needed it like he needed his next breath. Knowing she was submitting to him gave him peace and reassurance.

He didn't want her to run. He would never allow it. He fucked her mouth in short strokes. He groaned as her tongue whirled around the head. He would never let her go. If she ran from him, he would be right behind. She was his. His.

He pulled his cock out. "Not so simple, love. I want to come inside you. I want to pack you with cock." He leaned over and kissed her. "And I'm glad I've erased that fucker from your mind. He can't hurt you again, Kaja. I won't allow it."

She'd been thinking about Sven. He'd been there in the back of her mind. She'd had what seemed like a fleeting thought that Dante was her only lover. His touch was the only one that mattered. Her husband had heard her loud and clear. He didn't seem embarrassed that she wanted only him.

"You better." His eyes had narrowed. "I find out you want someone else and I'll have them taken out. Do you understand?" He stopped. "You didn't say that out loud, did you?"

She shook her head. Now he would get upset. "It is common when wolves bind themselves and the binding is strong, that they can hear each other's thoughts during times of great emotion."

His hand softened in her hair. "Cool. Um, if this is really going to happen a lot, you should know that I cuss in my head all the time and I think about your pussy most of the day."

She could handle that. She smiled and sent some thoughts his way. "This is what I think about."

His cock. His mouth on her. Everywhere.

His breath hitched. "Fuck, that's hot, Kaj. Hold that thought."

She wasn't sure what else she was supposed to do. She was chained and had a large, buzzing plug up her ass.

Dante was back in a second with another dildo, this one oddly shaped. It had a large cock but there was an extension that came off the base forming a tiny cup. There was a long strap that came out from each side. Dante moved behind her. "This one is for your pussy. It's the best on the market. Top of the line." He pressed her forward again. "This one doesn't even come out for another couple of months. Talbot Industries makes the best sex toys. Though they have terrible names. This one is called The Jennifer. I would have called it Superhot Cock with Clit Sucker."

She preferred The Jennifer. Dante shouldn't be allowed to name things. After all, he'd been the one to come up with shanimal first.

He slapped her ass. "I heard that."

She shrugged as best she could. "I've decided I prefer werewolf. Though we simply called ourselves wolves."

"I'll just call you mine." He parted her pussy and worked the vibrator inside.

She stopped thinking about anything but how full she was. She groaned as he placed the strap around her, and the vibe started to work. It was utterly soundless, but she could feel it fucking into her in slow, tortuous strokes.

"Here's the good part." Dante finished strapping it on.

She felt her eyes cross as the little cup latched onto her clitoris and began to suckle.

Dante fell to his knees. "Oh, fuck. I'm sending Talbot a case of Scotch. Fuck. Fuck. Fuck. It feels like it's milking my dick. Kaj, you have to shield that or I'm going to come. Please. Have mercy."

She thought of a wall between them. She could still feel him. He wasn't shielding. His thoughts flowed over her wall like it didn't exist. Perfect.

He was shaking a bit as he stood. "Thanks. I have plans that don't include premature ejaculation."

But she wasn't going to wait. Her lower body was humming. Her pussy, her ass, and her clit were vibrating, and it sent her into shockwaves of pleasure. Her whole body shook as she let the orgasm run its course.

Dante's hand ran down her back. "Bad girl. I would spank you again, but your ass is the most perfect pink. I don't want to ruin it. No more orgasms until I get inside you."

He pulled the dildo in her ass out. Kaja bit her lip as something even bigger than the dildo began to invade. Dante's thoughts battered her.

So good. He'd waited so long for this. For her.

He pressed his cock to her ring and pushed inside. "That's right, baby. Open for me. Let me in."

It felt so good. She was tight around him. Different. Darker.

She closed her eyes and let Dante take over. His cock was squeezed deliciously. The pounding pulse of the vibe hit him like a rocket. He was caught between the vise of her anus and the vibration in her pussy. He wasn't going to last.

He gripped her hips. The sight of her naked and bound and submitting filled him with satisfaction. She was beautiful. So fucking gorgeous. She was his, and he wasn't going to let a bunch of hack reporters make her feel like she was less than she was.

What was she? *Everything*. She was his everything.

He fucked into her ass. "Do you hear me, consort? I know what I'm thinking. I mean every word."

Tears blurred her eyes. More than his words, she felt him.

I am a better man for loving you, Kaja.

He was close. So close. She felt his orgasm start, but he kept pushing his feelings at her.

She saw a picture of herself in his brain. She glowed. She was love and light and healing to him. She was comfort.

"I love you, Kaja. I love you." He gave over and let the orgasm take him.

Kaja felt herself surrounded by Dante. His strength, his power, his love flowed through her system. He overpowered her. All of his thoughts, his feelings, his memories hit her as strongly as his pleasure. Her vision faded, and the world blinked off.

She came to with the most languorous sense of awakening. And the feel of someone biting her thigh.

She looked down her body, which was now on their bed. Her hands were free. She was spread out.

And Dante was feeding.

Such pleasure. He flooded her with it.

He released her. "I was right. I like this vein because I can smell your pussy."

There was a drop of blood on his lips. He licked it up but didn't move beyond letting his head nuzzle her pussy. He laid his head down on it as if it was a pillow. "Although, I swear, I can smell you all the time. I can smell everything, actually. And my eyesight is better. I have a theory."

She let her hand find his hair. Peace, blessed peace. "What's your theory, my love?"

His head came up. A smile crinkled his face. "I like that.

222

Anyway, I noticed that I'm stronger."

She'd noticed, too. He carried her around like she weighed nothing. He was faster than he used to be.

"I can see better than before. Everything physical about me is better." He kissed her pussy, an affectionate gesture. "Pretty pink parts."

He was easily distractible. "Dante."

"Fine. I think it's you. I think it's your blood." His arms surrounded her thighs. "When we're connected, I see the world the way you see it. Experience it through your eyes, so to speak. You have better senses than I do. Feeding from you makes me stronger than I could have imagined."

"That's good," she said, but she wasn't truly listening. She was thinking about fitting in. She couldn't leave. She couldn't ever leave him. Now that she'd felt his love for her, he would have to deal with her for the rest of his preternaturally long life. He would never be rid of her. She was the best part of him.

"A fat lot of good all this strength is going to do me behind a desk." He sat up, a frown on his face. "I have to meet Lodge. If I hurry, I can still make it in time."

He was leaving, but this time she was calm. He wasn't leaving her. "I will wait up."

He got off the bed and walked to the closet. He pulled out a pair of pants. "I don't want that."

She frowned. Well, she was tired. "I can go to sleep."

"No, Kaj. I want you with me." He put on the pants and walked to the bed, holding out his hand. "Come with me."

She put her hand in his because she would follow him anywhere.

Chapter Seventeen

"And how do you know where they're going to be?" Chalen asked his former mistress over their video connection.

"I pay one of the maids to keep tabs on him," Amanda replied.

He had to give it to her. The girl was smart. "Did the maid tell you when he would be there?"

"I know he and the shanimal left about a half an hour ago. They didn't take the limo, and they left from one of the lower levels. The maid was surprised the beast was with Dante. They had been fighting earlier in the evening. She said they were arguing over the press coverage from earlier today."

Chalen felt a satisfied grin split his face. "I'm not surprised that he would try to evade the press. I'm sure the Dellacourts are perfectly horrified that their son is involved with an animal. Although I am a bit curious about her. Get dressed. I'll pick you up in twenty minutes. I think it's time for you to have a talk with Kaja. I think I've found another use for that tape you made of Dante. I'm not going to release it publicly. I like the narrative that he couldn't find another consort. But I wonder what his new wife will think about the plan you helped him cook up. She might not like the fact that he married her to embarrass his parents. I belong to that club. I'll get us in."

Amanda's eyes widened in confusion. "Why would I talk to her? Everything is going along exactly as you planned. The press is tearing the Dellacourts apart. I just watched a news editorial on how we will all be copulating with animals if we don't recognize Torin's right to rule."

Oh, the net was tightening, but Chalen had plans for Dante that didn't include simply hurting his feelings. And if he could make a profit while he was at it, that was all the better. The shanimal would be interesting to his medical division.

"I don't pay you to tell me what to do," Chalen said. "I'll pick you up in twenty minutes."

He closed the link between them and let the head of medical research know that he would have a new subject to test very soon.

* * * *

Dante held Kaja's hand. He barely restrained himself from wrapping an arm around her and keeping her close to his body. He wanted contact with her. He craved it. He'd been fighting his instincts for weeks in a vain attempt to look normal.

Normal wasn't going to work for Kaja. Normal was going to stifle her. It was going to kill that sweet soul of hers in a way violence and neglect hadn't.

"Good evening, Mr. Dellacourt," the desk clerk said.

Dante nodded at the man who probably was well armed and trained. The doors to The Club opened, and he led his wife through.

One day he would bring her here as a sub, not a guest. The BDSM club was known for its exclusivity. Royals only, and royals with money. Everyone else was well-vetted staff.

He didn't miss the way Kaja's eyes took in the grandeur of the space. Julian Lodge didn't do anything halfway. His entryway was a monument to decadence.

"Dante." Julian walked out of his office and into the grand entry. A mass of muscle was at his side, but then Julian rarely went anywhere without a bodyguard. It looked like that was the big guy's job tonight. "You know Mr. Taggart."

Ian Taggart was the head of Lodge's security branch. Lodge Corp was well diversified but in the last few years had come on strong when it came to security, and the turning point had been the hiring of Taggart. The massive vampire was one of those royals whose family hit hard times. He'd gone into the military and when he'd retired, every corporation on the plane had tried to hire him. Including his. Lodge had sweetened the deal by offering Taggart a membership to the exclusive club. It had also been said that Taggart brought with him a network of spies. Lodge would definitely know how to use that. "Taggart. I promise I'm not going to mangle your boss."

Taggart grinned, a completely predatory look. "Oh, please, feel free. I would pay to see that show."

Lodge simply sighed and held out a hand. "Welcome back. It's been a long time since you came in."

He shuddered. "Well, seeing my sister bound to a Saint Andrew's Cross while her consort whipped her made me swear off sex for a long time."

Kaja stared up at him.

"Three days is very long for me," Dante conceded.

Julian laughed. "Truly, it is. This is your consort." Julian bowed in the formal fashion. "Greetings, consort."

She smiled at Julian. That smile. Gods, it got to him. Especially since he knew she'd never smiled before she met him.

"Hello," Kaja said.

Taggart bowed her way as well. "Welcome to The Club, Mrs. Dellacourt."

Dante gave in and pulled her close. Another royal was staring at his consort. Despite the fact that he knew Julian had a consort of his own—if rumors had it right, he had two—Dante felt his fangs lengthen. His hold on Kaja tightened. Julian wasn't exactly ugly, and all the subs lusted after the big blond guy. Taggart was actually quite brutal when he wanted to be. He was very alpha. Taggart hadn't taken a consort yet.

Kaja snorted. "He is not my type."

It would take a while to get used to this whole telepathic thing. She'd obviously heard his thoughts. "I better be your type."

"Yes. You are my type."

She looked gorgeous, her brown-and-gold hair forming a halo around her head. Her blue eyes were wide and dominated her pretty face. She was everything to him. How had that happened? She'd become the sun in his sky. He'd fought it, but now he couldn't remember why.

He was going to leave his home to save her.

"Dante, if you'll join us." Julian gestured toward his office door.

He pulled Kaja along.

Julian stared at him. "Your consort is welcome to have a drink at the bar."

"Or she could come with me." He didn't want her running around an infamous BDSM club alone.

Kaja patted his hand. "I would love a drink. Don't worry. I won't allow myself to be carried off. If anyone tries to harm me, I will show them my beast."

His beast. He loved the beast inside Kaja. And she was the reason he would leave his home. Kaja needed something she couldn't get on this plane. And she also needed trust.

He leaned over and brushed his lips to her forehead. She understood. He'd felt her love. She loved him. He was her world as she was his. Even when she shielded, she couldn't hide that fact from him. It made him feel ten fucking feet tall. "Go on, love. Have a nice drink and meet the other subs. I won't be long."

She went up on her tiptoes and planted the sweetest kiss on his lips. She was his. "I will wait for you, my love."

She'd started using the endearment, and it went straight to his cock. She'd only ever called him *First* or *Dante* before. *My love* was new. "I love you, Kaj."

That was new, too. He wouldn't stop. He loved her. He was better for loving her. His heart was different—fuller. Everything was different. He'd gone into this relationship with bad intentions, and now he couldn't imagine his life without her. How quickly that had changed.

She merely smiled as though she knew. He didn't have to tell her. He merely had to open himself and she could feel how much a part of him she was.

"I love you, too. I will not stare at strange vampires. I will tell

227

everyone that I am taken and require nothing more than my husband." She wrapped her arms around him, squeezed, and walked away. Her glorious ass swayed as she walked. "I still feel your hand and your cock there, love."

Oh, she was *his* fucking mate.

"You seem to have chosen well," Julian said with a self-assured smile.

"I was infinitely lucky." Dante watched her until the moment the door closed and she was no longer visible.

"If you need someone to deal with the press, I'll do it for free," Taggart said, a fierce frown on his face. "I might even pay you."

Letting Taggart murder a couple dozen members of the press would make him feel better, but it wouldn't help Kaja. They would always look down on her. "I appreciate the offer. I think my wife would have a problem with it."

Taggart shrugged. "Wasn't planning on telling her."

"You've obviously never been married. They always find out." He turned back to Julian. "Now, tell me why you pulled me from my bonding time."

A shadow moved from the corner. A familiar British voice spoke up. "I'm afraid that's my doing, Mr. Dellacourt."

And just like that his mood went from sunny to kill.

Without a thought, he moved, his legs crossing the distance between them. Instinct led him. Dante had his claws around Roan's throat before the fucker could think to move. He slammed Roan against the wall and could smell the other man's fear.

"Now see, this is why I'm here," Taggart drawled. "I wanted to see if you could kill Roan. Hey, my offer is rescinded if he kills you."

"You're faster than I suspected," Julian Lodge said. If he was angry about the violence in his establishment, it didn't show.

Roan held himself perfectly still. "He's much faster than the last time we tussled."

Anger pulsed through him. "Tussled? Is that what you call nearly getting my consort killed?"

Roan's eyes held his. "It wasn't your consort who nearly died. It was you. She was the one who brought you back. And I was the one who told you how. Now you can take off my head because I can't

228

seem to stop you or you can listen to me."

"I am not cleaning that up," Taggart said, taking a step back. "I told you we should have put down a tarp."

Julian crossed his arms over his chest and leaned negligently against the wall beside them. "He didn't come here to fight. He came here to talk to you. He has information."

"I don't care about his information. This motherfucker has tried to kill me twice. I don't think I trust him to tell me the truth." A nasty thought ran through his head. Kaja. He'd sent Kaja to the bar alone. "If you took my consort, I swear they will be picking up pieces of you for weeks."

Now Julian didn't look so unconcerned. "Back down, Dellacourt. I don't give a shit if you don't trust him, but don't you dare accuse me of allowing a consort to be abused in my club."

The club owner and, if rumors were true, mobster, was frowning ferociously, his fangs out. Julian Lodge could be a friend or a foe. Dante's choice.

And he had an easy way to check on his consort. Hopefully the whole telepathic thing worked when he didn't have his mouth on her pussy. *Kaja?*

He felt her surprise, and her deep satisfaction, at the connection. *Yes?*

How did he put this without scaring her? *You don't happen to be surrounded by mercenaries?* He'd never been good with subtlety.

And she was smiling. He couldn't see her, but he felt that smile. *No. I am surrounded by liquor, however. I like margaritas, Dante. They taste good.*

Behave, love. He wanted to be there with her as she tried tequila for the first time, but he shut down their connection. She was safe. He let the fucker-asshat-cocksucker fall to the ground and turned to Julian and Taggart.

"So, you're willing to vouch for him?"

Tag nodded and the tension in the room seemed to deflate. "Yeah, I worked with him when I was in the military. He's a proud dumbass who should have come to me when he cashed out, but no, he had to form his own crew and take on a bunch of shitty jobs to prove he could."

Julian's fangs receded. "Many of those jobs were for me. He's done good work for me over the years, including retrieving my promised consort from the Seelie plane a few years back. Though he brought along an extra bit of baggage."

Roan's hand was on his throat. "Well, I couldn't kill the young man. He wouldn't allow your consort to go without him. He was lucky you're a vampire with an open mind."

Julian smiled, a genuine, affectionate smile. "I've forgiven you for that bit of business, Roan. It all worked out in the end and after this is over, Roan's decided to join the team."

"Well, I am sick of working for unsavory characters," Roan admitted. "Taggart can't be worse."

"I can try," Taggart quipped. "And I plan on you working with the Unseelie, so you might want to rethink your stance on unsavory characters."

He'd really only heard one thing in that exchange. "You can get on the Seelie plane?"

"See, I told you he can learn," Taggart said. "Roan and his men can get on and off the Seelie plane. They've been smuggling for years now."

"It isn't hard, if you know where to go," Roan said, his voice still raspy. "And who to kill."

Julian stepped back. "I thought he might prove useful to you, Dellacourt. You see, I know something the rest of the world doesn't know yet. According to Taggart's sources, the Council is meeting secretly tonight. They're voting on a resolution concerning Torin and his place on the Seelie throne."

Dante's stomach took a deep dive. "We're going to lose."

Julian nodded, his mouth a grim line. "Yes, I believe so. I think that by morning, the Vampire plane will officially open negotiations with King Torin, and your cousins will become the most hunted men on all the planes."

It was happening too fast. Gods, it had been thirteen years and it was still happening too fast.

"I have more bad news," Taggart said. "I got a call from a man I have on the inside at the door that separates our plane from the Refugee plane. Your cousins are on their way here, to the Vampire plane. They'll be here in a couple of hours."

They would be walking into a trap. "They haven't called. I don't know how to stop them."

"Calm down," Roan said. "They're smart and apparently can call the trees to their aid."

But there weren't any trees on this plane for Cian to work with. He might find the occasional houseplant, but he would have to be on the surface to find trees. This fight wasn't going to happen on the surface. This was all about the royals and the lack of available consorts.

Torin was going to win.

"I have to find them." He would get on a bike and head for the south door. He knew the route they would take.

"I already have men on it," Taggart promised. "They're waiting at the door and will make sure the kings get to the Dellacourt building. We'll make arrangements to protect them."

"I picked my side of this fight long ago." Lodge nodded toward the door at the end of the hall. "I'm related to the Unseelie king. He doesn't want the true Seelie kings dead. Torin killed his daughter, my cousin, Gillian. We've been looking for revenge ever since."

"And I just think Torin is an asshole and we're way better off with the twins on the throne," Taggart added.

"Good, then please go and protect them. I know you've got men on it, but I want to know you're watching out for them." He didn't know Taggart's men. He wanted the best.

Taggart looked from him to Roan. "You going to kill my new hire?"

So that's why Taggart had really been here. "No. He's safe. But my cousins aren't."

Taggart nodded. "I'll make sure they're safe."

Lodge watched him leave before turning to Dante. "Now, come into my office. Roan here has some things to go over with you. Your night is going to be rough, I'm afraid."

Roan straightened his clothes. He looked odd out of camos, as though street clothes didn't quite suit him. "I took a job I shouldn't have taken. I made a mistake, but I'm here to make it right. What do you know about Chalen Palgrave?"

"I know he's a douchebag who can't run a company." Why were they worried about someone like Chalen Palgrave? They had much bigger problems.

"He's a douchebag who's trying to kill you, your wife, and your cousins. He's the man who hired me."

Then he would be the man Dante killed. "Tell me everything."

He followed Roan and Julian into Julian's private office.

* * * *

The lovely blonde woman passed Kaja another drink.

"I don't know if I should." Kaja giggled just a bit. The drink was doing strange things to her head. She knew she really shouldn't drink more. She was becoming intoxicated. Yes. That was the word she was becoming. Drunk. Funny feeling. Still, when the glass was pushed in front of her, she leaned forward and took another sip.

"Oh, live a little," her new friend said. "Come on, it's only two. Julian doesn't allow anyone more than two drinks here. Although, we might be able to get the bartender to sneak us one more."

Kaja focused on the bartender. He was an attractive young vampire with dark hair and a slender body. *Jeremy*. He'd introduced himself as Jeremy. Well, Jeremy might be attractive, but he had nothing on her Dante. Her Dante was the most beautiful man in the world. He was kind and gave a very good spanking. He had all the best sex toys.

She giggled again. She was losing it. "I don't think I can handle another one, Ashton."

"It's Amanda, sweetie," the woman said. "And I'm surprised you've made it this long. You have some kind of crazy metabolism."

She wasn't sure what the pretty blonde was talking about, but she seemed so nice. Everyone was being nice to her. "I will have to tell the machine at home that I like these drinks. And when it is rude to me from now on, I will make it pay."

Amanda regarded her. "You should. Those machines can really get you. Today, my mirror told me my hair didn't look good. Bastard. Bad programming. It's supposed to be supportive. It's supposed to tell me I look good."

"You do look nice," Kaja offered. In the few weeks she had been on this plane, she had noticed that women liked to be told they looked pretty. She liked it herself. "My mate tells me I look nice."

Amanda smiled, but it seemed a bland thing. "Does he? He never really noticed with me."

"He tells me often, though mostly when I am naked. He likes me to be naked. A lot. He gave me the option of coming to this place naked. I did not think it was a good idea. You vampires seem extremely concerned with clothing. Alana is always trying to buy me more clothing. And shoes. I only have two feet."

Something Amanda had said skittered at the back of her brain. What had she said?

Oh, her mind was foggy. It had felt good just a minute before, but now there was a queasy feeling in her stomach.

"I thought she had four." Jeremy, the bartender, was staring at her. He didn't look so nice now. There was menace in his gaze. "I saw the press coverage of the freak."

"Shanimal," Amanda said with a frown. "She's a shanimal, not a freak."

Kaja hated that word. The room was starting to spin. "I am not a shanimal. I am Kaja. I am Dante's."

He'd said it. She was his. She wasn't going to let these vampires make fun of her. She was the consort of Dante Dellacourt, and more than that, she was a good person. She was worth respect with or without her fur.

"Yeah, I know that's what he told you." Amanda sat forward. "You're different than I thought you would be. I'm actually sorry this is happening to you, but you should know that I'm Dante's mistress."

Kaja felt a growl deep in her throat, but she couldn't force it out. "You are not."

She pulled out one of the tablets that vampires seemed to always have on their persons. "I'm sorry, but this is who your husband really is."

A video started. There was her Dante and this woman. He lay back and allowed her to service him. His cock gradually became long and thick. He finally ordered her to climb on top of him.

"He never lets me do that," Kaja grumbled. "I told him it would be fun."

Amanda's mouth dropped open in apparent surprise.

"This was before we were married. I can see the date stamp. I know when we were married." And beyond that, it was so obvious to her that Dante wasn't engaged in the sex. Oh, Amanda was attractive, but he didn't even tie her up. He couldn't be too involved. This was how Dante had sex when he wasn't in love.

Dante loved her. Some silly video wasn't going to make her question that. She'd felt it in her bones.

"Fine. How about our afterglow? Maybe that will convince you he isn't what you think he is." Amanda turned the volume up.

They were talking. It penetrated her brain. They were talking about Dante finding a consort. His father had demanded it. Amanda told him to find someone unsuitable.

Kaja turned and smiled at Amanda. "Oh, I know this about my husband." She groped for the proper words. What had Susan called him? It seemed like the right word for him now. "He is a dumbass."

He was. He'd gotten caught in his own trap. He'd sought out a consort who would horrify his family. And she'd managed that. He'd sought a consort so unsuitable no one would question him when he set her aside. He'd found the perfect one. No one would say a word against Dante if he found her someplace far away to live.

He could never let her go. She was half of him.

Kaja bet he'd never expected that.

She tried to get to her feet. It was time to find her gorgeous, sexy, dumbass husband and explain a few facts of life to him. She wanted to be on top from time to time. It looked like a nice position, and she refused to accept less than his ex-mistress. "I do not know why you seek to hurt me, but this will not work. I know he makes foolish plans from time to time. I was the odd plan of his that worked out for the best. And I will fit in here. I will make sure of it. You should understand that if you come near my husband again, you will find out how quick I am on four feet. I am not allowed to eat anything that speaks no matter how stupidly it speaks, but Dante never said anything about maiming. I will maim you."

Of course, she would have to be able to walk first. She grabbed onto the bar, trying to hold herself up. Where had Dante gone? She couldn't feel him anymore. She couldn't focus long enough to even make the attempt.

"How much did you give her?" Amanda asked. Her voice sounded far away to Kaja. "Gods, Jeremy, if you've killed her, Chalen will have both our heads."

Amanda's arms went under her shoulders. Kaja struggled to move. She was beginning to understand that she was in trouble. "I do not want to be killed."

She felt so weak. What was happening? Did they talk to the demon? Had they given her his elixir? It had made her weak before, but now it made everything fuzzy, and her limbs were limp and useless.

"I'll take her. I'm stronger than I look." Jeremy picked her up. "And I've carted more than one druggie out the door. Security won't think anything of it. I want my payout in cash. I'm going to have to leave Dallas. If my boss ever finds out what I did, he'll pull my fangs out of my head, and that will be the nice part of my day."

Her world had upended. Her mind sought Dante's but found only fog. She started to drift in and out of consciousness.

When she opened her eyes again, she was being placed in a large hovercar. A man with cold, dead eyes looked down at her.

"Hello, Mrs. Dellacourt. My name is Chalen Palgrave. I think you're going to like your new accommodations. Well, until the vivisection begins. Then you might not think it's so nice."

The car took off, but Kaja was out once more.

Chapter Eighteen

Dante felt older as he walked out of Julian's office. He'd only been in there for an hour and a half, but he would have sworn he'd aged ten years.

It was really happening. After all these years, the fight was finally here. Torin would come after Beck and Cian, and he would have the Vampire Council's support. Well, maybe not their support, but they would look the other way if it meant royals once again had full access to consorts.

Torin was going to be the acknowledged king of the Seelie Fae, and Beck and Cian would be the rebels. He was having a hard time processing it.

And Chalen Palgrave was trying to kill him.

William Roan walked out behind Dante, a grim look on his face. "Mr. Dellacourt, I understand that you don't trust me, but I'm your best bet to stay unharmed until such time as this misunderstanding with Palgrave can be fixed."

He didn't want to fix the misunderstanding. He wanted to eviscerate Palgrave.

"Roan really is excellent at what he does," Julian said. "I'll vouch for him. Use him as a bodyguard for a while until we deal with Palgrave. He's insignificant compared to ensuring the safety of the true Seelie kings."

Dante wanted to growl his frustration to the world. He didn't need this shit with Palgrave while his cousins were in danger. "I didn't kill Kinsey Palgrave and neither did my cousins. If they had, I would have heard about it. If I had killed Kinsey, I damn straight wouldn't hide it. And, if I'd killed him, it would have been because he was doing something he shouldn't have."

Julian walked out, closing the door behind him. "Ian has been working on the problem. According to his sources, Kinsey Palgrave went to the Refugee plane and didn't come back. He received a message from someone. We managed to find a record of the call. I have excellent government contacts. They'll tell you they're all about privacy, but there's little on this plane that doesn't get recorded somehow. It's fuzzy. I can only make out a blonde woman telling him to come pick up a consort. Kinsey left shortly after receiving the call. Am I correct in saying there was a hag stalking the kings?"

Julian's sources were utterly impeccable. Dante bit back a surge of bile. He could still see that hag. "You're right. She's dead now." He'd had a hand in killing her. "And she was blonde. Her name was Liadan. She was sent by Torin to kill the twins. When she couldn't manage that, she caused trouble."

"I wouldn't be surprised if the hag was responsible," Julian said. "She would be strong enough to kill a vampire. It doesn't matter now. I doubt Chalen will listen to anything I say. You need to get your consort and return to the Dellacorp building. Let Roan handle Palgrave while Ian figures out where to stash the kings until I can get them to the Unseelie plane. I'm in contact with King Fergus. He's offering them asylum."

"In exchange for what?" He wasn't stupid. The last thing he wanted was to walk his cousins into an ambush.

Julian's lips turned up. "He's my uncle, you know. King Fergus married my mother's sister."

No. Dante hadn't known that. The Unseelie were secretive. "Are the twins part vampire?"

Now Julian was full-on smiling, but the fangs he showed off gave it all a menacing feel. "Worse. They're half-Unseelie-royal, half-royal-vampire, and all symbiotic twins. Lachlan and Shim are more dangerous than you can imagine. And they've matured past an age where they must bond. I could smuggle a mate off the Seelie plane, but they insist on only one."

"That's insane. They can bond with any bondmate." Dante thought about how fast Beck and Ci would have taken a mate if they could have found one. They might not have loved her the way they did Meg, but they would have done it.

Julian shook his head. "They've dreamed about this one for years. Don't you think my uncle has offered up any female who could bond? He's promised the Planeswalkers a multitude of riches if they would bring him a bondmate his sons would accept. But they want the princess in the tower. That's what they call her. They insist that Beck and Cian Finn hold the key to finding her and bringing them into their true power."

As Meg had brought Beck and Ci into theirs. He didn't want to think about what kind of powers the Unseelie princes would gain from bonding with the perfect mate.

Julian stared at him. "Please trust me when I tell you my uncle will do anything to save his sons. The Seelie kings are in no danger."

It was almost too much to take in. He nodded at Julian. His mind wasn't made up, but it wouldn't do any good to argue now. He would discuss it with his cousins.

He knew Julian was right, but it rankled. He wanted to wrap his claws around Palgrave's throat and not stop until the fucker's head popped off. But Kaja had to be his first concern. He had to get her home to the safety of his family's building. Once he had her back in the penthouse he would set security on her ass. At least six. A full unit. Then he could take care of Palgrave and decide what to do about his cousins.

A worried-looking young man strode up to Julian and spoke in hushed tones. He had to go up on his toes to reach his master's ears. Julian's face went stone-cold, his eyes darkening with every word the young man spoke.

"Show me," Julian said.

The younger man held up a tablet, and within minutes, Julian was cursing a blue streak.

"What?" Dante asked. If there was going to be trouble in The Club, he wanted to get Kaja out as soon as possible.

Roan was on high alert, his every muscle rigid. "What's going on?"

"Your consort is gone," Julian said flatly, every word a knife to Dante's gut. He held out the tablet, showing him a still picture of Kaja sitting at the bar next to a familiar face. "Do you know this woman?"

Amanda. Fuck. He'd sent her a nice note and a large check, but it looked like she hadn't appreciated being given her walking papers. "She was my mistress until I got married."

Roan cleared his throat. "I think you'll find she has ties to Chalen Palgrave. I saw a picture of her in his office."

A fucking spy and now a kidnapper. He'd never had the best of taste in women until he'd met his Kaja. "Where would he have taken her?"

"Not to his penthouse," Roan said. "I would bet he took her to his company headquarters. It's one of the reasons I broke the contract. I suspected he wanted to hurt the consorts, both yours and the queen. I didn't spend much time there. I know the main office, but again, I think he'll avoid it. If we call the cops in, it would be the first place they would look. Palgrave Industries has a couple of different arms. Some of the small divisions are in other buildings across the city. Can we look up the building plans?"

Julian whispered something to his employee who turned and took off running. "I'll do one better. I can get you a guide."

Dante didn't want a guide. He wanted that gun Meg carried around. It was still buried where Kaja had hidden it.

While everyone else kept talking, Dante closed his eyes and tried to find her. Acting on pure instinct, he opened his mind and called to her.

Nothing at first. He practically screamed in his head and then a tiny whimper. If he hadn't felt it before, he would have blown it off as an incidental sound, but now he grabbed on to that one tiny sound and held on for dear life. He focused, forcing away the rest of the noise in his head. Her mind was cloudy, unable to think in a clear pattern.

She was afraid. He heard one word play in her drug-addled brain over and over again.

Dante.

She wanted him to come for her. His whole body ached at her fear. He wanted to kill Chalen Palgrave, but more than that, he wanted to comfort her. He'd brought her to this plane where she would never be accepted. He'd brought her to this.

Hush, sweetheart. I'm coming. I am going to be there, and you're going to be fine.

He forced his own panic to a much deeper place, one that Kaja couldn't feel. She needed him to be calm. She was alone and scared and had no idea why she couldn't think straight. Dante knew. He'd been to enough parties in college to recognize the drugs they'd given Kaja. He sent out soothing thoughts.

He got a flash of white—so white. All the lights were white, and the man was white, and she was in a cage. The entire vision was disorienting. His stomach churned. Kaja was handling the drugs well. Gods, how much had they given her?

He opened his eyes. And then narrowed them because he couldn't quite believe what he was seeing. "Meg?"

The queen of the Seelie Fae stood there dressed outrageously in a red leather bustier and what Dante worried was a thong. She was wearing stilettos that added at least four and a half inches to her petite frame.

"Does Beck know you're here? Gods, Meggie, he's not just going to spank you this time. He's going to go crazy. You go and change into something decent right now. Do you understand me? I do not have time for this. You will change, and you will get in the car I'm going to call for you, and you will go back to my house. You will not step foot outside the Dellacorp building, or Beck won't be the only one who spanks you."

Meg's eyes went wide, and then she fell to her knees in a perfect submissive pose. She turned her face up to Julian, and there was a placid smile on her lips. "Oh, he's lovely, Sir. Is he my new Master? You promised to find me one. He's so commanding."

Roan elbowed him with a shake of his head. "Take another look. She doesn't glow, Dellacourt."

Fuck him. Roan was right. This woman looked like Meg, but she didn't have Meg's glow. This Meg was a vampire. It was odd to see her like this, but it was only fair. After all, according to Meg, she'd met Dante's human self when she was on the Earth plane.

Julian placed a hand on Vampire Meg's head. "Sorry, Megan, he's taken. But I will pair you with a Master when I find the right one. I need your help for another reason. I need to know how to get into the Palgrave Industries building."

Her familiar face went blank, and her eyes cast down. "I'm sure they're closed at this time of night, Sir."

Julian was obviously having none of it. "Yes, and you, you clever and bratty sub, know how to get around that, don't you? You know how to get in and how to do it quietly, so no one knows you're coming."

Her auburn hair shook. "I'm not allowed to do anything illegal. I remember everything you said to me after the last time you bailed me out of jail. I am a very good girl."

No, she wasn't. She was lying. Even Dante could see that.

"You're a masochist is what you are, Megan." Julian gently pulled her head back. "If I didn't already have a couple of beloved submissives, I would take care of your discipline on my own. I'll leave it to Master Leo. It's not going to go well for you, but I might tell him to allow you to come if you fess up right now. Otherwise, you'll be on the cross for hours with no relief."

That threat had her talking. "It was just a little raid. You don't understand, Sir. Palgrave Medical is running horrible tests on bunnies and monkeys. I snuck in and freed a few of them."

Julian hauled her up from her slave position. "Megan here is a bit of a protester and part-time criminal."

"I am not a criminal. What they do to those animals is criminal," she argued.

"You were in the medical facility?" Dante asked, making connections. "Is it mostly white? With cages?"

Vampire Meg nodded. "It's a terrible place. They keep it so cold. They don't even understand that animals need soothing colors, too."

"I don't think soothing colors mean much to animals who are being tested on." Julian sighed as though he'd gone over this with her before.

Tested on. That fucker had his consort in a cage. Chalen Palgrave meant to treat her like a beast to experiment on. Dante's heart raced, but something dark opened inside him. If Chalen Palgrave wanted a beast—Dante would give him one.

Megan took a step back. "Is he going to hurt me?"

Julian put a fatherly hand on the woman's shoulder. "No. But I suspect I can't say the same thing about Palgrave."

Meg smiled brightly. "Oh, good. He's a horrible person. I'm a pacifist by nature, but I will totally help get him in the building if he's going to kill that man. You'll let me keep the bunnies, right?"

Dante turned without speaking. Roan fell in beside him.

"I'm going to call some of my contacts in the police force. We'll keep it quiet. I wouldn't want Palgrave to destroy evidence, if you know what I mean," Julian called out.

There was the click-clack of stilettos as Meg raced to catch up with them. She had Julian's dark shirt wrapped around her body like a robe.

"This should be fun. I know the best way into that building." She walked on like they were going on a shopping trip rather than into battle. "And now that I have a minute with you, Mr. Dellacourt, I can talk to you about organic meal pills. There's this rancher who has come up with a way to organically produce meal pills that doesn't even kill the cow."

He growled her way as his car was brought from the garage.

He wanted the real Meg back.

* * * *

Kaja came to in fits and starts. The world was a weird mix of past and present. She dreamed of her home, but this time she ran with Dante at her side. She on four legs and he on his two powerful ones. He ran as naked in his skin as she was in her fur, his fangs and claws on display. It was full summer, and the forests were alive with prey. Deer and stag and moose all fled in terror at their approach, but it wouldn't matter. They would select the fattest and feast. They were unstoppable. Stronger because they were together.

She reached out to him.

I'm coming, love. I'm coming.

He wasn't coming. He was here beside her. As it should be.

Then it was white, so white. When had the snows begun? The world was coated in white and silver and cold. So cold. She shivered despite her fur.

Where was Dante? She wanted Dante. She didn't want to be alone again. *Dante?*

Hush, love. I'm coming.

But he wasn't here, and she was sick. She felt it in her brain. She was ill and in pain. *Dante!*

Kaj! Calm down now.

The voice in her head had taken on a distinctly domineering tone, and she responded to it. She forced herself to stop. Her head was muddy, but she could move. The ground beneath her was cold, but it wasn't soft and wet like snow. It was hard and unnatural. Metal. She opened her eyes and closed them quickly. Too bright. Far, far too bright.

"I think it's awake."

The voice that spoke was cold as well. Through slitted eyes, she looked up. She was in a cage, though not one as nice as the gnome's cages. This was utilitarian. Metal bars and cold floor beneath her. There were two men standing beside a long metal table looking down at her. One was in a white coat that reached his knees. He wore a dress shirt and slacks underneath, and had strange gloves covering his hands. The other wore a suit much like her Dante's.

"Funny how she changed when she lost consciousness."

"I didn't think so. It was disgusting. She's a fucking dog. How does Dellacourt make himself touch that?"

Kaja knew the second voice. It was the man who had been in the car. Why had he taken her?

She was in her wolf form. She knew why she had changed. Her body needed to heal, to dispel whatever illness the drink had given her. She was physically stronger in this form. Already she felt better, though still so weak.

She would not drink again. Ever. Her mind sought the connection to her husband.

"I wouldn't know, Mr. Palgrave. I don't understand the lure. I would much rather discover how she ticks. I'd like to start with some stimuli to see if I can get her to change back to her human form."

Dante. I am afraid.

I know, baby. But I'm coming. I won't leave you there. How many vampires are around you?

She forced her head up. Weary. She was so weary, but she looked around. She opened her senses and let the sights and smells of the place wash over her.

Two men. One woman. Amanda. She thought the name with a sneer.

Dante seemed to get the message. His next thoughts were hesitant. *Um, I can explain about her, love. You see...*

Kaja growled.

I love you, Kaj.

She would see about that. For now, she had a job to do. *I'm in a small cage. I can smell three others, but they are outside the door.*

And then she forgot to breathe, the pain was so great. It came up from her paws and radiated through her body, sending fire through her veins. Her lungs felt tight and breath was impossible. She howled with the ache that went on and on and on.

"It doesn't seem to be doing anything," the man in the white coat said. She watched as he took his hand off some form of button.

Her body sagged as the pain stopped. Her legs shook. She had no control.

There was a kick to her cage that sent the whole thing rattling. The man in the suit stared down at her, disgust apparent on his face. "Hey, dummy, change. We want to see your human form. Do you think it has a brain in this form?"

White Coat frowned. "I believe so. That was only a medium setting though. Perhaps we should try one higher. I don't want to push it, Mr. Palgrave. The higher settings tend to kill off the subject or at least fry its brains."

Kaja, what the fuck was that? What are they doing to you?

Dante's panicked voice screamed in her head. It was too much. They wanted her to change, but she couldn't risk it. She could handle more in this form. If she changed and they turned on the machine, there was a chance that she could die. She needed time. Dante would come. He would come, and she needed to be alive when he got here.

She would take the pain.

Kaja! You talk to me right now. I felt that. What are they doing?

He'd caught her pain? That wouldn't do. She would have to shut down their connection. She was loathe to do it. Feeling Dante was the only thing that was keeping her going.

That was why she'd been afraid. She'd been afraid of loving him. She'd been unwilling to fight for him because when she couldn't directly feel him, she didn't trust him. It was time to move past that. It was time to believe.

They are killing me. Come quickly. I love you, my Dante.

She closed the connection between them as the pain began again. This time she was alone, with no physical sense of Dante. As the shaking began, she realized he was still with her. No matter what. She didn't need to feel him to know he was coming.

He would always come.

Kaja howled and held on to the pain. As long as she hurt, she was still alive.

Chapter Nineteen

The hovercar stopped in midair.

Dante's brain felt numb. Oh, every nerve in his body felt alive. His heart was beating so fast, he was surprised the fucker didn't set off some alarm. His senses seemed far sharper than ever before. He could see farther, smell more. Even his hearing seemed to be on some type of steroids. He'd noticed it as they had left The Club. He'd been able to hear whispered conversations from yards away. His every sense had come to full life, but there was a hole at his center. A dead space.

She'd cut their connection. He couldn't feel her anymore. He was numb so the pain and panic didn't take over.

He strained to see through the thick fog that coated the air, making it hard to see anything, even with his enhanced vision. He managed to make out the name on the building. Palgrave. Palgrave Industries would own all the upper space. He checked the side of the building. Twenty-three. Damn. They were into the lower quarter. No wonder he couldn't see much. Visibility was extremely poor below the fiftieth floor. And under twenty was nothing but tenements. It was where his people stuffed the poor so they wouldn't have to look at them.

His people had more in common with Kaja's than he liked to think about.

"This is it." Meg pointed to a small ventilation shaft. She seemed excited to see the grubby thing. "It has sensors, but they don't work. The pollution level here is off the charts. The building next door manufactures something that screws with the sensors. Heavy metals, I think. I've been able to get into the building, no trouble."

"And where is the lab?" Roan asked.

"Thirty floors up," Meg said without a pause. "We have to get to the fifty-fourth floor and go across. The first air duct you come to drops directly into the medical lab. If your consort and her captors are in there, you'll be able to hear them."

He would be able to find Kaja no matter where she was, but that wasn't the point. "You want me to climb thirty stories up a ventilation shaft? Tell me something, Meg. Does it have ladders?"

She bit into her bottom lip, looking so much like her human counterpart when she had to tell her warrior husband something she knew he wouldn't like. "Not exactly. Um, I've always used a hover lift. I probably should have mentioned that. I have one at home. We could go get it."

Kaja was dying now. He didn't have time to find a hover lift. And a hover lift would only take one of them up at a time.

Suddenly, he just knew. He had the strength to do this. Kaja had given it to him. He had the strength to save her.

"Fuck that." He opened the door to the hovercar. Even with the inertial dampeners, the car swayed slightly. He pulled open the access door. It was big enough for him to crouch in. His eyes adjusted to the darkness. Strange. He could see in the dark. More than that, he could smell. Kaja. She was here in this building. She was holding on. "Roan, if you can't follow me, then get to the cops. I need a couple of minutes to get up there and protect her, but then send them all in."

"What are you talking about? You can't make it up there without a lift. Look, I've got some mag gloves that will let me climb, but that's a long way up." Roan was directly behind him. "Dellacourt, you aren't trained for anything like this. Let me go."

Roan might be trained, but he didn't love Kaja. And he didn't have Kaja's blood flowing through his system.

"Like I said, Roan, try to keep up." The edge of the opening was small, but he felt an odd grace come to his limbs. He stopped fighting his instincts. He allowed Kaja's blood to take over.

His claws popped through his skin, but he welcomed the pain. Longer. He needed them longer, and they pushed through another inch. His claws were long and thick, wickedly sharp on the end. They were made to rip and tear, but now they would carry him.

Dante leapt across the few feet that led to the opposite side of the shaft. His claws slid into the metal as though they belonged there. He dangled for a moment, all of his weight being held by his hands.

And he knew. He could do it. He would do it. And he would win.

"Dellacourt? Are you insane?"

Dante pulled his left hand out and pulled up with his right arm. He got up another couple of feet and dug in again. Easy as pie. He wasn't even winded. "Nope. I'm on werewolf blood. She likes to be called a werewolf. I've never been this strong. If you're coming with me, you better get going."

Dante swung up again, finding a rhythm.

Nothing was going to keep him from his consort. Though he knew she was shielding from him, he sent out the message anyway.

I'm coming, Kaj.

* * * *

Kaja tried to bring her head up, but she was so weary. The pain was past recognition. She felt it always now. She couldn't remember a time when it wasn't a part of her bones. It seemed like hours or days had passed since she'd felt something other than pain.

No. She'd known pleasure and passion. She'd known her lover's cock diving deep and the feel of his fangs penetrating. She'd known what it felt to feed him, to love him, and to be loved in return.

Kaja felt a bit of strength return. *Stay alive.* That was all she had to do. Dante would take care of the rest.

Except that she wanted to help. She wanted to be there when these people went down. They would go down, because Dante would not allow them to live.

"How much more can she take?" The one named Palgrave had taken off his suit coat. He held a stick in his hand. It was an odd stick. It was dark colored, and fire shot from it. He'd touched it to her flesh, and she had burned.

"Why can't you leave her alone? She's not going to change." Amanda had stood back the whole time. Kaja had sensed her reluctance. Amanda had even shed a tear or two, but Kaja didn't care. The blonde still stood there. Her tears hadn't saved Kaja a moment's pain. They hadn't given her strength. Amanda's compassion was a useless, weak thing. Amanda obviously hadn't figured out what Kaja had. Compassion meant it was time to act.

Compassion meant it was time to risk.

Palgrave sighed. "If she isn't willing to do what we want, then maybe we should change the game a bit. Do you have any thoughts, Doctor? I admit, I'm getting bored watching her shake."

The man in the white coat regarded her. She growled at him, satisfied when he moved back a bit.

"She's feisty for what we've put her through. Her vitals are still incredibly strong. Watch them." He gestured to a small panel at the back of her cage. Numbers played there in red colors.

"She gets stronger every moment we don't inflict pain. She heals at an incredible rate." Palgrave stared at the monitor. "What do you think causes that? If we could isolate the gene that gives her that healing ability, we could make a fortune. Do you have any idea what peasants and royals without a consort would pay for that?"

"I need to take some samples. I'm sure I can isolate it with a bit of work." White Coat turned around and began gathering materials. Kaja tried to shrink back.

"You're going to keep her alive, right?" Amanda's voice seemed strained. She clung to the wall as though she didn't want to get any closer to the crime she'd taken part in.

Palgrave's chest puffed, and a vicious laugh came out of his mouth. "For a while, though I suspect she's going to wish she's dead."

"The Dellacourts aren't simply going to let you take Dante's consort." Amanda's arms came over her chest.

"I'm sure they'll thank me. Did you see the press coverage

today? She's a freak. Everyone is talking about what an embarrassment the bitch is. Donald Dellacourt will more than likely shake my hand."

"I don't think you understand them."

Palgrave's eyes narrowed. "And you do, peasant?"

Amanda's back stiffened. "Well, I know Dante well enough to know that he won't let it go. I know he started out with a stupid plan, but this is what he does. In the end, he almost always does the right thing. He broke up with me. I certainly didn't expect that. Why would he break it off with me if he intended to put her aside?"

Palgrave's lips turned distinctly cruel. "I think you overestimate your charms, dear." He stalked toward her.

Kaja began to growl. She could sense Palgrave's intent, but Amanda didn't seem to have the same instincts. She stood there as the huge man walked up to her.

"He liked me," Amanda protested.

Kaja watched as Palgrave took the woman's head in both his hands. He cupped her cheeks in a mockery of affection. "Of course he liked you, dear. Every male likes a female who opens her legs for him. Every man likes a whore until she's served her purpose."

Palgrave's hands snapped around, and a loud crack reverberated through the room. The blonde slumped down, her eyes dead before she hit the floor.

"Doctor, do you have a morgue somewhere in here?" Palgrave asked the question with a lackadaisical tone, as though he was mentioning the weather.

Rage filled Kaja's gut. Amanda hadn't been a good person, but Palgrave was worse. This was what he would do to her. He would use her and dispose of her.

The doctor looked up from his work. He glanced down at the dead body. "I'll have someone take it to the harvesting room. I can always use organs. Although you could have told me you were going to dispose of her. Now I can only use the eyes, skin, and hair. You destroyed many organs that would have made this company money."

Palgrave waved it off. "I just wanted her to stop yapping. And she might be right about Dellacourt. He might come after her if only to save face. Luckily, he has no idea I'm the one behind everything.

I'm sure he thinks King Torin is doing this to fuck with him. He has an overinflated sense of his own worth. Now let's get back to this little bitch. Unlike the dead one, she can still make me some money."

And then Kaja smelled something wonderful. She opened her senses and caught the smell of sandalwood and hair gel. It smelled like home.

Dante was here. He had come for her.

Years of loneliness washed away in an instant, and she realized all her pain had led her to this place. Had the pack treated her with the smallest bit of kindness, she would never have left. She would have stayed and lived only half a life, never realizing what it meant to love. She would have told herself that this was the way the world worked and accepted what she was given.

Dante had shown her a different way. Her world, her love, her soul were all worth fighting for. She could see herself through her husband's eyes, and she was lovely.

She couldn't contain it one second longer. It had been there in her gut, churning and begging to be released ever since the moment she'd met him. The mating howl. The call of a wolf to her true mate.

Kaja threw her head back and howled.

"What the fuck is that?" Palgrave yelled, putting his hands over his ears.

Kaja opened herself and was flooded with him.

A couple minutes more, Kaj. I love you, baby.

She felt his intent. He'd heard her call and opened himself, too. He might not understand the formality of the call, but he'd recognized the meaning behind it.

Fight, Kaj. Fight.

She pulled her strength around her and charged the cage. The bars shook but held. She snarled and barked at her captors. She might not be able to get out of her cage, but she could buy Dante time and give him the edge of surprise.

"She's gone fucking insane. Do you think she has rabies?" Palgrave took a long step back. He reached into his pocket and pulled out a small device. When he flicked it on, a little charge pulsed through the room and a blue light flashed. "This is a sonic blade, you dumb bitch. Do you know what it can do to you?"

"I think she understands quite well what we're planning on doing to her. You see, this is why using animals without reasoning skills is better. This one understands English. She's not going to be distracted by a treat when she understands we're going to remove one of her limbs for study." White Coat shook his head. "I can get her to stop that infernal howling. If this kills her, at least we'll have some quiet."

He flipped the switch, and Kaja's howl stuck in her throat. The pain was even worse, but Dante's voice was there, comforting her, sharing the pain. She felt him. He was close, so close. The connection between them was a strong rope tethering her to the plane. She felt her heart beating too fast, but then it slowed, even as Dante took the pain for her.

Play dead, Kaj. Hurry. I can't hold out much longer.

Kaja dropped to her belly and let her eyes go blurry and unfocused. The pain wracked through her, but it was less now. No matter how bad it got, she wouldn't move because Dante needed her. She thought about closing the connection again but felt a low growl roll across her skin. It didn't come from her. Dante had sent it. It was a warning to obey him.

If she didn't, she would get the worst spanking. Kaja stopped breathing.

It was time.

The machine flicked off. It took every bit of concentration to keep her body still.

"Gods be damned, Doc. I didn't want the bitch dead." Palgrave still held his knife. Kaja could hear it humming.

"Bah, she's better dead. None of my techs would have been willing to get close to her. She's too dangerous. Now I can perform an autopsy and get everything I need."

There was a loud crash, and Kaja opened her eyes. He was here.

Dante fell from a hole in the ceiling. He landed on his feet and stared at her. She could feel his rage. He had understood that she was in a cage, but seeing it seemed to have opened something volcanic inside him. His eyes became orbs of pure forest green, and his claws were far longer than she'd ever seen.

"What the fuck?" Palgrave quickly yelled for security.

"Did you think you could take my consort and I would let her go?" Dante's voice was deep, his words clipped.

"I thought you would run around trying to figure out why that fucker Torin had your consort."

Another body fell from the ceiling. Kaja immediately recognized him as the mercenary who had taken Dante and Meg. He was out of breath, but he had a weapon in his hand. It was reassuring since he seemed to be working with Dante, not against him.

"I'm afraid I have a new friend, Palgrave." Dante wasn't out of breath. He stood there, a solid figure casting his shadow across the room. Roan moved to stand next to him. Neither one seemed to notice White Coat behind them. He was moving quietly, the needle in his hand.

Kaja barked a warning, but Dante was already in motion. He moved fluidly, his body twisting around. Before White Coat could raise the needle, Dante had a hand around his throat and he squeezed. His claws sank into White Coat's throat. Dante picked the smaller man up. White Coat's feet dangled, kicking out uselessly. After a moment, the man stopped moving, his face blue, his throat a mottled mess of blood and tissue.

Dante tossed him away like a rag doll.

"Whatever you're on, Dellacourt, it's some good shit." Roan watched him with obvious appreciation.

Dante ignored him, preferring to look at Palgrave, who now had the backing of three security guards. Each held a sonic Taser unit in his hand.

"I really should have come more prepared," Roan said. "I feel naked without my kit, but I can still take out the two on the left."

"Let my Kaj out, and she can take them all." Dante's lips quirked up as he looked over at her. She could feel his love and desire. "Kaja, when you get out, I want you to know that I release you from that whole 'no killing things that talk back.' You can kill any asshole in this place. Except that one." He pointed to Palgrave. "He's mine."

"Like you could take me," Palgrave preened. "You've never been a fighter, Dellacourt. You might be able to take a lightweight like Doctor Wilson there, but I doubt you can take a royal."

"I will kill you. You touched her. I would kill you if you had touched her with affection. I'll take you apart for touching her in

253

violence."

Roan was inching toward her cage. Kaja got prepared to pounce.

One of the security guards aimed and fired his Taser unit at Dante. The air crackled with electricity, but Dante ducked, his body bending backward with grace and precision. The dart bit into the wall behind him. Dante straightened up, and his hand was on the tether that connected the dart to the hand unit. He jerked the line back, and the guard moved with it. Before he could think to scream, the guard stood before Dante. With a quick flick of Dante's fist, the other man fell.

"Not so smart, Palgrave, but then I should have expected that from you. None of us killed your brother, you know." Dante stepped over the unconscious body of the guard.

"I know one of your cousins did the deed," Palgrave spat. "I'm not stupid."

Roan was close, so close. Dante seemed to be trying to keep Palgrave's attention on him. "Torin had a hag in the village. We believe she's the one who called your brother to the Refugee plane."

"You're lying. And it doesn't matter. I know what I know." Palgrave strengthened his stance and held the blade tightly.

The two guards behind him moved forward.

Roan leapt across the distance, his hand reaching for the button that released her cage. Both security guards fired and hit Roan. His body jumped, spasming as the electrical current ran through it. Struggling, his hand moved forward. His teeth gritted, but he slapped his hand on the button, and her cage opened.

Chaos reigned. The guards released the darts and brought their weapons back online. Palgrave moved forward, his sonic blade lifted and ready. Roan fell, utterly unconscious. Kaja leapt from her cage. Her body ached, but it didn't matter now. All that mattered was getting Dante out of here alive. She attacked the first person she saw. The guard screamed as she went for his throat. He tried to get the Taser unit to work, but he dropped it as she dug her teeth in. She felt the blood begin to flow and let go. She didn't have time to play with him.

When she looked up, Dante had caught the second guard's dart and had it wrapped around his throat, but Palgrave was coming for him. Before Kaja could jump, Palgrave was thrusting the blade into

Dante's back. She smelled the blood beginning to flow, felt the horrible pain, but she took it because it was halved. Dante was able to twist and block the next blow. He swung out, catching Palgrave in the chin.

Kaja leapt into action. She jumped up, trying to get Palgrave's throat, but he was fast with the knife. It caught her leg, and she fell.

"Kaja!" Dante screamed her name, but she felt it more than heard it.

He got to his feet and faced off with Palgrave.

"Give it up, Dellacourt. I have reinforcements coming. You can't win."

"You're not leaving here alive." Dante was unarmed, but he didn't back down. "Kaja, you get behind me."

Limping, she moved to his side.

He looked down at her. "Yes, I suppose that is your place. I love you, Kaj. I've never loved anyone before. You're half my soul and all of my heart. No matter what happens, I want you safe. When the time comes, you run and don't look back."

She heard the words, but she wouldn't heed them. She would never leave him. If this was the end for him, then she would take out whoever she could, and she would follow him. She didn't know what came after this life, but she would follow him.

Palgrave pounced. He raced forward, knife out. He hit Dante with the full force of his bulk, and the two men went down. They rolled, and then Dante got to his feet. He'd been hit again, this time low in his gut. Palgrave moved, circling her husband. Kaja growled and got ready to leap.

"Mine, Kaja. This kill is mine." Dante bared those magnificent fangs her way.

"You're not killing anything, Dellacourt. You're bleeding out. You're so fucking weak, I won't even have to try this time." Palgrave's lips curled in a sneer.

Dante was weak. Kaja could feel it. She remembered how females during the hunt sometimes sent their mates energy. She took a deep breath and sent every spare bit of energy she had his way. Her body sagged down, unable to stand a moment further. She was done. If Dante fell, she would go with him. She held tight to the invisible thread that bound them. If he went down, he would take her, and they would be together.

"That won't happen, baby." Dante could read her thoughts. He stood tall, his skin practically glowing. "I'm taking you out of here."

Palgrave ran, and Dante was with him. They met in the middle, and there was a horrible crack as Dante punched at Palgrave's chest. His fist met flesh and didn't stop. Kaja managed to lift her head as Palgrave's face took on a horrified, blank look.

Dante pulled his hand out of his opponent's chest. It didn't come back empty. Palgrave's heart was in Dante's hand.

"That was for my consort." Dante held the heart as it turned to dust and everything that was Chalen Palgrave became a pile of dirt on the floor.

Dante turned and raced to her. He got on his knees. "Baby. Gods, baby, tell me you're all right."

She was tired. So tired. She felt her body failing, but it was all right to go because Dante was safe. Dante was whole. The energy she'd sent him had healed and saved him. She wanted to hold him with two hands. Using the very last bit of strength she had, Kaja changed. She brought her hands up to touch his beautiful face. He was her magnificent beast.

She heard Dante curse. When she looked up, his eyes were still full green, but there was a sheen of tears in them. He clutched her with one hand but drew his other to his mouth. "Don't you leave me, Kaj. This has to work both ways."

He gouged at his own flesh, and his blood began to flow. He put his wrist to her mouth. "Drink, baby. I'm full of you. Your blood, your energy, your strength. Take it all back. Please. I need you."

Kaja felt the blood fill her mouth. Immediately she felt the healing begin.

"That's right, baby. Take it. I can handle it. Drink." He pressed his wrist to her mouth, cradling her head.

Kaja fell back the instant she knew she would be all right. She heard Roan groaning in the distance. Her body was laid across Dante's, and she could feel his soul reaching for hers, brushing and touching. Safe.

But he was still a vampire. He pulled out his phone. "Hey, Susie.

Yeah. Start a hostile takeover of Palgrave. No. He won't fight back. Why? Because I just pulled his heart out of his body. Yes, I'm serious. I want half."

Dante tossed his phone away and cuddled her against him as he stood.

"You all right, Kaja?"

She managed to nod. She was whole and happy to be alive.

Chapter Twenty

"It's official." Dante's father laid his tablet down with an audible thud. The silence in the room was utterly oppressive.

Dante looked between his cousins as they stood in his father's office.

Beck paled at the news. "We're renegades?"

Dante forced himself to speak. His cousins needed to understand how deeply fucked they were. "Every mercenary on the plane will be after you."

Dante's own heart seized even though he'd been expecting the news since Julian had told him what was going on only hours before. He knew he should be in bed, holding his wife while she recovered, but this couldn't wait.

His family surrounded him. His mother and sister were crying. Colin looked grim but kept holding Susan's hand. Kaja placed a hand on Meg's shoulder. Kaja looked tired but resolute.

Beck and Cian were silent for a long moment, something unspoken passing between them. Meg sat beside Kaja, her eyes tearing up, but her chin had settled into a stubborn lift. She wore casual clothes, but there was no mistaking who Megan Finn was. She was a queen.

"Can you get Meggie off this plane and back to the Earth plane?" Beck asked, his shoulders squaring as though he knew he was in for a fight.

Meg appeared ready to give him one. She stood and went toe to toe with her warrior husband. "I'm not going anywhere, Beckett Finn. Do you hear me?"

Cian got up and lent his strength to Beck. "Meggie, you can't stay."

"Try to get rid of me. I know the way home. You can dump me somewhere, but I'll be back." Meg's hands separated and grabbed a fistful of both her husbands' shirts. "I won't stop. I'll fight. I'll fight to my dying breath."

Beck's face was a mask of pain. It was mirrored by his brother's own face. "That's what we're afraid of, love. We can't lose you."

"Well, man up. This is war, and I won't be left behind." Meg let go, her hands shaking.

His father stepped in. "None of you can stay. The Council voted twenty minutes ago. The Vampire plane has aligned with Torin. I have guards at every access point, but by morning they will have warrants to extradite you both to the Seelie plane. We don't have much time to get you out of here."

Beck shook his head. "You can't get us out. They'll be on us the minute we leave the Dellacourt building. You can't save us, Uncle Don. It's fate that we came back here just as this happened."

Cian's mouth turned down. "Save Meg. Beck and I will find a way. Torin will wait to kill us. He'll want to make it public."

Dante's mother stood and grasped his father's hand. "Please, Don. You have to help them. We can't turn them over. They're all I have left of my sister."

His father looked down at his mother, love shining in his eyes. Gods, he loved his parents. Dante turned to Kaja and sent out his own love. His parents had taught him how to love. He'd always thought their wealth and position was the greatest gift they had given him, but now he could see. His parents' passion had informed his own. Kaja was a song in his soul.

"I would never turn them over, wife. They're my blood, too.

Dante and I have been talking to Mr. Taggart. We've come up with a plan." Donald waved to the servants.

The door opened and Taggart escorted a petite female inside. Vampire Meg walked in, and all eyes shifted her way.

"I found our brat and she's agreed to help us," Taggart announced.

"Holy shit, that's me." Meg stepped up and looked at the mirrorlike version of herself.

"That's so cool," they both said in unison.

"There are two of them," Cian breathed as he and Beck stepped up. "Will you look at that, brother? Are you thinking what I'm thinking?"

Beck slapped at his brother's chest. "No. I know what you're thinking. And you're crazy if you think she's going to do that. I'm thinking that's twice the trouble."

Real Meg turned, her face in a perfectly outraged mask. "Cian Finn. That is not happening."

Vampire Meg smiled at the brothers. "I don't know. That might be fun."

Meg's eyes narrowed.

Vampire Meg paled. "Or not."

"And they call you the smart one," Beck huffed under his breath.

Taggart nodded Dante's way. "I've got the other two in a hovercar on their way here and Roan is in place. We're ready when you are."

Kaja had come to Dante's side, and she slipped her hand into his. Just touching her brought him a feeling of peace. He kissed her hair and prayed he never ran into her twin. One Kaja was all he could handle. "Vampire Meg has agreed to pose as the queen. We found a set of vampire twins with the proper coloring. In thirty minutes, they are going to flee the building. Shortly after that, Beck, Cian, and Meg will leave quietly from the ground. We have a hovercar and a group of soldiers waiting to take us to the west door. It will be guarded, but William Roan assures me he'll kill anyone who tries to stop us."

Beck turned to him. "It sounds dangerous."

"Everything is dangerous from here on out, cos. You know the way this will go." Dante squeezed Kaja's hand.

Cian put a hand on his wife's shoulder. "Yes. There is no other path, brother. I know you wanted to live peacefully, but Torin won't allow it. And you know what he's doing. If he has his way, he'll purge the Seelie plane of undesirables, and then he will go after the other planes. We can't duck this fight anymore. It's time to stand. It's time to claim what is ours."

Beck seemed to grow taller. He took his place at Meg's side, the three connected in ways Dante knew most people couldn't dream of. "Then we'll go. We'll meet with Fergus and see what happens."

His mother hugged all three of them. "We'll work from here. We'll do everything we can."

Cian shook his head. "You have to be careful, Aunt Alana. You can't let them know you're helping. If it comes to it, you have to renounce us."

His father took his mother's hand and pulled her into a comforting embrace. Susan and Colin stood.

"It won't come to that," Susan said. "We have power, Ci. Once the Council realizes what our sunscreen can do, they will back off. We won't be able to openly defy them, but we'll have their balls in our hands, if you know what I mean."

That was his sister, a ballbuster to the end.

He was going to miss her.

"We need to move out soon. I want to be on our way the minute the decoys leave." Dante had a bag packed for both him and Kaja, but they wouldn't be taking much. He would have to learn to travel light.

The room erupted into chaos as his parents and sister began to argue. Dante listened to all the reasons he shouldn't go with a patient ear. This was why he hadn't mentioned this part of the plan until now. Meg started in on how it was too dangerous, and Cian told him to stay behind as well.

"Stop!" Beck's command had everyone taking a step back. The room quieted. The warrior king of the Seelie Fae looked at Dante. "You know what you're giving up, cos?"

Everything. And nothing. He was giving up everything he knew—money, power, luxury. It was nothing compared to what he gained. A cause worth fighting for. A real place for Kaja.

"I know."

Kaja's hand found his chest, and those brilliant blue eyes stared up at him. "Dante, you cannot leave your home. I know why you're doing this. Please. I will fit in. I will adjust."

He didn't want her to adjust. He wanted his wolf. And she was wholly mistaken. "This is what I need. I didn't understand it before. I'm a warrior. I'm a beast, and this is my cause. Come with me. Fight with me. And this isn't my home, Kaja. You are my home."

She wrapped her arms around him, her answer rolling across his brain.

Yes.

Beck nodded. "You're more than welcome, cos. You are needed."

Dante was surrounded by his family. They formed a tight circle.

"I love you, brother," Susan said. "You come home to us someday."

"My baby." His mother wept unashamedly. "I'm so proud of you."

They walked away one by one, each doing his or her part to get ready. Dante's father looked at him.

"Do you understand what you're doing?"

"I'm fighting for what's right." He waited for his father's lecture on how naïve he was being.

His father's strong jaw trembled. "I raised you well, son. I always knew it. You make me proud. Anything you need, you call your family. And Kaja, thank you. You're my daughter. Dante's told me a bit about your plane. Forget them. This is your pack. You are always welcome here, daughter."

Kaja held on to Dante, her chest shaking with emotion. He felt her great love for his family, but he was doing the right thing. She would never belong here, and he would never be happy without her.

Four hours later, Roan proved true to his word. The guards lay unconscious, and the door to the Refugee plane opened before them.

"Your Highnesses." Roan gestured to the doorway. "It will be a day's journey to the Unseelie plane. The decoys have not been caught yet. We will be safe. It is my great honor to serve you."

Beck thanked him, his face grim. He showed his wife and brother through the door.

They were on the run. They would win their throne or be buried beneath it.

Kaja smiled at Dante as she walked through the door.

He followed. He left his plane behind because his whole world was wrapped in one small woman. She held his heart, his future.

He would have it no other way.

The door closed behind Dante, and he faced his destiny.

Epilogue

The Seelie plane

The sun warmed her face, and Bronwyn Finn looked out over the meadow. The fields were filled with wheat. Tall stalks swayed in the wind, and dust blew up from the tiny dirt road that led to her tower. Her hands already ached from the thought of harvesting all that wheat. She put that reality aside. It was weeks before she would spend every day in the field. She could remember a time when she'd been a pampered princess.

Now all she had was this tower. From her vantage, it felt like she could see the whole world. Well, hers at least.

"Bron, it's time for supper." Gillian's voice drifted up from the bottom of the tower.

Bronwyn had to smile. Gillian still thought of her as the child she'd saved that terrible day in the White Palace. That day when she'd lost her mother and father, Bronwyn had found Gillian McIver. The Unseelie princess had become her healer, her savior, her surrogate mother. When she was younger, she would never have believed it. Unseelie and Seelie living together, dependant on each other. Loving each other as family. But Gillian had been her world for a very long time.

And Gillian was a slight pain in her ass. Bronwyn was twenty-seven years old and still being called to supper.

"I'm coming," Bronwyn called back, but she let her head drift to her hands as she stared out over the peaceful field where she'd spent the last thirteen years of her life.

She'd had the dream again last night. It was the same thing every night. When she closed her eyes, she tried to envision her brothers, alive and whole, but every night when conscious thought fled, they came to her.

The Dark Ones.

She'd dreamed of them for as long as she could remember. It was as though they had grown up with her. She'd lived a whole second life when she closed her eyes and went to sleep. Sometimes they were so real that she wondered which reality was the dream. She remembered them as children playing through her mind as she slept. As she grew, they did as well. They talked about everything in her dreams. She knew them as well as she'd known herself. And then they were gone for a long time.

The dreams stopped when you died.

So much had stopped when she'd taken that final breath and died in her brother's arms. She shook off the terrible memory. She'd died, but Gillian's magic had brought her back. Unseelie magic that would undoubtedly cost Gillian her life if Torin the Pretender ever caught them.

She got up from her perch. The sun was going down. It would be time to go to bed in a couple of hours. It would be time to dream again.

The dreams had only come back in the last few years, and they had taken on a distinctly adult tone.

Four hands caressing her. Two mouths vying for her attention. She didn't know their names, but she knew how they felt when they moved against her. She knew what it felt like to be between two hard bodies. Beloved. Wanted. Whole.

Bronwyn stood and smoothed out her dress. Sheer fancy. She was alone, and she would remain that way. She was untouched. A virgin at twenty-seven. It was pathetic, but true. Her only real experience was an attempted rape that her brother Cian had halted. She knew only violence. Nothing could change that.

The Dark Ones were merely a figment of her imagination. She'd latched on to her childhood fantasies in order to have a relationship— even one that only happened in her dreams.

But Bronwyn had left dreams behind long ago. She'd stopped believing the day Torin had slaughtered her family.

The Dark Ones weren't coming for her. No one was. She was alone. If Beckett and Cian were alive, she prayed they had found a safe place to live and some modicum of happiness.

Bronwyn went to the chest where she kept her meager possessions. She opened it and moved aside her second-best dress. She let her hand move under the fabric to wrap around the cold metal hilt of a knife.

It was the knife used to kill her.

It was the knife she intended to kill Torin with.

Bronwyn let the knife be, content that it was there. She closed the drawer and started down the stairs, a weary feeling stealing over her.

It was hours until she could slide into sleep and see them again. They were figments, but they were hers.

Her Dark Ones. Her loves.

If you're out there—come for me. Please come for me.

Tears blurring her eyes, Bronwyn started down the stairs.

* * * *

Bronwyn and the royals will continue the faery tale with *Beauty*, now available.

Author's Note

I'm often asked by generous readers how they can help get the word out about a book they enjoyed. There are so many ways to help an author you like. Leave a review. If your e-reader allows you to lend a book to a friend, please share it. Go to Goodreads and connect with others. Recommend the books you love because stories are meant to be shared. Thank you so much for reading this book and for supporting all the authors you love!

Beauty

A Faery Story, Book 3
By Lexi Blake writing as Sophie Oak

The princess in the tower

In one horrifying night, Bronwyn Finn lost her family, her kingdom, and the princes who had haunted her dreams for years. Left alone, years pass as she fights for survival and craves revenge against the uncle who took everything from her. But she's never forgotten her Dark Ones. Now she hides along with her guardian, but the war rages ever closer.

Two dark princes

A tragedy marred Lach and Shim's lives. The future kings of the Unseelie Fae are obsessed with finding their promised wife—Bronwyn. Lach and Shim have never stopped believing that Bronwyn is their mate. She is the bond that connects the halves of their shared soul.

A destiny that will change a kingdom

With the blessing of the renegade kings, Beck and Cian Finn, Lach and Shim begin a dangerous quest to find their bride before Torin and his hags take her life.

Across two planes, a war will rage. Lives will be lost. Love will be found. And the Seelie Fae will welcome their true kings home.

About Lexi Blake

Lexi Blake is the author of contemporary and urban fantasy romance. She started publishing in 2011 and has gone on to sell over two million copies of her books. Her books have appeared thirty-three times on the *USA Today*, *New York Times*, and *Wall Street Journal* bestseller lists. She lives in North Texas with her husband, kids, and two rescue dogs.

Connect with Lexi online:

Facebook: Lexi Blake
Twitter: authorlexiblake
Website: www.LexiBlake.net
Instagram: www.instagram.com/lexiblakeauthor